This book is a work of fiction. Names, characters, places, and incidents either are products of the author's imagination or are used fictitiously. Except where noted, any resemblance to actual events or locales or persons, living or dead, is coincidental.

Cover by Kristie Birdsong

ISBN 978-0-9860749-3-6

10 9 8 7 6 5 4 3 2 1

For Ilana…my soulmate.

This book is a work of fiction.

The Esther Code is REAL.

Chapter 1

Tonight is the night.

Tonight he is ready.

Simon is surprisingly calm considering what he is about to do. But why shouldn't he be? It is not the first time he has done it, nor will it be the last. He has planned every detail meticulously. He sits in his car, mentally rehearsing the sequence of events. Has he remembered everything? Yes. He has been here before, has become familiar with his target. The crisp air bites at his face as he crosses the parking lot to the visitors' entrance of Crestwood Assisted Living.

Again Simon wears his "visiting outfit": khaki pants, a yellow polo shirt with "Christian Fellowship" insignia over the left breast, an ID card on a chain around his neck, a baseball cap that allows his neatly combed, light brown ponytail to fall through the back, heavy-framed glasses, and a neatly trimmed mustache. A backpack is slung casually over his right shoulder.

Crestwood is a squat one-story building shaped like a boomerang, with the entrance in the middle of the bend. The place is clean and well lit, even from the outside. As Simon enters the assisted living center, he notices again the absence of that sanitized smell that generally infuses hospitals. Crestwood is the kind of place that convinces the suburban families of

Harwood Heights, Illinois, to surrender parents and grandparents to the care of strangers.

There is an expectable proliferation of faux flowers and indoor plants in the main foyer. So many electric potpourri burners pump out vanilla fragrance that Simon worries the smell will cling to him even after he leaves the building. The facility is secure and adequately staffed. A large plaque instructs all visitors to "Please Sign in" upon arrival.

Simon confidently strides directly to the frosted-glass sliding window, which is already open halfway. Despite management's best efforts to imbue Crestwood with the feel of home, there is something inescapably officious about the sign-in process. A clipboard with the sign-in sheet lies on a ledge in front of the open window. There is a pen chained nearby, but Simon produces his own from his shirt pocket. He signs his name sloppily with his left hand.

A young black man sits behind the desk, reading a large textbook. He glances up and recognizes the visitor.

"Back again?" After checking the clock on the wall behind him, the man, likely a student, smiles. "I bet the old guy appreciates you."

Simon peers at the same clock, but he omits writing the time next to his name.

"Yep. He had any visitors today?"

"Nope." The black man shakes his head. "Yesterday his son came by. Didn't stay long, though."

Simon nods, "That's how it goes sometimes. If I don't see you on my way out, I'll catch you next week."

"Cool. Next week. I'll be here. Keep it loose." The young man flashes a smile, and his attention returns to his textbook.

Simon walks the familiar hallway to room 128. The door bears a decorative sign with a little plastic window. Large letters inform visitors of the resident's name.

FRED SCHMIDT.

Simon pauses momentarily and ponders that they will soon be sliding that name out and replacing it with someone else's.

"You here to read to Mr. Schmidt again?" Simon starts at the voice of the plump, middle-aged nursing assistant behind him.

"Yes," he says. His heart is pounding, but he retains outward composure.

"How long you gonna be?" The nursing assistant's voice is nasal and unpleasant, but Simon does not allow his face to show irritation. She is shutting the door to room 129.

"We're going to finish the book tonight if he can stay awake long enough. Don't worry," he adds with a small smile, "I'll make sure he's tucked in for the night before I leave."

"Oh, I know you will. You always do."

"Thanks, have a good night."

Simon knocks first, then walks into the room. There is a compact living area with recliner, love seat, upright chair and small TV on a stand. This flows into the bedroom, which displays plenty of family photos. One baby picture has a place of honor on the dresser. Simon surmises that it must be a great-grandchild. Cute kid.

Mr. Schmidt is lying in the bed watching a television set that is mounted in the corner.

He is in his late eighties, bald, thin, and pale. The frailty of his body, however, does not extend to his mind. His connections still esteem him as both smart and sophisticated. He still enjoys reading, talking, and exercising his mind, which is why he enjoys Simon's visits. Mr. Schmidt immediately clicks off the TV when he sees Simon enter.

"Ah, I was hoping you would be here soon," he greets Simon in his thin, brittle voice. "Thank you for coming again. I am eager to hear what happens next."

"Tonight I wouldn't miss. It's a big night," Simon responds, with perhaps too much enthusiasm.

"Shall we pick up where we left off then?"

"Not tonight. No book tonight. Because tonight I have something better. Just relax, and give me a second to get dressed up."

Simon senses the vague confusion building in the old man's mind. He sees Mr. Schmidt staring into him, attempting to pierce Simon's mystery and find a logical agenda beneath.

Simon merely smiles and removes a pair of latex gloves from his backpack.

"We're not going to play doctor, are we?"

Simon does not respond as he pulls more items from his backpack.

"Because I think I get enough of that here," Schmidt continues with a weak chuckle.

"Good doctors are hard to come by. I've got another pair of gloves, too. Hang tight, you'll see."

From the backpack, he removes a white disposable jumpsuit, a surgical hat and mask, and shoe covers. He puts on each item with deliberation.

"Are you going to paint the room, or something?" The old man's voice grows sharper with each question. His chest is rising and falling faster too.

"Hold on, I'm not going to ruin the surprise for you." Simon pulls out a brand new pair of leather driving gloves from a plastic bag. The price tag is still attached to one, and the disconnected halves of the plastic connecting cord dangle pathetically from the leather. He puts these on over the latex gloves.

"Are we going to do some wood carving? What are we going to do that you don't want to get dirty?" Mr. Schmidt asks. The old man shows both age and nerves as he begins to button and unbutton the cuff of his light blue pajamas.

"One minute, one minute."

Simon bends over and takes his instrument from the bag. It is a simple thing, yet sinister, consisting of two handles connected by piano wire. Simon made it himself. He keeps it lower than the bed, so Mr. Schmidt cannot see that Simon possesses a weapon. Leaning in close to the old man, Simon whispers something into his ear. The old man's eyes swell grotesquely as he scrambles for the call light on his bedside table. Just as Simon predicted. His moment of opportunity!

In reaching for the button, Mr. Schmidt lifts his head off the pillow. With a quick twist of the wrist, Simon places his homemade garrote around Schmidt's neck and pulls the cord tight. Not a sound comes out of the old man—not even a last breath can escape. Mr. Schmidt's hands flail meaninglessly, too far to even touch the metal cord that digs into his skin. He makes a few weak attempts to kick his legs, but they are powerless under the comforter. Simon maintains a tight grip for several minutes, until he knows the old man's heart has stopped. It is done. The only breathing he can hear is his own, tense and ragged.

With forced calmness, Simon removes the garrote and double-bags it. He then removes a Ziploc bag that holds a small piece of paper. The paper is two inches square, with "F.S." in big typed letters in the center and "parmo sh ta" evenly spaced along the bottom in smaller letters. Simon positions the bag and shakes it gently, allowing the note to fall out and land near the lifeless left hand.

He then gently moves the body in a sleeping position facing away from the door and tucks Schmidt in as promised. Removing all the other items, Simon bags them and places everything into the backpack.

He then sits down, takes a book out and begins to read out-loud.

Chapter 2

A blinding light intensifies Jamie's headache. Her thoughts are slow, foggy. She does not know where she is. Blinking rapidly to adjust her eyes to the searing light, Jamie assesses her predicament. She is propped up on a table. Her legs are tied tightly, and she cannot move them. Jamie looks forward and sees her hands tied to the miter gauge of a table saw. She tries to scream for help, but her mouth is taped shut. Questions flood her mind. How did she get here? What case was she working on?

The small roar of a mechanical engine fills her ears. Sweat pours down Jamie's face as she watches the table-saw start spinning. The blades disappear completely into an illusion of round metal. Out of the darkness, a man's large hands take hold of the miter gauge. They start sliding Jamie's fingers towards the saw slowly, five little pieces of wood waiting helplessly for the cut. Jamie attempts another scream as her hands slide toward the threatening blur.

Adrenaline pumps through her veins. She has to save herself somehow. Jamie tries to bend and move her fingers in any way to escape the blade, but her body refuses to respond. Desperately she tries again, but the effect is the same. Looking for someone to help, Jamie registers that there she is surrounded mostly by darkness, interrupted only by a bright light focused on the saw blade. The darkness is thick and suffocating, and without hope. Jamie is truly alone.

Something is ringing. It must be a safety precaution to signal impending danger. Yet the hands ignore the warning bell and move the miter gauge closer and closer to the spinning blade. The ringing noise grows louder—Jamie desperately wants to block her ears from the keen sound, but she can only watch her fingers move closer to the saw. Her only hope is that the noise is so loud that someone else will hear it and come save her. But in a few seconds it will be too late. As the saw blade touches her skin, blood spews from her wounds and covers the table. Jamie screams as her terror peaks, forcing her awake.

Her breath comes in desperate gasps, as she looks around her bedroom, still afraid of impending danger. The room is empty, but eerie in the morning light. Jamie sighs in relief as she confirms that there is no table saw in her room. Her mind begins to grasp that she is safe and in her own home. No danger.

As the ringing continues, Jamie realizes it is her alarm. She picks up her cell phone from the bedside table and silences it. The time, 5:45 a.m., glares at her. With the echoes of the nightmare in her mind, she is relieved to be awake. Jamie slinks back to the middle of her bed and pulls the covers tight up under her chin. The cotton is soft, comforting, and the lingering smell of Chris's deodorant pushes the nightmare further back.

Her boyfriend, Chris, had spent the night, but he was already gone. *That is what happens when you date an orthopedic surgery resident.* It is also the source of the nightmare. As an FBI agent, Jamie Golding has encountered the most twisted, horrific images of murder and mutilation, and she has dealt with them well. Most of the time, she is able to leave her work at work. Death and brutality are tragic and awful, but at least the dead are gone and safe, she thinks. The dead feel no pain. She is proud of the fact that, despite all of the gruesome sights she has seen, she has never been physically ill. It has become a point of pride. Chris inflicts pain for the sake of healing. Yet the idea of power sawing off the end of a femur in order to do a knee replacement gives Jamie the willies.

If Chris had not been relating an incident right before she fell asleep, maybe Jamie would not have had her nightmare. He is several weeks into a month-long hand surgery rotation. The patient was a twenty-two year old construction worker who could not speak a word of English. The poor guy had cut off four fingers with a table saw. Chris had explained to Jamie that this was the cause of his all-nighter. He and his attending surgeon re-attached the fingers under a microscope. They were able to re-attach three out of four. A great bedtime story. For some strange reason, the suffering of the living disturbed Jamie more than the mutilation of the dead.

Out of bed and still shaking, Jamie throws the covers over the empty bed and smoothes them down. She changes into her running clothes. She quickly pulls back her wavy black hair and clips down the stray strands. Jamie checks the time on her cell phone. She only has a few minutes before she has to meet Seth outside her apartment for their morning run.

Most of her friends despise running, using it only to stave off the weight gain that comes with age. But to Jamie, running does much more than burn calories. She has invested in expensive Adidas Vigor Three TR W running shoes, the perfect choice to take on trails. She looks out the window; she can see the dawn breaking between the buildings of Montclair, Virginia. It is always a beautiful sight.

After preparing for the cold morning run with some hydration and stretching, Jamie heads outside and sees her friend Seth Cooper stretching his calf on the street curb. He looks up and grins, curly black hair falling into his eyes. Seth is slightly taller than Jamie, fit, with an average build.

"Hey!" Jamie greets him. "You ready for this?"

"Of course! I'm already loose. Let's go," Seth replies enthusiastically.

Jamie leads the way down to Waterway Drive, not too far from her apartment. Seth picks up her stride and begins to speed walk next to her. This is their quick warm-up before starting the hard run. Jamie runs the same path three times a week and saves her longer runs for the weekends. She is not always able to start her day with a run, but she loves it when she can. It gives her a morning coffee boost without the coffee. Today will be an easy day: three-and-a-half miles to start her Wednesday morning.

Jamie glances at Seth, and without a word, they both transition into a run. Together they find a comfortable pace. The cold air piercing her lungs gives Jamie the feeling of being alive.

The thump of her shoes on the pavement and gravel roads is her music. The rhythm is comforting. Jamie looks over and smiles at Seth, who runs beside her with a grin. She can tell he enjoys the morning runs as much as she does. He catches her eye.

"So, at which hospital is Chris doing his residency? He's almost done, right?"

"He's in his third year at George Wash. in D.C. Two more to go and then maybe a fellowship."

"Oh, that's all?" Seth teases. "I thought he was almost finished." They move to one side as another pair of runners comes down the path, and he feels Jamie's shoulder rub against his own. Seth feels a rush of excitement at her touch.

"Personally, I would like to see him more often. Right now, we can only get together about once or twice a week. Once on his post call day, and maybe once on the weekend. Needless to say, he hardly gets any sleep—between work, errands, and driving thirty miles to see me, there just isn't time."

"Sounds pretty crazy. I can't believe you guys make it work with such demanding jobs." Seth changes the subject. "So, how's work going? Using your radar lately?"

"It's not radar. Just good training."

"From your Masters in Forensic Psychology or from your work with the FBI?"

"Maybe a little of both. Seriously, though, pick someone—anyone—I'll show you it's not just a degree that enables you to read people." Jamie is always up for a challenge.

"Oh, I know what you can do. You don't have to prove anything to me," Seth assures her. Jamie looks determined, though, so Seth gives in to her game. "Okay, here comes a pair of runners. Do your magic."

Jamie rolls her eyes at his comment, then turns her attention to the challenge ahead. The couple running toward them are clearly college students. The girl wears a pink sorority jacket, while the guy has on a loose sweatshirt with a Greek fraternity's name plastered on the front. As Jamie and Seth pass, the male runner's eyes sweep in their direction. Jamie notices that he looks not at her, but at Seth. Once the couple is out of earshot, Jamie explains her observations.

"College-age couple. The young woman is more concerned about how she looks than actually getting any exercise. She's extra lean, had a boob job, and nobody works that hard on her hair just to go for a run. The boyfriend is just a trophy she wants; otherwise, she would have noticed he's bisexual."

"How do you do that?" Seth wonders. "Okay, then, what about this guy?"

An overweight man walks the trail toward them. He looks to be about sixty, and his tennis shoes are brand new. Jamie notices they do not even have the first scuff on them. Out of earshot, Jamie once again reveals her findings.

"He had bypass surgery not too long ago. This is probably one of his first attempts to 'workout'." She sketches the quote in the air. "I doubt he will keep it up for more than two or three weeks. After that, his most vigorous exercise will be finding the remote when it's lost between the couch cushions."

Seth whistles. "Harsh."

"The truth is hard, but we need it to change—to become better."

Chapter 3

Simon watches the national news on television. There is no mention of his handiwork. He checks the major news websites. Nothing. He can continue, unhindered. He needs the FBI. Where are they?

The Federal Bureau of Investigation. A crucial part of Simon's plan. He knows the FBI will have to get involved at some point. This part is for certain. But they are taking too long. Simon would not have cared if the FBI had come into the picture after the first, second, or even third job. But he definitely expected them by now. Where are they? Why is there nothing in the news? Where are the warnings to the vulnerable public of the USA? Maybe it is time for a more direct approach—to leave a note, to invite them in.

He gazes out his window at a flock of geese while he plays with this new idea.

Maybe it could say, "I want you to know that I want you to know about me." Or, "Well, hello there, what's taking so long? I've been waiting for you." Something whimsical. An invitation.

Chapter 4

My MEMOIR by Lola Englemann
I was born in the city of Propoc, not far from Kosice,
when it was originally part of Slovakia, in the year 1921. I
remember the sun and how it felt on those hot summer days in
Slovakia. The warm air mixed with the smell of rain on the wind.
My best friend, Mary, who lived across the street from our home,
and I would traverse around those back hills picking flowers and
making mud pies. Edit, my older cousin, would sometimes play
with us during the summers when her family came to visit ours
from Prague.
We would pretend to be birds flying through the hills as
the wind blew through our long braided hair. Sometimes we
would play hide-and-go-seek in the nearby woods, or follow a
stream as far as we dared. There was a group of boys in the
town, who my older brother was a part, and they would chase us.
It was one of my brother's friends that would change my life
forever.

Chapter 5

As they arrive back at Jamie's apartment, Seth broaches, "So…did you talk with Chris this morning?"

"No, he's usually gone before I wake up. It's a long drive to D.C. from my place. Plus traffic. Of course, it could be worse," Jamie concedes. "Things are pretty good between us, I guess."

"Good." Seth sets aside feelings and switches to logic. He had hoped that things would disintegrate long ago between Jamie and Chris, giving him a chance to move in. He is still hoping, waiting.

While trying to think of a way to extract relationship details, Seth realizes that Jamie's look is pensive—she is holding something back. As Jamie's best friend of several years, he knows that, if he gives her enough time, Jamie will tell him whatever is on her mind. After a few moments, she obliges.

"I've always seen myself as a low-maintenance. I don't do romantic nonsense. No swooning or primping, no flowers, no jewelry. That's not me. So why are things so complicated with Chris? I'm not jealous of his work. I want him to work. Besides, my job is also demanding. I think I just want him to make more of an effort."

"What are you looking for?"

"Something special, I guess. Exciting, you know? As for Chris, I'm not breaking up with him. And maybe, with time, he can prove to me that we have a deeper connection. I mean, I have feelings for him. I have to give him a chance." Jamie chuckles after she finishes explaining. "Thanks, Seth. Sometimes it helps to talk these things out. I don't know what I would do without you."

"Let's see, no FBI job that I helped you get. I think then you wouldn't have that nice apartment you live in. And you might have never even graduated without my help in Bio." Seth playfully counts off the reasons on his fingers, his eyes twinkling with the delight of anticipating Jamie's reaction.

"Hey, hey, hey. I know I owe you for so much. Believe me, you are my best friend." Jamie smiles. She teasingly pushes Seth in the shoulder.

"What time is it?"

Jamie looks down at her running watch. "Oh! About six-forty. I've gotta get moving."

"We both do. I'll see you around." Seth turns to make the short walk down the street to his house.

"Later!" Jamie waves and disappears into her apartment stairwell.

After a quick shower, she takes only seconds to apply a coat of mascara and a tasteful smidge of black eyeliner. That's all the makeup she ever needs. Jamie had roommates in college who would take hours to get ready for a date. Jamie would rather spend her time productively.

She enters the kitchen and grabs a yogurt from the fridge. Thanks to Chris, the coffee pot sits warm and ready. She takes both coffee and yogurt to the table. It is then that she spots a note on her tiny kitchen table. She must have missed it earlier.

> *Dearest Jamie,*
> *Would you please save a place for me on your calendar for a special date this Monday? I have made a very nice reservation at Bistro L'Hermitage restaurant. I'll pick you up at seven. Hopefully there will not be any work interference this time. Really looking forward to this.*
> *Love,*
> *Chris*

Jamie sighs and shoves the note into her purse. All she can think of is the last time Chris arranged a romantic dinner. Jamie found herself sipping a cup of white wine alone for an hour. When she finally received a text from Chris, it said he would not make it. He had to stay late to fix a hip fracture. "I can't control what time they fall and break their hips," was his justification. The worst part was that she could not argue.

Okay. Time to focus on work. That's what really matters to Jamie. Doing her utmost at the job she loves. Jamie slings her bag over one shoulder, picks up the coffee mug, and heads to Quantico, Virginia.

Chapter 6

Jamie pushes back a long strand of black hair and uses a key card to enter the main offices of the Federal Bureau of Investigation's National Center for the Analysis of Violent Crime (NCAVC). She presents her badge in order to bypass the scanners and metal detectors that screen visitors.

"Mornin', Ms. Golding," the young security guard salutes her with a wide grin.

"Hey, Jimmy. How's your son?"

"Becoming a basketball champ. He's got another game this afternoon!"

"Let me know how it turns out."

"You got it."

With a nod, she joins the rest of the employees heading toward the elevators, but she soon veers away from the crowd. Jamie prefers the stairs. The mingled colognes and perfumes of her coworkers make her dizzy. She takes a quick sip from her coffee cup to fortify her for the upward trek.

"Jamie!"

She turns to see the strawberry-blond Tyler ascending behind her. "Hi, Tyler. What's up?"

"Question for you," Tyler begins, falling into step with Jamie. "Is it because I'm new that Mr. Whitehouse is always that..."

"Grumpy, standoffish, and stiff?" Jamie laughs at her own descriptors, and at Tyler's conundrum. "Remember, he is not only your secretary. He has to serve six agents."

"No wonder he was so mad when I asked him to get me a Frappuccino from Starbucks," Tyler muses, a little breathless from the climb.

"You what?" Jamie wonders aloud, keeping step as she stares incredulously at Tyler. His face twists into bewilderment. Jamie looks back ahead and laughs heartily; Francis Whitehouse will never forgive poor Tyler for that. Tyler deflates a little, but Jamie goes on to advise him sincerely, "You're not in Kansas anymore, Toto, this is the NCAVC. You should be careful from now on. You have to get back on his good side, and it might take a while."

The key card gives them access to the inside offices. The wing is a large, open room, populated by cubicles. On the outer perimeter are offices that block the outside light from the cubes. Jamie makes her way through the maze to her own office. She is relieved to finally have an office with a view, instead of the repressive gray walls of the cubicles.

She unlocks the door identified as hers: "Special Agent Jamie Golding." The office itself holds only a heavy black desk, some office chairs, and a bookshelf. Prominently displayed on the top of the bookshelf is a picture of her crossing the finish line of the Potomac River Run Marathon. On the opposite wall is a motivational poster with a runner on a seemingly unending trail. The caption reads "TENACITY: Never look back. Just keep going."

Jamie finds a note conspicuously displayed on her desk: "0830, Conference Room A."

It is going to be an interesting Wednesday.

She sits in her chair and boots up her computer. She takes another sip of coffee. But before Jamie can even type in her password, a short man with thinning brown hair and a stern face leans in on her door frame.

"Did you get my note?" he drones, as if annoyed by the simple task.

"Yeah, what's up?"

"You know, they hardly tell me anything," Whitehouse responds with an eye roll. "I know it's something important, though. I was told to call Mr. Fredericks if I didn't see you by 8:10."

"What? Like I'm ever late? What's his problem?"

"You'll find out soon enough. Just be there early. I don't want him getting on my case. Mr. Fredericks is adamant about the 8:30 part." Whitehouse commands her as though he is her superior and not a secretary.

"Don't worry, I'll be plenty early."

"Anything you need in the interim?"

"No, I'm good, thanks."

Jamie knows very well what Francis Whitehouse's problem is. He has a Napoleon complex and is bitter about his male "Betty Bureau" status. He has worked in the same position for eighteen years and has watched agents come and go. He is good at what he does but lives with a chip on his shoulder.

Jamie heads to Conference Room A. Special Agent Joey Hughes sits at the long, cherry table. Joey grew up in Brooklyn with an Italian mother and American father. He is very street-smart, but he is also cocky, arrogant, and a self-perceived playboy. He is a seasoned agent who recounts his best stories over and over. Everything about him rubs Jamie the wrong way.

Across from Joey is Special Agent Phil Clark. Phil is a tall, lean, and handsome African-American with a near-genius IQ. He is laid back and would never tell anyone he has been a member of MENSA since the age of seven. He is very sociable, and his breadth of knowledge allows him talk to just about anybody. He has been with the Bureau a few years longer than Jamie, and he showed her the ropes when she began as an agent.

"Looking delicious this morning, Jamie," Joey sasses at her. His dark brown eyes watch carefully for a response. Jamie proudly displays her middle finger.

"You better watch it, Joey, I think you're beginning to recycle lines."

Jamie seats herself in the nearest chair (and farthest from Joey). Arranging her tablet and coffee mug on the conference table, she tries to ignore his continued attempts to engage her. "I should have known that you two would be here for a special meeting. I guess we are the best of the best, huh?"

At least he doesn't think of me as a "clagent" any more. That is what they call FBI agents that move up from clerical positions.

"Anyone know what happened between Whitehouse and that new kid, Tyler? Phil asks sincerely, addressing the table at large. "I overheard some heated give-and-take yesterday."

"He asked Whitehouse to run to Starbucks for a Frappuccino." Jamie divulges, although she immediately regrets giving Tyler's problem away.

"He didn't!" Joey's shock rapidly dissolves into hysterical laughter.

Phil also starts laughing the moment Jamie says the words. He pauses long enough between gasps of laughter to add, "I would have loved—to see Whitehouse's face—at that moment!"

Phil's words make Joey laugh even harder. Even Jamie cannot help chuckling as she imagines Whitehouse's reaction to Tyler's absurd request.

Phil wipes a tear from his eye and jokes, "Let Tyler know he's gotta sleep in the bed he's made."

"Yeah, I basically told him the same thing," Jamie confirms, trying to control her own laughter.

A blonde woman enters the room. "Good, you are all early, and...happy." She wears a curve-defining red dress and matching red heels and nail polish. "Mr. Fredericks will be pleased you are all here already." She begins setting up a laptop and preparing the overhead projector.

"Morning, Cynthia! Looking delicious as always. How are we?" Joey grins widely, clearly undressing her with his eyes. There is a near-collective eye roll.

"Busy. Mr. Fredericks will be here soon. You should move closer to this side of the room, Joey, but leave a chair open."

Joey watches her as she moves around the room, further preparing for Fredericks's arrival by pulling down the white projector screen. He makes no effort to hide his thoughts.

Jamie makes little attempt to mask her disgust. She turns her attention to a new email from Chris.

Good Morning Sweetheart,

I hope you found the note I left you this morning. It was tough not to kiss my sleeping beauty awake before I left. I'm on

call this weekend, but I really want to do a special dinner on
Monday. Please dress up for the occasion.
                    Love,
                Chris
          Interesting, Jamie thinks. He does not usually send her e-
mails. Has she ever e-mailed him before? How would she
address him? If she skipped playing the cutesy stuff (not her
style), would Chris be offended? Of course, replying more
formally could be even more insulting. Her better option is just
to answer him with a phone call. Yes, that will be safer.

Out of the corner of her eye, Jamie spies a tall, thin man
entering the room briskly. She could recognize her boss
anywhere, with his purposeful stride and commanding posture.
Howard Fredericks is in his early forties, but the stress and worry
etched into his gaunt face say otherwise. He is Special Agent in
Charge and Jamie's direct supervisor. He adjusts his glasses as
he stares down the room. Satisfied with what he sees, he turns
and, with a nod and a wave, introduces the man who stands
expectantly behind him.

"You all know Larry Thompson, the Assistant Director in
Charge of the NCAVC."

Jamie and Phil shoot each other looks of surprise to see
the ADIC. Larry Thompson is none other than Fredericks's boss.
The ADIC does not usually sit in on case discussions. Thompson
takes the open seat next to Joey, and they exchange polite smiles.
Joey sits up a little straighter.

"I apologize for the short notice, but Thompson needs to
report to H.Q. in D.C. at 10 a.m. We have no time for small talk.
So let's get straight to the point. This is a sensitive matter. We
have a serial killer. The victims are all elderly white males. There
is hardly any physical evidence. At each crime scene, a single
cryptic note is found."

Thompson clears his throat and continues, "The media is
currently unaware that the murders are connected, since they are
scattered around the country, and the victims are old men. Two
of the murders actually occurred in nursing homes. We need to
either solve this case quickly or go to the media ourselves.
Otherwise it will reflect very poorly on the Bureau."

"Exactly!" Fredericks agrees, staring down at Jamie, Phil, and Joey.

Thompson resumes his overview as if there had been no interruption. "The most recent murder occurred this past Sunday. The local detective in charge of the case asked for our help. Apparently the crime scene was abnormally clean—too clean. The Chicago office located three other murders that match the same M.O. over a three-year period. There are no leads in those cases either. And we must assume that there will be more murders to come.

"Let's hope the perp eventually slips up." Thompson looks slowly around the table, letting his gaze pause on each agent. He finishes by staring at Fredericks, who recognizes the signal that Thompson is finished.

"Cynthia," Fredericks directs, not missing a beat.

She jumps to start the PowerPoint slide presentation.

"The murders have been spread out over the last two-and-a-half years," she opens.

The screen reads, "Sep 29, 2010; Mar. 20, 2011; Mar 8, 2012; Feb 24, 2013." The next slide shows a map of the United States with red dots marking the places where the murders occurred.

"As you can see, we have victims in Salem, New York; Abilene, Texas; Flint, Michigan; and the latest one right outside Chicago, Illinois," Mr. Fredericks lists, using a laser pointer to indicate each of the already-highlighted cities.

"All four victims died in the same manner, strangled with wire, approximately ten-gauge." The slide shows four pictures of neck wounds. They appear to be identical. Fredericks continues, "All four had a note in the left hand with two or three large letters and a series of words across the bottom. We think they may be initials of some sort, but each set is different."

The slide changes to show a picture of an elderly man, an obvious postmortem.

"The first victim is Jules Henning, 88. He was apparently driven from his home in Schenectady, New York, almost fifty miles, to Salem, New York.

Another map, demonstrating the distance between Schenectady and Salem, appears on the screen. The next slide is of an elderly man, lying in front of a red building clearly identified as, "United States Postal Services, Post Office of Shushan, New York, 12873." The old man lying in the mud looks like a peacefully-sleeping homeless man.

"Here is the fatal wound on his neck." A new slide of the victim shows a close-up of the place where the wire bit into the skin, leaving angry red lacerations.

The next slide pictures a square note with the large, carefully-typed letters "J.V.R." right in the middle. In the bottom left-hand corner of the note, it says, "Pars", then "Hon" in the middle, and "Dota" in the right corner.

"No fingerprints or fibers—the notes are clear of any trace evidence. The other three victims had similar notes. Different words and letters, but the same format."

"Survived by wife and daughter. No possible motives for either. His daughter is unmarried, quite the cat enthusiast, but also a financially stable librarian and dedicated child. Wife now lives with the daughter."

Another picture of an elderly man in bed.

"Victim two is Hans Bierman, 94, found strangled in his own bed in a nursing home in Abilene, Texas."

Another close-up of a neck wound fills the screen.

Jamie is bursting with questions about these murders, but instead of asking, she furiously scribbles them down on her tablet. Experience has shown that Fredericks ignores anything that interrupts his presentation and berates any person who does the same. Jamie must wait until the end. She glances to the side and sees Phil also writing on his own tablet.

"Note the similarity of the wound."

Another note flashes on the screen. This time the big letters are "W.K." In the bottom right corner is "dol," and in the bottom left corner, "fon."

These notes have to be the key.

"An interesting fact about this murder is that Mr. Bierman was visited earlier that day by a female, and there were female hairs found near the victim. It's possible that the hair could belong to the perp, as no matches were made to employees of the nursing home. Either way, the hair hasn't brought any new leads. All of his relatives have solid alibis."

26

Another victim. This one is slumped behind the bar in his home.

"Third victim, Leon Farbor, 88, was found in his home in Flint, Michigan, by his cleaning lady. He had been dead for about a day. Mr. Farbor has one daughter. She is very financially secure—more so than her father, actually—as her husband is a successful stockbroker in Los Angeles. Local police found no forced entry, no possible motives, and, again, no usable evidence. The place was washed so clean as to suggest that the perp had considerable time to spend scrubbing away his presence."

Another mangled neck.

"Same wound."

Another note. "A.R." in big letters, with "por" in the bottom right-hand corner, "at in the middle and "ha" in the left-hand corner.

The next slide depicts a new victim, in his bed.

"The fourth victim, Fred Schmidt, 91, was murdered this past Sunday, near Chicago, in a nicer, more expensive assisted living facility. He was discovered early Monday morning. His time of death is estimated to be around 9 p.m. on Sunday night. Local police questioned the staff. Evidence points to a man in his thirties, with long hair, who was the last non-staff person to see Mr. Schmidt alive. The staff of the facility said the man had visited frequently on the weekends to read to the victim. He claimed to be from a church group, but no one can verify which group or whether it's even true. Mr. Schmidt has a son who was unaware of anyone visiting his father. Again the room was spotless. No solid evidence, but we are still awaiting trace."

A final neck close-up.

"Again, same wound."

And the last note. "F.S." in big letters on the card. Spaced across the bottom: "parmo", "sh", and "ta."

Fredericks begins to say something, but is cut off as Thompson clears his throat and resumes, "VICAP has connected all of these cases, and now I need NCVAC to pick them up. I can't stay, but I expect to be kept fully up-to-date. Alert me if another victim turns up, and I will decide when and what, the local police should be told about the others. We are checking databases for a similar M.O. and to find possible leads. I do not want the idea of a serial killer to come from some local police detective. It should come from us. But I want to see what you dig up first before we come out that we are on the case."

When he finishes, Thompson pauses a moment, perhaps expecting everyone to stand up. No one does. He briskly exits the room. Fredericks reestablishes control.

"Cynthia, get the Chicago cops on the line." He turns to the agents. "Do you have any questions?"

"Do the victims have anything in common?" Phil raises a finger and opens the discussion.

"We are researching the victims, but there's nothing so far. I expect all of you to further delve into the victims' lives and find any connections that might exist."

"Was it possible that Jules Henning was already in Salem? Does he have family or friends in that town?" Jamie asks.

"According to his wife, he was home when she left him that morning. Next."

Joey jumps in. "So his car was not found in the post office parking lot?"

"No, it was still at his residence in Schenectady."

"Did the local police find a possible crime scene in Mr. Henning's home?" Jamie fires at him, not looking up as she scans her list of questions.

"There is no evidence of a crime scene in the home."

Before Jamie can ask another question, Cynthia catches Fredericks's eye.

"Detective Ragsdale, please hold for Mr. Fredericks," she intones automatically into the receiver of the conference table phone. Then she announces," Mr. Fredericks, I have Detective Ragsdale from the Harwood Heights Police Department on the line."

"Good. Put him on speaker." The crackle of new work becomes suddenly still as all pause to listen.

Cynthia presses a button and then nods seriously to her boss.

"Detective Ragsdale, this is Howard Fredericks, we spoke earlier. I have Special Agents Jamie Golding, Phil Clark and Joey Hughes listening in. Please tell us what you have so far?"

A deep, gruff voice begins with a sigh, "In two decades on the job, I've never seen anything like this." His tone becomes businesslike. "The victim was killed in a well-staffed assisted living center. One that costs a pretty penny, too. Secondly, all the surfaces in the room were wiped down with a strong cleaner. There wasn't even dust around the legs of the bed. In other rooms you could find dust and debris under the bed, but this had been cleaned beyond what the best facility staff can do. The garbage can was newly emptied. Nothing...."

"Can you explain to my team where and how the victim was found?"

"The nursing assistant who found Mr. Schmidt said he was tucked in like a baby. Here's where it gets ugly. She was sure he died in his sleep. The nurse practitioner that pronounced him dead didn't even notice his neck at first. Mr. Schmidt's sons were contacted and told that he died in his sleep. It was the funeral directors that saw the neck wound when they went to transfer him out of his bed and onto the gurney. After that a real nightmare ensued. They had to tell the family, and by the time I arrived, it had become heated, to say the least."

"Right. Now, the room? Maybe someone from the facility cleaned the room while Mr. Schmidt was sleeping?"

"No, sir. I checked. The staff is adamant that they did not clean the room that night. Disturbs the residents, and all."

"There were no hairs or fibers near the wound? No prints? Nothing at all?" Fredericks asks.

"Our guys are pretty good. They went over that room with a fine-tooth comb. In the end, they left with only one or two vials of nearly nothing, just some specks of dust, if you ask me. I'll get you the results as soon as they are in, but the prelim doesn't look like much. Won't be too much help there."

"Detective Ragsdale, I am giving the file to Special Agent Golding. She will also be given your contact info. Tomorrow she will be flying out to Harwood Heights to meet with you and examine the crime scene. In the interim, Cynthia will get you her number, in case there are any new developments. Golding, any questions for the detective before we hang up?"

"Do we know if there's a way to contact the man who last saw Mr. Schmidt?"

"No one knows who he is or where to start looking for him. His name was a fake and a dead end."

"Anything else?" Fredericks adds.

"No, sir."

"Call us if anything changes. Thank you."

Before Detective Ragsdale can give a response, Cynthia hangs up the phone.

"Jamie, for now this is essentially going to be your case." At a nod from Fredericks, Cynthia gives several large file folders to Jamie. "Clark should have some time to help, but Hughes is too swamped."

Joey smiles gloatingly as he leans back in his chair and crosses his arms.

Jamie is relieved she will not have to work with Joey. Joey is the kind of agent that jumps in towards the end of an investigation and tries to take credit for everyone else's work. Jamie prefers working with Phil, who is much more reliable, trustworthy, and, generally upright.

Mr. Fredericks continues undeterred. "They will, however, both make themselves available to you if you turn up any leads. I want you to keep them apprised, as well as myself. Clark, Hughes, I do expect you to help her out when you can. I especially do not want any of you to do anything without backup. There is no telling what we are up against. When it is time to move in, I want it coordinated to the last detail. Absolutely no screw-ups here. I want a full team on the arrest with the best forensics possible. We're going to have to hang this perp with the smallest thread of evidence that he leaves us. It has to be just right, or we'll miss him. And we do not want him out on the streets any longer."

Mr. Fredericks glares straight into Jamie's eyes. His face is gaunt, pale. "Jamie, I want you to go through the files and visit each crime scene. Then compose a profile to get to Behavioral. After that we can regroup and see how far we've gotten."

"Yes, sir."

"Cynthia will arrange any accommodations you need, and she will be giving you the information. I have other business to attend to."

"I'll email you an itinerary ASAP." Cynthia briskly collects the laptop and powers down the projector. She dashes out of the room after Mr. Fredericks.

"Good luck, Jamie! Let me know if I can help you with anything." Joey smirks as he leaves the conference room.

"Well, I don't envy you too much with this case," Phil says, gathering his tablet and coffee mug. Standing up, he adds, "I promise you can count on me if you need any help."

"You're already first on my list, Phil." Jamie returns the smile he gives her. "Joey drives me nuts—thinks he's some kind of prima donna."

"Well said," Phil chuckles. "Maybe he is."

Chapter 7

Of course, not all of summer was just playing in the hills and following the wind. My mother and I lived with my grandparents, who owned the dry goods store. Most days during the summer I would work in the store helping. My chores included sweeping the floor, tidying up, and, with Mother's help, stocking the shelves. As I grew older, my jobs increased. I could help write the prices, cut fabric, and take money for the penny candy.

In the fall we would start school. Since my family was well off, I went to the private Neolog school, and Mary went to regular school. Mary was always eagerly waiting for me to come home, as my school finished a half hour later. We would often head to my grandparents' dry goods store and get a piece of hard candy. My school offered a snack every morning, which was rare back then. We had uniforms that were required for school, sailor suits with a skirt. I always enjoyed learning and did well. I received ones in all my subjects. I was eager to learn more. Mary was not as interested in school and was prone to even get threes or fours in her subjects.

Winter was always full of excitement. We would go ice-skating as often as our mothers would allow it and looked forward to sleigh rides through the snow. I also had a wooden sled that Mary and I would use to sled down the hills. We would come in half frozen but get quickly warmed up by hot stew for dinner.

I wish now that those carefree years would have lasted forever. Sometimes as a child, you never realize how wonderful life is. Instead, you enjoy it without a thought of what is to come next. Those moments when we could escape into nature and play are memories I still treasure to this day.

Chapter 8

Jamie dodges people as she makes her way back through the wing. Relieved to be out of the parade in the hallways, Jamie steps into her office and receives a surprise: Seth Cooper is waiting there for her. He looks good in his work clothes, with his dark and curly hair combed. Smiling, Jamie puts the files on her desk and slumps into her chair with a quick, "Hey, what's up?"

Seth smiles back. "Up for a beer after work tonight? I've got no plans." He takes a seat in the chair across from Jamie.

"I don't know. I just got a huge case." She wants to go out, but with the conference fresh in her mind, she feels stressed by the importance of the new assignment.

Seth eyes the pile on her desk. "What is it?"

Jamie pauses for effect. She can always count on Seth. He's been there for her since college. It is Seth who talked her into joining the Bureau and even helped her get on there.

"It's a serial killer case. Strange one if you ask me. Unusual, I mean. I will have to spend the night combing through these files for leads."

Seth rubs his chin thoughtfully. "Well, you do have to eat. Let's get a quick bite around six. You can't pull an all-nighter on an empty stomach."

Jamie half smiles at Seth, then caves. "Alright, sure."

"Great!" Seth jumps up from the chair. "Got to get back to the Forensics lab."

"Oh I know. The FBI Crime Lab is lost without you, their amazing supervisor." Jamie loves teasing Seth. She feels her tightness dissolving with laughter.

"That's right," Seth says confidently, putting his hands in his pants pockets. "See you tonight."

"Call me." Jamie moves her chair closer to her desk and grabs the top file off the stack.

"Yeah." Seth walks out of the room. He takes a quick glance back at Jamie, who is lost in her work before he has even left.

*   *   *   *

Jamie rubs her eyes for the third time in the last ten minutes. She has studied each file. She had hoped that there might be something there to link these four victims. Something that, by itself, might not seem relevant to the local homicide detective, but that would show up in all four files together. The only commonality is that the victims are elderly white males strangled with a wire ligature. Maybe the trips to the crime scenes will turn up some kind of pattern. She does think it very odd that they are so spread out. More often serial killers start close to home and stay within a confined radius.

She picks up her coffee cup, only to find it is already empty. Standing up to go refill it, she recalls that she has already had three cups. Jamie sinks back into her chair and reads each file again. Her mind is trying to wrap itself around the fact someone would purposely kill elderly males who only have years, if not months, left to live. Why kill a man who is in his eighties or nineties? What is the point?

It could be that the elderly do not put up as much resistance. Easy to overpower. Possibly, the murderer might be physically weak with a strong psychopathic desire to kill. For some reason his demons direct him to kill males, and he simply cannot succeed against someone younger and stronger. Maybe that is why the murderer is using a ligature of some sort as his weapon. He wants to watch the victim die, but he lacks the strength to inflict a mortal wound.

Maybe the murderer had some sort of abusive relationship with a father figure, which would explain why he kills older men. If these men represented his father, that would place the murderer in his fifties or sixties. Looking over the report again, Jamie notices that the latest victim had a visitor from a man in his thirties, and the man in Abilene had a visitor from a female, also in her thirties. Same perp? It is possible. Master of Disguise? What if it is not the same killer? These are elderly men after all. With the right tools, a woman could easily strangle an old man. Even so, how did the perp get close enough to slip a wire around their necks without being stopped?

Could it be a grandfather figure? Is the perp someone who grew up with an abusive grandfather? Do the victims resemble each other? If so, the victims might look like the abusive father or grandfather. If it is someone out to kill his "grandfather", then the killer may have similar physical characteristics as well. The ages of the victims are a very tight range, 88-94. *That should be significant.*

Another consideration. Are elderly men more trusting, and thereby more willing to let a stranger into their homes? How did the perp know that they would be alone? And not all of them *were* alone. Why take the risk of getting caught by killing someone in a nursing home? Then again, if you want targets in their eighties and nineties, then that is where you would find them. But what drives a need to kill men in this age range? Very bizarre. It is interesting that none of the victims were found right away. The killer had plenty of time to disappear back into society.

Jamie again reads the statements from the people who found each of the bodies, along with the shocking discovery by a funeral home director. There has to be a link to all of these cases.

The geography is also perplexing. If the perp is fixated on killing his abusive grandfather, or someone who resembles him, what is the explanation for the vast distances between the victims? Often, the first victim is someone very close to home. Someone the killer might see several times, until the demons talk the killer into acting on those sick thoughts. That might explain the first victim, but the others...why so far apart?

With the advent of social media, maybe the perp sees pictures of the victims on the Internet, and the sight of his "grandfather" triggers his rage. If only people really knew what the bad guys can get from pictures online. So many pictures now are taken by smartphones with a GPS. The same geo-tracking technology that enables location services also puts a geotag on the pictures. A perp can find a picture online, then access the data file and determine exactly where the picture was taken. So maybe our perp chose his victims based solely on what they looked like, then tracked their location via geotagging.

The planning is so meticulous. A true compulsive behavior would lead to a more spontaneous attack and therefore be disorganized. This perp, like a lot of psychopaths, is highly intelligent and is organized.

The notes found at each murder seem to be the most linking factor. Why leave a note with your murder victim? To prove some sort of point? Maybe to leave a calling card? A signature?

Her next thought is that it might be some sort of code. Maybe the words are scrambled. She takes the first note "Pars" ,"hon", and "dota." Rap, hons, toad? Maybe all the words on the bottom are meant to be strung together as one. Sharp, tharps, donts, stood, shot, rash, rasp. She needs to use all the letters which would make it that much harder. That's what computers are good for.

A young and very pretty brunette taps lightly on Jamie's door. "Special Agent Golding?"

"Yes."

"Hi, I'm Kim Hammond from Research. I found another murder with the same description. White male, 89, on October 19, 2011."

"No way! Where?"

"New Orleans."

"Are we getting the file?"

"Already done—they just faxed it over. Here is what I've got." Kim hands a file off to Jamie.

"Good work, thanks."

With a nod, Kim leaves the office, and Jamie picks up her office phone. She is connected to Whitehouse immediately.

"Whitehouse, I need you to book me a flight to New Orleans for Friday."

"Fine. Do you want a window seat?"

"No, but I need a return trip the same day." Jamie informs him, ignoring his sarcasm.

"OK."

Jamie can practically see him rolling his eyes. "Thanks."

She does not have time to waste dealing with Whitehouse. She is itching to open the new file. She compares the October date with the other dates. There is one in February, two in March, then September and October. Perhaps the killer likes the cooler weather. She carefully reads the newest file. Janos Kerekes, 89, married. Also strangled with a wire ligature. Murdered right at the front door of his house. His wife was home at the time and heard the knock. Someone called out to her to call 9-1-1 because her husband was having a heart attack. The wife is wheelchair-bound and did not see anything. They have a visiting assistant every day from 8 A.M. until 5 p.m., who helps them with activities of daily living and with light housework. The nursing assistant prepares dinner before she leaves. The murder took place at 6:30 p.m. Neither the wife nor the assistant reported any visitors or strange occurrences leading up to the murder.

A note left at the scene had the initials "E.K." in the middle and "a"…"spat"…"a" spaced along the bottom. No fingerprints. Police hypothesize that it was a random murder, maybe some sort of gang initiation. The Kerekes lived in a low income, high crime part of town. "The neighborhood has changed over the years," was a comment one of their sons made. "I've been trying to get them to move for some time, but the house is paid off, and my father would not hear of it. They have lived in the same house for over fifty years."

Jamie enters the initials and cryptic words into a computer program to see what words can be unscrambled. The program generates a long list of potential words of varying lengths. No cogent sentences use all of the letters. She will have to peruse the list and see if anything jumps out at her.

The phone rings on her desk, and Jamie answers, "Special Agent Golding here."

"Hey, you ready?" Seth's smooth voice comes over the phone. She knows him well enough to hear his grin.

"Whoa, it can't be six already! I just got started." Jamie continues to read through the random words. At this point she is trying to use all of the words from each of the notes. She knows it is a long shot, but maybe she will catch something.

"I know you love your work, but Jamie it's almost six. You need to eat. Come on."

"Just pick me up something and drop it by." Jamie tries to remember which letter she has left out in her attempt to make sense of the notes.

"You need to take a break. It will be my treat, okay?"

Jamie recognizes the stubborn tone in his voice. "Alright." Maybe a break could stop the oncoming headache and refresh her perspective. "Where we going?"

"How about we just drive together. The car is warm and ready. We'll just go to the pub so it will be quick."

"Warm car" finally convinces Jamie. "Fine, you win. I'm on my way down."

Seth attempts a British butler's accent. "I live to please you."

Jamie hangs up, gathers her things, and leaves her office in a hurry.

She walks past a few offices that have agents still working within. Jamie knows she will not be working a late night alone.

Jamie sees Seth waiting outside of her building, washed in the dying sunlight.

"Hey, I'm glad you came. You already look exhausted."

"That bad, eh?" Jamie delivers him a playful poke in the shoulder.

"That hurt!" Seth rubs his arm as though in actual pain. Then he states seriously, "Sorry, I didn't mean that. I just meant that you need a break, and I'm glad you're taking it with me."

"Of course! Besides, Chris is busy tonight." A chill wind disrupts her thoughts. "Let's go. It's getting cold out here."

"That, and my stomach is growling." Seth offers his arm and leads her to the BMW waiting at the curb. He opens the car door for her and watches Jamie gracefully slide into the seat. Seth slips into the driver's seat and starts to maneuver through the campus roads and out past the guard booth and gate. Although there is quiet between them, it is not uncomfortable. They do not have to fill every second with conversation.

Jamie finally breaks the silence. "So how are things going at the lab?"

"A few of the guys are testing my limits. Normally I don't like to rein the employees in too tight—it's not my style."

"Really? I remember you were quite the task master as a T.A. in biology."

"I was young and eager."

"So what are they trying to get away with?"

"The usual. Coming to work late, leaving early, taking extra long lunches. It's always the same group, the repeat offenders."

Seth stops at a red light. Jamie carefully watches some pedestrians cross the street.

"I guess they're not as dedicated to the job as you are."

The light turns, and Seth takes a left around the corner. "Yeah, I have to remind them of the importance of their work. Our forensics can put away a criminal and save lives. Nothing can be more satisfying than discovering the real bad guy and stopping them for good."

"Hate to break your bubble, Captain America, but they do get away sometimes." She admires Seth for his dedication to catching criminals, but there is a reality he sometimes forgets. There is a legal process that does not always keep the bad guys in jail.

"I know. Of course, we can only analyze what you guys bring us. There are still cases that bother me because we might be able to prove someone was at the scene, but we don't get the hard evidence to back it up. I guess that's why I do what I can so that as few as possible slip through the cracks."

"Speaking of cracks," Jamie points out, "there's a parking spot!"

"Perfect."

They enter the warm pub and find an empty table for two. When the waitress arrives they order without even looking at the menu. They both have their favorites. Minutes later, the waitress brings their drinks.

Jamie sighs and sips the beer that the waitress put before her. "So. I had a nightmare last night."

"You didn't say anything this morning."

"I know. I was hoping to forget about it. Last night, Chris told me about how he had a patient who'd had a fight with a circular saw. Obviously, the saw won." Jamie pauses, and Seth grimaces at the thought.

"I know, really. I guess I am just shocked at how I am affected more by a complete stranger whose fingers were cut off and then reattached than I am about my last case. You know, the one with the psychopath who dismembered the guy and stored him in his freezer."

"Must be your fear of table saws." Seth also takes a drink from his beer, then adds, "Seriously, I wouldn't worry about it. You have a very different job from Chris, and the two of you tackle your work in different ways. Besides, I would have nightmares about that too if it was the last thing I heard before bed."

Jamie laughs. "Good point. I really shouldn't let him tell me those things right before I go to sleep."

Seth nods, taking another sip of beer. The waitress interrupts them by bringing a turkey burger for Jamie and a large bowl of chili, no cheese or sour cream, for Seth. After the waitress leaves, Jamie picks the tomato off her burger, then picks up the conversation again.

"You see, he sent me an email today. I don't know. It was weird. An email invitation to a fancy dinner with all of these cutesy names in it. And that was after he left a note this morning with the same invitation. I mean, an email? He is promising me another amazing romantic date to make up for all the other times it didn't work out." Jamie stops to take a huge bite out of the burger. "And now I've got this case."

She chews thoughtfully before continuing, "I haven't given him an answer yet. Hey, how are things with Marcy?"

Margie. Seth tries to overlook this fact and replies, "She is okay, but nothing really special." He eats a spoonful of hot chili and tears off a bit of his side of corn bread. "So tell me about this new case." Her immediate frown speaks volumes to Seth.

"Well, it's really strange. There have been a total of five murders. All the victims are eighty years or older. I cannot figure

out why someone would want to kill a bunch of old, white men."
She picks up the dill pickle and slowly munches it.

"That is strange. All in the same area?"

Jamie puts down her turkey burger. "The murders are
scattered around the U.S." She pauses, then adds, "I wish they
were all in the same place; might make my job easier. But no, all
five happened in different locations."

"So what's your next step?"

"I am actually heading to Chicago tomorrow. Friday I'm
going to New Orleans, and then back here to spend the weekend
researching the files. I'll be in Schenectady Monday morning."

"Schenectady?"

"The first murder happened there. Well, we think that's
the first murder." Jamie munches a French fry.

"You weren't joking that they are across the country.
That's a good haul from Chicago. Don't serial killers usually stay
closer to home?"

"Like I said, this is a very strange case."

Two women walking into the bar catch Jamie's eye. As
they take off their coats, Jamie sees that they are dressed to kill.
They wear stilettos, tight black mini-skirts, and loose-fitting
halter-tops. Both women saunter past Jamie's table and up to the
bar behind her. She watches Seth, who does not even flinch or
divert his eyes from her own face.

"You're not turning gay are you?"

"What?" Seth is comically incredulous. "Why would you
ask that?"

"You didn't see those women? Even *I* was staring at
them. Chris would have tried to hide it, but he still would have
been obvious about checking them out. And, of course, he would
think I didn't catch him. It would be funny, actually."

Seth shrugs and responds, "I'm here with you—why
would I look at them? Besides, I never get tired of talking to
you."

Chapter 9

Simon sits at a table at his favorite Starbucks. There is a Starbucks much closer to his home, but Simon prefers this one. This Starbucks sits at the end of a strip mall that has a major chain grocery store in the middle, surrounded by several mom-and-pop stores and a few other franchises. Outside, the parking lot is very busy, but that is not what makes this Starbucks attractive. Most of the orders at this Starbucks are to-go, allowing Simon to find a small table to himself against the wall. It is the perfect place to set up his laptop so that the screen is not visible to anyone walking past. Simon casually glances around to see if he will have to deal with any nosy neighbors. But those around him are too deeply entranced by their own laptops to care about Simon.

He sets up his special black laptop. It is special because Simon only uses it when at a public Wi-Fi hotspot. He has made sure to never even turn on the computer at or near his house. When he is not using it, Simon keeps it carefully hidden in a locked file cabinet in a self-storage unit. He even takes the precaution of buying a brand new computer whenever he has finished research on the next victim. He pays cash for each laptop. Simon completely destroys the computer before he strikes. He knows that no matter how many times someone scrubs clean a hard drive, the Feds can see every keystroke that person has ever made, every website they ever visited, and every email they ever received.

Simon accesses the Internet and loads Google maps. He types in the next victim's address. In seconds, a clear image of the home appears. Simon smiles to see the old man's twenty-year-old Buick in the driveway on the satellite image.

The car is probably in the exact same spot right now.

The house is a traditional, two-story colonial home in an old, established neighborhood in the Buckhead area in Atlanta, Georgia.

He studies the tall, thick hardwoods and pines that surround the home. It is so dense that Simon can hardly see the neighbors' houses on either side. He checks his notes. A unique feature of the house is that the driveway extends past the right side of the house toward a two-car garage that is perpendicular to the street and connects to the breakfast room at the back of the house. Perfect. His plan to gain access to the house is based on this very useful feature.

Laughter pulls him away from the computer. Most of the crowd is gone now, and a blonde girl is flirting with her male coworker behind the counter. Together they wipe down the counters and clean the machines. They are so busy with each other that Simon feels secure in his privacy. Yet he still remains mindful of the noises and action around him. He sips his coffee and returns to his computer.

As he peruses his notes, Simon thinks to himself that this will be the easiest kill of all. The old man rarely leaves his house. He lives with his wife of over fifty years. No maid, no other family members, and no visitors. All Simon has to do is catch the old man when his chubby wife is at water aerobics. There is nothing like a bunch of fat old women bouncing in the water at the YMCA, thinking that they are exercising. They probably get more exercise from walking across the parking lot, changing into their bathing suits, and getting into the pool, than they actually do *in* the water. He assumes it gives them something to look forward to other than doctor visits. In this case, it provides the perfect window of opportunity for Simon to get his business done.

One more down. Although Simon had at first felt a sense of euphoria from his work, it has now become a tedious task. An annoying chore that never seems to be finished. It is unsettling to

Simon that the excitement so quickly dissipated into a feeling of burden. The nightmares do not help either. He should be sleeping better, knowing that he is destroying the monsters.

In a way, it does feel good to get so much "work" done, Simon thinks to himself. His progress is better than he could have imagined. And there is no guilt associated with any of these acts. Instead, each one brings him a step closer to freedom from the demons. The rest of the world seems so loose and carefree, but Simon is suffocating in the tight grip of the monsters. He will be done soon enough, and then he can move on and be finally free.

As he takes another drink of coffee, his eyes scan the name "Martin Rossi." Mr. Rossi will be so easy to eliminate that it could be done at any time. Well, any Tuesday between 9 a.m. and 11 a.m.

Glancing at the clock in the corner of his laptop screen, Simon decides that he has spent long enough at the Starbucks. No one marks his departure, neither the employees nor the constant stream of customers in and out of the store. Just the way Simon likes it.

Chapter 10

Seth Cooper sits at his desk, looking over the control results of one of the toxicology analyzers. The work is not exactly glamorous, but someone has to do it. The results to several cases are stacked neatly in one corner. Once again, he must double-check the work of others. Every once in a while, someone makes a mistake. Forensics is very tedious, but a botched sample can sway the outcome of the investigation, or even turn a court case. Seth works through most of his lunches to stay on top of the mountains of paper. But today he lets his mind wander. Jamie occupies his thoughts once again.

He remembers the first moment he laid eyes on Jamie Golding. It was at the University of Maryland, where Seth was a teacher's assistant and lab instructor for several science courses. This is not an unusual fate for a graduate student in Forensic Science. It was one fall semester that Jamie Golding took an undergraduate biology class as a prerequisite to get into the Masters in Forensic Psychology program. Seth was her TA and lab instructor.

He can still see her walking into his first lab session and taking a seat at the front of the class. Her satin black hair framed her beautiful face and accentuated her hazel eyes. Seth admired her tight jeans, which were intriguingly set off by a baggy university sweatshirt. Seth was definitely interested to know more about her. He also noticed that Jamie wore a gold necklace with a Jewish star. During their time in the class together, Seth and Jamie discovered that they had plenty in common. Even though Forensic Psych and Forensic Science share only a common term, Seth was able to spend more time talking with Jamie after classes or study sessions.

Ever since that first lab, Seth had been trying to get her attention. He could not help himself; he was stricken. Unfortunately, Seth's attempts to engage Jamie led to an uphill battle. The timing just never seemed to work. At first, Jamie saw him as only an instructor and could not bridge the student/teacher gap. At the end of the semester, she seemed to relax around him, but she was dating someone else. He invited her into his circle of friends, introducing her to other people who were studying different types of forensics. There was Barry Shapiro, or "Shap," who also went on to the FBI crime lab, and Steve Lansing, who went to an independent lab, and Richie Nguyen, who moved back to California. It was a fun group, while it lasted. Right under Seth's nose, Jamie broke up with her boyfriend and started dating Steve Lansing. After that, Seth began to date one of Jamie's Forensic Psychology friends, Karen. He was not going to sit around and wait for Jamie.

Once Jamie ended her relationship with Steve, Seth tried to pick things up with her. He invited her to his place to hang out and casually asked her to dinner. She pushed him away quickly. At first Seth had been confused, but then he realized that Jamie rejected him because he was still dating Karen. It was an awkward moment. By the time Seth broke things off with Karen, Jamie had already moved on to date a guy from her Criminal Psych class. Timing was still not in Seth's favor. Yet one thing Seth could hold on to was their friendship. Their mutual Forensics friends became a group that hung out constantly. By the end of his schooling, Seth was the best of friends with Jamie.

Seth graduated first and found a job working with the FBI at the National Crime Lab in Quantico, Virginia. It became a cycle: Jamie would pick up a new boyfriend, and Seth would miss his chance. Seth would drive the hour to double-date with Jamie and her new guy. He knew that it often annoyed his own dates, who did not want to spend two hours in the car on a Saturday night. Over time, Seth stopped looking at Jamie as someone he wanted to date and accepted that they would just be friends. But whenever he found himself without a girlfriend, those romantic feelings he still had towards Jamie would creep up.

Jamie had initially planned on pursuing a Ph.D. in Psychology. Seth suggested that she come to work for the Bureau, which encourages its employees to continue higher education. To his delight, Jamie was interested in this prospect. She was close to graduating and looking for direction, which the Bureau could provide. Seth helped introduce her to important contacts and advised her to take classes that would make her stand out against the myriad of applicants. Jamie relied on him for these contacts and for information.

Once Jamie finished her Masters in Forensic Psychology, their combined efforts paid off, and she received a very competitive and sought-after job with the FBI. She started as an analyst with the National Center for the Analysis of Violent Crime in Quantico. It was a great entry-level job for a recent graduate.

Seth was elated to have Jamie working at the Bureau. He helped her find an apartment not far from his own. They began to hang out more often. When she started, she never imagined she would go on to be a Special Agent. But she began to shine right away as an analyst and drew the attention of her superiors. Jamie proved that she was gifted in critical thinking and analysis. She also became interested in investigative fieldwork, rather than just analyzing data that was collected by someone else.

It is no easy task to make it to the FBI Academy to become a Special Agent. After three years with the NCAVC, Jamie submitted her application. Seth remembers the phone call he received from an ecstatic Jamie saying that she had passed the first hurdle and would be scheduled for the first phase of testing. Seth was happy for her and frightened at the same time, for she could be transferred almost anywhere in the country once she became a Special Agent.

Jamie did well with the battery of written tests and breezed through the fitness test. Then she was off to the Academy for twenty weeks of intensive training. When Jamie was in the Academy, Seth found himself again without a girlfriend. The thought of dating Jamie surfaced again. But he knew that one of the surest ways to lose a good friend is to date them. Besides, having a female best friend was useful. Jamie answered all of his questions, even personal questions. He could get advice, from dating rules to sex tips. With someone like Jamie, it was beneficial to stay friends. That had been his conundrum. It still is. He likes her, and he loves her.

By the time Jamie finished at the Academy, they had been through so much together that it seemed a good time to make a move. But it was also likely that she would be transferred to another part of the country, so they might end up parting ways anyway. After all of his efforts, Seth could not catch a break. The twenty weeks in the Academy had pretty much ended Jamie's relationship with her boyfriend, but it was near the holidays, and she did not want to break up officially and be alone.

Seth remembers well the New Year's Eve party at Barry Shapiro's house. Jamie brought her boyfriend, and Seth brought a date.

As the festivities wore on into a long night, Seth found himself alone with Jamie. He hoped it would be a magical moment and thus invited Jamie to accompany him to the backyard. There was a warm, welcoming fire pit with people milling about. The night was crisp and clear. It was romantic to watch the fire dance toward the stars.

They sat down on a log, and Jamie huddled close to Seth, away from the cold. He took her hand without thinking and rubbed it between his own two hands to keep it warm. She giggled slightly and put her head on his shoulder. Seth looked down at her, and there was a moment that the world around them seemed to stop. He leaned down, and she moved her lips closer to his—the long-awaited kiss was only a brush away.

"There you are! I've been looking for you."

Seth and Jamie froze and both looked up to see Seth's date tottering from one side to the other.

"Hey...aren't you guys cold?" she asked, ostentatiously rubbing her arms and shoulders.

After that awkwardness, Seth had second thoughts. He decided to see if Jamie acted differently towards him after she broke up with her boyfriend. Were there any signals? Was he looking too hard for them? His fear of rejection from his best friend kept him from making a move. If he had had a chance, he had blown it…and he knew it.

A knock on his office door jerks Seth back to the present. A young man his own age stands in the doorway. The newcomer has short, curly brown hair. His normally-large brown eyes are swollen with an obvious lack of sleep.

"Shap, what have you been up to lately?" Seth hails his friend and subordinate. "Not women and booze again?"

Shap just shrugs and offers his excuses, "Sorry I was late again today. I promise to work extra tonight to make up for the time this morning. And I can work over the weekend to make up for the couple of days I missed last week."

Seth considers for a moment, watching Shap closely. He met Barry Shapiro the first week of college. Actually, Shap was the person who made Seth look into forensic science in the first place. Looking back, Seth could hardly have imagined that they would end up working in the same lab at the FBI. The group of friends that Shap had led had been, in the best of times, tightly knit. Shap and Seth started on the same day at Quantico, and now Seth is Shap's supervisor. They have always been close, but lately their bonds are looser. Still, their past makes it difficult for Seth to be stern with Shap.

Seth sighs and consents, "Alright, that is a good compromise. I can handle that. Just promise me you will be on time to from now on."

"You bet," Shap smiles.

"I don't want to lose a man like you. You're one of the best guys I have in this lab." Seth speaks sincerely, but he instantly regrets what he has said. Hopefully, Shap will not use that honesty to manipulate Seth in the future.

"Thanks, Seth, I appreciate the vote of confidence. Well, I better get back to it."

"Great, thanks." Shap withdraws from the doorway and heads to his station.

Seth stands a moment, thinking to himself. Shap could easily be sitting at this desk if he had just been a little more driven. Soon enough, memories of Jamie drive Shap from Seth's mind.

A few years had passed since the New Year's Eve party, and they were still best friends. If given the opportunity, would he go for it again? There were good arguments on both sides. Another opportunity did finally present itself, and that was how Chris came into the picture.

It was four months ago. Jamie had just broken up with her boyfriend. Seth had not been dating anyone. It seemed like he finally had the timing right. Of course, he had to be careful about approaching Jamie right after a breakup. There should be a cooling-off period, or Seth might find himself the "rebound" guy. On the other hand, waiting too long always gave Jamie time to meet someone else. It was a delicate situation.

A Halloween party at Shap's house created the perfect opportunity for a romantic overture. He asked Jamie to go with him, and she accepted. Seth spent a pretty penny to rent the perfect costumes for them both. They needed to match, so that everyone would know they were together. He would be the Dread Pirate Roberts, and she, Princess Buttercup. Seth had overlooked the outrageous price because, if he was going to let Jamie know his true feelings for her, he had to do things right.

Seth can still remember the pain he felt when they arrived at the Halloween party. Jamie started scanning the crowd for prospects—not for herself, but for him! Despite this setback, Seth determined to continue with his plan and let her know how much he loved her. There would be plenty of time during the night, or even on the ride home, for him to find the right moment to tell her. After a couple of dances and cups of punch, Seth left to use the restroom. When he returned, he was irritated that Jamie stood talking to Chris, who was wearing surgical scrubs. As Seth approached them, Jamie signaled with her hand for him to come over.

Seth can still remember every bit of conversation from that night. He had spent hours before the party examining each of his past mistakes. He would not let Jamie slip through his fingers again.

"Seth, this is Chris. He's a 'doctor'." Air quotes accompanied the word "doctor."

"Yes, I can see that." Seth was not impressed.

"No, I really am a doctor. I came straight from the hospital," Chris asserted with ill-concealed pride.

"Oh, then nice 'costume'." Seth matched Jamie's quotation gesture.

The music in the background changed, and Chris announced, "Man, I love this song! Come on, let's dance."

He pulled Jamie into the middle of the crowded dance floor. There were thirty or forty people already there, bobbing and bouncing to the music.

"You guys go, I'll be right here," Seth called out, though he knew they would never hear him over the pounding music. Shap must have seen what happened because he walked up a minute later and gave Seth some punch and a sympathetic look.

At that moment, Seth's only consolation was the knowledge that he had Jamie all to himself on the ride home. Since Jamie had just met this "doctor", surely she would not go home with him. But this consolation was short-lived. The ride turned out to be unforgettably unpleasant. Jamie was a little tipsy and talking incessantly.

"What did you think of Chris?"

"He was a bit pretentious, don't you think? I mean, here we are together at the party with matching costumes, and he hits on you big time. How did he know we weren't a couple? Seems kind of arrogant to me."

"No, it's not like that. You missed it. He came up to me and was like, 'Hey Buttercup, where's Westley?' So, I told him you were in the bathroom. Chris goes, 'I always wanted my own Buttercup. He's a lucky guy.' So I told him we weren't dating."

"He still seemed a little cocky to me."

"Maybe. I'll find out this weekend."

"This weekend?" Seth attempted to push down his anger and surprise.

"Yep. I gave him my number. We're going out Saturday night."

Seth looked over and saw the smile on Jamie's face. "Shit! I really blew it," he muttered under his breath.

"What?"

"Nothing. Never mind."

Seth sighs, coming back to the work in front of him. These are painful memories. But he still clings to the hope that, maybe through all the mistakes, complications, and misunderstandings, he might one day catch Jamie's eye. He shakes his head and declares to the empty room, "I can't help it. I love her."

Chapter 11

Jamie slouches into her office chair. She has read each file at least twice, hoping to see something that would give her a lead to follow. As with any case, there are many things to consider, but this case is also quite different. She sees the similarities in the evidence, but they do not provide a direction. There is nothing that might lead to a suspect.

Her scrambles of the words produced nothing but gibberish, with no discernible significance. She pulls out the list to try once more to find a clue.

"pars hon dota"…pandora shot, hot pandoras, harpoon tads, hap donators, shap tornado, tornado haps, toad orphans, toads orphan, north posada, hoard pantos, photo sandra, torah dapson, radon pathos, adapt honors, host a pardon, oaths pardon, shoot pander, honda pastor, arad photons, dash patroon, adopt sharon, drant shampoo, than parados, stop hornada, hood spartan, ana dropshot….

Most of Jamie's results are not even real words. The computer-generated list does not differ much from her own, and none of them make any sense. Why kill an old man and leave a note that says, "adopt sharon," or, "host a pardon"? Shaking her head, Jamie moves on to the next note.

"por ot ha"…para hot, par oath, rap oath, oar path, harp oat, apt hora, hot para, pah tora…

There are not as many outcomes for the second note. It is pretty much worthless, unless some rapper has a song called "rap oath." Jamie doubts it, but she looks it up on the Internet. There are quite a few results and several YouTube videos, but nothing connecting it to murdering old men.

"dol fon"…fond ol', no fold, flood n, nod flo, fondlo, fool dn, lo fond…

The third note also yields nothing. Knowing that her efforts might be fruitless, Jamie forges ahead.

"parmo sh ta"…ham pastor, port masha, mast pharo, mats aroph, prom hasta, soap thram, amah sport, hoar stamp, asap morth, tora phasm, maps torah, host param, shot param, sam haptor, oath ramps, mash porta, arm pathos, ram pathos, past mohar, amor paths, roam paths, atop harms, atop shram, pram oaths, atom sharp, atom shrap, rap thomas…

It is another dead end, unless there is a pastor named Ham. Jamie sighs again and files the scrambled words into a new folder of her own research and work. It is time to go back to the concrete facts.

She does an exhaustive search of the individual names of the victims. The search returns nothing that stands out. She finds only the usual life achievements, and nothing revealing a motive for murder.

Jamie rubs her forehead pensively and erases the names in the search bar. An idea pops into her mind, and she types in the individual words from the notes. Each search brings up nonsense. Searching further, Jamie tries all of the words from the notes together in the search bar. Yet another dead end. Typing in the initials from each note also returns nothing. Jamie combs her fingers through her long black hair, then twists it behind her head and secures it with a pencil. There must be something that can give her a lead. A knock on her door makes startles Jamie, makes her look up immediately.

"Hey Jamie, I've got the information you wanted on the victims—backgrounds, police records, and tax info." Phil Clark towers in Jamie's doorway, holding up the files. "A couple of them were quite well off. Could be a case of follow-the-money."

"I hope it turns out to be that simple. Thanks, Phil. You're the best."

"No problem." With a smile, Phil ambles into her office and sits in the chair across from her desk. He thumps his large fingers on the wooden arm of the chair. "But I'm afraid I don't have good news for you."

"Not surprising. This case is all dead ends. Watcha got?"

He hands her the files. "Here are all the police reports and criminal records on the victims. Needless to say, they were normal, law-abiding citizens, and nothing more."

"Really?" She had been hoping for something in their backgrounds, a connection that would lead her to answers. Something. Anything. "Nothing at all?"

"Well, two of them had quite the lead foot. But aside from speeding tickets, these old guys are clean. No big crimes, no little crimes, just a parking ticket along with speeding tickets, all of which were paid on time and with no complications," Phil summarizes, still tapping his knuckles to an unheard beat.

"Great. Thanks."

"No problem." Phil stands up to leave. "Before I go, is there anything else I can do?"

"I'm good, thanks."

Jamie delves into the files that Phil brought. Pulling out each record, she arranges the files side-by-side to examine them. Not one of the victims had ever lived in the same city, or even the same state for that matter. No similarities in occupation. There is nothing connecting any of the murdered men to each other.

Moving on, Jamie searches through their family histories. They have no apparent relation through marriage or cousins. Rubbing her forehead again, Jamie starts looking at birthplaces. That might give her some insight.

Two of the victims were born in Germany, two in Argentina, and one in Poland. Each of the victims immigrated to the U.S., but it is not unusual for men in their late eighties and nineties to be immigrants. If the perp only wanted to kill immigrants, he would not have needed to travel so widely around the United States.

Jamie reviews the information again, and this time, something catches her eye. Hans Bierman was born in Argentina. It is a strange name. She would expect Jesus or Paco, not Hans. Jamie remembers from her history class in college that there were lots of families that fled to North and South America during

World War I and World War II. Maybe Hans Bierman's parents were among the lucky few who escaped the war.

Glancing back at the other three files, Jamie notes that not one of the victims emigrated from his country of birth. Two came from Brazil, one from France, and one from South Africa. Jamie discovers that Fred Schmidt legally changed his name from Friedrich Seiler before coming to the U.S. Of course, many immigrants changed their names before entering the country.

Although Phil already gave her an overview, Jamie carefully combs through the criminal records. When looking for a needle in a haystack, one has to be very thorough. But each victim is clean, except for one or two speeding tickets and some parking tickets. Model citizens in every way.

Jamie concludes that, if nothing connects their pasts, then the victims are connected in the present, by their deaths. Something has to link them. She looks at the timing of the murders. September, March, October, March, and February—the months seem as random as the victims. It is strange that the killer waited nearly a year between victims four and five. The previous four were spaced about six months apart. Why wait so long? Normally, serial killers are sporadic, taking advantage of an opportunity that presents itself. They hardly ever go a whole year without killing again. To Jamie, this anomaly suggests organization.

Why these months? Why not December or June? None in the summer. Is it about availability? Is there a seasonal factor? It is quite the enigma.

Another odd thing Jamie discovers about the murders is that, in all cases, there is no sign of forced entry. Each victim must have let the killer into his home. Checking the file again, Jamie notices that the Jules Henning case is slightly different. He was fifty miles from his home when he was found. How did he end up in Salem, New York? So far, this is Jamie's best clue— Hennings is the first victim and is different from the rest. And why drive fifty miles and then dump the old guy in a place where he is sure to be found?

It is time to go to the source. Jamie picks up her cell phone and dials the number for her contact at the County Sheriff's Office in Salem.

A man with a thick New York accent answers. "This is Sheriff Foster; how may I help you?"

"Hi, this is FBI Special Agent Golding. I am calling you regarding the murder of Jules Henning."

"So the guys in Schenectady finally called the Feds, huh?"

"Well, not exactly..."

Foster clearly apprehends that he should not ask any further. "Okay. So what can I do for you?"

"Since Henning was found near a post office, I was wondering whether you were able to gather any video surveillance, either from the post office, nearby stores, or gas stations?"

"Nope. There was nothing to get." Foster chuckles. "Salem is in the country. Way at the end of Washington County. Population of 2,700. We don't have much in the way of surveillance in these parts."

"Where exactly is Salem?"

"Let me put it this way, you step out of Salem to the east and you're in Vermont. Literally."

"Must be beautiful."

"Oh, it is. You should come see us sometime."

"I'm coming next week."

"Really? Well, I'll be happy to show you where the body was found. Unfortunately there's not much else to see."

"I understand. But, just to double check, there were no tire tracks found? No footprints near the victim?" Jamie again confirms this information with her own files.

"No, it was raining that morning. I remember it well. We don't get a lot of abandoned murder victims out here."

"If it was raining, I would think it would be more likely to find footprints around the body."

"Well, we found two, six-inch impressions right near the body. I have a theory that the killer used a couple of long two-by-sixes and made a ramp from his vehicle. Then he dragged the body down the ramp and pushed it over, so it looked like a guy sleeping against the building. We have pictures in the file. Not much else, though."

"Have you found any leads?"

"Nope. We've essentially turned it over to the folks in Schenectady."

"Okay, thanks. I'll call you next week before I head out there."

"That's fine," Foster confirms before hanging up.

Jamie chews on her lip thoughtfully. She is going to be in Chicago in a few hours; it is time to start preparing her questions for them. Pulling out her tablet, she begins to make a list of things to do, ask, and look into while she is there.

Jamie looks again at the file on Fred Schmidt and to critically examine the information before her. The report shows that there is not much trace evidence being cooked at the lab. Why were there no hairs or DNA evidence found from any of the nursing home staff members? Surely they had had contact with the victim before he died, unless they were negligent. Jamie doubts it. It is a high-end facility, after all. They would have had regular interaction with Fred Schmidt. How is the crime scene so clean?

In fact, how were all the sites wiped so clean? It would take so much time to clean every surface, time that would increase the killer's chances of being caught. How did the perp know he had time to sanitize the area? How did he do it so quickly without being seen? It is all so perplexing to Jamie.

Her phone rings, and Whitehouse notifies her that the taxi has arrived to take her to the airport.

Jamie takes her bags and exits her office. On her way to the stairs, Jamie stops by Mr. Whitehouse's desk. "I'm off."

Without waiting for a comment from the all-too-grumpy assistant, Jamie heads out the door and down the stairs. Outside the building and across the grounds, a taxi waits. Jamie slides nimbly into the backseat. "Ronald Reagan Airport, please."

The driver nods, and the car begins its journey. Jamie directs her attention to the tablet she has already removed from her bag. She pulls up her list of questions and looks them over again.

Questions:
-Did Forensics come up with any trace evidence?
-Any DNA or trace chemicals found in the wound?
-How often does the staff clean the rooms?

-Why is there no DNA from staff members?

-How long was Fred Schmidt living at the nursing home?

Information Needed:

-Records of who visited the patient in the last six months.

-Names and numbers of the people working the day of the murder.

-Any video surveillance.

Jamie really hopes being on the scene of the crime and talking with people personally will make a difference. It is not that she does not trust the reports of the local law officers in Chicago, but it never hurts to make your own inquires. By analyzing each scene, she hopes to find a method in the madness.

"Here we are," the taxi driver announces as he pulls up to the airport. "Which airline?"

"Here is fine, thanks." She hands him the credit card she only uses for reimbursable expenses and requests a receipt. Minutes later she is walking towards the check-in counter. She does not have the luxury of printing her boarding pass and going straight to the gate, not if she wants to board with her weapon. Jamie always travels with her gun. Whitehouse is good about notifying the airline that Law Enforcement Officers (LEO) intend to board with their weapons. An hour's notice is required. She shows her identification and gets her boarding pass at the counter. The airline has to know where any armed LEO is seated, so she lets them assign her seat.

Jamie rolls her eyes as she approaches a TSA officer. The TSA guards are highly variable. Some are courteous to agents, while others show their aggravation at having to take a few extra steps. She presents the boarding pass, with the special stamp for those who fly armed, as well as her credentials, her proof of completion of the necessary training program, and the TSA code number sent to Whitehouse when he filed the NLETS. Once on the plane, she will meet the pilot and any air marshal or LEO that happens to be aboard. After jumping through all of the hoops, Jamie is thrilled to get through without any hassles.

Jamie ponders Fred Schmidt's name change. Did he want his family to stand out less among society? Maybe he had a grudge against his parents and did not want to carry on their family name? His wife might have hated the name, so they both took her last name? Jamie could not remember Fred Schmidt's wife's maiden name. She makes a mental note to look that up later.

What about the professions of all of these old men? Perhaps they had a business connection that brought them together? Maybe a deal went sour, and someone is out for revenge. Jamie turns over in her mind the various occupations of the victims. One of them had been an accountant, another was a small business owner, one worked in chemical sales, one had a prosthetics business, and one owned a small grocery store. It is possible that an accountant and business owner could have had come into contact through business transactions.

Once she lands at O'Hare she hails a cab to take her to the Harwood Heights police department. To pass the time, she removes her cell phone to check her email. Seeing herself with Chris on her background gives Jamie a pang of unease. She remembers that she still has to tell him that she will not be there for their special dinner date. Looking at the time, Jamie dials him, hoping to catch him between surgeries.

No answer. She decides to send him a quick text letting him know she will be traveling that day for work and will not be back in time. Jamie waits and watches the buildings of Chicago go by. There is no response. She can only assume that he is in the operating room. The car suddenly stops in front of a brick building. Jamie pockets her cell phone, gathers her things and goes in the police station.

Detective Matt Ragsdale is in his late fifties. He is a seasoned detective that does not easily show any emotion. He hands her a copy of the file.

Ragsdale seems happy to bump this case over to some young Quantico hotshot, like Jamie. When his superiors ask about the case, he can refer them to Quantico.

She indicates the folder in her lap. "Slim pickings, huh?"

"Yep. I've never seen a crime scene that clean. Ever."

"What about the report from Forensics? I don't see it in here."

"Yeah, they are overwhelmed at the lab. It is Chicago after all. Lots of crime here. Although, if we hover, we will probably get results sooner," Ragsdale wagers, checking the old-fashioned clock on his desk.

"Sounds like a good idea," Jamie agrees, standing up to encourage Ragsdale.

"Alright, I'll take you there," Ragsdale nods, also standing. He removes his jacket from the back of his chair. "I need to go down there anyway," Ragsdale responds. "Follow me."

In the car, Ragsdale returns to the matter at hand. "So...any other questions about the case?"

"I can guess the answer to this question already, but I should ask. Do you have any leads?"

"None. Like the file says, no leads so far and no motive."

"Isn't it strange that there's no DNA evidence from employees of the nursing home?"

"I've never seen a crime scene so spotless. It's like the murderer hired a cleaning crew," Ragsdale remarks with apparent disbelief.

They head downtown and finally reach the crime lab. Inside, Ragsdale leads the way through security and informs Jamie that they are visiting a friend of his.

"They actually have pretty good coffee here. You want some?"

"Sure."

Ragsdale leads the way to the employee break room and they each fill a Styrofoam cup with coffee.

"Hide the coffee under your coat until we get to his office."

The lab is filled with different types of analyzers, small and large. There are a few workers moving around, putting samples into tabletop machines, or looking into special microscopes. Jamie thinks the lab does not look much different from Seth's, except that this one is much smaller.

Ragsdale walks up to a young man in a lab coat. He has light brown hair and piercing blue eyes. Ragsdale gives the man a glimpse of the coffee and gestures toward the side of the room. The man turns around and leads them to a small office. They pass more employees doing experiments, dropping substances onto the surfaces of slides, and putting blood into centrifuges.

Ragsdale begins by introducing them. "Special Agent Golding, this is Will Hastings."

"Hi," Jamie responds. She moves her coffee from under her coat and shakes his hand.

"What case are you working on now?" Will queries, eyeing both agents.

"Schmidt. D.C. is giving the case to her," Ragsdale answers, stuffing a hand in one of his coat pockets. He takes another long drink from his coffee.

"You here for the results?" Will assumes, surveying Jamie, who simply rolls her eyes.

"You have anything ready or is it all still cooking?" Ragsdale quips as he leans on the desk.

"Oh, the baking is all done. But you won't like the results," Will cautions them.

He searches through the stacks of files on his desk. "Usually I'm more organized," he mutters, embarrassed.

"Believe me, it's always this way. He just wants to impress you," Ragsdale whispers to Jamie with a wink.

"Here it is!" Will proclaims, pulling out a file from under a mug of moldy coffee. "For me, coffee is more like a moving paperweight." He holds out the file to Jamie.

Hesitantly she accepts it, slightly disgusted. She opens the folder and looks over the test results.

"As you can see, we found nothing. We ran the few samples we had, and none of them contained DNA. A fiber that was found at the scene also matches the blanket at the foot of the victim's bed."

"What about the sample from the neck wound?" Jamie interjects.

"Yes, the sample from the neck wound shows that it had been washed with a bactericidal, ammonium-based agent similar to the chemicals used to wipe down surfaces in hospitals. It's pretty caustic on skin, though. Especially on an old guy's thin skin. Check out the photo on the next page."

Jamie turns the page over and sees the picture of Fred Schmidt's neck wound.

Will moves to stand next to her and continues, "You can see it if you are looking for it. There's a line of demarcation where the chemical was applied. The skin around it is normal looking. The perp took the time to clean the wound."

"Did you find out anything else?" Jamie pursues, vexed by the lack of results.

"Well, the samples from the skin were very clean and irrigated. I did find a few threads embedded in a fold of the wound itself. Its pattern is that of a hexagonal embossed polypropylene cloth material."

"A disinfectant wipe?" Jamie asks.

"Exactly. Typical in bactericidal wipes."

"Is it an easy chemical to get?"

"Actually, yeah, you can order it online. Comes in a dispenser similar to Clorox wipes that you buy at the grocery store. See, I have some over here." Will grabs a plastic tube from the corner of his desk. "This is what we use to wipe down the lab. Actually, this shouldn't be in my office. Never mind that. The one used on the victim is similar but this one is bleach-based. We are trying to trace down the exact manufacturer, but there are several options."

"Okay. What else are you running?"

"Everything is done and in the file." Will is apologetic, but the lack of evidence is not his fault. "They didn't bring us much trace."

"Great, thanks," Jamic says, trying to hold back her disappointment.

"No problem."

Jamie turns to Ragsdale. "Can you take me to Crestwood Assisted Living in Harwood Heights?"

"Sure," Ragsdale responds.

Jamie and Ragsdale turn to leave the messy little office.

"Agent Golding, you wanna have dinner tonight?" Will calls to Jamie.

"Sure, if you're paying," Ragsdale answers, turning to see Will's bewilderment. Then Ragsdale chortles, his laugh deep and loud, and continues out of the office.

"How far is it to Harwood Heights?"

"Not far—twenty minutes, or so. I hate Chicago traffic," Ragsdale growls. "Better call ahead, so they are ready for us when we get there."

"Right." Jamie finds the number in the file and calls on her cell phone. She alerts the director that they are coming.

Jamie shuts the phone and looks out the window. Ragsdale enumerates various points of interest as they cross the Chicago River on the Eisenhower Expressway, but nothing particularly impresses Jamie. Her mind is on the case, and she has begun to feel concerned. All she can think is, if an experienced detective like Ragsdale has no evidence and no leads, then what is she supposed to find?

Soon enough, Ragsdale is pulling into the long driveway of the facility. A white sign with gold lettering tells them that they are at Crestwood Assisted Living. It is a short, brick building, which is clearly well kept and not very old. They park in a side lot and enter through the main door.

As she walks through the door with Ragsdale, Jamie becomes aware of the strong smell of vanilla plug-ins. The plants are decorative, and they look nice. A few residents sit in the spacious foyer with visitors. Jamie walks up to the reception desk, which resembles that of a doctor's office.

"How can I help you?" a Hispanic girl asks from behind the glass window.

"I'm Special Agent Golding. I'm here to speak with Ms. Applegate," Jamie explains, flashing her badge.

"I will let Ms. Applegate know you are here."

"Did you work last Sunday night?" Jamie adds, before the girl can pick up the phone at her desk.

"Oh no. I don't work weekends," the girl replies. "But I bet Terrence was here that night. He only works the weekends because he's in business school."

"Thanks." Jamie starts checking the case file and sees that it was, in fact, someone named Terrence working that night.

"Oh, by the way, I need you both to sign in," the receptionist requests as she picks up the phone.

Jamie signs her name, then hands the pen to Ragsdale. They wander the reception area. Ragsdale takes a seat, but Jamie continues to move around the area, taking in the details. She tries to imagine the murderer walking through the front doors, signing in, killing an old man, and leaving without a trace. It boggles her mind that someone could get away with murder in an assisted living center, with employees nearby constantly.

"Hi, I'm Juanita Applegate." A short black woman comes forward with her hand out to shake Jamie's. She wears a tight professional black skirt with a lurid blouse in hues of red, orange, and yellow.

"I'm Special Agent Golding and..."

"Ah, Detective Ragsdale, I remember you," Juanita cuts across Jamie, holding out her hand to receive Ragsdale's.

"Before we start, I want to you know we intend to cooperate fully. I've already given statements to Detective Ragsdale and the police. The sooner we get this solved, the better for my residents. Some of them are a little nervous right now. I hardly understand how something like this would happen here, in my center. It's just unbelievable."

"I'm glad to have your assistance. I promise I won't take too much of your time, but I would like to see the room and speak with Terrence and the other staff that were on duty that night."

Juanita looks off to the side, her expression a little terse. "I can't let you see the room. There is a new resident already occupying that room."

"WHAT?!"

"You see, we have a waiting list. The room was released yesterday. I had to call five times to get it released. After all, they had already been in and taken photos and whatever else," Juanita argues, standing her ground.

"Oh! I forgot to mention that," Ragsdale pipes up from beside Jamie.

She sighs, "Fine. Well, I would like to see the room anyway."

Again, Juanita becomes agitated. "We couldn't possibly do that—privacy and all."

"You can't honestly expect me to believe that. How do prospective residents preview their rooms?" Jamie demands, losing a bit of her cool.

"We get permission from some of our guests to show their rooms to new clients, who are escorted by me, of course,"

Juanita informs them with a self-satisfied smile at her own professionalism.

"Well, then, I'm your newest potential customer, and I want to put Granny on your waiting list. Let's go. Room 128. It's her favorite number. And you'd better find something for your new resident to do outside of his room for a few minutes—get some fresh air, perhaps," Jamie orders the woman with a determined glare. The time for diplomacy was before a new occupant was settled on top of Jamie's crime scene.

Juanita's smile slowly transforms into an indignant glare. She opens her mouth, and closes it again with a twitch of her lips. "Fine. I'll arrange it. Just a moment."

With that, Juanita disappears around the corner.

"You've got some spunk, kid!" Ragsdale exclaims once Juanita is out of earshot.

Jamie ignores him, her mind still on the retreating Juanita. Jamie follows her down the hallway toward room 128. Juanita knocks on the door and slinks inside. Jamie leans against the wall and waits patiently. Glancing over, she sees that Ragsdale has followed her and is standing behind her looking at his phone. It takes about three minutes, but Juanita finally convinces the old man in the room to go for a walk outside. As she guides him to the back door, which leads into a garden, she waves Jamie into the room. Juanita's brown eyes still burn, but Jamie has more important considerations.

Not waiting for Juanita's signal, Jamie starts into the room as soon as the old man turns his back to her, seconds before Juanita waves. Jamie enters through a tiny sitting room, complete with recliner, armchair, and television. She follows the room's "L"-shape around the corner to find that the rest of the apartment is a small bedroom and a bathroom. Jamie figures that the room next to this one will fit into the crook of the L, so the whole center is one big jigsaw of rooms, maximizing the given space.

The new tenant has already set up pictures of family and friends. As Jamie expected, the place is clean. But at least she now has a concept of the room and can clearly imagine the steps the killer would have taken. The bedroom would have provided more privacy for a murder than the sitting room. Jamie examines the bedroom, even looking under the bed. Clean. She exits the room and finds Ragsdale still leaning against the wall. His bored expression tells Jamie everything she needs to know.

Jamie looks each way down the hallway and realizes that the room is not tucked into a distant corner. The killer must have had a reason to pick this room, instead of a less visible corner room, or a room near an emergency exit. It is perplexing. It further solidifies the idea that the murder was not random, but that Fred Schmidt was the intended victim.

A nursing assistant is wheeling out the neighboring resident. Jamie assumes the poor old guy is off to the dining hall, or maybe therapy, or to visit a friend. Glancing at Ragsdale, Jamie grins slyly before ducking into the room. As she suspected, the room fits, puzzle-like, with Schmidt's old room. She heads to the bedroom, where she gets down on her hands and knees to see under the bed. There is plenty of dust, hair, crumbs, and even a strand of rope from a mop caught in the wheels of the bed legs. This further confirms that the killer cleaned the victim's entire room quite thoroughly.

Exiting the room, Jamie spies Juanita returning without the older gentlemen. Juanita's face radiates anger.

"What do you think you're doing?" Juanita hisses, none too quietly.

"I need to see the sign-in sheet for last Sunday," Jamie replies coolly, ignoring the question.

Juanita mumbles something under her breath, then stalks away down the hallway.

"You sure know how to push people's buttons," Ragsdale snickers.

"You coming?" Jamie retorts, following Juanita down the hallway.

"I wouldn't miss this," Ragsdale mutters, falling into step beside Jamie.

Juanita throws open an office door so that it hits the wall and recoils towards Jamie. Reaching out an arm, Jamie catches the door before it shuts and enters the room, with Ragsdale on her heels.

Juanita shoves the clipboard at Jamie. "Here."

Jamie accepts with a smile and a "Thanks."

The clipboard is just like the register Jamie signed earlier. Since so many people have touched it, Jamie doubts that there will be any usable evidence from it, but that did not stop the police from fingerprinting it. Jamie sees a small residue of black powder left on one of the corners of the clipboard. At least they followed protocol. She looks at the names on the list for Sunday night. Toward the bottom is an entry that reads, "Simon W," with no time given. The handwriting is very poor, as if this person used his non-dominant hand. The previous signature was written at 6:46, and the one after Simon checked in at 7:10.

"I need to speak with..." Jamie begins, then pauses to check her notes, "Terrence and Bertha...Bertha Ames, the nursing assistant from the night of the murder."

"Terrence won't be in 'til Saturday. He only works weekends," Juanita informs them with obvious pleasure. "And Bertha doesn't come in until 3 p.m."

"That's okay. I'm sure they both have cell phones. I need to speak to Terrence before I leave," Jamie says, motioning to the telephone.

"He won't answer if he's in class."

"I'll take my chances."

Juanita hesitates for a moment. "We have to go to my office, so I can look up their numbers."

"Lead the way," Jamie replies with a mocking smile.

They follow Juanita back out of the office and down the opposite hallway to a room next to the dining room. Jamie smells cilantro as soon as the door opens. The room is filled with obnoxious colors and strange Aztec statues like those at tourist traps in Mexico.

Sitting in her comfy business chair, Juanita loads something on the computer. She picks up the phone on the desk and dials, all the while stonily watching Jamie. Ragsdale slumps into one of the chairs on the other side of the desk, a smug look on his face.

"Hi, Terrence. It's Ms. Applegate. I have someone here who needs to speak with you," Juanita says briskly, her face unchanged. "Between classes? Okay, perfect—this should just take a few moments."

Jamie takes the phone Juanita holds out to her. "Terrence, I'm Special Agent Golding of the FBI. I have a few quick questions for you."

"I've got fifteen minutes before class so, okay, cool, shoot," Terrence answers nonchalantly.

"That's great." Jamie jumps right in. "Do you recall a visitor to your facility named Simon W.?"

"Yeah, he came to see Mr. Schmidt."

"And how often did this Simon come to visit Mr. Schmidt?"

"I dunno. I think I've seen the dude maybe two or three other times, before that last time, that is. I can't really remember. A lot of people come through there, you know."

"When did you see him last, before this past Sunday?"

"Uh...probably two weeks ago."

"Also a Sunday? Also in the evening?"

"Can't remember for sure. I guess it could have been a Saturday. But yeah, he always came in the evening, probably around seven or so," Terrence recounts.

"Interesting. And did he look the same each time? Similarly dressed? Did he bring anything with him? Tell me all that you remember about his appearance," Jamie requests.

"Well, he had essentially the same thing on. Wore a nametag from the group he was with. Same hat on each time. Always carried a backpack."

"The group he was with?"

"Yeah—some church or something."

"Anything else you may have remembered since, anything that might not be in the other reports?"

"No, that's really it. He was a pretty friendly guy. Always addressed me by name. He never seemed suspicious to me. Totally double-cool with ice, you know," Terrence expounds thoughtfully.

"Thanks, Terrence. I appreciate your help. Can I call you again if I need anything else?"

"For sure."

"Okay, thanks again."

"Bye."

Jamie hangs up and looks at Juanita, who is glowering.

"Now Bertha," Jamie reminds her.

While Juanita looks up the number and starts to call Bertha, Jamie again peruses the register in her hands. She flips back the pages and searches for a similar sign-in. She sees "Simon W" the week before on Saturday evening. She checks the preceding week as well, but sees nothing. Another week back, however, "Simon W." again appears on a Saturday night. All of them are in the same handwriting, most likely, the same guy.

"It's Bertha," Juanita snarls, again holding out the receiver for Jamie.

Jamie takes the phone. "Hi, Bertha? This is Special Agent Golding, FBI. I have a few questions for you."

"Now's not a good time." The woman on the other end sounds hurried.

"Well, I'm only in town for today. I absolutely have to speak with you; can I meet you somewhere in the next half hour or so?"

"Fine, you can come to my house. Half an hour. You got a paper and pen, Hon? Here's my address."

Jamie writes down the address that Bertha gives before hanging up abruptly. Jamie hands the phone back to Juanita.

"Is that everything?" Juanita snaps, her right eye twitching slightly.

"Yes. Thank you for your compliance. I'll see myself out."

Jamie exits the room and confidently walks down the hallway. She does not turn to see if Ragsdale is following, but she can hear his footsteps behind her. "Can you take me to this address?" Jamie passes a piece of paper over her shoulder.

He takes it from her hand and answers sincerely. "Sure."

"Great. Let's get going," Jamie says as she picks up her stride.

"You're one hell of an agent," Ragsdale responds with bemusement.

"I'm getting there." Jamie is glad he cannot see her lip curve up a little.

Fifteen minutes later, Ragsdale pulls the car to a stop in front of a small, older home. The house is painted dark brown, and the paint is chipped here and there, giving it a leopard-print appearance. The grass is not overgrown, but most of it is crabgrass. No other shrubbery is visible. There is a frail, chain-link fence enclosing the yard. The fence is bent and twisted in places, so one could conceivably sneak underneath it. The gate is missing altogether.

"I'm going to sit this one out," Ragsdale decides, making himself comfortable in his seat.

"I'll only be a second."

She strides briskly through the almost nonexistent yard and up the creaking wooden porch steps to the front door. The cold is still unbearable to her, as she knocks on the door. After a few seconds, Jamie starts to bounce on the balls of her feet to keep herself warm.

A series of metallic rattling sounds on the other side precedes the door opening, and a black woman peeks out through the small crack. "Yeah?" her voice challenges.

"I'm Special Agent Golding. I came to ask you a few questions."

"You're early."

"Sorry, I'm just on a tight schedule because I only have today before I fly home. I just need to ask a few questions," Jamie says, motioning to the door.

"Fine, Hon, ask away. I had just gotten out of the bath when you called, getting ready for work," Bertha explains, still looking out through the inch-wide gap between door and frame.

"Can I come in? It's freezing out here."

"Of course." Bertha pulls the door open wide enough to admit Jamie. "I'm just a little nervous and all, after what happened to poor Mr. Schmidt."

The smell of frying oil and batter welcomes her warmly. The modest home is tidy and neat. From the smeared handprints on the wall, Jamie assumes that Bertha has at least a couple of children as well.

"So what can I help you with?" Bertha asks, not unkindly, pulling her cornrows back into an elastic band.

Jamie gets right down to business. "What do you remember about the man who visited Fred Schmidt the night he died?"

"He was a nice man. He would come and read to Mr. Schmidt and then tuck him in for the night."

"Did you talk to him the night Mr. Schmidt died? See him later that evening, when he left, or anything?"

"I did walk by and heard him reading to Fred. Most of the time, when he left, he would let me know Mr. Schmidt was all set and sleeping. I figured I didn't need to check on Fred. He always sleeps through the night without any problems."

"How did Simon act that night? Was he composed?"

"Well, he wasn't nervous. Wasn't in a hurry. Said he'd be back in a week or two. Nothing outta the ordinary."

"Would you recognize him if you saw him?"

"Lord, yes!"

"Anything else you remembered that you maybe didn't report earlier?" Jamie presses.

"Nope, Honey, that's all I remember. Do you think he done it?" Bertha questions her nervously. "What if he comes back for me? You know, since I seen him?"

"Trust me, he won't be coming back. Are you sure there were no other suspicious persons that night? Just the regular staff? Even housekeeping?"

"Nope, nobody. Do you think I need to move? I've slept at my sister's the last four nights. She don't like it on account of I don't get to her house until almost midnight."

"You don't need to move." Jamie tries to sound reassuring. He won't be back, believe me. He doesn't live in Chicago, or even Illinois for that matter. And," Jamie weighs her words, "he doesn't care about you. Trust me, you'll be fine. Thank you for your help, and here's my card. Please call me if you think of anything else."

"Sure will. You find him, you hear, and quick!"

"We're doing our best. Again, call me if you think of something. Anything." Jamie reiterates, as she sees herself out.

As she descends the porch, Jamie can hear the metal rattling again, then footsteps walking away. Then silence. Jamie stands still in the yard for a moment. Her mind is doing somersaults. He could have killed Fred Schmidt on any of the other nights. Why did he wait for this particular Sunday? On the one hand, it was shrewd of the murderer to make his visits a norm, so no one would suspect anything. That move provided him several hours before anyone even noticed the crime. However, more visits also meant more chances of being remembered when the authorities came around. With a normal killer, Bertha would be right to be afraid.

But Simon W. was not a normal killer. And his kills were not random. So why that time? Why that date?

Jamie starts walking again, but a buzzing in her pocket holds Jamie up at the car. She retrieves her cell phone, which announces a new text from Chris. Jamie opens the message and reads, "it figures." What is that supposed to mean? Chris is no doubt angry with her for breaking their dinner date. Of course, he has done the same to her, several times. Irked, she puts the phone away and slides into Ragsdale's car.

Chapter 12

At night, my family used to gather around the radio. My mother and grandparents were mostly interested in the news that would be broadcast. I, on the other hand, would endure the tedious reports in anticipation of hearing the latest installment of my favorite radio show. Of course, I could only listen to the radio at night as long as my schoolwork and chores were done for the day.

Aside from the radio, my grandparents' dry goods store was the center for gossip and news in Propoc. Many people gathered and talked with my grandparents, imparting tidbits of information, gossip, and other types of news. I never felt lonely working in the store with my family. The local folk would come and buy goods, then stand around and chat. Sometimes people came who were not even customers—they just wanted to be up-to-date on the local happenings.

Once, I did overhear a conversation questioning the absence of my father by someone new to the community. I, too, had pondered this question. Like myself, my grandparents never discussed my father at all. When I questioned my mother about my father, she would tell me that she has me and that was enough for her. All I ever gathered about my father is that he disappeared not long after I was born.

Despite my unusual family dynamics in those days, I was still accepted by the community. And since I excelled so well on my marks in school, I became sort of a wonder to people. Especially since my older brother did not receive as high marks as me. I was a young girl who was just as intelligent as the boys at my school.

I was also privileged enough to receive piano lessons. Not many people in our town knew how to play a piano, and even fewer owned a piano. My grandmother played the piano and taught me how to play. Although I never applied myself to it as I did to my studies, I still learned enough piano to play well. Even now, sitting down at a piano and playing brings back those memories of my grandmother gently and patiently teaching me to play.

As time passed and my childhood slipped away, I began to be interested in the boys at school. Mary and I started becoming aware of our own style and trying to push limits that the older generation felt were sinful. I never truly defied my mother or grandparents, but I did start wearing makeup and perfume too early for my grandmother's taste. Mother seemed unconcerned, as other issues were more important to her.

I had a beau for a little while. His name was Edvard. He walked me home from school for a whole week. Once, he stole a kiss when we sat on a rock, and Mary's younger sister caught us. As expected, when the word got out, my mother and grandparents worked to end the little crush. I envied Mary. Her parents would allow any of the boys she liked to court her, unlike my family. They were much more picky about whom I could and could not be courted by. Sadly, there were hardly any boys in the town that I was interested in more than Edvard.

One summer we traveled to Prague to see my cousin Edit. The ride on the train was quite an exhilarating experience. We did not have many modern advancements in our small town. I was amazed at how fast the train could go and the country scenes that flew by my window. Once in Prague, Edit and her family greeted us at the train station.

Uncle Adolph owned a restaurant and cooked some of the best food I have ever eaten in my life. Edit and I enjoyed those summer days, giggling about boys, walking the streets of Prague looking through the windows of the shops, and imagining what it would be like to wear the beautiful clothes we saw inside. She showed me the wonders of Prague—the statues, fountains, and more. We shared a room during my stay and talked ourselves to sleep every night. That summer brought Edit and me closer than ever.

By the time I graduated school, my concern for boys was minimal, as my grandparents had prepared for me to attend college. It was rare and a privilege for a woman to attend college in those days. I was so excited for this opportunity that I could hardly think of much else. Mary and I had drifted apart slightly, as she was dating to marry. By the time I was looking to start college in the fall, she and I were no longer best friends, but just friends. I could never imagine what she would do to me in the near future.

Chapter 13

The bank is fairly crowded on this particular morning. A medium-sized line winds between the stanchions. He patiently waits, trying to conceal his face from the cameras as much as possible. Although he knows there is nothing to worry about, Simon has a tight knot in his stomach. It is nothing serious. After all, it is his bank.

"Next, please?" an Indian woman calls out.

Simon walks up to the teller, who stands behind a tall counter. He says nothing, but hands her a check for two-thousand dollars, his driver's license, and the banking slip.

Looking at the slip, the teller asks, "How would you like it?"

"Three envelopes, each with one-hundred dollars in twenties. One envelope with a hundred dollars in tens and fives. The fourth with sixteen hundreds," Simon tells her quietly. No reason to share with the whole bank.

The teller nods and prepares the cash.

"Beautiful day today," Simon remarks while waiting for the teller to fulfill his request.

"Yes, it is," the woman replies cordially. "Alright, here you are. Three envelopes of a hundred in twenties and one of tens and fives."

She counts each one while Simon watches carefully.

"The last with sixteen hundreds," she tells him, counting those as well. She looks up to see if Simon approves.

Simon nods, and the woman holds the envelopes out to him. He carefully takes the envelopes, touching only one corner. Simon thanks her and leaves.

"Have a good day," the woman calls after him.

He leaves the bank and walks to his car in the parking lot. Once inside his car, Simon has a large Ziploc bag waiting for him in the passenger's seat. He drops the envelopes into the bag and closes it. He drives out of the bank parking lot and heads to the back of a strip mall. Simon pulls out a cap from the glove compartment. The cap sits on top of a dark red wig. Simon puts the hat on his head and adjusts it. The mirror reflects a redheaded man wearing a trucker's hat. It looks perfect. Simon pulls his car out again and drives to his real destination. He parks his car in the lot of the local FedEx Office.

He purchases time on one of the computers. He chooses the most secluded computer of the bunch and begins his work. Simon opens a word processor and starts typing out a paragraph, copied word-for-word, from one of the print shop's circulars. Then he skips to page two of the document and types a couple of lines before scrolling down to the lower corner of page two and typing his real note.

There is a method behind this odd behavior. The printing process requires one to first save the file in a certain folder, so the shared printer knows which file to print. A user cannot just print what you typed. Even though Simon will delete the file when he is finished, he does not want anything linking his printouts to the murders. If, for some unlikely reason, anyone did open his file, the person would not see his note right away, but merely a random excerpt from a brochure, which would probably not arouse suspicion. It would be even less likely that the person would continue to page two and see his note. To Simon, it is just another step in covering his tracks. He stops to think about how crazy this might seem, but he nonetheless takes every precaution, every time.

When the paper leaves the printer, Simon again takes care to touch it only by the corner. He takes the paper across the room to the large guillotine paper cutter. He meticulously cuts it so that the square that contains his message remains on the surface of the cutter, and the scraps fall away. He removes a pair of tweezers from his shirt pocket and a plastic bag from his jeans pocket, then uses the tweezers to gently slide the note into the Ziploc. Satisfied, Simon puts his utensils back in his shirt pocket, along with the closed sandwich bag.

Now it is time to buy a silk flower arrangement.

Simon returns to his car and uses the main roads to get to the nearest craft store. He had originally planned to use a tiny, mom-and-pop florist located an hour from his home, but Simon fears that the arrangement could then be traced. They may have imported some rare flower with pollen that might have ended up on his arrangement, which would allow the Feds to determine where it was bought. There is no reason to give the FBI a point on the map, even if it is an hour away. He decided against the small family business and will instead use a national chain store. It would be more difficult to discover from which store the silk flowers originated.

Simon still wears his disguise while browsing in the craft store. Simon finally discovers a silk flower arrangement in a decorative porcelain bowl. The bowl could be traceable to this large retailer. Since this chain has stores across the country, it would not necessarily point to him, but he does not want to give the FBI any leads. Simon carries the arrangement to the employee who is assembling them in the back of the store.

"I really like this arrangement, but I would like it in a simple glass vase," Simon tells her. He puts on a desperate-yet-hopeful face.

"I'm sorry, but it is already priced, as-is. I can't change this one, but I could make you a custom one if you would like to come back in an hour," she informs him, an apologetic tone in her voice.

"An hour?"

"You could try aisle nine. I think there are some silk flowers in vases over there."

"Okay, I'll try that. Oh, and can you spare one of those pitchfork note holders?"

"We sell them. Aisle fourteen."

"Great, thanks."

"No problem."

On aisle nine, Simon discovers numerous silk flower arrangements in glass bowls and vases. He returns to his car to fetch a cardboard box, along with a new pair of leather driving gloves in a plastic bag. He reenters the store and puts the box down in aisle nine. He dons the gloves and carefully places his chosen arrangement in the box. Once this is done, he takes off the gloves. He will carefully wipe everything down later. He cannot guarantee that the employee who arranged the flowers does not have a criminal record. A good fingerprint will lead the police to this store. He obtains a pack of ten plastic pitchfork note holders from aisle fourteen, then heads to checkout.

At the register, Simon places the box on the counter. The clerk raises an eyebrow at the box before looking up at Simon.

"My own box," Simon explains calmly.

The male clerk shrugs and pulls the hand scanner from its holder to scan the arrangement without removing it. The young man states the price, and Simon gives him cash. At his car, he opens his trunk and carefully places the box inside a larger box, leaving both open, so he can still see the arrangement.

Simon seals up the box with packing tape. *I can't have any carpet fibers from the trunk getting into the box and clinging to the silk of the flowers.*

He slides into the driver's seat and looks at himself in the mirror. He sees the face with the red hair and cap. "Who have I become?" he asks himself softly. The knot in his stomach feels a little tighter. *I can't worry about that now,* he decides. *Got to keep going.* Simon decides that it is about time to tell his staff at work that he is finally going to have that root canal he has been postponing. This Tuesday sounds reasonable.

Chapter 14

Despite the heavy traffic and high volume of noise at the airport, Jamie can still hear her cell phone. She fishes it out of her coat pocket and answers it.

"Hey Jamie, how's it going?" Seth's familiar voice addresses her from the other end.

Jamie looks around and spots a less-crowded corner of the airport, so she makes her way over. "Doing well. And yourself?"

"Not bad at all. So when will you be back in town?"

"I should be at my apartment about seven-thirty," Jamie replies. She hears the relief in her own voice even as she tells him.

"Ah, so you are already in town. I was just checking on you—I want to hear about your trip."

"Okay, I'll call you later."

She shuts the phone and rejoins the throng. She passes through the terminal and walks past the baggage claim. Jamie is surprised to see so many people standing at the carousels. Checking a bag is expensive these days. She has only her small, rolling suitcase behind her as she exits the airport. Jamie stops the first taxi she sees and hops in. Her stomach growls unexpectedly. Now she realizes why the airport pizza place smelled so good. It is too bad that Chris will not be waiting for her with dinner at her apartment. It is going to be lonely without him. Well, Jamie does not want to think about that problem either.

The taxi pulls up to her complex. Jamie punches in the code to open the front door, then takes the stairs up to the third floor. She walks down the newly dark red-carpeted hallway to the door bearing the golden numbers 325. The door is already unlocked and slightly ajar. She pulls her Glock .40 pistol from her purse and slowly pushes the door wider. She enters silently. With her pistol aimed straight ahead, she creeps into her living room, all the while scanning the room for movement. She makes her way down the hall toward her bedroom, stopping and listening before she enters. She hears a noise in the kitchen. She follows the sound with her weapon at the ready. She hears the refrigerator door close.

"Hello?"

"Hi! I'm in here," Seth's voice responds.

Not long after she moved into her apartment, she exchanged keys with Seth. It actually comes in handy quite often. Although some notice would lower the chances of Jamie shooting him. She slides her pistol back into her purse and returns to the front entrance.

Jamie doffs her coat and drops her keys on the small table next to the door. She sighs with relief when she sees Seth with two subs on the kitchen counter.

"I knew you would be famished. I hope you don't mind the surprise. I got your favorite," Seth says, welcoming Jamie with a hug. She hugs him tightly back.

"Thanks a million. I'm going to jump in the shower real quick. I've been traveling all day," Jamie tells him, pulling away.

"That's fine. I can warm it up for you when you are done." Seth picks up both subs and puts them in the microwave.

"I'll be quick," Jamie assures him before she disappears into her bedroom. She leaves her bedroom door half-open so she can hear Seth, in case he needs anything. She jumps in the shower and washes her hair. After she dries off, she pulls on her comfy, oversized t-shirt. After running the brush a few times through her wet hair, Jamie looks in the mirror and is satisfied with her reflection.

"Much better!" Jamie declares as she exits her bedroom and joins Seth in the living room. He has been flipping through channels on her television.

Seth looks over at her. Then he takes a second, longer look. Her tan legs are shapely and long. A huge white t-shirt covers much of her thighs, but it is clear that the shirt is all she has on. The color also brings out the richness of her dark, shiny hair. Seth can hardly shut his gaping mouth as she comes into the room and slumps down on the couch next to him. Even as she sits, the t-shirt slides further up her thigh.

Jamie does not see that Seth is eyeing her closely. She is totally comfortable around him. She is wrapped in her own thoughts, but she is also accustomed to Chris, who usually does not look away from the television.

"Anything interesting on?"

"Not really."

"Well, I'm starved. Let's get those subs." Jamie stands up and heads into the kitchen.

"Sure," Seth answers as he follows her.

"Thank you so much for getting these! You really are a lifesaver." Jamie pulls one of the subs out of the microwave and offers it to Seth.

"I do what I can," Seth quips with a wink, accepting his sub.

She grabs the other sandwich and unwraps it on the grey granite counter top of her kitchen island. She pulls up one of the stools and offers the other to Seth.

"Wait, this one is yours." Seth slides the sub across to Jamie.

"Good, because I can't say I'm fond of jalapenos," Jamie laughs, looking with disgust at the contents of the sandwich she unwrapped. She trades with Seth and rips into her roast-beef-and-provolone sub.

"Wow! This is delicious!" Jamie exclaims with her mouth still full.

Seth grins. "You must be really hungry."

After swallowing, Jamie affirms, "Starving."

Seth takes a bite of his own sandwich, chews for a while, then asks, "So how was your trip?"

"Sometimes I cannot believe what a pain it is to travel," Jamie replies in between bites.

"I hear you. By the time you get home you're always tired and hungry. That's why I brought food," Seth says, then removes a jalapeno from his sandwich and eats it alone.

"How's the lab? Everyone behaving?" Jamie asks, getting up from her seat and crossing the kitchen.

"Not really. Having to be Shap's supervisor is hard sometimes."

"You mean Barry Shapiro is the one giving you the hard time?" Jamie wonders, obviously shocked. She stops in front of the counter.

"Yeah, it's weird. He'll be fine for a while and then suddenly he starts missing work, or coming in late and looking like hell."

"Poor guy, must be having a rough time. I wonder what's up. I should call him—find out what's up. I haven't talked to him in a long time."

"So how was Chicago?"

"Not a great start. Came away empty. You want some water?" Jamie offers as she takes a glass out of the cupboard.

"Okay, thanks."

"Anyways, I talked to everyone I could there. No real evidence, no witnesses, no leads of any kind. I feel like that is becoming all-too common with this case," she laments as she fills up one of the glasses with water. She brings it to Seth.

"Thanks."

Filling up her own glass, Jamie continues, "I could not believe how fast the detective in Chicago was willing to hand the file over. It was like a grenade to him. I could almost hear him saying, 'Tag! You're it!' when he dropped the file in my hands."

"Sorry you couldn't turn up any leads. I'm sure you will find something soon." Seth's eyes continue to follow Jamie as she moves to resume her seat on the stool across from him.

"You know what is really a strain?" Jamie continues without pausing. "This case has me traveling across the country practically all week long. I won't even be able to see Chris this weekend because he is on call. I was totally hoping to get some special time with him. And I may need sex to let go of all this stress from the case."

I can take care of that for you, Seth allows his mind to reply, keeping a straight face, so as not to give away his thoughts.

"I guess some extra running will have to do the job," Jamie concludes.

Seth adopts a sympathetic attitude. "Yeah, things with Margie and me are not going so well. She has been giving me the excuse of being too busy."

"Chris totally thinks I'm doing the same thing to him. You might want to give Margie a break. She could actually be as busy as I have been. I bet what she needs is a bit of patience," Jamie responds thoughtfully. She takes another bite of her sub.

"So have you talked to Chris?" Seth probes, testing the waters.

"Not exactly. He sent me a really rude text," Jamie growls.

"What happened?" Seth encourages her to explain. He sets aside his sub, so he can give her his full attention.

"I tried to call him to say that I couldn't make our dinner date Monday night, but he didn't answer. So I texted him, thinking that was better than forgetting to call him later, since I'm so busy with the case. Several hours later, I get a two-word text that reads, 'It figures.'"

"What is that supposed to mean?"

Here I go again. Dying to make a move but afraid to pull the trigger.

"Your guess is as good as mine." She throws her hands up in defeat. She takes a vicious bite of her sub and chews angrily.

"It seems pretty hostile to me."

"Exactly! Like I would rather be alone in a hotel room than eating a nice dinner with my boyfriend? And, for once I have to travel for work, and he can't be understanding? I am always understanding about his work schedule. I mean, seriously?" She takes a gulp of water and a deep breath to calm herself down.

Seth watches her calmly, not interrupting.

Jamie blows the air out of her mouth in exasperation. "I feel like it is me keeping this relationship together. Why should I have to make all the sacrifices?" Jamie finishes.

"A one-sided relationship does not work," Seth agrees quietly. *I would be so good to you.*

"You're right. She thinks for a moment, then finally sees Seth watching her with concern. "Thanks for letting me rant. I appreciate it."

"Any time." He returns to his sandwich.

Jamie polishes off the last bite of her dinner. She rolls up the sub wrappings and throws them in the trash under the kitchen sink.

"You might think about dating someone who is Jewish," Seth suggests. "It might make things easier. And it would be less complicated if you did get serious."

"Really, Seth? You're kidding, right?" Jamie questions him, heading toward her refrigerator.

"It is important, you know. My father would turn over in his grave if I married out," Seth explains, standing up and throwing the rest of his sandwich in the trash.

"I'm dying for a glass of wine. Do you want some?" She pulls a bottle out of the fridge. She pours wine into her empty water glass, until it is about one-third full.

Seth nods, and Jamie fills his glass too.

"Let's talk in here—it's more comfortable," Jamie suggests, already heading across the hallway to the living room.

"Sure." Seth follows Jamie at just enough distance to enjoy the view.

"What about your mother? Would she care if you 'married out'?" She takes a seat on one side of the brown leather couch. She tucks her knees up under her chin, making sure to pull the shirt down as she sits, covering her legs a little better.

Seth sits nearer the middle of the couch, close to Jamie but not too close. He takes a sip of wine before setting it on the coffee table. "Well, since I'm an only child, my mother just wants me to get married. She wants grandchildren so badly, but really she still expects my wife to be Jewish. And Shap gives me grief if I even look at a non-Jewish girl. He makes me feel more guilt than all of my relatives put together."

"My parents aren't really dedicated to the whole Jewish heritage thing. I mean, they never give me the big dose of 'Jewish guilt' or lecture me about 'marrying in'. Look at my brother. He married out, and his kids were even baptized Christians. So, yeah, not a big deal."

Seth decides to change the subject. "So, you flying out again tomorrow?"

"Yep, I'm going to New Orleans tomorrow, for a case with the same M.O.—I'm going to check it out. Then I fly out again on Monday morning. The onsite investigations are going to keep me busy," Jamie finishes, resting her chin on her knees.

"What about this weekend?"

"I'm going to be working on this case, getting all my facts together. I have to make a profile for Behavioral. I've gotta fill in as many holes as I can, so I can give the best picture to Psych when I get back. I want to go over it beforehand, so I can make the most of my trip. What about you?"

"Margie and I are supposed to get together, if she doesn't blow me off like she did earlier this week." Seth harrumphs his annoyance.

"Uh oh!"

"Yeah, I just don't think it is going anywhere. She seems bored with me. And I can't figure out where it went wrong."

"I doubt it is you," Jamie reassures him. "You're the nicest guy in the world and no doubt the best boyfriend ever. She's stupid not to snatch you up."

"Maybe."

"Seth, give yourself more credit than that. Dump her, and find a better girl. She isn't worth it."

"We'll see."

"Don't worry, you'll find a nice Jewish girl soon enough."

"I'm sure you're right."

There is a lull in the conversation. Jamie smiles at Seth. She feels almost warm inside as he gazes back into her eyes. She reaches out a hand, which he takes. The hand surrounding hers is soft and warm.

A ringing breaks the silence. Jamie jumps up and puts her glass of wine on the coffee table. She runs down the hallway to her bedroom to find her cell phone going off loudly. Jamie checks it, only to see that it is several texts from Joey asking for her to meet him at a local dance club. He must be drunk. Exasperated, she returns to the living room.

"Joey is such a dick," Jamie remarks snidely, showing Seth her phone. "I can't even imagine why he would think I would meet him at a club to talk about 'work'. Yeah, right, how stupid does he think I am?"

"He needs backup," Seth jokes.

"Probably." Jamie chuckles appreciatively at the thought.

"Well, I'm traveling tomorrow, so I should probably get to bed early," Jamie says apologetically.

If I had any balls at all, I would be joining you.

"Yeah, I should get home," Seth concedes falsely, trying to hide his disappointment. He finishes off the rest of the wine and sets his glass on the coffee table next to Jamie's. He stands up and starts to walk toward the front door.

Jamie follows him. "Thanks for coming over."

"No problem. Hope you sleep well after all that traveling, and good luck on your research," Seth exhorts her.

"Thanks. I think I will sleep just fine. Oh, and thanks again for the subs."

"Anytime." Seth smiles and gives Jamie a goodbye hug.

She squeezes him back, glad to have such a close friend. They both step back and stand awkwardly in her entryway for a moment.

"Well, bye," Seth says and opens the door.

"See you later!" Jamie calls as he disappears down the stairs. She locks her door before he makes it out of the building.

Heading to her bedroom she cannot help thinking about what a great guy Seth is. Why hasn't some nice Jewish girl taken him off the market?

Like she always does when she has a big case, Jamie reads over her notes before bed. Often, as her brain relaxes on its way to sleep, she gets a sudden epiphany. An "Aha!" moment. She keeps a pad of paper and a pen on her nightstand, so she can capture those moments of insight when they occur.

As she reads her notes, one thing bothers Jamie. Are the dates of the murders really random? If so, why did the killer in

Harwood Heights not kill on an earlier visit when he would also have had the chance? Jamie looks closely at the dates, then pulls up Google and types in the date of the first murder.

September 29, 2010. It was a Wednesday. There is a Wikipedia article for that day. Jamie clicks on the link; maybe it will provide her with something she does not already know. Apparently, September 29, 2010, is the 272nd day in the Gregorian calendar. She scrolls down the page, reviewing at all of the events that occurred on September 29th. The entry includes dates from 522 B.C. until present. It includes events like the adjournment of the first United States Congress and a tsunami near the Samoan Islands. But none of it clearly relates to murdering old men. September 29, 1982, saw the start of the Chicago Tylenol murders. That case was never solved. This could be something—sometimes "copycat" killers idolize other serial killers and try to mimic them. All of the Tylenol victims were in Illinois, and so was one of Jamie's. A possible clue?

She returns to her Wiki article and scrolls down to find that English serial killer Fred West was born on the same date in 1942. Another possibility, which Jamie adds to her list. She finishes reading the page. Under "Holidays and Observances", Jamie sees nothing interesting, unless International Coffee Day counts as a reason to kill an old man. She mentally chuckles at the ridiculous idea.

Sticking with Wikipedia, Jamie searches the site for March 20, 2011. A Sunday. She reads through another list of links to moments in history. There is nothing interesting in births, deaths, or other events. Holidays include Earth Day, Sparrow Day, Storytelling Day, and International Happiness Day. A gas attack on the Tokyo subway killed twelve and wounded 1300. Pope Clement III died on that date in 1130.

October 11, 2011. Another Wednesday. No events stand out to her.

Next is March 18, 2012. Another Sunday. Flag Day in Aruba and Men's and Soldiers' Day in Mongolia. The largest art theft in U.S. history, twelve paintings, collectively worth around $300 million, were stolen from the Isabella Stewart Gardner Museum in Boston. Maybe the victims were art thieves, and their killer, a crusader for justice.

She enters the last date, February 24, 2013. Yet another Sunday. Jamie sighs and notes that it was an Independence Day for Estonia (one of several), Flag Day in Mexico, and National Artist Day in Thailand. The National Constitution in Cuba was proclaimed in 1976, and Cuban president Fidel Castro retired from the position in 2008.

She notes that three of the murders happened on a Sunday and two on a Wednesday. Convenience? Coincidence? Or perhaps it is something else.

Chapter 15

As Jamie gets ready for the day, she is still ruminating on the information from the night before. The birth of an English serial killer or the day the Chicago Tylenol murders started does not provide an obvious connection to her killer. She would have to research each one individually, but Jamie's hunch is that both of them are dead ends. She packs a bag to take to New Orleans for the day.

Soon enough, she is driving a rental car to the home of the late Jonas Kerekes.

As she drives through the Bywater neighborhood, Jamie hits the power locks. She feels the eyes of the locals watching her drive through their turf. The houses are shotgun homes, more like little cottages stacked right next to one another. Having done some research while waiting to board the plane, Jamie knows that Katrina did not flood this part of New Orleans. But she can see the wind damage from the hurricane. The trees are so broken and twisted that, even several years later, they are not fully recovered.

As the voice on the GPS announces, "You have arrived at your destination," Jamie looks at the house to her right. Like all of the other houses on the street, this one has only a front door and a single window on its face. Huge wrought-iron bars barricade both door and window. Jamie cautiously pulls the car up to the curb. When she knocks on the front door, it opens almost immediately, but a screen blocks Jamie from entering.

"Whaddya want?" grunts a gruff, male voice through the screen and the bars.

"Hi, is Mrs. Kerekes at home?" Jamie asks politely. Her eyes examine the layout of the home quickly and make a mental picture, so she can later reenact the crime in her mind.

"Nobody with that name lives here." The man slams the door.

Not exactly what Jamie had been hoping for. She lingers a moment longer on the porch, taking in all aspects of the view. She tries to imagine the perp walking right up to the door, murdering the old man just inside his house, then signaling the wife to call 9-1-1 by claiming that her husband is having a heart attack. The paramedics come in and, not realizing it is a crime scene, start trying to resuscitate the victim, in the process disturbing any evidence that might be there. Unbelievably bold, yet also brilliant.

Jamie sees a black man slowly rocking in his rocking chair on the porch across the street. She remembers from the report that it was from the home across the street that someone saw something. She leaves the porch and crosses the street to the bright yellow house.

When Jamie reaches the porch, she sees that the man's eyes are closed. Jamie clears her throat, wanting to raise the man without scaring him. When she gets no response, she ascends the steps of the porch and knocks on the door.

"She ain't gonna hear ya." The statement issues from the vicinity of the seemingly asleep man.

"I wanted to ask about the murder of Mr. Kerekes. I am looking for the witness who gave a statement."

"Another reporter, huh?"

"Something like that." Jamie shrugs, trying to appear more like a reporter than an FBI agent. It might help her get more information from him, especially in this neighborhood. The man does not stir from his current position. Leaning against the rail, Jamie looks at him expectantly.

"I was just sittin' here an' saw a pizza delivery man drive up to Mr. Kerekes' about 6:30 p.m. or so. Like any normal pizza guy, he just went to the door and all."

She is amazed at how little his lips move when he talks. Hastily she asks, "Did he have a pizza box? Or a pizza delivery bag?"

"Yeah, I think I remember a blue bag."

Jamie pauses thoughtfully. There was no report of a pizza box found at the crime scene. The killer could have just carried a pizza delivery bag, and no one would have known whether or not there was pizza inside.

"Did the car have a sign on top?" Jamie pursues, trying to sound like a top reporter.

"If it did, it didn't have no light in it."

"What did the car look like?"

"Nothing special. A beat-up old car."

"And the pizza guy's appearance?"

"It was dusk, not much to see other than he was just as black as me."

"Anything else you remember about that pizza delivery guy? Something you thought of after you spoke with the police?"

The man's lips curl into his mouth, and his features scrunch up for a moment. "Nope."

"Was there anyone else who might have seen something that night? A fellow neighbor out on their porch?"

"Uh uh," the man grunts.

"Well thank you for your time." Jamie smiles.

"Yep."

The man keeps rocking without moving any other muscle. Jamie watches him for a second and then makes her way down the porch stairs.

She makes for the local police station, only to find a swamped detective who has the Kerekes file in the "Too Hard Box." This is an FBI slang term for the place that files go when they belong somewhere between the inbox and the outbox, but instead the file sits, undisturbed and forgotten. The detective is not pursuing any leads and has dubbed the murder a random and senseless act of violence on par with what he sees every day. His precinct teems with gangs. When Jamie asks about the pizza deliveryman and the witness across the street, the detective replies that the witness "couldn't tell the difference between a pizza delivery car and a Ferrari." Jamie disagrees but finds it pointless to argue. The detective informs her that the wife went to live with her son and died three months after her husband.

The one thing she will be able take back with her is the overwhelming fact that these two men were targeted. One, while in a well-staffed assisted living center, and the other, in a densely inhabited neighborhood.

You are good, Simon W. Very good. Who the hell are you?

Chapter 16

The phone alarm rings, but Jamie is already awake. Sitting up, she retrieves her phone and silences it. The flight home last night left her slightly restless. She stands up and starts to get ready for a long run. What sleep Jamie managed to get was not refreshing—her brain buzzed all night, creating weird nonsense dreams. Even now, her mind is still trying to comprehend all of the information on the case. She stretches a bit and changes into her loose-fitting running clothes.

Jamie grabs her CamelBak and fills it with water. She tightens it and walks out of her front door. Like she always does when she goes running, Jamie uses her spare key to lock the door, then ties up the key in the laces of her right shoe. The less she has to carry on a run, the better.

Pushing open the outer door of the apartment complex, Jamie breathes in the crisp morning frost. She stretches out her calves on the stone steps of her building, still enjoying the cold air in her lungs. After a few more stretches, Jamie begins to walk briskly. She does not go towards the trail, but instead goes on Waterway Drive toward Spriggs Road. It is six miles exactly from her apartment to the end of Spriggs, which dead-ends at

Hoadly Road. The way is familiar to her—her body follows the route automatically, allowing her thoughts to roam.

The empty quiet of Saturday morning helps Jamie to concentrate solely on brainstorming about the case. She begins to wonder if maybe the killer was in contact with the other victims before they were killed. This train of thought draws Jamie back to her main questions. How did the killer pick his victims? Is he a paid hitman? There is more to this than just randomly picking out a name in the phonebook. What made these victims different from other older gentlemen? Why these guys?

Looking up, Jamie sees the Beth Israel synagogue on Spriggs. An eight-foot banner catches her eye. Festively decorated, it announces the Purim holiday and the carnival and costume contest being held at the synagogue. Jamie's mind is flooded with memories.

In the first grade, she had dressed up as Queen Esther. Jamie remembers feeling pretty in her regal costume. She remembers her excitement to enter the costume contest. She did not win. Images of Hebrew school come to her as well. She can vaguely remember making noisemakers. What are they called? Ah, groggers. Hebrew school was such a joke. There was a pervasive feeling that nobody wanted to be there on Sunday mornings. Even the teachers had no passion and a lack of faith in what they were teaching. Despite the attempts to make it fun for the children, Hebrew school was nothing but a disaster.

A specific memory stands out. In third grade, one of her friends had asked the teacher if the Red Sea really split in two for the Israelites. The other kids and Jamie eagerly watched the teacher, whose face turned red as she stammered on about something no one understood. Jamie's friend was persistent and asked the teacher more bluntly: did it, or did it not, happen? The teacher was obviously flustered and replied that it probably did not happen. Jamie recalls sitting there and wondering why, then, did she have to come here and learn about it?

When Jamie was in fourth grade, her parents moved, and the nearest synagogue was twenty-five miles away. They might have gone once or twice when they first moved in, but they did not join, and Jamie stopped attending Hebrew school altogether. She has seldom since been to a synagogue. Barry Shapiro is the only person she knows with a strong connection to anything Jewish.

Jamie turns around at the end of Spriggs Road and returns to the synagogue. She looks with curiosity at the sign and wonders when Purim starts this year. She is shocked to see that it has actually already passed, that it was this past Sunday. Jamie almost stops mid-stride. This past Sunday was also when Fred Schmidt was murdered in Harwood Heights, Illinois. Coincidence?

She wonders why she had not noticed the date of the celebration before. She checks both sides of the banner noting that they are exactly the same. She starts back into her run again, away from the synagogue and toward her apartment. She had not seen any Jewish holidays listed on Wikipedia. She now contemplates what else she might have missed. Maybe this past Sunday was another holiday or special day in another religion or country. Maybe it was a special day in Islam or Buddhism? Maybe she should research it again. The return run to her apartment goes by faster than ever as Jamie is lost in her thoughts.

Despite the smell of sweat, Jamie skips the usual post-run shower and instead retrieves her tablet from where it lies on the desk in her room.

Within seconds, she has Google running again and searching for March 20th. The results include the usual holidays, International Day of Happiness, World Sparrow Day, and U.N. French Language Day. Jamie tries a different tack, putting both dates in March and adding the word "calendar." The first result is a snowfall report from a ski resort in Idaho. The second result is titled, "Jewish Holidays 2001-2020."

"Huh?" Jamie responds aloud.

She clicks on the link, and a chart appears with the years going down the right column and the various holidays across the top. She notices that her two dates in March are each on the Jewish holiday of Purim.

The Jewish calendar does not coincide with the Gregorian calendar. Therefore Jewish holidays are always on the same Hebrew date, but they appear on different days in the regular calendar. For example, Purim is always on the fourteenth of the

Jewish month Adar, and Passover is always on the fifteenth of Nissan.

Interesting, so does that mean that the perp waited until Purim? Is that why he did not act during an earlier visit? Yet what does Purim have to do with murdering old men? Jamie starts to think about each victim. Fred Schmidt was not Jewish, was he? Were any of the victims?

Jamie looks up each victim's religious affiliations. Two of them were Catholics, two were Protestant, and one had no stated affiliation. If the murders were intended to be on Purim, did the date matter to the killer or to the victims? Maybe both. Hopefully they can tell her something.

Jamie turns back to her desk and searches for Purim. She finds some useful websites and discovers that Purim is mentioned in the Book of Esther. It commemorates the day that a plot by Haman to annihilate the Jewish people was foiled and the Jews were saved.

To celebrate the holiday, costumes are worn in honor of Esther, who hid her Jewish background. Traditionally the costumes are based on characters from the book of Esther, but, over the years, they have become anything, from Batman to fairies.

Jamie wonders about the other dates. She searches for the murder dates in October. They also both coincide with a Jewish holiday! September 29th and October 19th are on the chart as Hoshana Raba. *Whatever that is.*

She then searches for an online Jewish calendar. Several are available. She finds Hoshana Raba to be the last day of the holiday of Tabernacles. Interesting. Jamie starts a new search for Hoshana Raba. Clicking on the first reliable-looking source, Jamie finds a jackpot of information.

Hoshana Raba is also known as the Day of Final Judgment. Maybe the murderer has been making his judgment final for old white men. She discovers that, in the Jewish religion, Hoshana Raba is the last of the Days of Judgment that begin on Rosh Hashana and also include Yom Kippur.

Could the killer be Jewish? That is a big matzo ball to swallow. On the bright side, she is finally getting a possible lead.

She has three murders occurring on Purim and two on Hoshana Raba.

Someone is killing old men on Jewish holidays!

Chapter 17

Although she was raised Jewish, Jamie can remember hardly anything about Purim. Why celebrate a holiday of people trying to kill Jews? Her father used to tell her that all Jewish holidays are the same. Someone tried to kill us. God miraculously saved us. We eat!

Miraculously saved.

Jamie turns to the tall, cherry bookshelf, which sits against the wall. Her eyes peruse the volumes on the shelves. Jamie kept all of her books from college, including A Casebook of Forensic Detection, Criminalistics: An Introduction to Forensic Science, The Forensic Psychology of Criminal Minds, Handbook of Forensic Neuropsychology, and others. After reading through a few more titles, she moves to the next shelf.

Jamie spots her copy of Crime and Punishment and feels a burst of affection. Maybe, when this case is over, she will read it again. But right now it is not what she is looking for. This shelf does not have what she needs. On the next shelf, hidden between a Spanish textbook and a European History book sits the Jewish Bible. Jamie's aunt Cheryl gave it to her right after Jamie graduated from high school.

Aunt Cheryl was much more connected to Jewish things and was very active in her own synagogue. She gave Jamie the Bible because she was certain that Jamie's college roommate would be a born-again Christian set on conversion. Jamie should be armed with her own Bible, if the need arose.

"I think I'll be fine. Where do you come up with these things anyway?" Jamie remembers saying to her aunt.

"I'm just saying, you are going to a big school, and you never know who your roommate will be," Aunt Cheryl insisted. She probably would have pursued the subject, but Jamie's mom chimed in and put it to rest.

"She'll take it with her, thank you. Won't you, Jamie?"

"Of course, thanks."

As promised, she took the large volume with her to college. She never opened it. She thinks now about her aunt's warnings and smiles. Jamie begins flipping through the Jewish Bible until she finally sees the book of Esther. To Jamie's surprise, it is short. Only ten small chapters.

Esther is a complex story. The King of Persia wants to show off his trophy wife, and the Queen refuses. The King deposes her and is then in need of a new wife. All of the young virgins are forcibly taken to the King, and among them is Esther, an orphan. Esther is Jewish, but she hides that fact at the suggestion of her cousin, Mordechai. She is picked by the King and becomes the new queen.

Right after Esther becomes queen, Mordechai overhears two courtiers planning to assassinate the King. He exposes their plot; the conspirators are caught and hanged. Mordechai's actions are recorded in the chronicles of the King. Not long after, Haman, the villain of the story, receives appointment to viceroy, second only to the King himself. But, because of his religion, Mordechai refuses to bow to Haman when commanded to do so. *Men haven't changed a bit.* Jamie smiles to herself.

Haman discovers that Mordechai is Jewish. To punish Mordechai for his disrespect, Haman convinces the King to agree to a day on which they can massacre all of the Jews and seize their property. The decree is sent out, and Mordechai, along with his people, begins to mourn and fast.

Mordechai tells Esther about the decree, and he begs her to appeal to the King. She is hesitant to approach the King without a summons, as it could lead to her death. After fasting and praying for three days and having her people do the same,

Esther comes to the King without being summoned. He acknowledges her with his scepter, which saves her life. The queen invites the King and Haman to a feast. At the feast, Esther requests their presence again at a feast the next night.

Haman returns home from the feast, once again offended that Mordechai refused to bow to him. He builds a gallows in hopes of seeing Mordechai hang there. Then he goes back to the King's palace to ask the King if he can hang Mordechai. The King is having his chronicles read to him because he cannot sleep. Right before Haman approaches him, the King hears again how Mordechai saved his life. The King asks Haman how to honor a man for services rendered. Haman thinks the King is referring to himself, so he tells him to put that man in the King's clothes, on the King's horse, and to proclaim through the city how the King rewards his loyal people.

The King instructs Haman to do so unto Mordechai! Haman is enraged that he has to parade his enemy around town. Then Haman attends the second feast hosted by Esther. There at the feast, Esther tells the King that she is Jewish and that the decree made by Haman will kill her people...and herself. The King is outraged by this information and leaves the feast. Haman panics and begs Esther to save him. He becomes hysterical in his pleas, and the King returns to see Haman falling on the Queen. The King quickly orders Haman to be hanged on the gallows that were built for Mordechai. Unfortunately, the King cannot repeal the decree to exterminate the Jews, so he amends the law to allow the Jews to defend themselves.

The appointed day comes, and five hundred attackers, as well as Haman's ten sons, are killed by Jews.

Jamie bolts upright, her body pumping with adrenaline. There, in the middle of chapter nine, are the names of Haman's sons: Parshandatha, Dalphon, Aspatha, Poratha, Aridatha, Parmashta, Arisai, Aridai and Vaizatha.

Jamie grabs for the nearest case folder off of her desk. She checks the note found with the victim. "pars hon dota." Parshandatha is the first name listed in the book of Esther. She looks back at the other notes.

"dol fon" - "dolfon" - *Dalphon!*

"a spat a" - "aspata" - *Aspatha!*

"por ot ha" - "porota" - *Poratha!*
"parmo sh ta" - "parmoshta" - *Parmashta!*

Her brain is racing forward with this new finding. She notes the variant spellings of the names. Was the killer trying to make it difficult to draw a connection using the internet?

Where are Adalia and Aridatha? He has gone in order of the biblical list, so why would he skip those names? Or did he? Maybe there are more murders.

What is the connection with Purim? Purim takes place in Persia, now Iran. Could the killer be Iranian? Is he taking revenge against the Persians killed 2,500 years ago in the Purim story? No, the October dates were on the little known Jewish holiday of Hoshana Raba. He used the Jewish calendar. The killer must be Jewish.

Why Purim? The victims do not seem to have any connection to Purim or Persia.

Most serial killers prey on their own race. Most are males in their twenties or thirties. Serial killers have a typical "cooling off" period until the demons come back. Serials fantasize about the crime for a long time before committing it, which is why most serial killers start close to home, with someone familiar. Schenectady, New York, was first, and the victim was lured away from his home. Maybe the perp had been fantasizing about killing him for some time.

Maybe the murderer actually knew him….

Chapter 18

Jamie wakes up on Monday feeling ready to head to Schenectady. She had to take a Benadryl the night before to help her get to sleep because her mind was racing from her new discovery. Jamie had assumed that the killer had to be Jewish, but after some rest, she realizes she may have jumped to conclusions.

Esther is not only in the Jewish Bible, but in the Christian Bible as well. The only conclusion she can safely draw is that the killer is religious, possibly some sort of zealot.

After she lands at Albany International Airport, she rents a car, and, using her portable GPS system, she drives to the Schenectady Police station.

Detective Hunt informs her that he has no leads and no idea why Henning was driven almost fifty miles from his house. There were no signs of forced entry. She does not mention that she is dealing with a serial killer. Jamie will thoroughly investigate all of his neighbors. It is possible that he knew the killer, which would explain why there was no forced entry. Henning may have gotten into the killer's car willingly. Detective Hunt tells Jamie that Lacy Henning-Smith, the deceased's daughter, still calls every Monday, asking if there are any new leads. Jamie hates to put fuel on the fire, but she has to call the daughter and ask her if her father had any Jewish connections. Now the daughter will probably call Jamie every

Monday as well. Jamie asks her the same questions she will ask all family members: Did he ever mention anyone that you never met? Was there anything unique about him? Something uncommon? Any clubs or affiliations? Was he a churchgoer? Any secrets? Any involvement with the Jewish community? Any suspicious neighbors? She gets nothing from Lacy but a barrage of questions about why the FBI has been brought in and what is Jamie not telling her. Jamie remains polite and leaves Schenectady with full confidence that she will be hearing a lot from Lacy Henning-Smith.

She traverses the low, rolling hills and farmhouses and arrives forty-five minutes later in the quaint historic town of Salem. She passes the Revolutionary War Cemetery that dates back to 1762 and the school that has been in use since 1780. The Sheriff's Department is located south of the village. Sheriff Richard Foster is a small man in his fifties who reminds Jamie of Barney Fife from The Andy Griffith Show. He drives Jamie to the hamlet of Shushan, where the body was found propped up against the Shushan Post Office building. An awkward silence passes, but Jamie imagines it is probably much more awkward for her than for him. The police radio is silent. The hum of the car engine is the only noise that fills the calm. Jamie looks back out the window again, watching the unfamiliar countryside. They drive along the beautiful Battenkill River and pass the **Shushan Covered Bridge**, constructed in 1858, which is now a museum.

The post office is a red brick A-frame building that used to be a train depot. On the side of the building, there is a small strip of grass right next to the wall and some handicapped-parking spaces.

Jamie compares what she is seeing to the picture from her file. Henning's body was found on the side of the Post Office, in the strip of grass, centered right below the two white-framed windows. Directly over the body the lettering on the side of the building reads: United States Post Office, Shushan, NY 12873.

The name Shushan sounds familiar to Jamie. She thinks for a moment and then remembers. Shushan is the capital city of the Persian Empire and the setting for the book of Esther. No wonder it sounded familiar, for she had just read about it. Another link to the book of Esther! Statistically speaking, most criminals get caught trying to hide their crimes, not while committing them. *This guy wanted us to find out about his crime and intentionally placed the body under the name "Shushan". He went to a lot of trouble...and considerable risk.*

Foster reiterates his theory that the perp made a ramp out of some two-by-sixes and used it to place the body against the post office. It was raining when Foster found the body, around 8:30 a.m. He has essentially handed the case to the folks in Schenectady. Jamie surveys the surrounding area. Route 64 runs behind the post office. She can make out a few houses on the other side of Route 64, but they are not close enough to have heard anything in the middle of the night.

Her only success in this journey is finding another tie to the book of Esther. What it all means is still a mystery.

She spends the night in a hotel near the Albany airport and eats some Chinese take-out while watching Clint Eastwood in <u>Escape from Alcatraz</u>.

Chapter 19

Simon relaxes as the limo driver pulls up at the small municipal airport. He glances at his watch as the driver parks close to a private Cessna Citation Mustang. 5:50 a.m. Perfect timing. The driver exits the limo and opens Simon's door.

"Shall I get your bags, sir?" The limo driver offers courteously.

"No, thanks, I can handle them." Simon steps out of the car. He reaches in and pulls out the rolling bag and a big cardboard box. With a wave to the limo driver, Simon approaches the private plane.

"Hey! I assume you're Mr. Maddox." A short, stocky man looks Simon over. "My name is Brad, and I'll be your pilot for today. Here, let me take the box for you!"

"No thank you," Simon dismisses him, "It's fragile. But you can take my bag." Simon holds out handle on the rolling bag.

Brad takes the bag and falls into step with Simon. "Everything is in order. We will be in the air shortly."

"Great! Thanks."

They board the plane, and Simon makes his way to the back seats. Brad puts the rollaway bag on the ledge behind the cockpit and secures it there, then secures the cardboard box behind the last row of seats. Simon watches Brad slide into his

108

pilot's chair and prepare the plane for takeoff. About five minutes later, the plane is taxiing on the runway.

Simon watches the clouds zoom by. He has an hour and forty-five minutes before they arrive at Peachtree DeKalb Airport in Chamblee, Georgia, which is a suburb just ten minutes north of Atlanta. The cost of this entire mission will be around $8,000. It may seem like a lot, but it is really a drop in the bucket. Money is no object when it comes to achieving his goals.

He begins to play out in his mind over and over again exactly how it will all happen. The thrill of the kill has all but left him. The first kill was something Simon will never forget. He remembers the cushy life the old codger was living and the anger linked to that knowledge. He is going to get the deed done today, but he no longer savors it and wishes that someone else would take over the task.

But there is no one else.

Simon is proud of his achievements, though. His progress has been amazing, and fulfilling his promise has been much easier than he imagined. Swift. Simple. Righteous.

Brad starts to radio the air traffic controller, waking Simon from his reverie. He looks out the window and sees the small world beneath him. How little do people know that their lives are infested with vermin. He will act as exterminator. Simon looks to the cockpit, as Brad receives the okay to land the plane.

Simon stares out the window as the small jet makes a smooth landing. Brad deftly slows the plane and turns it off the runway and onto a taxiway. As the plane turns it shows Simon the limo that awaits him. In minutes, Brad helps Simon disembark and transfers the rolling bag to the limo.

"How long will you be?" Brad asks before letting Simon disappear into the limousine.

"Just a couple of hours." Simon has already planned that, if either the limo driver or pilot asks about the trip, he will say that he is coming to Atlanta for a real estate closing. Luckily, Brad does not seem curious, and Simon departs.

Simon instructs the driver to take him to Tower Place in Buckhead. The driver nods and turns the car onto the side streets leading from Peachtree DeKalb to Peachtree Industrial

Boulevard. After some Atlanta traffic, the limo finally pulls into the multi-building complex. As he enters the circle drive in front of the main building, Simon instructs the driver, "You don't have to wait for me here. I will call you when I am ready. It'll be a couple of hours." He hands the driver a twenty. "Why not go get some breakfast or something," Simon suggests pleasantly, climbing out of the car with the rolling suitcase and cardboard box.

The limo driver nods and smiles. Simon walks away from the limo, and the car pulls back into the busy streets. He walks past a nicely-landscaped square in front of the office building. Inside there is a classy lobby with leather chairs surrounded by tall, leafy potted plants and large oriental rugs that cover the polished stone floor. A uniformed security guard sits behind a concierge desk. Check-in is not required.

Towards the back of the lobby, past the elevators, Simon sees the restroom signs pointing around the corner. He weaves through a few people waiting for the elevators and turns the corner to find the men's restroom. The bathroom is just as luxurious as the rest of the building, with granite counters, sensor spigots, and several toilet stalls. Simon picks the handicapped stall and locks the door. He retrieves a burner phone and calls a Hispanic taxi company to arrange a pick-up. He then opens the package of a brand new bed sheet and uses it to cover the floor of the bathroom stall. Simon puts the box down and starts to change.

He begins his transformation by placing a tight-fitting hair net over his thick hair. He then removes the clothes he is wearing and places them in a plastic garbage bag. Opening the suitcase, he removes his new clothing, each piece of which is still in the original plastic from the store. The pants and shirt are identical to what he currently wears. Simon pulls out a one-piece, white, disposable coverall suit and puts it over his clothes. He removes a brand new pair of shoes, three sizes too big, and slides them on. Simon has already placed weights inside the toes of the shoes, to fill the extra space. He places shoe covers over the new shoes. He tops off his outfit with a baseball cap and adds some dark sunglasses.

Simon unlocks the stall door and throws away the plastic wrappings. He folds up the bed sheet and places it back in the suitcase, along with his tightly-bagged original clothes.

The building is perfect for his plan, since there are exits on both sides leading to different parts of the complex. Simon turns and leaves the building through the opposite door from where he entered. A taxi waits at the drop-off curb of the building. The words on the side of the car are in Spanish. Simon approaches the car, and the cab driver greets him.

"Hello, Señor!" He jumps out of the front seat to help Simon put his things in the back.

Simon nods, pleased with what he sees. He is hoping the driver's English is not good enough to comfortably watch the evening news. He gives the driver the address of a house situated near the victim's street. Even if the driver radios in the destination, there will be no record matching the crime scene and no familiar address for the driver or dispatch to recognize. The taxi driver nods, and away the car takes off into the maze of Atlanta streets.

Despite the early morning traffic, the taxi driver arrives at the address of the last house at the corner of the victim's street in Simon's desired window of time. He then tells the driver to make a right turn and go to the fifth house on the right. The taxi turns into the driveway, and Simon directs the driver to pull all the way up to the side of the house, blocking the driver's view of the front door.

Simon reaches into his rolling suitcase and pulls out a fanny pack from the front pocket, along with a Playboy magazine. He hands the magazine to the driver saying, "I'll be right back. Keep the meter running."

The driver smiles again, accepting the magazine and delving into its pages.

Simon opens his door and carefully removes his shoe covers, making sure his shoes do not touch anything in the car. He wants the first contact made by the brand new shoes to be with the driveway. He leaves the shoe covers on the floor of the back seat. Strapping the fanny pack around his waist, he reaches for the cardboard box, then exits the taxi, shutting the door behind him. Simon carries the box to the front door and sets it on the ground. He removes a pair of latex gloves from his fanny pack and puts them on. He opens the box and removes the smaller box with the flower arrangement. Without a second's delay, he rings the doorbell.

Simon waits a few seconds, then hears the removal of the deadbolt. The door opens only a crack. Martin Rossi's eye glares through the space. "What?" the old man spits at him.

"Floral delivery." Simon replies with a smile, undeterred.

"Fine, fine," Mr. Rossi mumbles, shutting the door. Simon can hear him unlatch the chain lock. The door swings open, and Mr. Rossi stands there, wearing a bathrobe over white pajamas with light green stripes.

"This is for Annette Rossi. Let me put it on the table for you." Simon does not wait for an answer, but walks right into the foyer. He takes the flowers out of the cardboard box and sets the arrangement on a small side table. "There is a card here, too," Simon announces, stepping back to let Mr. Rossi take a look.

As soon as the old man's back is turned, Simon swiftly pulls the garrote out of his fanny pack.

Mr. Rossi reads the note aloud, mumbling, "I know who you are and what you have done. It is time for you to die for your crimes."

Before Mr. Rossi can even react to the note, the garrote is around his neck. It is over in a couple of minutes. Simon leaves the old man's body slumped where it falls. He removes the garrote and places it in a large Ziploc bag, then puts it back in his fanny pack. Simon takes the note that Mr. Rossi read and also places it in the pack. He opens a Ziploc bag, and with a pair of tweezers he removes a small note from the bag and places it on the cardholder.

It reads, "A.J. Ari Sai."

And, on the back:

Fools

Behaving

Irresponsibly

Simon smiles to himself. He always enjoys his finishing touch. The note seals the deal for him. It defines his work. With a quick movement, Simon snatches up the cardboard box and walks out the front door without touching anything else. He drops the cardboard box back into the one sitting outside. Then, picking up the larger one, he makes his way back to the taxi.

The driver hardly looks up from the magazine as Simon opens the car door. He sits down and replaces the shoe covers before pulling his feet inside the taxi. Simon then directs the driver to take him to the nearest MARTA station. As the taxi backs out of the driveway, Simon pulls out a disinfecting wipe. He discreetly wipes down the door handle and anything else he might have touched.

In no time at all, the taxi arrives at the MARTA station and parks behind a line of taxis waiting for the next train to arrive with its potential fares. With his latex gloves still on, Simon removes the correct amount of cash from the envelope with the tens and fives. Simon exits with his personal belongings and slowly walks along the line of taxis.

The taxi Simon just exited leaves the station and disappears into traffic. Simon times his stride just right so that, as the taxi turns out of view, he stands right next to the first taxi in the line. Simon tells this driver, an African American, to take him to the Starbucks in the strip mall at the corner of Piedmont and Peachtree. The Starbucks is directly across from Tower Place.

Simon has an envelope ready with money and pays the taxi driver in cash. Using a disinfectant wipe, he opens the taxi door and removes his belongings.

Once the taxi drives off into the street, Simon walks around to the rear of the Starbucks, where several large dumpsters serve the stores in the strip mall. The most important step is to dispose of the murder weapon. He removes the garrote from his bag and wipes it down thoroughly with the disinfecting wipes. It consists of a three-quarter-inch wooden dowel cut into two, four-inch pieces. Simon drilled a hole through the middle of the dowel allowing enough room for the ten-gauge wire to pass through. He tied the wire in double-knots on either side of the dowel, producing a thirty-inch piece of wire with a handle on each end. A simple garrote.

Simon is actually proud of his perfect weapon. He cuts the wire into approximately three-inch pieces with wire cutters. He pulls out a plastic jar of peanut butter and stabs each of the pieces of wire into the peanut butter, until it is submerged. He then wraps the peanut butter jar completely using two-inch-wide white bandage tape, until it is unrecognizable. Simon does not want some dumpster diver digging out a jar of peanut butter to eat and finding the most damning evidence. Once the jar is effectively mummified, he puts it into another garbage bag.

He collapses both cardboard boxes and wipes them down until they are wet with disinfectant and places them in the dumpster. He removes the coveralls, hat, and shoe covers, and places them in a heavy-duty garbage bag from his carry-on. He changes back into his regular shoes.

He walks a bit farther to the next store's dumpster and shakes the weights out of the shoes and into the bottom of the trash. He disposes of the clothes he wore on the plane. Pulling out a different heavy duty bag, Simon puts the large shoes in it, ties it up, and tosses it into a third dumpster.

At the next store's dumpster, he trashes the bag with the peanut butter. He bags the rolling luggage, with the hat and fanny pack concealed inside, into a large, black garbage bag and throws them away as well. He walks around to the storefronts and heads across the street to the high-rise. Inside the foyer, he informs the concierge that his cell phone has died and asks the man to call the limo for him.

Once the limo arrives, Simon tells the driver to head back to Peachtree DeKalb Airport, where his private plane is waiting. He pays for the limo from the envelope full of hundreds. Once in the air, Simon smiles.

In and out before the old fart's wife even gets home.

Chapter 20

The next day, Jamie meets with detective Joe Haley in Abilene, Texas. He is tall, built, and strikingly good-looking. His accent is so stereotypical Texan that Jamie is taken aback. Together they go over the file, which includes photos, reports, forensics, and the surveillance camera footage from the nursing home lobby. Human hair was found on the sheets. No DNA could be obtained because there was no follicle. Detective Haley informs Jamie that the hair did not match any of the nursing home employees. Haley reviews the timeline of events. At 9 a.m., Elizabeth Bierman-Colier, the daughter, visits the victim. At 11:30 a.m., Mr. Bierman is wheeled to the dining room for lunch. After enjoying gourmet macaroni and cheese with green beans and tapioca pudding, Mr. Bierman is returned to his room, between 12:15 and 12:30 p.m. On the sign-in register there is one female visitor with an unknown relationship to Bierman. The name is Esther Shushan. Esther Shushan? Here is Shushan again, this time paired with Esther. This all but confirms the connection. Jamie flips back to the pictures and looks again at the sign in sheet. The handwriting seems to match the strange, sloppy signature of "Simon W." from Harwood Heights. In addition, the pen ink is not the same as the others on the sign-in sheet.

They review the surveillance video. The surveillance camera is perched above the receptionist's desk, looking out at the foyer. A woman comes into the frame. She wears a stylish pantsuit, wide-brimmed hat, and sunglasses. She signs in at the desk with her left hand. Immediately, Jamie notices that the woman's hands are covered with white, lacy gloves. Perhaps to hide a man's hands, Jamie surmises. As Jamie watches the woman in the footage, she can tell immediately from the woman's behavior that the woman knew where the camera was—her head is turned down and away as she comes into view. Long black hair hangs down from under her hat. A time stamp on the screen shows 11:00 a.m.

"She doesn't sign out for another fifty minutes," Haley explains as he moves the footage ahead a bit.

The woman reappears at the front desk to sign out. The time stamp says it is 11:48 a.m. After signing out, the woman leaves.

"Interesting," Jamie mutters thoughtfully. Her brows are furrowed, and her eyes look past the screen. She is trying to put the pieces of the puzzle together.

The woman returns to the sign-in window. After a brief conversation with the receptionist, she goes back into the nursing home. According to the time stamp, this occurs at 1:02 p.m.

"The receptionist did report that the woman returned and claimed to have forgotten her cell phone and that she would only be a second. The lady returned to the front reception area, and the receptionist remembers the woman waving to her as she left," Haley recounts, watching for Jamie's reaction to the footage.

"He probably hoped he could get back in unnoticed, and the cell phone ploy was a backup if he was spotted," Jamie hypothesizes, not taking her eyes from the woman on surveillance, who waves a cordial goodbye. The woman leaves at 1:09 p.m.

"He?" Haley queries, raising a dark eyebrow.

"Yes. Esther Shushan is a man, hence the gloves, which hide his hairy, or otherwise masculine, hands," Jamie informs him confidently. She continues, "He knew we would figure it out. I believe he even wants us to. The ploy was for the immediate aftermath, so that, in the crucial minutes after the body was discovered, the lady in the snappy suit would be in the clear."

Haley nods in response. "They did not discover the body until 3:15 p.m."

"The perp was long gone," Jamie avers. "He was really smart. Most of the residents there probably take naps after lunch and that is probably when the staff breaks for their lunch. He came in during the '*residents*' lunchtime. Probably prepared the room for his return. He then breezed back in after the staff went on break."

"Makes sense, but what about the hair we found? It does belong to a woman," Haley counters.

"The hair they found was probably human hair from his wig. A lot of human-hair wigs come from India. That would match the Asian characteristics they found at the lab. There is a ritual in India where women and even men grow their hair long and then cut it and offer it to one of their gods in the temple. The temple then collects the hair and sells it to wig makers and uses the money to maintain the temple. It's a multi-million dollar business," Jamie explains. "He planted it. How many did you find?"

"Six. But, come to think of it, that's a lot in one spot, isn't it?" Haley does not wait for a response. "I'm sure one of his kids did it. Do you know how much that nursing home costs per month? It will drain even a huge nest egg pretty quickly. And Bierman was still relatively healthy—could have lived for years more. Someone would rather have the money than dear old dad," Haley avows, looking at the file in front of Jamie.

"Possible, but which one? He has four kids, plus sons-in-law and daughters-in-law," Jamie points out.

"Oh, I've suspected them all at one point or another. We've got nothing other than family members as potential suspects. We even considered that it might be a crazy staff member. But the staff here has been stable, with not a lot of turnover. And all the staff said the victim was a very pleasant guy. Not an ornery old grinch that pissed people off and not someone that they would want to get out of the home," Haley expounds.

"And what about the note?"

"Strangest part is how clean it is. As if it has never been touched by a human hand. Clearly planted. Something to divert us away from a family member. Makes it seem more like a mysterious serial killer or something. We've had nothing even remotely similar from here to Dallas."

"My only question is why a family member wouldn't poison him or do something else to make it look like he died of old age. This is so obviously murder."

"Yeah, that has bothered me. But you know, if this was well-thought-out, they could use that as part of their alibi, that it would be too obvious to use a conventional cover-up. They could possibly have thought it out that far," Haley rebuts. "What do you think?"

"My hunch is that he was targeted by a non-family-member." Jamie replies with a shrug. After a pause she abruptly closes, "Here is my card, and I have your info. Please let me know if anything turns up. I'll do the same."

"Will do," Haley assures her, nodding his head again.

With a quick handshake, they part ways. Jamie exits through the busy reception area and walks to her car. She punches in the address of the nursing home, then tucks the file into the front pocket of her suitcase.

The nursing home is quite luxurious. An ostentatious water fountain sits in the middle of the circular driveway in front of the entrance. A roof over the drive is held up by some Grecian-style pillars. She pulls the rental car into the stall closest to the entrance, since the front door is blocked by a short bus, which is unloading a wheelchair-bound senior.

Jamie wants to re-trace the killer's moves. She does not need to interview any staff members, as only the receptionist saw "the woman", and even then they hardly spoke. There is no point in raising flags with her FBI credentials. Jamie is not looking for evidence. She is just trying to accurately envision the murder.

Walking through the sliding glass doors, Jamie is engulfed by the smell of cleaning products. Ignoring that overwhelming scent, she looks past the ornate furniture of the waiting room, to a camera placed precariously at a fixed angle. She sees for herself that it is easy for a person to prevent the camera from getting a head-on view. If the nursing home has any sense, Jamie is sure they will have fixed the security problem by now. Sure enough, she spots a new camera positioned at the top of a brick fireplace in the foyer; it pans the whole area. Jamie smirks to see her idea confirmed.

The receptionist's computer is at an angle so that she is behind a small hutch connected to her desk. The woman does not even observe Jamie walking past. Jamie concludes that the killer probably thought he had a decent chance to get by unnoticed. When he did not, and instead had to sign in, the killer left without doing anything. Trying to sneak in a second time, he was seen again, so he used the "Forgot my phone, I'll be right back" line. Clearly, it worked.

From the receptionist's perspective, "she" went in and had a normal visit. Then she came back, but only for a moment. It would not seem like enough time to commit the crime. That is all that matters for the first fifteen minutes after the body is discovered.

Jamie walks down the hospital-like corridor, which is lined with railings for the elderly to use if they want to walk. She examines the length of the hallway and the staff there. The place is pretty empty. It would have been possible for the killer to enter the room of the victim and exit again without being seen by a staff member. Jamie finally reaches the room where the murder transpired. Once again, it is not the most convenient room in which to murder someone. In fact, it is only two rooms away from the nurses' station. She peers into the room.

"Who are you?" a grumpy old man grunts. He is sitting in a medical bed, propped up and facing a television.

The room is furnished cozily, with nice wood floors, lush potted plants, and large windows through which to view the outside world. Every decoration, from the white cornice around the top of the room, to the lavish decorative lights, reveals to Jamie just how much a room in this nursing home would cost.

"Sorry, wrong room," Jamie excuses herself, trying to act embarrassed by looking down and away. But she hesitates a moment longer, soaking in all the details before scurrying away.

Jamie is again able to pass through the foyer without the receptionist seeing her. Once outside, she sees that the short bus and the old man in the wheelchair are gone. A moment later, so is Jamie.

She calls Gary Bierman, the victim's oldest son, and asks the usual questions. It turns out that Mr. Bierman owned his own business selling oil and gas pipe. A self-made man.

He had been president of the Abilene Business Association, on the boards of the local hospital, Rotary Club, and the United Way. He was very religious and an active member in his church. She asked him if his father had any contact with the Jewish community, and he responded, "Where? Here in Abilene? Is there one?" It turns out that there is a small Jewish temple in Abilene with around twenty-five members. Now Jamie has to suppress Gary's barrage of questions about the Jewish connection. After she hangs up with him, she calls Kim Hammond from Research, to get an update on how the victims could have been associated during their lives. There seems to be nothing linking them.

She is off to Flint, Michigan, in the morning. She figures that, in the meantime, she might as well see a little of Texas. She heads to the Lucky Mule Saloon for a bite to eat and some line dancing. The crowd of cowboy hats and giant belt buckles amuses Jamie. She gets hit on several times before she calls it an early night. She arrives back at her hotel around ten o'clock. The flight will leave at 5:25 a.m., and will include a stop in Dallas. It is the only way to get to Flint from Abilene.

Chapter 21

The private jet comes to a stop. Peering out the window, Simon sees a taxi waiting for him not far from the hangar. He will return to work and create his alibi. He gives the driver instructions, and, when the taxi arrives at the mall where his car is parked, Simon pays with cash. A reporter's voice floats out of the speakers, assessing the traffic for that hour. He drives to his workplace and arrives at 1:05 in the afternoon. He makes sure several people see him as he walks to his office. It is pretty tough to get all the way from Atlanta as fast as he did. He immediately opens a file on his computer, makes a few changes, and saves it again. Now he has a permanent record on his computer of being 620 miles from the crime scene, less than four hours after the murder. His computer at work is locked very tightly, with automatic backups every fifteen minutes. He has made an indelible mark that places him far away from the death of Mr. Martin Rossi.

With the pay period ending, it is time to fill out his timesheet. He has worked for the same company for many years. He knows quite well that the comptroller merely transfers the timesheet data to a spreadsheet, which is then forwarded to a payroll company. No one will scrutinize his time.

Now he needs to get some real work done. Soon enough, he becomes lost in his work, until he leaves the office at 5:30 p.m.

He climbs into his four-door sedan and begins the drive home. As the engine turns over, talk radio comes on. Simon turns it down, a little shocked that he was listening to it so loudly before. Once the car gets going, he smiles to himself and turns the radio back up, switching it to a music station.

At home, Simon performs his routine walk-through, to make sure that there is nothing that could link him to the crime. Simon buys everything new for each murder. He makes his purchases the day before and does not bring any articles of clothing home, so he does not have to worry about hiding any evidence; the shoes, hat, clothes, gloves, sunglasses, fanny pack, and wig, if used, are all untraceable to him. It is his workshop in the basement that will require his attention instead.

Simon walks down his stairs into the basement and looks over his workbench. He has already thrown away the leftover piano wire used to make the garrote and cleaned up the wood shavings from drilling the holes in the wooden dowels. Simon had put a sheet on the basement floor to collect all the bits of wood from his work. Once finished, he folded up the sheet, careful not to let any scraps of wood fall onto the floor. Such precautions might seem ridiculous to a normal person, but Simon knows that Forensics teams can match wood samples. He even threw away the drill bit after making the garrote. Typically anal-retentive, Simon now sweeps the basement floor again, but he collects nothing beyond the normal dust of life.

Simon had double-bagged the trash and taken it behind different strip malls, to dispose of the bags in different dumpsters. One of his favorite dumpsters is located behind a busy restaurant. That dumpster gets full fast, so his bags are covered by the end of the night.

Simon has no data on any of his targets at his house. Nothing on his computer and not one piece of paper from any of the files. He had rented a five-by-five storage space using a fake ID and paid cash in advance for the entire year. Simon even made the renewal date easy to remember, so the contract would not lapse. August 8, or 8/8. Eighty-eight. That number has become a neo-Nazi symbol. The letter "H" is the eighth letter of the alphabet. So eighty-eight stands for "HH", which is short for "Heil Hitler."

Inside the storage unit sits a lone double file cabinet. The top cabinet is now empty. That is where he keeps the laptop he uses for each victim. The bottom cabinet is where he keeps his files. There are only two files left.

He momentarily reflects on this past Sunday evening's ceremonial laptop burning. Simon destroys each computer the same way. First he unscrews the outer case and then exposes the hard drive. He them places the laptop in a metal garbage can, douses it with charcoal lighter fluid and throws in his file on the latest victim. One match later, all that is left is a charred and melted mess. Once it cools, he wraps it in two-inch bandaging tape until it is completely indistinguishable like the peanut butter. He then double-bags it and places it in one of the dumpsters.

Simon unbuttons the top button of his shirt, which seems to have tightened suddenly around his neck. He worries, "Am I missing something? No." Another job executed exactly as planned.

It is time to make the phone call. He automatically reaches to take his cell phone out of the holster on his hip and realizes it is not there. He did not take it with him today. No change of plans could have made him use his cell phone in Atlanta, no matter how dire the circumstances. He could not have his phone locate a cell anywhere but at home on the day of a murder. He goes to his bedroom where he finds his phone on his dresser connected to the charger. Simon always makes this particular call after each job. He hears the aged voice on the other end. They are mutually assured that the other is fine. Simon is satisfied.

Chapter 22

Jamie turns on her phone as the plane lands in Flint, Michigan. Her short nap has refreshed her. She waits for the plane to taxi up to the gate. Her phone vibrates twice, and Jamie sees two new texts. Both of them are from Phil Clark. She opens them up, eager to see why two texts are necessary.

The first text reads, "Call me ASAP. Perp struck yesterday, Atlanta GA."

"You've got to be shitting me!" Jamie exclaims fiercely to herself. She is in so much shock that she does not know if she said it aloud or in her mind. Right now, she does not care. She scrolls to the next text, anxious to see what it says.

"Going to Atlanta."

Jamie wants to scream. She just spent six hours traveling in the wrong direction. A waste of time. *Damn it.* She needs to get to Atlanta immediately. Jamie does not bother calling Phil. She calls Francis Whitehouse instead.

"Ah, Ms. Golding. I've been trying to get hold of you," Whitehouse answers very matter-of-factly.

"I know. I just got the texts from Phil. I've been on a plane for the last few hours," Jamie snaps bitterly. "When can I get to Atlanta?"

"Well, Mr. Fredericks requested that you stay in Flint and finish up there first. Then you can meet Phil in Atlanta," Whitehouse directs her in a monotone.

"Absolutely not!" Jamie's spits with fire. "I've got to get to Atlanta. Screw Flint! I'm not going to find anything here. It's just procedure."

"Let me look up the soonest flight I can get you on. Until then, Fredericks wants you to check into the murder there," Whitehouse answers.

"Thanks, Whitehouse."

"Let's see," Whitehouse mumbles to himself. Jamie can hear his fingers working madly on a keyboard. "There aren't a lot of flights from Flint to Atlanta. Your options are to leave today at 5:40 p.m. and arrive in Atlanta at 7:53 tonight. Or you can wait for the 6:00 a.m. flight in the morning and arrive at 7:56."

Jamie will not wait. "I'll take the one tonight," Jamie tells him. *Atlanta traffic is atrocious. It would be a nightmare, trying to get anywhere at 8:30 in the morning. Besides, if it's too late to go to the crime scene, I can go to the morgue.*

"Alright, I've got you a ticket."

"Okay. Whitehouse, don't forget to file the NLETS. I've got my weapon with me," Jamie reminds him. He does not usually forget, but today there is no time for error.

"Of course. I will have Phil pick you up at the airport," Whitehouse tells her with a sigh.

"Thanks Whitehouse. I owe you one."

"I'll remember that."

Jamie's next call is to Phil. It goes immediately to voicemail. He is probably on the way to Atlanta. She grabs her things and joins the last trickle of passengers off of the plane. As she exits the gate, Jamie sees a large clock. She has five hours before she needs to be back at the airport, which is enough time to see the Flint police.

Jamie makes her way to the airport entrance and climbs into the nearest taxi. She tells the driver to take her to the Flint Police Department. Jamie's mind is still reeling from the news of another murder. It just does not fit. Where is the typical "cool down" period? The killer just struck ten days ago. It seems like something has changed the game. What prompted him to kill again so soon? Is he acting compulsively, or is he still meticulous in his planning? Has something unexpected set off the killer?

All Jamie can think is that Atlanta has her answers, and Flint is just a waste of time. A cold crime scene is devoid of leads. Five hours to kill on an old trail when a fresh one is waiting for her.

The taxi arrives at the police station, and Jamie pays the cab driver. She enters the police station and immediately finds Reception. Jamie introduces herself, and an officer shows her to Detective Moore's office.

"Hey," Moore hails her, standing up. He grabs a napkin and wipes his greying mustache. "I'm Keith Moore. What can I do for you, Ms. Golding?"

"I'm here to talk about the murder of Leon Farbor." Jamie shakes Moore's hand. She tries to hide her irritation at having to waste her time talking to this detective, who she is sure cannot provide her with new information.

"Have a seat," Moore directs her, sitting in his own chair. He leans over the side of his desk. "I've got the file right here." After a couple of seconds, he sits up again and holds out a folder for Jamie.

Leon Farbor was in good shape, for an 88-year-old man. His wife died four years ago, but he is survived by a daughter, who lives in L.A. She was not the type of daughter who called every day, but she happened to call the morning that her father was murdered. Farbor's daughter has lots of money. She told detectives that for years she has been trying to get her father to move out to L.A, or at least to move in to a retirement community.

"Are you sure there was no forced entry?" Jamie verifies, flipping through the crime scene photos and notes.

"We checked and double-checked, but, to the best of my knowledge, there wasn't any forced entry points at any of the doors, windows, or other possible entrances." Moore takes another bite of his sandwich, which has been perched on top of the mess of files.

"Do you have any leads?"

"Well, the obvious suspect is the only surviving daughter, but, since she has more money than the old man, it doesn't make any sense for her to kill him. And she talked to him that morning from L.A. So I guess, no," Moore reasons, scratching his beer belly.

"Have you heard from her?"

"Oh, yes. I still get calls every week or two—from her, her husband, or their lawyer—asking if we have any leads. What can I tell them? The person who did this is a ghost. No evidence, no motive. We haven't had any remotely similar crimes around here. So where are we supposed to look? But how did the Feds get involved? I didn't notify them. Was he Mafia or something?"

"Not exactly. Can I go see the house where he was murdered, or did the family sell the estate?" Jamie inquires, starting to feel the fatigue of flying, which does not improve her mood.

"Yep, the house is already sold. So all you have to go by is the pictures from the crime scene," Moore affirms with a shrug and a dubious look.

"Well, thanks, here's my card if anything turns up." Jamie stands up to leave. No point in asking any more questions. There is no new information here, as with the rest of the murders. Jamie just wants to be in Atlanta.

"No problem, good luck," Moore bids her with a goodbye nod. He does not rise from his chair but opens up another case file. Moore takes a bite of his sandwich and is lost in more pressing business.

She enters the taxi, thanks the driver, and gives him the address of the home. Even though Jamie cannot actually enter the house, she might learn something about the perp. Jamie has seen all of the other crime scenes; maybe there is something similar to show what the killer prefers as a layout or makes an easy target. But it is really just a formality. It is clear that these victims were each targeted, probably without regard to their locations.

Mr. Farbor's home is a cluster home, probably containing only three small bedrooms. The house is a part of a tract of fairly new, brick homes. Jamie checks the file and discovers that the victim had lived there for fifteen years. The neighbors are practically on top of each other, so it is strange that no one saw or heard anything on the day of the murder. With so little privacy, someone should at least have seen a strange car or van.

There is nothing about this house that would make it an ideal site for a murder. In fact, it is the last place a clever serial killer would pick. Farbor, like the others, was not a random victim. He was targeted. They all were. But why?

They are connected somehow. If only she could get some clue as to what link she should be looking for.

*　　　　*　　　　*　　　　*

Jamie finally arrives at Hartsfield-Jackson International Airport in Atlanta. Following the flow of the crowd, she enters the train that speeds passengers through the miles of tunnels. Once outside, she sees Phil Clark sitting in a car parked on the curb, right behind a police vehicle.

Jamie opens the passenger door of the dark blue sedan and greets Phil. Phil hands her a sub sandwich.

As he drives, he fills Jamie in. "The newest victim is a Martin Rossi. White male, age 89. It's the same M.O. There are no witnesses. Also strangled with a ligature; wound is exactly like the others. And yes, there is a note."

"Let me guess, it had 'Arisai' on it."

"Whoa, how did you know that? You figured it out?" Phil quizzes her, his tone impressed.

"Not completely. The strange word on each one of the notes is from the book of Esther. From the Bible. Each name is one of the sons of Haman," Jamie explains.

"Sons of who?" Phil crinkles his forehead in confusion.

"Haman, the villain in the book of Esther, had ten sons. Each one of these notes has had the name of one of his sons on it. Did the new note also have some initials?"

"You know what those mean too?"

"That I have no clue about," Jamie admits. "I'm good, but not that good."

"There were more than just initials on this note. The note said 'Ari' and 'sai' and the initials 'A.J.' But get this: the note also had the words 'Fools Behaving Irresponsibly' written on the back."

"So?" Jamie replies between bites, her eyebrows furrowed in confusion.

"Fools Behaving Irresponsibly. F-B-I. It's like he knew we would eventually get involved, and he is taunting us. This time, the note was in a flower arrangement. Probably how he got into the house." Phil gets on I-85 heading north, straight for downtown Atlanta.

"You think he posed as a deliveryman? What kind of flowers were they? Could you tell what florist it came from? Any clues there."

"Actually, the flowers are fake. Silk. They were already taken to the crime lab."

"What else? Did you find anything else that could help us catch this guy?" Jamie persists, pulling her Nalgene bottle out of her suitcase pocket. She takes a long drink.

"Not really. I was hoping you'd found something," Phil confesses, deflating a little.

"Hah," Jamie says humorlessly. "I visited five different crime scenes. Spoke with five different detectives. Not one of them has a lead. Not one of them has any good trace evidence, except Abilene. They found some women's hairs that seem to have been planted."

"So much for Locard's Exchange Principle."

"What?"

"You know, Locard's Exchange Principle. When any two people meet they exchange trace materials, like hair and fibers."

"Oh gosh, it's been too long since I've heard that term. I don't have the photographic memory that you have," Jamie says with a laugh. There is a lull in the conversation. Then Jamie shares, "The guy is really good. Thorough. I'm not sure how he does it. And he doesn't take any souvenirs like a lot of serial killers."

"He did leave the flowers behind," Phil points out, "but don't get your hopes up. There was a glass vase, and the note, but no fingerprints. Not even from the victim. No trace evidence that looks even remotely specific or useful. Nothing we could pin on the perp right now. They combed for the usual fibers, but it's not like the Forensics team walked away with anything to be excited about." Jamie can hear Phil's frustration, which mirrors her own.

"None of the neighbors saw anything?"

"Atlanta P.D. knocked on doors yesterday. I asked around today. It's been all over the news. No one has come forward who saw a van or anything. Once you see the house, you will know why there wouldn't be witnesses even if they were looking. The house is on a big lot with a long driveway, so you can barely see the house from the street. The neighborhood is old, with a lot of big trees. There's nothing to see."

After a brief pause, Phil snaps his fingers and adds, "I forgot, we are going to the M.E. tonight. They finished their autopsy and said we could come by, ask questions."

"Wonderful!" Jamie confirms with an actual grin. She had not been looking forward to meeting with another police detective. They simply do not have the larger picture. It will be a relief to get the information straight from the source.

"I talked to Fredericks earlier today..." Phil begins, then trails off.

"How's he taking this?"

"Fit to be tied, as they would say down here. The good news is, once it gets out that there's a serial killer, we will have a dozen people calling to confess," Phil speculates with an eye roll.

"It's sad, really..." Jamie reflects, frowning, "Strange that people can hear about a case so much they think they have done it themselves. Then there's the other half, those that think they should be punished for past sins, and, of course, the plain crazy people who want attention or who should just be in a mental hospital. I'm not excited about getting a bunch of calls that I will have to look into. But, you never know, one of them could be the call that gives me a suspect."

"So true." Phil pauses before changing the subject. "So what did you find out?"

"Not much, but a start. The answer has to be with the victims. These aren't random at all. It's almost as if they are all part of a secret society or something. Maybe they pulled off a bank heist or some white-collar crime thirty or forty years ago, and one of them snapped or something. Maybe one's conscience got to him, and he was going to come clean. You know, nark on the others." Jamie pulls out her tablet.

Phil exits the freeway. "So tell me about the names on the notes. I'm still confused about that."

"The names on the notes are straight from the Bible. They are the ten sons of the villain in the book of Esther. Not only that, but two murders were on the Jewish holiday of Purim, which is also based on Esther. I've decided absolutely that it can't be a coincidence," Jamie elucidates, looking at the notes on her tablet. "The first victim was found leaning on the Shushan post office. Shushan is also mentioned in the Book of Esther. And, in Abilene, the perp signed in as Esther Shushan. Also, two murders took place on an even-lesser-known Jewish holiday called Hoshana Raba."

"Interesting. What does it all mean?"

"I think it means that the killer is Jewish."

"You're sure?"

"No. But I've thought about it a lot. And I think that's the best explanation."

"Well, that's something. Were any of the victims Jewish? This last guy wasn't," Phil adds. He pulls the car into the parking lot of the Fulton County Medical Examiner's Office.

"No, but there has to be something linking them."

Phil turns off the car. "Maybe our killer is a hired gun and not a serial?"

"I'm starting to think so as well," Jamie concedes. "He's professional enough."

"Yeah, but then who's calling the shots?"

"Your guess is as good as mine."

Jamie sends a quick text to Chris before getting out of the car.

"Gone to Atlanta for my case. I'll be away a few extra days."

Walking into the Fulton County Morgue, Jamie reminds herself that she has never succumbed to the nausea triggered by a case. No matter what she sees, she will uphold that tradition. She checks her phone, but Chris still has not texted her back. Jamie suddenly realizes that it is Wednesday night. Chris is post call and would have been spending the night with Jamie, if she had been home. Jamie suspects he will be chafed at her for only telling him about her extra trip at the last minute, especially via text message. It is too late to fix that now.

Dr. Alphonse Davis is in his late fifties, with salt-and-pepper hair and eyes as dark as his skin. He extends his arm and shakes first Jamie's, then Phil's hands. "Nice to meet you."

"Thanks for squeezing us in. I really appreciate it," Jamie tells him sincerely, as they follow him down the stairs to the coroner's office. "I wanted to see the body before it was released to the family for burial. And I very much wanted to know what you, as the Medical Examiner, think about the body."

"Well, I've been an M.E. for a long time. You wouldn't believe how many murders I have seen and how many autopsies I've done. This murder was very clean, very professional," Dr. Davis apprises them, leading the way to his office. "Did you fill out the paperwork with the receptionist?"

"Yes sir," Phil assures him.

"Great, then we can go see the body."

Jamie and Phil follow Dr. Davis down the hall to the large county morgue. The room is much colder than the rest of the building. The walls are covered with the pale green tiles distinctive to the 1970s. Inside, there are several autopsy rooms with long slabs of cold metal. White sheets cover some of these tables. Jamie assumes these bodies are waiting for their turns. Across the room, on the wall, is an immense refrigerator with drawers containing the dead. There are techs transferring bodies from the fridge to the tables and back again. In some rooms, you can see through the glass, at the bodies being inspected and dissected.

Dr. Davis approaches the fridge and slides out the gurney on which lies Martin Rossi's body. The stiff body is wrinkly and old. Jamie looks immediately at the neck and sees the familiar and deadly wound.

"Martin Rossi, age 89, cause of death: asphyxiation via strangulation. Nice furrow from approximately ten-gauge wire wound around the neck, petechiae in both eyes, and evidence of congestion in the cheeks. The killer stood behind the victim. Snuck up on him, or put the wire around his neck as he turned. Internal exam did not show anything except advanced atherosclerosis of the aorta, with a small, three-centimeter abdominal aortic aneurysm." Dr. Davis pauses, then adds, "Not unusual for a man this age. There is no head trauma or blunt trauma. He did not fall from a sitting or standing position, but was carefully placed on the floor. Blood work was drawn for toxicology. Gastric contents have been sampled and sent to crime lab, as well as a urine sample. Now, his wife gave us a list of the drugs he was taking regularly. One cholesterol and two blood pressure meds. Nothing unusual," Dr. Davis remarks, finishing his report.

"Any signs of a struggle?" Phil inquires, looking across the body at Dr. Davis.

"Yes. A small amount of blood on his fingers and under his nails. Probably his own, from where he would have reached up to loosen the ligature. He might have scratched his assailant, though."

"Can you estimate the killer's height from the neck wound? Based on what I've heard, there's a good chance the victim was standing up when attacked," Jamie asks.

"The victim measured out to be six-foot-two." It appears the killer was shorter or that he came at the victim from a lower angle and from the rear. The two sides of the wound angle slightly downward at the sides," Dr. Clark explains, pointing to the neck wound to indicate the curvature. He resumes, "The killer is most likely right-handed; the marks on the left side are deeper and more uniform."

Phil takes a closer look at the neck wound. "And the time of death? His wife said she left at 9:00 a.m."

"Without that knowledge, and based solely on the conditions of body temp, rigor mortis, and lividity, I would say the victim died between nine and eleven a.m. I arrived at the scene at three p.m. Rigor mortis had not fully set in, so that means less than eight hours had passed. His temp was thirty-three point two. That's puts it around five or six hours after his death. He had a decent amount of lividity on his right side, which had time to form and then to shift to his shoulders and sacrum. He was on his right side a good two hours and wasn't moved, then was rolled over, onto his back. His wife claims she found him on his right side and rolled him over around 12:45 p.m., when she came home. Her story holds up against my findings—she told the cops that he had egg, toast, and black coffee for breakfast, and that's what we found in his stomach." Much of this, Dr. Davis reads from his notes, adding his own editorials, as needed.

"I doubt she did it. I'm certain we've got a serial here. There are at least five others victims, almost exactly the same, all over the country. I've spent the last two days visiting all of them," Jamie discloses, examining the dead face in front of her.

"The word is not out about the nature of these murders yet," Phil reminds her furtively, nudging her with his elbow.

"I think it will be now," Jamie counters, as she gestures to Mr. Rossi's cold body.

"Well, you don't have to worry about me letting it out," Dr. Davis assures them bluntly.

"Thanks," Jamie nods, recognizing that she can trust Davis. He has nothing to gain by sharing that information. Besides, Jamie is sure that, with the murders still occurring, the FBI is going to have to inform the public soon.

"Anything else?" Dr. Davis inquires.

"Was there a good transport of the body? I mean, this perp does not leave much; we are going to have to nab him on next to nothing."

"It was very clean. Totally by the book. We bagged his hands, bagged the body, crime lab was at the scene. Everything was done correctly. Combed the scene for trace. We get a lot of murders here in Atlanta," Dr. Davis reminds her staunchly, his look challenging.

"Anything special about the ligature used?" Jamie asks, ignoring Dr. Davis' stare.

"I cut out a sample of the neck wound here," Dr. Davis points out, indicating a square of neck with no skin. "Approximately ten-gauge wire, like typical piano wire. You can buy it at any music shop or hardware store."

"Nothing else about the body?" Phil queries, putting his hands in his pockets.

"All of the evidence was sent to the GBI crime lab in Decatur. Ask for Rudy."

"Thanks," Phil replies, as Dr. Davis returns the body to the fridge and closes the door.

With a nod, Dr. Davis walks away, holding his file.

Jamie and Phil make the fifteen-minute drive to the GBI Crime Lab. They ask the first white coat they see about Rudy. She points him out where he stands, in a glass room, surrounded by machines used for various types of analysis.

Jamie guesses that Rudy is in his late twenties. He is black, of medium height, and dressed casually under his lab coat. Two wires lead to the earbuds in his ears. Jamie knows the music is playing because she can hear it as they approach.

"Rudy?" she calls.

He hears, but waits for the chorus to finish before he takes out the headphones and responds. "Let me guess, FBI? I can always finger the Feds," he tells them proudly. "Which case y'all working on?"

"Rossi."

Rudy pulls up the file on his computer, singing a few bars while it loads. He motions to the agents to come around his desk, so they can see the monitor. "I personally combed the body, clothes, and body bag for any trace evidence," Rudy asserts cadently, still in the flow of his music.

"Let's see, prelim toxicology is negative for the basic 'drugs of abuse' panel, the narcotics, benzos, barbies, alcohol, and so forth. Looks like the comprehensive panel will not be back for another seven days. But I can tell you that the blood under his nails was his own. Tissue samples aren't ready yet," Rudy reads out from his file.

"Doubtful we'll find anything useful from the victim. We know how he died. What's going on with trace? What did they remove from the scene or find on the body? Who's working on that?" Jamie fires at him, scanning the information on the computer screen.

Rudy shrugs then hollers across the room, "LaShondra! You started on the Rossi trace yet?"

"Yeah, got the footprints, just printed my report," the black woman hollers back. It happens to be the same woman who helped them to locate Rudy.

"Footprints?" Jamie echoes with surprise.

She glances at Phil, her face registering shock. Swiftly she crosses the room to talk to LaShondra. The black woman is in her early thirties, super skinny, and painted with a ridiculous amount of makeup.

"I forgot to tell you we got some good footprints on the freshly-vacuumed carpet," Phil says apologetically as he approaches Jamie.

"So what about the footprints?" Jamie asks.

"Men's twelve. Converse All Stars. The easiest sole to recognize. Classic pattern, hasn't changed since the '40s. And this shoe seems brand new. No sign of wear at all," LaShondra explains.

"Can I see some photos from the crime scene?"

"Sure," LaShondra replies and pulls out several photographs, taken at the scene, showing impressions in the plush carpet. There are different angles with measuring tape next to them.

"Here is where the uniform impressions of the pattern enforcing the shoes are new. One interesting thing: the person who made the prints walks more on the balls of their feet. Not uncommon, but particularly noticeable here," LaShondra elaborates as she shows them how the clearest impression is near the ball of the foot. She is obviously proud of her work.

"There were no similar footprints anywhere else in the house. Only in the living room, just off the foyer. Nothing is missing. It looks like the perp came in, did his thing, and went right back out the front door," Phil reflects aloud, examining the pictures over Jamie's shoulder.

"Any other trace evidence being processed?" Jamie asks eagerly, looking to LaShondra.

"We are running samples from within the footprints and have some samples from the outside of the residence as a control. Hopefully they won't match, and we will have something that the perp brought with him from outside the scene."

"What about the silk flowers?" Phil inquires, as an afterthought.

"Ah, yes, we received a silk flower arrangement, and that is being thoroughly checked over," LaShondra expounds to Phil. "No fingerprints found on the vase, though, or any of the flowers. The thing was scrubbed well. A few fibers and strands on the arrangement. They are being processed and recorded, but we do not have a control to compare them to yet."

"You won't get one either," Jamie grumbles under her breath.

"What was that?" LaShondra pursues, flashing a suspicious look at Jamie.

"Oh, nothing. I just said there probably won't be any. The perp is really good."

"Rudy said the killer came from behind. Do we have any trace on the back of the victim's shirt?" Phil continues hopefully, in an attempt to draw LaShondra's attention from Jamie.

"Yeah we got some fibers and hairs. They are all being processed and recorded. Again, we have no comparisons." LaShondra pauses then remembers, "Wait, not true, we did get some control hairs from his wife. But I figured you knew that and were asking about something else."

Jamie thanks LaShondra with a smile.

"Anytime," is LaShondra's friendly reply before she returns to her work.

Jamie and Phil go back to Rudy's office.

"Here's my contact info if something turns up." Jamie hands Rudy her business card. "If you could, fax all reports as they come in and a full copy of the file when it is complete."

"Sure," Rudy nods, still moving his head in time to an inaudible beat.

Jamie and Phil leave the crime lab and walk out to their car in the parking lot.

"Too late to head to the Rossi's, I presume," Phil submits with a grin.

"Yeah," Jamie sighs, looking at her watch and frowning. "I sure wish we could, though."

"I've got the number to the Rossi house. I'll call the wife first thing in the morning and tell her we are coming," Phil offers as they approach the car.

"Perfect. I want to see that crime scene as soon as possible," Jamie states adamantly. She feels grateful to have Phil as a partner. After working so long together, they seem to understand each other very well.

"No problem." Phil unlocks the car doors and slides into the driver's seat.

"I'm telling you these victims were marked. They have to be." Jamie's voice wavers. She wants so badly for this lead to be sound.

"Like you said, the stiff may tell us more than the lab," Phil says. He casts a sympathetic glance in Jamie's direction, as he pulls into the hotel parking lot.

"Let's hope so; otherwise we're at another dead end."

They walk into the hotel and check in. Together they walk down the hallway and find their rooms, next door to each other.

"It's been a long day, see you tomorrow morning," Phil bids her, swiping his room key.

"Agreed, goodnight," Jamie wishes him back. Once in the door, she drops the handle of her suitcase and turns on the water to fill the bathtub. She then lets herself fall backward onto the mattress. After resting a few seconds, exhaling a few deep breaths, she pulls out her cell phone. She writes another text message to Chris, hoping this time to receive some sort of response.

Without waiting for a reply, she slides into the bathtub and lets her tension melt into the hot water. After a good soak, she heads to bed. She is planning to wake up extra early, so she can get to the crime scene as soon as possible. Chris is clearly ignoring her. Jamie grunts angrily and throws her phone on the side table. She lies down and is asleep instantly, as soon as her head touches the pillow.

*　*　*　*　*

As usual, her cell phone alarm wakes her up. She turns on the news to help her get reoriented from all of the traveling. She is getting dressed when her phone rings. Jamie answers it, expecting Phil. She is surprised to hear Fredericks's voice instead.

"Ms. Golding, what is going on?" Fredericks demands over the phone.

"I flew in last night to Atlanta. I haven't seen the crime scene yet. The murder is definitely done by our perp. I will talk with the family and see the crime scene today. I'll get you the report as soon as we get back," Jamie lists off, undaunted by her superior's tone.

"Alright," Fredericks replies curtly. "Bring me something I can use."

"Yes, sir," Jamie promises, "I won't let you down."

"Keep me updated."

"Right," Jamie confirms to the dead phone connection. Now there is even more pressure for her to deliver.

A fresh crime scene with untouched evidence might provide the answers Fredericks is demanding. But Jamie is still a little uneasy. None of the other crime scenes yielded either evidence or leads. *What can I expect to turn up, especially after the other detectives, forensics teams, and crime scene investigators didn't find anything?* Maybe the family can provide her with the missing pieces she needs. Surely, Jamie will have something to bring to Fredericks by the end of the day. *Surely.*

Heading downstairs to the hotel lobby, Jamie sees that Phil is already present and enjoying a toasted bagel from the continental breakfast. Jamie grabs a yogurt and a bagel for herself before joining him.

Phil speaks first, updating Jamie on the plan. "I just got off the phone with Mrs. Rossi. She says we can come by anytime this morning. Nice lady, really. She was grateful that we gave her a warning call."

"It's sad that bad things happen to good people," Jamie remarks, before putting a spoonful of yogurt in her mouth.

"Bad things happen to everyone; it's just something we all have to deal with. I think Mrs. Rossi will be fine," Phil counters, his aspect pensive. After a moment's pause, he stands. "Shall we?"

Jamie gathers her bagel and yogurt and follows him out of the lobby area.

Chapter 23

Jamie picks out the Rossi home when they are still down the street. The giveaway is that the house is an epicenter of parked cars, eight or so, pulled into every available spot around the home and street. It looks like the house where the party is, but this is not the right type of celebration.

"Must have lots of family," Jamie speculates, stepping onto the curb.

"'Lots of family' is an understatement," Phil marvels, turning off the car engine and jumping out to follow Jamie.

Jamie looks up at the house. She cannot see the front door, due to the mass of thick trees blocking her view. Before she can even take a few steps, a man in his fifties, slightly pudgy and looking very stern, marches determinedly up to her. He wears khaki pants and a plaid button-up, complete with pen in the breast pocket. Before Jamie and Phil can say a word, the man begins his tirade.

"Peter Rossi—I'm his son—what can you tell me?" The words stream out of him. "When are they going to release the body—we have a funeral to plan—who is the sonofabitch who did this—is he arrested yet?"

Jamie remembers that name from the report. Peter Rossi is the son from Charlotte. Phil did not meet him the day before because Peter was at the coroner's office harassing them about releasing the body. Jamie could already see that Peter would be a hindrance to the investigation.

"Mr. Rossi. Phil Clark, Special Agent with the FBI. And this is Special Agent Golding. So sorry about your loss, Sir," Phil introduces, putting a hand out cordially.

"Oh my God! Forget the niceties! Answer my damn questions! When do I get to see the bastard who did this? When do we get the body? No one is telling us shit!" Peter shouts at Phil, ignoring the extended hand.

All Jamie needs is someone who is borderline hysterical. She calmly explains, "The police and FBI are still doing their investigative work. Right now, the best way to help us is with your cooperation. When we have the answers, you will get the answers. It's important that I speak with Mrs. Rossi first."

"Absolutely not!" Peter storms, his eyes bulging and the vessels in his neck distended. "She has been through enough damn harassment. The police fingerprinting her like some criminal! She is about to have a nervous breakdown. Shit! We need answers, not more questions! My brother is a lawyer; talk to him. He's inside."

"Alright, we will speak first with your brother," Phil assents, attempting to disarm the time bomb.

Peter stalks up the driveway and onto a concrete path that leads to the front door. Jamie and Phil trail him closely, preparing themselves for another outburst. As soon as Peter walks in the front door, he proclaims, "Kent, the Feds are here!"

Inside the elegant home, a crowd of people stands around, as if the funeral has already started. Mrs. Rossi sits in the middle of the group, at the kitchen table. In front of her, a photo album lies open. A granddaughter and daughter sit on either side of the old woman, whispering quietly to try to comfort her. A few people sitting at the table are busy conversing on their cell phones. As Jamie and Phil walk into the room, some members of the gathering rise from their chairs.

Out of nowhere, Peter barks, "Don't get excited; they don't know shit!"

A man on the back porch hastily ends his phone call when he catches sight of the agents entering the kitchen. He resembles Peter, but slightly taller and much leaner. Jamie assumes he must be the lawyer brother, and she hopes he might be the peacekeeper. He also wears khaki slacks, but with a designer polo shirt.

"Hi, I'm Kent Rossi."

"Special Agent Phil Clark."

"You were here yesterday, right?" Kent asks Phil.

"Yes. This is Special Agent Jamie Golding," Phil informs the brother, who shakes Jamie's hand.

Jamie motions out of the room, requesting, "Can I speak with you alone?"

"Sure," Kent answers with a nod of his head.

"Phil, could you do some crowd control, while I try and get the wife alone?" Jamie whispers with a hopeful smile.

"Yeah, but you owe me one," Phil admonishes her playfully. He turns to the crowd and announces, "I want to update you all on the case."

Jamie smirks as she follows Kent down the hallway to a formal dining room. She can only imagine what baloney Phil is going to have to give them until she finishes questioning the wife.

Secluded in the dining room, Kent starts, "What can I do for you?"

Jamie decides to be straightforward. "I need to talk to your mother. I know the stress and anxiety is high around here, but it's crucial that I speak with her, alone if possible. Can you make that happen?" she petitions him seriously.

"Yeah, sure. Give me some time to set it up."

"First," Jamie adds, stopping him from leaving, "could you show me where it happened?"

"Yeah, this way," Kent beckons. He leads Jamie out of the room and farther down the hallway.

In the background, Jamie can hear Phil explaining that the Atlanta police are doing their best. He reiterates that the FBI is here to help, and imploring the family to be patient in allowing them to do their job. Several voices begin talking at once, but Phil speaks over them, urging them to stay in the room while Special Agent Golding examines the crime scene. He ends his briefing by inviting their questions.

"Here...here it is," Kent informs Jamie. His face is pale and tired.

"Thanks." Jamie looks at the ground where the body was found, and at the table on which the flowers were placed. The plush carpet betrays the killer, showing clear prints where his feet fell. Jamie tries to imagine the scene as it unfolded. In her mind, she sees the killer enter the front door, set the arrangement down, kill Mr. Rossi, and leave through the front door. That matches the report, which stated that there were no footprints found leading up the carpeted stairs, or in any other room in the house. The only footprints were those from the front door to the body, and back again.

Approaching the front door, Jamie examines the round brass knob. The reports indicate that the prints on the door's handle belonged to the victim and to Mrs. Rossi. After the killer entered the home, how did he exit without touching the inner doorknob? Jamie surmises that the door was left ajar on purpose. Posing as a floral delivery, the killer might have entered the home on the pretext of setting the flowers down for Mr. Rossi.

Jamie briefly surveys each of the other rooms in the house. She is searching for something that might tell her about the victim. The family photos on the walls look normal. The books on the shelves do not stand out as particularly revealing. The plump, flowery, overstuffed couch makes the living room cozy, but it holds nothing special, as far as Jamie can see. Kent follows her from room to room, seemingly too tired to invest himself in her examination.

"Did your father have a personal office or desk? "

"Yeah, he has a little alcove in his bedroom where he kept his desk and important documents," Kent recalls. "You don't think someone in the family is responsible?"

"No, I don't believe any of your family is involved—especially not Mrs. Rossi. The FBI has seen some similar crimes lately," Jamie discloses vaguely.

"Really?"

"Is there any way you could arrange for Mrs. Rossi to show me their bedroom?" Jamie requests delicately.

Kent raises an eyebrow.

"You're welcome to join us, but not really anyone else," Jamie clarifies.

Kent bows his head in consent and leads the way back to the kitchen.

Jamie hopes that Kent will be more cooperative if he feels included and trusted by the FBI agent. She follows him back down the hallway but hangs back from entering the kitchen.

"Mom? Can I see you for a minute?"

From her spot in the shadows of the hall, Jamie can see Peter as he instantly stands and demands, "What for? What's this about?"

Kent raises his hand like a stop sign. "Peter, don't worry. It's nothing. Please stay here, and I'll handle this. Mom?"

Peter's face turns a dark red, but, as he looks around the room, he sees that others are glaring at him. He sits, sulking, glaring daggers at everyone and no one.

"What do you do for a living?" Phil inquires politely of Peter, trying to distract him from his mother, who has gotten up from her chair and is disappearing down the hallway.

Kent offers his mother his elbow, to help her walk. "Mom," he addresses her gently, "this FBI agent needs to see your bedroom."

Startled, the old woman shoots a cautious look at her son, then over her shoulder, at Jamie.

"I know this must be difficult, but it's important that you show me your husband's desk," Jamie adds solemnly.

"It's alright. I understand," Mrs. Rossi's affirms quietly in a strong European accent.

"I'll be with you the whole time, Mom. It will be fine," Kent tells her bracingly, helping her up the stairs.

"Thanks, Kent, I appreciate your help. I can do the stairs by myself," Mrs. Rossi assures him.

Jamie follows them up and through a corridor to the master bedroom. The room smells like old things, which Jamie attributes to the antique bed and dresser. Even the desk in the alcove looks worn enough to have antique appeal. A couple of easy chairs sit next to the desk, facing each other. Across from the alcove, there is a spacious walk-in closet and, next to it, the entrance to the master bathroom. The bed sits in the middle of the room, against the wall opposite Jamie.

"His desk is there," Mrs. Rossi informs Jamie, pointing her bony, wrinkled finger. "Feel free to search it thoroughly, if it will help."

"Thank you. I will try not to disturb too many of his things," Jamie promises, approaching the desk.

"None of the drawers are locked, so you shouldn't have any problems," Mrs. Rossi continues, coming over to stand next to Jamie.

Looking over the papers on the desk, Jamie does not immediately see anything that raises a red flag. There are passports in one drawer, along with some old letters.

"I can't believe he kept them," Mrs. Rossi exclaims quietly, tears suddenly spilling from her eyes. She turns away, as though it is too much to bear.

Jamie picks up the letters. They are little love notes, from Mrs. Rossi to Mr. Rossi. None of them are postmarked. "They're not letters…" Jamie observes, inviting Mrs. Rossi to explain. She turns to the old woman, one eyebrow arched questioningly.

"No. I used to put one in his lunch every month, marking the date we were married. I never knew he kept them," Mrs. Rossi says with difficulty. Her tears still fall, unabated.

Kent puts his arms around his mother and lets her cry on his shoulder.

Jamie is speechless as she returns to searching the desk. She cannot help but wonder if that kind of love could ever exist between Chris and herself. Trying to ignore her own emotions, Jamie refocuses on searching the desk. She finds a revolver in the second top drawer.

"Does he own any other guns?" she asks without turning around, trying to intrude as little as possible.

"He has a hunting rifle locked in a cabinet downstairs. He used to go on hunting trips every year."

The large file drawer at the bottom on the other side of the desk is filled with years of tax documents. Jamie pulls out one year's taxes and looks for any LLCs or partnerships. There are none.

"Did he have any business partners? Go into a real estate venture with someone?"

"No, he has been retired for over twenty years."

"What kind of work did he do?"

"He had his own business repairing and selling parts for electron microscopes," Kent answers.

Continuing her search through the desk, Jamie finds only sticky notes, pens, writing pads, paper clips. Everything seems to have its proper place. On the top of the desk are small drawers, which Jamie also digs through, only to find random keys, a collection of buttons, some forgotten pennies, and a few pins from the 1996 Olympics in Atlanta.

In one small drawer, Jamie finds Mr. Rossi's address book. *Perfect.* It might hold contacts that could connect him to the other victims. "I'm going to take this address book, Mrs. Rossi. I promise to return it when the investigation is over," Jamie tells her, holding it out.

"Okay, fine," Mrs. Rossi consents. Her weeping has slowed, but her eyes are still teary.

"He didn't have a computer of some sort? Like a laptop?" Jamie wonders aloud, taking one last look through the desk. She starts checking to make sure there are no false drawers or other hiding places that she missed.

"Dad wasn't exactly tech savvy. He hates...I mean, he hated computers."

"Right," Jamie nods. Jamie's grandparents are the same way.

"Here, Mom, come sit down," Kent urges, looking at his mother. Mrs. Rossi's face is blanched and her eyes droopy, and she does not respond.

"Is it okay if I have a look around the room?" Jamie asks politely.

Mrs. Rossi shrugs and shakes her head again, almost completely indifferent to what is happening around her.

"Mom?" Kent gently asks. He steers his mother into one of the maroon leather armchairs. Fetching her a blanket, Kent covers his mother's lap, then stands behind her protectively.

Jamie enters the master bathroom and searches the cabinets and drawers. In here, she also checks for false drawers and other hiding places. Searching through the toiletries, Jamie sees nothing unusual. She checks the walls for hidden places and finds none. Finishing the bathroom, Jamie heads back out to investigate the dresser.

Mrs. Rossi watches Jamie sift through her personal belongings, but Jamie is sure the woman could not care less. The grief has completely eaten away her ability to feel. Jamie digs through an underwear drawer, only to find some jewelry in an old cigar box. None of the pieces stands out. She continues through the other drawers, but finds only the usual clothing, all folded neatly.

Next, Jamie inspects the room, taking in each detail. She examines a picture of Mr. and Mrs. Rossi that must have been taken only a few years ago, as Mrs. Rossi does not look too different. Jamie turns to the wife and asks, "Where are you from? Originally."

A quiet pause, then Mrs. Rossi responds, "Poland."

"And Mr. Rossi? Where was he born?" Jamie pursues, picking up another photo of a grandchild from off of the dresser.

"Italy," Mrs. Rossi answers, her voice trembling.

"Interesting. Where in Italy?" Jamie asks. She takes a seat in the easy chair across from Mrs. Rossi, feeling a bit of tension in the air between them.

"Uh, he was born in northern Italy, near Austria," Mrs. Rossi murmurs. Her body is now visibly tense.

Jamie senses the hesitation, and even defensiveness, in the old woman's voice. Time to play a few of her cards, to gain trust. "Mrs. Rossi, there is no doubt in my mind that you are innocent in this crime. I believe someone outside of your family circle is responsible."

Jamie pauses, watching for signs that her words have soothed Mrs. Rossi. When there is no change, Jamie elaborates, "You see, there have been other murders similar to your husband's, and I believe there is some kind of link between them. In order to catch his killer, I need to know everything you can tell me about your husband."

Mrs. Rossi gives a nod of understanding. Her features relax slightly. "What do you want to know?"

"How long were you married?"

"Sixty-eight beautiful years," Mrs. Rossi answers, tears glistening in her eyes. In the next moment, she smiles faintly, as though reliving those years.

Jamie smiles sympathetically. "Is it okay if I ask you some more questions?"

Mrs. Rossi pulls a handkerchief out of her pocket and dabs her eyes. "Yes, it is fine. Go ahead."

"Did your husband know anyone whom you have never met?"

"Not really."

"Any enemies, death threats, or blackmailing?"

"None that I know of," Mrs. Rossi responds, her forehead crinkling with the effort of remembering.

"Was he in any clubs? It could be something serious, like a political organization, or something as simple as a membership to a golf club," Jamie expounds.

"A poker group? They met every third Thursday night. But he hasn't been going as of late," Mrs. Rossi explains, emotionless.

"Why did he stop going?"

"Just got bored with it." Mrs. Rossi shrugs.

"Did he lose a lot of money? Or were there fights over money at these poker games?" Jamie presses, desperate for information.

"No, they play for nickels and dimes."

The response catches Jamie off-guard. She represses a chuckle as she imagines a group of old men fighting over four or five dollars.

"None of them were going to gamble away their retirement money," Mrs. Rossi assures Jamie. "Well, we wives wouldn't let them."

"Right," Jamie confirms, trying to understand a poker game played with only petty change. No wonder the old guy got bored of it. "Can you get me the names of those men involved in the poker group?"

"Yes." Mrs. Rossi begins to rise from her chair.

"Oh, it doesn't have to be right now," Jamie protests with a kind smile and a wave of her hand.

Mrs. Rossi leans back into her seat, and Jamie catches Kent's smile of appreciation.

"Was he a Freemason?"

"No."

"Member of a church?"

"Yes."

"Which one?"

"Catholic."

"Did he hold a position with the Catholic church, or maybe have connections with the priests, pastors, bishops, or other leaders?"

"No."

"Did he possibly belong to a secret society? A private group? Or have a group of school friends? Maybe some people on the Internet?"

"No, no. His whole life was our family," Mrs. Rossi states sadly.

"He wouldn't have been able to make Internet friends. I couldn't even get him to check the email account I set up for him," Kent laments to Jamie.

"Well, how about a long-lost family member, perhaps someone with a bad past?" Jamie presses, trying to stretch her mind to find any possible connections.

"No, nothing like that," Mr. Rossi denies.

"Any shady old friends or questionable people from his past?"

Mrs. Rossi sighs, obviously fatigued by all of the questions, "No."

"Did he loan any money to anyone recently?"

"No chance," Mrs. Rossi jumps in, "I keep the finances."

"Any secrets he might have kept from your family or you?"

The old woman quietly thinks for a moment, then answers honestly, "No. He told me everything. At least I think so."

"If you knew his secrets, were there things he rarely talks about or doesn't want people to know about? Maybe from his past, his job, or other financial dealings?" Jamie pursues, trying to logically follow the flow of questions and answers.

Mrs. Rossi glances subtly towards the closet while biting her lower lip. It is so quick an action, barely more than a twitch, but Jamie notes the involuntary reflex.

Flipping her wedding ring on her finger, the old woman replies shakily, "Everyone has their own secrets and sins they like to keep quiet."

Jamie slowly shakes her head. She thinks she might be close. "Any affairs of that sort? Children from other lovers?"

"Oh no, no!" Mrs. Rossi exclaims, defensively but without malice. "He loved me dearly."

Jamie stands up and walks toward one of the antique dressers, so she can look at the pictures again. The faces of children and grandchildren are clustered on a large, oblong doily that rests on the top of the bureau. A picture in the back catches Jamie's eye. It is a wedding picture in an old frame. She picks it up and brings it back to the easy chairs. Pointing to the beautiful young woman in the picture, Jamie asks, "Is this you?"

"Yes," Mrs. Rossi acknowledges sadly, examining the picture. For a couple of seconds, it is obvious that her mind is in her memories, and not in the present.

"Where were you married?" Jamie continues, handing the picture to Mrs. Rossi.

"Switzerland," Mrs. Rossi tells her dreamily, accepting the framed picture.

"Wow! Switzerland! It must have been a beautiful wedding. What year?" Jamie wonders aloud. Her mind is still calculating her approach, even while she is trying to make a sincere emotional connection with the widow.

"September, 1945. We eloped." Mrs. Rossi's eyes are still seeing things from the past instead of the present.

"Romantic. How did you guys have money for such a trip right after the war? You must have been quite young," Jamie reflects, leading Mrs. Rossi on to answer the question.

"He was twenty one, and I was eighteen," she replies. One more tear escapes from her eye and runs down her cheek. "He had saved some money during the war, so we could elope."

Jamie's knows it was highly unusual for a young person to amass any amount of money during the war that ravaged

Europe. Her questions instantly become more precise. "Was he in the army?"

"Yes, for the Austrians."

"Why not for the Italians? Did his family move to Austria after he was born?" Jamie is fishing as casually as possible, but Mrs. Rossi is not blind to the net.

"Something like that," the old woman responds blandly, essentially avoiding the question.

Standing up, Jamie returns the wedding photo to its place on the dresser. She slowly examines a few of the pictures on the wall before she continues her questioning.

Jamie casually walks to the bedroom closet. "May I?"

"Yes, of course."

She enters the closet and looks around. She keeps the door open, to have an unobstructed view of Mrs. Rossi. "Did he have anything that he didn't tell anyone about, except for you?" Jamie words her question carefully. Despite the lack of specificity, however, Jamie has no doubt that Mrs. Rossi fully comprehends her meaning.

Mrs. Rossi again gazes, apparently without thinking, towards the top shelf of the closet. Jamie marks the look, which confirms for her that there is something significant hiding in the closet. Some kind of secret that Mr. Rossi would want to keep from his family, from everyone, from the world. It is time to ask the hard questions.

"Mrs. Rossi, this is important." Jamie's tone is apologetic, but also insistent. She points at the top shelf. "I need to know what he was hiding. It may be the only way we have to catch the guy. You do want us to catch your husband's killer?"

Jamie pauses, but Mrs. Rossi does not reply. Jamie persists, "I'm going to ask you again directly. Does your husband have any secrets in his past?"

The old woman cannot look Jamie in the face. Her eyes dart around the room, as though she is searching for an escape from the question. Jamie senses an internal struggle as Mrs. Rossi rapidly twists her wedding ring over and over again on her finger. Then, strangely, Mrs. Rossi stops and stares into space for a few seconds. She shakes her head slightly, ending the silent reverie. At this point, Jamie is sure that she will get an answer from Mrs. Rossi, but she cannot tell if it will be the answer she needs.

Swallowing hard, Mrs. Rossi begins, "I'm sure this is nothing...."

"Mom, you don't have to divulge anything you don't want to," Kent interrupts. His demeanor and tone are suddenly strong and professional. But his eyes are afraid. *He doesn't know either.*

"Kent, your father would never want you to hear this, so please leave the room," Mrs. Rossi implores him.

"Mom, I'm not leaving. I can handle whatever you have to tell me about Dad's past."

"Honestly, it will be a relief for me, in a way, to finally take this burden off my shoulders," Mrs. Rossi muses, almost to herself. "I hate secrets."

The words transform Mrs. Rossi into a feeble old woman. She tries to stand, but her face goes pale, and her body shakes as if bitterly cold.

"No, Mom, sit. What do you need? I can get it for you." Kent tries to coax Mrs. Rossi back into the chair.

She looks at her son, and her eyes give him permission to witness this moment. "It's in the closet. Top shelf in the back. A small, brown shoe box," Mrs. Rossi instructs, as she slumps in her chair.

Kent crosses the room to the closet. Jamie moves aside as he reaches up to the top shelf and begins pulling small boxes out of the way. He carefully forms a stack on the floor. This goes on for a few silent moments, until Kent finally removes a small, brown shoebox. He stares at it for a second, then glances at Jamie. She feels for this family, for the horrible secret that is finally going to come out. But she also needs answers.

Kent takes the box back to his mother, who accepts it reluctantly, as though it is a time bomb. "Help me to the bed," she requests of him. With his aid, she rises and shuffles over, motions for Jamie to follow.

As Jamie comes to help Kent with Mrs. Rossi, the old woman places the shoebox heavily into Jamie's hands, as though passing off her yoke. Mrs. Rossi slouches down onto the mattress and, with Kent's help, leans back into the pillows that are propped at the top of the bed. She then bows her head, as if she is ashamed. Kent takes a seat next to his mother and puts a comforting arm around her shoulders. He watches Jamie closely, clearly blaming her for her role in his mother's pain and discomfort.

Jamie opens the shoebox. Although it is old, the box has hardly been handled or used. Curious, Jamie lifts the lid slowly, but she is taken aback by the contents of the box. With confusion, she realizes the box contains WWII memorabilia. An old pocketknife with the SS insignia, a few patches removed from a uniform, some photos, and an old passport. Jamie sets aside the pocketknife and instead examines the patches. The colored thread still clings raggedly to their edges. One of the patches bears the name "Kleiss." The pictures are mostly of the same soldier.

"Are these…" Jamie begins to ask, but she cannot wrap her head around it. She walks around the bed and sits down on the other side, where she starts laying out all of the items in the box.

"What are these things, Mom?" Kent inquires, watching Jamie remove objects and set them on the bed.

"They belong, or once belonged to, your father," Mrs. Rossi quietly replies to her lap.

Jamie scrutinizes the photographs more closely. She assumes that the soldier, who appears in picture after picture, is Mr. Rossi. Sometimes he is posing with an army buddy, while other pictures show him and his buddies with their arms around the waists of beautiful young women. After laying out all of the pictures, Jamie turns her attention to the passport. Inside is a picture of a young man, the same as the soldier in the photographs. The name on the passport was not "Martin Rossi." The name on the passport was "Stefan Kleiss."

"Mom, what does this mean?" Kent asks, astounded. "Dad was a Nazi?"

Mrs. Rossi nods her confirmation without lifting her head to face her son.

"Wait. What exactly did he do during the war?" Jamie, despite her incredulity, stays on point.

"He was a guard at Auschwitz," Mrs. Rossi tells them before she breaks down, sobbing.

Kent leaps to his feet and begins pacing the bedroom floor intoning, "Oh my God, oh my God!" over and over in a low, anguished tone. All the color has drained from his face, and his eyes are bogging.

"I have some more questions for you," Jamie tries to resume, almost in a daze. "But first I can give the two of you a moment alone."

Jamie exits to the sound of Mrs. Rossi's continued sobs. She can hear Kent beseeching, "Why didn't you tell us?"

Jamie stands a moment in the hallway to let all of this information sink in. She will suppress her excitement, but she is sure this is the connection she has been searching for. Jamie walks down the hallway and descends the stairs to find Phil and the rest of the guests sitting in the family room next to the kitchen.

Jamie notices that many more people, probably relatives or friends, have arrived. They all sit solemnly, holding plates full of bagels and vegetables. Glancing back at the kitchen table, Jamie notices someone, maybe a neighbor, has brought a deli tray. She gladly interrupts an intense conversation between Phil and Peter. More accurately, she saves Phil from a verbal assault by Peter. It is obvious that everyone else knows that Peter is making an ass of himself.

"I insist you call the coroner and get me a time when they will release the body! We need to be able to plan this funeral, and we can't without a body," Peter yells, spraying Phil with spit.

"I'm sorry, but that is not possible. The Forensics department has the body for as long as they need. That is how we get evidence for the investigation," Phil replies in a monotone, blinking his eyes placidly against the flying saliva.

"Fine! What do you have to offer us then? Huh?" Peter demands, trying to rally the people around him to help him.

Jamie can see this turning into a witch-hunt pretty quickly. "Hey, Special Agent Clark," she calls, trying to defuse the situation.

"Special Agent Golding!" Phil's face beams relief as he addresses her. "What can I do for you?"

"Can I see you outside for a moment?" Jamie points towards the exterior door. They step outside, onto the walkway, and Jamie begins, "I need a bit more time. I have found some important information, or so I hope." She checks the area around them, then drops her voice and continues, "The victim was a guard at Auschwitz. It might be what ties our victims together."

"Interesting. It sounds like it could be the clue we've been looking for," Phil agrees. Then his face changes to a look of astonishment as he gasps, "Wait, are you telling me I have to go back in there? Well, in that case I need combat pay!" His humor is a relief, but Jamie will not be distracted.

"Just a bit longer. I promise I will try and be quick," Jamie entreats him, as Phil makes his way back into the house. "At least don't let Peter up the stairs. That's really the most important thing."

"I'll take care of it."

Jamie then retrieves her cell phone from her pocket. She dials Quantico and is connected shortly.

"Whitehouse, here."

"Hi, it's Golding. I need you to get an analyst to find out where my victims were from 1940 to 1945."

"Okay. I will get right on it," Whitehouse replies dryly.

"Thanks, Whitehouse." Jamie hangs up. She heads back inside and to the murder scene and inspects the entire area one more time. The killer simply came in, strangled him, and walked out. She climbs the stairs and makes her way to the bedroom door. From inside she hears an intense conversation going on, but the talking stops when Jamie knocks on the bedroom door. She enters without waiting for a reply.

Mrs. Rossi has returned to the armchair. Her eyes are blotched from more crying, and she slumps low, watching Kent, who still paces the room.

"I'm sorry I couldn't give you more time, but I have some questions and some things to explain to you both." Jamie pauses. Neither mother nor son says a word. "First of all, I want to tell you that no one is going to try to stir up your husband's past now that he is gone. Also, I'm not saying that your husband's past has anything to do with what happened, but I will tell you that it does seem to fit. Now, I need to know as much as you can tell me. Any and all details."

Mrs. Rossi takes a steadying breath and nods a few times. "Alright. I will tell you everything I know. And the whole truth this time."

"Perfect," Jamie says, pulling out her tablet to record the information. "Where was your husband born?"

"He was born in Austria."

"As Stefan Kleiss?"

"Yes."

"How did he become affiliated with the Nazi party?"

"His parents joined the Nazi party in the 1930s. Martin's older brother became part of the SS first, in 1940. At the age of seventeen, Martin joined the army and became part of the SS, in 1943. His first station was as an SS guard at Auschwitz. He was there until it was evacuated," Mrs. Rossi recounts sadly.

"How did you meet your late husband?"

"I lived in a small village called Brzezinka. It was only a thirty-minute walk from Oswiecim," Mrs. Rossi answers quietly, using the town's Polish name.

"Wait! Mom! So you're saying that you met Dad while he was a guard at Auschwitz? You knew that, and you married him?" Kent interrupts, flabbergasted.

"I don't understand?" Jamie continues, "You lived near Auschwitz?"

"Auschwitz and Birkenau were right outside of the town of Oswiecim. There were about 16,000 people living in Oswiecim during the war. It was not uncommon for the girls between seventeen and twenty-five to meet up with the soldiers there. I first met Martin there, at the local dance hall. Of course, back then he was Stefan. When he had time away from the camp, we would meet in town. A couple of times he actually invited me to Auschwitz. The guards' quarters were really nice, but the part I will never forget is the luxury that the officers had. It was like being at a retreat. They did host many high-ranking Nazi guests there." Mrs. Rossi spoke in even tones. "Officers would even vacation there." She looks straight at the wall, keeping her face blank as she gives these answers.

"Did you know what was happening in those camps?" Kent demands, his grief subsumed by horror.

"Of course, we did. Nobody was allowed to visit the inside of the concentration camp, but the smell from the smokestacks came to my home when the wind was blowing it toward our town. I cannot ever forget that smell." Her face is suddenly dark and fearful.

"What happened when Auschwitz was evacuated? Did Mr. Rossi escape?" Jamie asks. She remembers from her school days that it had been bad enough to be in Auschwitz itself, but it was no better when they moved the Jews out of the camp. Jamie fears that Mr. Rossi may have been involved with all of these horrors.

Mrs. Rossi's eyes fill again with very different tears. "No." Her whole body shudders with the pain of recollection. "Martin participated in the death march to Wodzislaw, which was thirty-five miles away. It was something he always regretted. In Wodzislaw, he was assigned to put the women on the train. There were open-air cattle cars, and he loaded them into those cars, in the snow, to go to Ravensbruck concentration camp. That was more than Martin could handle. After he had them loaded, he fled, despite the freezing temperature and falling snow. He was supposed to go on to Ravensbruck and then receive further assignment, but he chose to make a run for it."

"Where did he go?"

"He escaped to Brzezinka and found me. By then, we were already engaged to be married, but he was afraid for us to be married in Poland because he didn't want any records for the SS to come and find him. He hoped that they would assume he had been killed or captured. Our neighbors hid us in their basement when the Russians came through in late January 1945. For months, we were separated while in hiding, until that summer." Mrs. Rossi stops, her eyes seeing the scenes of her past as clearly as though it had happened yesterday.

"Why did you go into hiding?"

"They never tell you in the history books about the Russian liberating force that came into Poland, and about the mass rapes of the native women. My own mother was raped four times in a single day. I thank God we were able to hide and were not found. The Russians would have executed Martin," Mrs. Rossi answers through thick tears.

"How did you escape Poland?"

"Martin had money, gold, and other valuables that he had taken from the...that he got in Auschwitz. We made our way to Switzerland by the end of the summer. We immediately got married and moved to Innsbruck. After a couple of years living there, we heard the rumors about Auschwitz guards being arrested, tried, and even executed. It was time to leave. Our plans were to immigrate to Brazil in 1948 using his real name, but he changed it in Italy instead. He changed it to Rossi, a common Portuguese name. In 1953, we came to the U.S. and made a new life hiding from the past. All of our children were born in this country."

"Did your husband ever know anyone else with a similar story, or was he ever in contact with someone in the same predicament?"

Mrs. Rossi thinks for a moment, and then replies, "No, not that I am aware of."

Kent had stopped pacing half way through Jamie's questions. He now stands off to the side, still with shock, seeing his mother—and his father—with new eyes.

Jamie crouches next to the bed and puts her hand on Mrs. Rossi's. She looks up into the old, tired eyes. As horrified as she is by the truth, Jamie sympathizes with the cost to Mrs. Rossi to reveal it. "Thank you for the truth. I appreciate you sharing your tale, despite the hardship of reliving those memories. I want you to know that it could be extremely useful in finding and stopping your husband's killer. I will try to keep you updated. And, if you think of anything else, please call me," Jamie says gently, handing Mrs. Rossi her business card.

Mrs. Rossi mutely accepts the card, her tears still flowing freely. Jamie leaves the room, and the zombie-like mother and son, closing the door behind her. Once the door is shut, Jamie makes her way downstairs and finds Phil.

When he sees Jamie waving him to leave the room, Phil politely excuses himself. He leaves Peter with a polite "I will have a police officer address your concerns until I can get back to you."

"Worthless assholes!" Peter yells angrily at Phil's back.

Jamie leads Phil out the front door.

"So?" Phil inquires expectantly.

"I think we have a Nazi-hunter on our hands."

Chapter 24

At the same time, the politics of the country turned for the worse, and things around the world became more chaotic. My dream of college died as World War II broke out. Over the next few years, I would see and live through things that should never be repeated. You see, I am a Jew. The nightmares that I lived through cannot be adequately described, but I feel I must write them down and pass them along. Maybe someday in the future, such events will be thwarted before they happen again. I also write this memoir, in a way, to heal myself. Maybe once it is down on paper I will be free from the horrors I have experienced. Just maybe.

After World War I, Slovakia became a part of Czechoslovakia. During those days, you either told people you were Czech or Hungarian, since the Slovaks were more anti-Semitic. I actually never experienced any real anti-Semitism growing up in Propoc, Slovakia, not far from Kosice. My best friend, Mary, was a Christian. Living in a small town and owning the only dry goods store meant we were quite well off. As a child growing up, I had no idea that my grandparents actually wielded some influence throughout the community.

It was during World War II that Hitler took over and gave what was originally Slovakia to Hungary. It sounds terrible, but this is what actually protected many Jews for a little while, that Hungary and Germany were allies. Some of the local Jews tried to leave, going to the United States, France, or England. Others, like my family, believed that Jews had withstood persecution in the past, and it could be done again. Little did any of us know what persecution, horrors, and hatred we would see in the coming years.

Chapter 25

Heading to the kitchen, Simon retrieves a beer from his refrigerator and sits down at the small breakfast table. Screwing off the top of the beer, Simon lets his mind wander back to his father. He takes a sip, then leans back, reminiscing. Simon remembers it clearly.

He is seven-years-old, sitting on the porch, waiting for his father to come home. Dad has been away for what seemed like months, but which was probably only a couple of weeks. Sitting next to Simon are his baseball and mitt, waiting as anxiously as him. The family car drives down the street. Simon stands up, ready, wearing a smile wider than his face as he watches the car pull into the driveway. Racing up to the driver's-side door, Simon opens it, ready to greet Dad with a hug. Inside the car, his father reaches for his suitcases and briefcase, completely missing Simon's gesture.

Please, please let him be in a good mood, Simon prays as he reaches in to grab a suitcase.

"Thanks," grumbles his father, stepping out of the car.

Simon's prayer is not to be answered this time.

With profound disappointment, Simon senses that his father is frustrated and angry, just like the last time. His pale face shows too much work and not enough sleep. His father drags his feet up the driveway. Simon shuts the door, watching his father climb the steps to his house. So much for his hope of playing catch with Dad.

Simon goes running after his father, hoping that the sight of his mother may make his dad happy again. As he opens the screen door and walks inside, Simon hears his father's voice speaking rapidly and angrily from the kitchen. Knowing better than to get in the middle of another fight, Simon heads to the closest room to listen.

"I cannot believe it!"

"Milton, what did you expect? It has been the same result every time since you started this."

"I practically handed them all the information they needed to prosecute them!"

"Why do you do this to yourself? I will never understand it," Simon's mom counters, slamming a cupboard door.

"If you were the only son of a Holocaust survivor, growing up hearing her tales every day, you'd be just as vigilant. Everything was stolen from my mother. Her whole family, gone! She was the only one to survive. They took away her home and replaced it with the gas chambers, the crematories, the torture, and the murder of children. These monsters need to be punished for their crimes! What? You want them to get away with it?!"

Simon feels slightly squeamish hearing his father talk. He does not understand all of it, but what he does understand makes him nervous. As the quiet settles in for a moment, Simon holds his breath. When his mother begins talking, he releases it.

"You've been chasing these guys for years! What has it gotten you? Ulcers! And what about us? You are using your own money, time, and life, wasting it on chasing criminals that no one else cares about. You said this case was going to be different. The look on your face tells me it wasn't any different."

"I have concrete proof this Rossi guy is really Kleiss, and the government won't do anything to prosecute him. I literally handed over the evidence to the Department of Justice's Office of Special Investigations three months ago, and you know what they have done with that information? Nothing. Absolutely nothing!" Simon's father yells vehemently.

"It's the same old story, and it's not going to change. I'm sick of it. You said that this time they would do something. And what about Simon Wiesenthal, in Vienna? Send him the information. He will take care of it, so you don't have to be leaving us all the time. Leave it to the professionals, and stay here, be my husband, be a father," his mother pleads.

"It's not that simple. The system is the problem. Remember Kuester? I was able to prove he was in the SS and participated in the Piotrkow massacre. The U.S tried and convicted him of lying on his immigration papers and sentenced him to deportation. Where is he today? Still living in his home in Massachusetts. No country will take him, so he goes on like it never happened. Is that justice? Then there are the others. They are not interested in convicting these murderers, even though they were clearly at the concentration camp. Even if they looked at all my evidence, they won't do anything because they make an excuse that it costs too much money to go after these men and women who are in their seventies or eighties, especially if they have records of being good US citizens," Simon's father bitterly shouts.

"Oh no!" Simon's mother calls out. A pan slams against the stove. "Look at this! I just burnt our lunch."

"You are worried about lunch when your next door neighbor is a murderer!"

"Milton, really. You've been obsessed with locating Nazis hiding out in the U.S. since before we met. You even got several tried without any notoriety of your own, but this needs to stop now. No more long nights doing research or trips away from home for weeks at a time. It's enough already!"

"Just because interest in convicting Nazis seems like a waste of time to people who live in comfort, it does not make the pain, the horror, and the murders disappear. If Simon Wiesenthal is not giving up, then neither will I!"

"And what about your family here? Do you even know how your three dry cleaning stores are doing? What do you know about your son? Sometimes I wonder if you even remember that you have a wife and child."

"Rachel, I do this for both of you, and for my mother. You want to hear the craziest thing in the world? Evidence from communist countries is not admissible in court in West Germany! Where do you think most of these crimes took place, south Florida? The Communists could care less about prosecuting them, and the Germans won't accept my evidence. It's ludicrous! These monsters should not be free!"

Simon can hear his father starting to pace the kitchen floor. His mother is done fighting and is trying to calm his father down. Simon leaves his closet and heads back out the front door. Picking up his glove and ball, he stands alone in the middle of the yard. On each side of him, the neighbors are out. On one side, some younger children are running through the sprinklers; on the other, an old man is tending his garden. Simon looks at the old man, wondering if he is one of the monsters his father talks about.

A beeping from Simon's phone awakens him from his past. He runs to his bedroom, where his phone is still plugged in to the charger. He sees it is a text message from a friend. He ignores it and takes another sip of his beer, his thoughts returning to his father. Simon had a strange relationship with his father. There were times when he spent endless hours with him, when his father would have gladly thrown the ball with him. Then there were the times when his father was angry and frustrated. It was often centered around his frequent trips. His father would eventually settle down, and, in the meantime, Simon would slink away and spend a lot of time alone in his room. It was for this reason, Simon knew, that his mother had finally divorced his father after many years of patient loyalty. Simon even attributed his father's massive, deadly heart attack, which killed him at the age of fifty-three, to the constant stress and obsession of hunting down Nazis.

After his father's death, Simon, as the only son, had the task of cleaning out his father's things. Among them were files containing years of research on each purported Nazi. Some of them his grandmother had personally recognized from Auschwitz. Simon could not throw any of the information away. Simon had promised Dad, on his hospital deathbed, that he would keep up the work and not let these animals get away with it, no matter how old they were.

Simon was well-aware of cases such as Dr. Heinrich Gross, who was head of the Spiegelgrund Children's Psychiatric Clinic during the Holocaust. It was there that children with physical and mental handicaps were sent to be killed as part of the Nazi Euthanasia Program. Gross was tried and convicted after the war, but the conviction was overturned due to a technicality. In 1997, they opened a basement vault at Spiegelgrund and found hundreds of children's brains in well-labeled jars, which had been there since the Holocaust. At this point, Gross was deemed unfit to stand trial, due to his advanced age. He lived another eight years and died in 2005. There were so many other stories just like this, where the evidence was clear, and nothing was done due to lack of cooperation between governments and other obstacles.

His father's method, destroying his own life trying to bring justice through the legal system, did not appeal to Simon. So, he had instituted his own method, which, thus far, had proved to be highly successful. Simon sips some more beer and sighs, thinking that so many of the people in the files had already received their justice. Time was running out. He would fulfill his father's mission. If the legal system would not bring justice, then Simon would make his own justice. It is the only way.

Chapter 26

Jamie arrives at the NCAVC around 8 p.m. She goes in through the side door, using her key card to access the building. A night guard is there on watch and nods to her as she flashes her I.D. Phil has left for home. Besides, she does not need him for this. She has to make her presentation alone.

Before Jamie can even start climbing the stairs, her cell phone rings. From the ringtone, she knows it is Chris calling. She wavers for a moment, then decides to answer it.

"Hey, Babe," Chris greets her. "I'm here at your apartment. I thought we could do a make-up date tonight for missing Monday."

"Oh no! I'm sorry, I have to go in to work. Something came up. You haven't been waiting too long have you?"

"Nah, been watching television. Why don't you blow off work for tonight? It could wait until tomorrow, right?"

"No it can't. I wish it could though. I know how your time off is precious, but I have a huge presentation tomorrow."

"Well, this is frustrating. I would've stayed in the city and hung out with Scott and Alex if I'd known you were going to work."

"I said I'm sorry." She starts up the stairs to the fourth floor, trying to let out some of her pent-up anger.

"Is it that important? I mean, life and death? It's not like saving someone's hand or something."

"My job is just as much about life and death as your job. I thought you, of all people, could understand that."

"Sorry. I didn't mean that. I'm just exhausted."

"It's alright," Jamie groans, still bitter from his words. "Let's just plan the date together, later, maybe when this case calms down."

"I'm going to sleep at your place tonight. Too tired to drive back. If you get done early enough, you know where to find me."

"I promise I will be home as soon as I can."

"Later," Chris says and is gone.

Jamie hangs up the phone and finishes her climb. She is pricked by her boyfriend's words. He is always breaking dates and having to work, but, when the role is reversed, it is suddenly not fair.

There are a few lights still shining brightly through office doors. Tomorrow she will present to the team all of her findings from her trips. Fredericks, Phil, Joey, and maybe even Thompson, will be there early in the morning to hear what Jamie has discovered.

At 12:38 a.m., Jamie finally saves her finished presentation. Exhausted, she wants nothing but to go home and sleep. Shutting down her computer, Jamie remembers that Chris is in her bed.

As she walks toward her apartment building, Jamie can smell spring on its way. The chirping of the first crickets of the season interrupts the still dark of a moonless night. She is unafraid, knowing her Glock is readily available. Jamie enters her apartment and sets her things down quietly. She sees a faint light coming from her kitchen. The freezer door is open about an inch, and the narrow light faintly illuminates the otherwise-dark room.

There is a half-eaten bowl of popcorn sitting next to the kitchen sink. A wine glass and a drinking glass sit randomly on the counters.

"Thanks a lot," Jamie whispers. She leaves the kitchen and heads to the bedroom.

Before she even makes it down the hallway, she can hear Chris' snoring. She enters her bedroom and swiftly changes into her pajamas, all the while watching Chris skeptically as he continues to snore. Jamie stands in the bathroom doorway looking sourly at her bed.

Her decision to sleep on the couch is made when she hears another loud snore from Chris. She heads to the living room and curls up on the sofa.

Chapter 27

Jamie arrives in the conference room early. Within minutes, she has her presentation ready to go. Joey Hughes and Phil Clark come in talking about March Madness. Fredericks and Thompson arrive right at eight o'clock.

With a polite glance at those seated, Jamie jumps right in.

"Great. Thanks for coming. I have visited all of the murder scenes. I am going to present the data in the chronological order of the murders. The first victim lived in Schenectady and was found in front of the Post Office in Salem." She quickly scrolls through several pictures that provide a panoramic view of the road, forests, and post office.

"As you can see, this is a very secluded spot. No one lives nearby, and there were no witnesses whatsoever. The Sheriff's Department in Salem, which has jurisdiction over the small hamlet of Shushan, suspects the killer used some boards to make a ramp and dump the body without leaving any footprints in the dirt. It also rained after the perp left the body."

Jamie moves on. "The second murder took place in a nursing home in Abilene, Texas. As you can see, this is not the place a serial killer heads to find a victim. It's full of staff and people. The victim's room was not at the end of the hallway, near the exits, but close to the nursing station instead. He was clearly not a random victim.

"This is a video recording from the nursing home in Abilene. As you can see, here is the perp signing in. Note the wide-brimmed hat shielding her face. She is using her left hand. Note the lace gloves. And here she is leaving. She was in the nursing home for about fifty minutes. No crime was committed during that time. Here is the footage of her returning. The receptionist that day says the woman forgot her cell phone and wanted to run and get it. In seven minutes, she returns—the murder was done then."

"So what is the gender of the perp?" Thompson interjects with a frown.

"Although dressed as a female, I am certain that the murderer is male. Here is a picture of the perp's signature," Jamie explains, as the next slide comes on the screen, showing the name Esther Shushan. "The name is significant, and I will address that in a moment. It looks like it could have been written by a right-handed person, using their left hand. It is easy to see that the handwriting matches the name 'Simon W.' that was left in Illinois. I am convinced that the woman in Abilene is the same perp. He knew right where the cameras were, so he could avoid a direct shot; he wore a wide hat and gloves to cover his face and man-hands.

"Third. This next set of pictures is from New Orleans, the Bywater neighborhood. These homes are practically built on top of each other. There are plenty of prying eyes, and, in fact, a neighbor did see the killer, but thought nothing of it because the perp was dressed as a pizza delivery guy. The witness said it was dark, and he only thought he saw a black man. We are dealing with a person who spares no details in his disguises, down to the beat-up car. Note that this is the murder Kim Hammond from Research found. It was not in our original presentation. The police attributed this to some sort of gang initiation, as it appeared so random. The perp actually spoke to the wife, who was in another room, and said that her husband was having a heart attack and instructed her to call 9-1-1. He then said he was going to go get help. This kept her from screaming while he was getting away. He is clearly very clever.

"Fourth. The next set of slides shows the home in Flint, Michigan. If you recall, this victim was found the next day, by the cleaning lady."

"Fifth. A week and a half ago." She continues to the next set of slides, which show the inside of the Crestwood Assisted Living Center. "This assisted living facility has a full staff, and even requires visitors to sign in with their names and times of arrival. He signed in as 'Simon W.', with no time. The victim's room is again in the middle of the corridor, not near any exits. There are many residents roaming the hallways at all hours. Again, these murders are not crimes of opportunity."

"What about the most recent murder?" Fredericks asks, interrupting Jamie.

"Sixth. Tuesday. Atlanta, Georgia." Jamie advances the slide presentation with the shots taken from the Rossi house. "His home is very secluded. This was the first scene that afforded the perp some cover. I've talked with all of the detectives, and the files have essentially gone cold. Nothing was stolen or missing from any crime scene."

Clicking to the next slide, Jamie continues, "Here is a report prepared by the analysts. I had them check flight arrivals in each of the cities three days before and after looking for similarities of passengers, and nothing was found."

"Is it possible the perp could be driving across the U.S.?" Phil inquires, holding up a hand.

"That is entirely possible. Now, let's go over the newest victim. Martin Rossi, age eighty-nine, found dead in his home three days ago. His wife returned from her once-a-week water aerobics class and discovered her husband's dead body in the living room right off of the entryway." Jamie brings up the next slide. On the screen behind her are the pictures of Martin Rossi, post mortem, and a few pictures of the crime scene in the home.

"The Coroner in Atlanta believes the perp to be right-handed and under six feet tall, based on the wound on the victim," Jamie adds before she clicks over to the next slide.

The slide shows a close-up of the flower arrangement sitting in the middle of the side table near the front door. "The perp gained access to the home by posing as a flower deliveryman. A note was found that was similar to the others, but this one had the following on the reverse side."

Fools
Behaving
Irresponsibly

Fredericks's expression does not change. Moving along, Jamie comments, "This taunt only adds to the fact that this perp thinks he will not be caught."

The next slide shows pictures of the footprints on the freshly-vacuumed carpet.

"One significant finding is these footprints, discovered at the scene of the crime. Forensics tells us the shoe is a size twelve, men's Converse All Stars. From the tread marks, we know that the shoes are new and that the perp tends to walk on the balls of his feet."

A photo of the wound on Mr. Rossi's neck appears on the screen.

"According to the Medical Examiner, Rossi was killed from asphyxiation by a ten-gauge wire ligature, just like all of the others."

The next slide is the picture of the note. Jamie looks around at the small group, preparing to explain her discovery. She takes a moment to gather herself, then says, "Thus far, the notes have been a mystery. After some research, I've discovered that the words here," Jamie points, "comprise a phonetic spelling of a name from the Bible, from the book of Esther. The names are probably chopped into pieces just to make them harder to decipher. Taking out the space, each name on the notes matches the name of one of the sons of Haman. The names are assigned chronologically to the murders."

"Haman?" Fredericks echoes doubtfully.

"He was the enemy of the Jews in the Biblical story of Esther. His ten sons were all hanged, and each of their names is listed in the Bible," Jamie answers, putting the next slide up on the screen.

pars hon dota	Parshandata
dol fon	Dolphon
a spat a	Aspata
por ot ha	Porata

	Adalia
	Aridata
parmo sh ta	Parmashta
Ari Sai	Arisai

Displayed is a close-up of the book of Esther with the verse containing the names of Haman's sons. The next slides pop up next to the names, each one coordinating with notes found near the victims. "As you can see here, the names match almost perfectly," Jamie points out. "And he skipped two names. I'm going to look into why the names Adalia and Aridata may have been skipped. It is possible that they weren't skipped and that we are still missing some victims. As soon as we are done here, I'm going to start research to find out if there are more murders."

"Interesting," Thompson says.

"What about the initials on the notes?" Fredericks asks.

"Honestly, I still have no idea what the initials on the notes mean. I am still researching those as well."

Jamie moves on to the next slide, which shows side-by-side images of the post office with "Shushan" written in white letters, and the sign-in sheet with "Esther Shushan" written on it. "On an interesting note, there are two murders where the name Shushan comes up. Shushan is the city in which the book of Esther takes place. The book of Esther chronicles the Jewish holiday of Purim, which is a festival in the early spring. Three of our murders took place on Purim. So we have the names of the ten sons of Haman from the book of Esther; we have Shushan and Esther Shushan, both from the book of Esther; and we have some of the murders occurring on the Jewish holiday of Purim, which is celebrated in the book of Esther. It seems obvious that the perp is trying to make a statement.

"The other two murders occurred on another, lesser-known Jewish holiday called Hoshana Raba. It is some sort of minor judgment day."

"So does this point to a Jewish killer?" Fredericks asks without emotion.

"It might be. There is more to consider here, sir. I uncovered some crucial information when speaking to our last victim's wife."

The next slide that comes up on the screen is a black-and-white picture of a young man in a Nazi uniform, his arm wrapped around a young girl.

"Martin Rossi was a former Nazi soldier stationed at Auschwitz in 1943. His real name was Stefan Kleiss," Jamie informs the group. "He changed his name in Italy and then moved to Brazil. It was from Brazil that he and his wife immigrated to the United States."

Fredericks gives her a thoughtful frown, looking carefully at the old picture. Phil subtly glances over at Fredericks, then at Thompson. Jamie also pauses, letting the information sink in.

"I am currently tracking down the other victims' whereabouts during World War II, but I feel confident in saying that we have a Nazi-hunter on our hands."

Fredericks says nothing; his expressionless eyes are still staring at the photograph on the screen.

"A Nazi hunter?" Thompson echoes.

"I suspect that our perp is, in fact, Jewish, based on the Biblical connections and the Rossi's Nazi background. Instead of a serial killer, I am convinced that we have a vigilante."

"Maybe it is the Mossad or some other organization. What makes you so sure it is an individual vigilante?" Phil proposes, as the others pause to ponder the question.

"I don't think the Mossad would leave the cryptic notes or include the other symbolic elements. The perp could, however, be a paid professional hired by a wealthy individual or organization."

"Get the background information on the other victims, and discover if they also have Nazi ties of some kind. Otherwise, it could be a coincidence, and the victims are linked in a different way," Fredericks surmises.

The group is silent. Jamie senses their astonishment at the connection, their struggle to comprehend the consequences of such a possibility.

"I will email you all a copy of my presentation," Jamie concludes, turning off the projector.

"Good work, Golding," Fredericks pronounces. "Keep me informed."

"Of course," Jamie agrees. She begins to gather her things together.

"We have to go public with this," Fredericks says with a commanding voice. He glances over at Thompson, who gives an ever-so-slight nod of approval. "Let's see, it is 8:15. I'll call a press conference for 11:00 A.M. I'll prepare a statement, and we'll send out a wire to law enforcement across the country. As always, the exact details of the murders will be withheld, but we could use the help of the public, as well as local law enforcement, to look out for this guy."

Jamie and Phil both bob their heads briskly.

"Jamie, I would like you to attend the press conference. It will be at H.Q. in D.C.

"Yes, sir."

"Great. Now I have to prepare my remarks," Fredericks states, by way of farewell, as he departs.

Phil stands up and leans in, saying, "Good work. You wrapped that up all nice like a present."

"Thanks," Jamie smiles.

"You want to ride together to the press conference?"

"Great, I'll drive."

Jamie leaves the room. She expected a press conference, but she did not think it would be today, and she certainly did not think she would have less than three hours. Jamie heads back to her office. After putting her things away, she sends an email with her presentation to the group.

At 10:45 Jamie arrives at the pressroom, where she sees the familiar FBI seal displayed prominently behind a solid mahogany lectern. Even with such little notice, all of the major national news agencies are present: Fox News, CNN, USA Today, MSNBC, and others. Jamie stays off to the side, against the wall. After a few minutes, Phil arrives and takes the position next to the wall directly behind her.

"Ready for this?" Phil asks, his voice quiet, but still audible in the noisy room.

"Yeah. Except that now I'm going to be inundated with hundreds of leads to filter through."

"Maybe it will spook him and cause him to slip up. Or maybe he'll confess to a buddy or something. Sometimes this works to our advantage," Phil reminds her.

"I don't think so. Not this guy."

Jamie has already thought of those scenarios, but this guy is not like the usual serial killers. This guy wants the FBI to be looking for him. The result will be hundreds of tips pouring in, and each of them will need to be looked into, no matter how fruitless. Of course, a good tip could break the case for her. Maybe all of those extra eyes will help, but, either way, the perp is too intelligent to be found by just any nosy lady in the neighborhood.

Phil looks at his watch and remarks, "Fredericks is always right on time."

Jamie looks at her cell phone to check the time. At precisely eleven o'clock, Fredericks and Cynthia walk into the room. Fredericks places his notes on the lectern and adjusts the microphone. Cynthia stands to his right and a few feet behind.

With barely a scan of the eager faces in front of him, Fredericks starts in his formal, no-nonsense manner. He does not even clear his throat.

"Good morning. Thank you for coming. My name is Howard Fredericks, Special Agent in Charge at the NCAVC at Quantico. The purpose of this press conference is to inform the public and law enforcement agencies at the state, county, and local jurisdictions, of six murders that have taken place over the last two-and-a-half years. The first murder occurred on September 29, 2010, and the most recent occurred on Tuesday of this week. The murders were committed in Schenectady, New York; Abilene, Texas; New Orleans, Louisiana; Flint, Michigan; Harwood Heights, Illinois (which is right outside of Chicago); and the most recent was in Atlanta, Georgia. All six victims were elderly white males with ages ranging from eighty-eight to ninety-four years old. All were strangled with a wire ligature. The murders are likely to have been committed by the same individual or group of individuals. We believe that one perpetrator is a white male in his late twenties or early thirties. We are here today promoting public awareness and soliciting the public's help in amassing any and all information about these murders and who might be responsible. We deem the perpetrator or perpetrators to be extremely dangerous, and we believe that they pose a serious threat to our communities. Anyone with any information is strongly encouraged to contact their local police department or the FBI, via our online tip center or telephone tip center, 1-800-C-A-L-L-F-B-I.

"I will not be taking questions right now. We plan on having another press conference in the near future, when we have more facts. Thank you."

With his statement read, Fredericks turns and heads toward the door, followed by Cynthia. A roar breaks out from the crowd. Immediately, five or six simultaneous questions are called out to them as they leave. Fredericks does not slow down his gait or even slightly divert his eyes from the door. Jamie admires his steadfastness and focus. She turns to Phil, who merely shrugs his shoulders.

"My sentiments exactly," Jamie concurs with a smile as they both make their way out of the pressroom.

Chapter 28

Jamie stares blankly at the computer screen in her office.

Now, with the press conference, and this thing going national, the pressure is really going to be on her to get an arrest. She needs to make the most of her time before she gets inundated with loonies claiming to be the killer.

Who are you, Simon W.? A serial? A vigilante? A paid professional?

The buzzing in her mind is so irritating that she needs a diversion before she dives back into the case. She tries her luck at calling Chris, but the phone goes to voicemail. She does not leave a message. By the time Chris calls her back, she will most likely be busy and not want to be disrupted.

Where do I find a Nazi hunter? Are you alone or part of an organization? Is it revenge, or are you just taking the law into your own hands?

She Googles "Nazi hunters" and sees several articles about active crusaders. Even today, there are rewards advertised on the Internet for information leading to the arrest of Nazis in hiding. She clicks on the Wikipedia page for "Nazi Hunter" and sees a picture of Simon Wiesenthal.

That explains the use of the name Simon W.

She searches for the name. Apparently, Simon Wiesenthal was a Holocaust survivor who became famous as a Nazi hunter after the war. He died in 2005. His whole life, he worked to bring justice to war criminals. He had many notable successes. There is nothing to suggest that he ever promoted outright vengeance. The Simon Wiesenthal Center is a U.S.-based organization that fights for social justice and promotes Holocaust education. As she gathers more and more information, Jamie becomes convinced she is dealing with an individual. She cannot imagine any of the organizations she finds turning to outright murder as a means of justice. She especially does not think they would use Simon W. as a cover, thereby smearing the name of the most respected Nazi hunter.

This is an individual who, in a distorted way, considers himself to be the next Simon Wiesenthal.

The leaving of a note also points to an individual. She has thought that from the beginning. All of the cases are too uniform to consider this is a small band of vigilantes.

Leaning back in her chair, Jamie sighs. But what is the Purim connection? Why leave notes with names from the book of Esther? And do those facts really point to the killer being Jewish? It could be a Jewish sympathizer. And, to add to the mix, what do the initials on the notes mean?

Her cell phone buzzes, interrupting Jamie's thoughts. She retrieves her phone off the desk and spares a glance for the text. It is from Chris. He just finished a really unusual case at work and promises to call her and tell her, after he gets the post-op orders done and does the surgical dictation.

"Great! I can't wait," Jamie says sarcastically to the empty office, rolling her eyes.

What do the book of Esther and the sons of Haman have to do with anything? I need a rabbi.

Her phone rings. Jamie hits her Bluetooth. "Hello?"

"Hey, guess what? I just finished a case involving necrotizing fasciitis," Chris blurts excitedly.

"That is...?" Jamie pauses, waiting for him to fill in the blank.

"Oh, it's a flesh-eating bacteria. Get this, the guy's been getting ninety percent of his calories from beer. While at work one day, he accidentally drives a construction staple into the palm of his hand. It left some nice puncture wounds right below his middle finger. He does not get it cleaned out properly and throws a Band-Aid on it. Now, a week later, the bacteria has tracked via the fascia about three-fourths of the way up his arm. His arm is hideously swollen, red, and hot to the touch," Chris continues rapidly.

"Ew! Gross."

"The hand surgeon and I filleted his entire hand and arm, from the base of his middle finger, all the way to under his armpit. There were whole sections of tendons and parts of muscle bellies that were completely dead. We debrided everything and left the wound open. He will be coming back multiple times for us to clean it out and remove any dead tissue," Chris delineates.

"Wait, so is it really flesh-eating?"

"Not actually. Flesh-eating bacteria do not eat human flesh, but they release toxins that kill human tissue. We are actually hoping to save his arm. It will take several wash-outs and high-dose antibiotics. The hope is that this first surgery will stop it from spreading up the arm."

"Ouch."

There is a long pause in the conversation.

"How's work going for you?" Chris inquires, almost as an afterthought.

"Oy, this case is becoming bigger every day. I can't believe how many places I've traveled to in the last week or so. Fredericks is really going to be on my back, and there is no letup in sight," Jamie confesses, feeling the strain in her body. She rubs her neck, feeling the tight muscles and the knots in her shoulders.

"So when can I sleep over again?" Chris asks. Jamie hears the doubt in his voice.

Great, he just wants to sleep with me again. This whole relationship is nothing but sex anymore.

Jamie replies, "Uh, probably not anytime soon, with this case."

"Right," Chris replies, some resentment in his voice. "Well, you can take a break sometime, right? When you do, call me."

"Just like you squeeze me in between your cases," Jamie retorts, trying to keep the anger out of her voice.

In the background on Chris's end, Jamie can hear some commotion. "I've gotta go," he says, then immediately hangs up.

"Later," Jamie bitterly tells no one. She clenches and unclenches her jaw. It is hardly fair that he should be pissed about her having to work. She always plans around his schedule, and, now that she needs him to be flexible, he is acting like a spoiled brat. Before Jamie can fester any further over Chris, her phone rings again.

"Hello?" Jamie spits, unable to hide her irritation.

"Whoa! You alright, Jamie?" Even though he sounds taken aback, Seth's voice is warm.

"Oh, I'll tell you later," Jamie mutters with a sigh, relaxing a bit.

"So what time are you working 'til?"

"Not much longer, I'm about spent."

"How'd your presentation go?"

"As well as could be expected. I laid out everything that we know this morning and then we had a press conference. Now the whole world knows about this insane case, and everyone is looking to me to solve it."

"Sounds stressful. How about I bring you by some takeout when I get off of work, so you can have one less thing to worry about tonight," Seth offers kindly. "I won't stay long, I promise."

"That would be great," Jamie accepts.

"I've got something to tell you as well," Seth hints, but Jamie's head is already back in her work.

"Okay, I'll see you later."

As she focuses back on the case, Jamie is bothered by one piece of evidence—the footprints. Why would the killer leave obvious tread marks? It appears he had time to clean up after himself, since the body was not found for several hours. All of the other cases had no such evidence. Of course, none of the other victims had such pristine carpet that had also been recently vacuumed. Jamie starts to wonder if this is the break she has been looking for in the case. Maybe, for once, the killer made a mistake. Criminals have been caught before with as little as a good footprint, especially since Forensics said he has an identifiable weight bearing.

Once at her apartment, Jamie thinks that, after her stressful day, she needs nothing more than to unwind and get comfortable. She takes a long, hot bath, then puts on a loose black tank top and a pair of comfortable, green pajama shorts. She wanders to the kitchen and makes some tea.

Sitting on her couch with her tablet and her tea, Jamie begins her search for a rabbi. Her first order of business is to look online for nearby synagogues. To her surprise, she discovers that there are a lot of them close to her. Jamie looks over a few of their websites, to see if any strike her as the best to call. Nothing stands out, so Jamie decides to email several of them.

Should she say she is a special agent for the FBI? Disclosing that fact might also get her paired up with someone who is only interested in the FBI angle, and who is not interested in her questions. It is safer to not to divulge that information, Jamie thinks, until she knows if it will help.

She begins typing her email.

Hi,

My name is Jamie Golding, and I would like to set up an appointment to meet and discuss some matters of Jewish significance. I am specifically interested in the book of Esther, Purim, and how those things relate to the Holocaust. Please contact me at your earliest convenience.

Thanks,

Jamie Golding

703-555-7662

To save time, Jamie cuts and pastes her email, sending it out to as many rabbis as she can. She figures she will meet with whoever responds first. Rabbis are probably pretty busy, and they may not have time for a non-congregant. Either way, she has to try.

While she has her account pulled up, Jamie tries to catch up on personal emails that came in while she was gone. It never ceases to amaze her that she can receive so many emails in such a short time. After reading a few of them and deleting the junk, Jamie notices that she already has a response. That is much quicker than she had expected. She eagerly opens the email and scans it.

Dear Jamie,
There have been many attempts of late to link the ancient Purim story with the recent Holocaust. The connection is supposedly through mysterious hidden codes and coincidences within the book of Esther. This is nothing more than science fiction. If you would like to learn more about each one individually, I recommend going to the library and getting books on each subject separately.
Please drop in on a Shabbat so I can meet you.
Sincerely,
Rabbi Judy Lankowitz

That is a bizarre response. *Many attempts to link the Purim story and the Holocaust.* What? Regardless of what it means, this rabbi does not seem to have any time for her. *I am definitely not going on a Saturday. When could I speak to her then, with a bunch of people at services?*

She checks her email again, hoping to hear from another rabbi.

A knock at the door heralds Seth's arrival. She opens the door to find him standing in the hallway, two take-out boxes in one hand and a jug of 100% white grape juice in the other. His black hair is messy in an attractive way, Jamie notes. He is still wearing his work attire, along with his quirky, lovable smile. "Hungry?" He asks, holding up the takeout boxes.

Seth can see that all of the traveling and late nights on the job are wearing on Jamie. Her eyes are droopy from lack of sleep and look bruised underneath. Her straight black hair is pulled up and held in place by a single pencil. Some strands of hair have escaped the updo, and now fall about her face. The effect is flattering. But what really catch Seth's attention are Jamie's long, slender legs and low top.

"Very," Jamie answers, opening the door and extending her arm. The motion knocks the shirt strap off her shoulder, revealing an inch more cleavage.

Seth tries valiantly to keep his mind on the conversation, striding past Jamie and to the kitchen, saying "Good, I hope you're in the mood for a veggie burger with French fries. And, yes, 'veggie' means 'tofu'," he teases her playfully.

"Please tell me that's for you," Jamie quips with a grimace, following Seth into the kitchen.

He laughs. "Okay, that's mine. I got you your favorite. Curried orange chicken salad." Seth opens one of the takeout boxes and shows her the contents.

"Yes!" Jamie exclaims. She takes the box out of his hands and grabs a fork from the kitchen drawer. She does not wait for Seth, but starts eating. She had hardly noticed her hunger until the smell of the food overtook her.

"Are you going to eat? Or is this all for me?" Jamie jests, pointing her fork to the other takeout box.

"I'm getting there. You want some?" Seth inquires, holding up the jug.

"Yes, please...I love white grape juice."

Seth pours two glasses of juice. He opens his own box, revealing chicken salad without cheese, and begins to eat.

Jamie bursts out in actual laughter. "You're such a tease!"

"Tofu is amazing, but I prefer a chicken salad." He gets himself a fork and starts eating slowly. He directs his full attention to Jamie. "So how were all of your trips?"

"Pretty worthless. Except for Atlanta," Jamie states baldly, then takes another bite of lettuce and tomato.

"What's in Atlanta? I thought your last stop was in Michigan or something."

"Well, you wouldn't believe this, but while I was out visiting all the crime scenes, the perp struck again." Jamie shares excitedly, leaving her fork in the salad.

"Really?"

"Yeah, I cut my trip to Flint short and headed out to Atlanta as soon as I could," Jamie tells him enthusiastically. "Nothing is better than having a fresh crime scene to investigate."

"That's wonderful!...Well, I mean, not for the victim, but awesome for you," Seth amends with an awkward grin.

"So how's it going with you?" Jamie asks, moving the subject away from her case.

"It's going okay. I broke things off with Margie. It wasn't going anywhere."

"Oh man, sorry to hear that. I'm sure it's for the best, but it still sucks."

"Eh. I'll be fine."

"I'll have to start keeping my eyes out for another girl for you."

My eyes are working just fine. It's you who can't see what I see.

"I'm hopefully going to be meeting with a rabbi soon. Maybe I can ask him if he knows anyone."

"Please don't."

"Hey, I'm kidding. You know I would never do a thing like that!"

"Maybe ask him what he thinks about you dating Chris!" A joking simper accompanies this statement.

"Very funny." Jamie rolls her eyes. "But touché. Point well-made."

Seth throws his empty takeout box in the trash and puts Jamie's leftovers in the fridge, along with the juice. Retrieving his own glass of juice, Seth joins Jamie where she has retired to the couch. She is sitting with her knees pulled up to her chest. He sits as close as he dares. As usual, Jamie does not seem to notice.

"You're more helpful than Chris today. I couldn't believe his snide remark to me," Jamie blurts angrily, remembering the conversation.

"What did he say?"

"About how I am not available when *he* has time off," Jamie recounts, venting the bitterness she had felt earlier.

"Wow, that's uncalled for."

"I know, really! I have always worked around his schedule, and suddenly, when I am busy at work, I'm *never* available to him."

"It's not like you are flying around the country that often," Seth points out sympathetically.

"Exactly. For once I have a hard case to work on, but if I'm not around for Chris when he has time for me, then I'm selfish?" She stands up from the couch and starts pacing the floor.

Seth stares surreptitiously as the muscles in her legs flex and relax. "I hardly think you are selfish," he says encouragingly, making every effort to focus on Jamie's problem, and not on her body.

"I know. You'd think it would be my turn to be busy and for him to be understanding, like I always am for him. I don't know. I'm really starting to doubt this relationship. I'm starting to see how one-sided it is—how one-sided it has always been," she fumes, still pacing the floor.

"You've got a point there. In a relationship, both parties have to give it their all; otherwise it won't work. That's why I broke it off with Margie. And I think maybe Chris is asking a little too much of you," Seth adds reasonably, watching Jamie's face for a reaction.

"It's so true! I have given plenty, and he's still not satisfied." Jamie is almost shouting. At this moment, she realizes she is overwrought. She stops pacing and breathes slowly for a couple of seconds, trying not to let herself lose control.

"Sorry, I got lost there for a moment," Jamie apologizes. "I just want things to be different with Chris, but whatever. I'll give him some time to think about it, or even talk this over with him."

"Just wait until you cool off a bit before approaching him. It's better to be calm then to be angry and say words you can never take back again," Seth advises her cautiously.

"You're right," Jamie sighs again, plopping on the couch right next to Seth. It feels good to be close to him. She turns to look him full in the face. "I really do appreciate you Seth. You have always been there for me, no matter what...." Her heart seems to be beating slightly faster. His face is so close to hers that she can see the flecks in his eyes. Jamie feels an electric thrill pulse in her veins.

Jamie is so close to Seth that her soft skin brushes his own. Her hazel eyes, staring straight into his own, make Seth's heart skip a beat. He slowly moves in to put his arm around her, his lips coming closer to hers. Seth notices that Jamie is also leaning in, ready to receive him.

This is it.

A ringing breaks the moment. Jamie looks down and answers her phone, her mind still swirling with anticipation and thrill.

"H-hello," she stutters.

"Hello, is this Jamie Golding?" a gentle male voice asks.

"Yes."

"Hi, this is Rabbi Daniel Silverman. I received your email today and wanted to arrange a meeting, with me or with one of the other kollel rabbis, either tomorrow or another day this week. Will that work for you?" the man explains respectfully.

"Tomorrow would be fine. What time?" Jamie asks, shaking her head clear.

"I actually have some time around one tomorrow afternoon."

"Perfect. Where are you located?" Jamie stands up. She retrieves a pencil and notepad from the kitchen. Rabbi Silverman gives her the address—a synagogue not far from D.C. "Thanks, I look forward to the meeting."

"No problem. I hope we can find what you are searching for," Rabbi Silverman replies sincerely.

"Thank you. I'll see you tomorrow." Jamie hangs up the phone. She is standing at the kitchen counter with the paper in front of her.

"Hey, Seth, do you know what a kollel is?" Jamie calls as she returns to the living room.

"Nope, never heard of it," Seth tells her with a shrug. "Why? What is it?"

"No idea. I'm just going to meet with one tomorrow," Jamie informs him, sitting on the couch again. This time she puts a cautious distance between them.

"Well, I better be going," Seth announces, noticing her distance.

"You've got some work to do tonight?" A part of her does not want him to leave.

"We've been overwhelmed lately, so I'm trying to do some damage control," Seth expounds with a look of distaste. "The worst part is that I have to check up on Shap; he was behind again on some reports. I'm worried about him. I can't let him slack off just because we are friends. It's just a hard dynamic."

"I meant to call him, but I haven't had the time. Tell him I said to shape up! Not really, though." She pauses and looks at

Seth wistfully. "Thanks again for dinner, and for your help. I really appreciate it."

Seth puts on his jacket and turns to her with a smile. "Anytime."

Before he leaves, Jamie kisses Seth on the check. His smile expands, taking over his face. "See you later," Jamie titters nervously.

"Count on it," Seth assures her, beaming.

He walks down the hallway and disappears down the steps. Jamie watches for a moment, her heart beating faster. She is confused and excited at the same time. Jamie begins to wonder if Seth is starting to mean more to her than just a friend.

Chapter 29

My cousin Edit Engelmann was still living in Prague when World War II broke out. She had decided to work for her father in their glatt kosher restaurant, located at 1 Maiselova Street in Prague. It was the only glatt kosher restaurant in Prague. I think back how her father's name was Adolph. Can you imagine that name today, Adolph? Amram was his Hebrew name. Her father originally moved to Prague to learn Torah in a Yeshiva, an advanced school for Torah studies. Eventually, Edit's father was told by her grandfather that he could not keep learning forever. It was then that the restaurant in Prague was born.

Since Prague was part of Czechoslovakia and did not belong to Hungary, the Jews there were transported off to concentration camps in 1942. At the time, I had little knowledge of my cousin's whereabouts. We worried for their family and prayed for their safety. It wouldn't be until later that I learned her fate was none other than Auschwitz.

Our own fates hung in the balance as well. Many of the Jews were exiled to the Slovakian border or later, as we learned, to the Garany concentration camp. Those of us who were allowed to stay did not know what the future would hold for war-torn Europe. But life went on.

Many of the men from our town were conscripted into the Hungarian labor force. This was to be both a blessing and a curse. You see, the Hungarian Forced Labor Corps were brutal. Prisoners lived in inhumane conditions, with limited food, and endured terrible winters building railroads, supervised by sadistic Capos, beaten and abused. But, unlike the Nazis, there were some humanitarian Hungarians who kept the conditions from deteriorating too badly. In the end, living in this tiny slice of Europe, protected until 1944 from Nazi control and deportation to concentration camps, would save many lives. There were casualties, though. One of my uncles suffered this fate. Some who went to work for the Hungarian labor force were never seen again. Until I meet with God, I will never know the fate of my Uncle Moshe, who disappeared.

Chapter 30

The morning light streams in the windows at the NCAVC as Jamie enters the building.

She goes into her office, sits down, and checks her email. She has received three new messages from rabbis—one apologizing because he cannot help her, one saying he can meet next Thursday, and one recommending she contact Rabbi Silverman. This furthers Jamie's hopes that Rabbi Silverman will be able to shed some light on her case.

She remembers that she wants to find out what a kollel is. She does not like surprises. She pulls up Google and types in the word "kollel."

Kollel turns out to be a Hebrew term meaning "collection" or "gathering", specifically in reference to scholars. Jamie smirks. It is perfect. That is what she needs, a group of rabbis who do nothing but study the Jewish texts and hash out Jewish philosophy and theories. They should have some sort of answers to her questions about Purim and the Holocaust.

*   *   *   *   *

The Beth David Synagogue is built of white granite. A large window is decorated with the Star of David. It is, in fact, a humble sort of synagogue otherwise. Jamie enters the building feeling slightly out of place. There is an office, not far away from the entrance, where a woman greets her.

"I have an appointment with Rabbi Silverman."

"Rabbi Silverman, he is with the kollel." The woman pauses, then points. "Located around the back of the building."

Jamie thanks her, then leaves through the doors she just entered. Out the front door of the synagogue, Jamie turns and finds a side path, which she follows to the back of the building. A brass plaque on the brick next to a door reads, "The Francis and David Katz Kollel Learning Center." Jamie opens the door and finds herself in an anteroom with access to coat closets and bathrooms. The rest of the chamber opens up to a single large room with wall-to-wall books. In the middle of the large library room are several tables and chairs.

Jamie walks slowly forward, trying not to attract attention. Four of the tables in the middle are occupied, each with two rabbis each sitting opposite of each other. Jamie notices that several large volumes are lie between them on the table. All of the rabbis are dressed the same, dark pants and long-sleeved, white dress shirt.

As Jamie draws closer to entering the book room, one of the rabbis stands up suddenly. The man starts yelling at the rabbi sitting opposite him. Jamie jumps back a couple of steps, startled by the outburst. She notices that the other rabbis in the room do not flinch. They do not even seem to notice. Curious about the show of temper, Jamie watches cautiously from her vantage point, still unseen by the rabbis.

"That's not what Tosafos is saying at all! He disagrees with the Ri!" the standing rabbi shouts with vehemence.
The sitting rabbi shakes his head in clear disagreement. "Let's read it again, and the Rashi."
But the Ri agrees with Rashi!"
The sitting rabbi states calmly, "I realize that, but the Rif argues with Rashi, and so does the Ritva. Let's look at the Ritva."

"Fine," the standing rabbi mumbles, regaining his seat and, apparently, his composure. He starts flipping to the back of the large volume in front of him and says, "Okay, here it is...."

At this point, one of the other rabbis spots Jamie. He puts on his jacket and large-brimmed black fedora and comes into the antechamber to greet her.

"Jamie?"

"Yes," Jamie answers. "Rabbi Silverman, I presume?"

"Come on in," the rabbi invites, motioning her into the large room. He is of medium height, probably in his mid-twenties, Jamie suspects. His carefully-trimmed beard makes it difficult to pinpoint his age. The rabbi's hair is dark brown, matching his eyes.

"Jamie Golding," Jamie says amiably, holding out her hand to shake his.

"It's a pleasure to meet with you," Silverman replies. He quickly retrieves a book off of the table and acts like he does not see her hand. "Here, let me put this book back on the shelf. We are just finishing our morning learning session." He crosses the room and returns the volume to its space on one of the bookcases.

Jamie follows behind him and admits, "I'm so sorry for being a little early, but I wasn't exactly sure how to get here, or how bad traffic would be."

"Understandable. It's not a problem. I'm happy to help," Silverman assures her.

"What was he so upset about?" Jamie inquires, jerking her head toward the rabbi who stood up during the session.

Silverman explains, "Oh, he is not upset. He is just excited about his opinion. Let's go where we can talk."

"He sounded upset to me." Jamie cautiously eyes the two rabbis involved in the argument. "I thought it was going to come to blows there for a second."

"No," Rabbi Silverman answers gently. "They just disagree on what one of the commentaries means. Here, have a seat."

Rabbi Silverman takes a seat at the nearest empty table. Jamie looks at him doubtfully.

"Could we go somewhere a little more private?" Jamie requests, surveying the room.

"Sorry, this is as private as it gets. It's a modesty thing. We don't seclude ourselves with women, other than our wives," Silverman tells her with a smile.

Oh. Right.

Seeing her hesitation, Silverman assures her, "No one will hear us."

Jamie pauses as she considers presenting her badge, but she decides against it and instead takes another moment to observe her surroundings. She hears a mixture of Hebrew, English, and Aramaic, being bantered back and forth. The intensity of the rabbis in their own studies and discussions reaffirms the rabbis claim: no one is going to be listening to their conversation.

"So, are you married?" Rabbi Silverman opens politely.

"No, why do you ask?"

"Oh, if you were, I was going to ask if your husband was also interested in things Jewish, and, if not, I might know someone…you just never know," he says, a twinkle in his eye.

"Right, okay," Jamie concedes, sitting in a chair across from Rabbi Silverman. "So you're married, then?"

"Yes, and we have four kids, and one on the way, bli ayin hora," Silverman declares.

"Congratulations," Jamie wishes him with a smile, looking more closely at his face, searching for signs of age. *Five kids? He looks twenty-five!*

"Thanks. We are excited too," Rabbi Silverman agrees, also smiling. "But now we should talk about the reason for your visit. What can I do for you?"

"I am Jewish, but I'm not very religious. I am also a Special Agent for the FBI. I'm working on a case for which I cannot disclose many details, but I need to know as much as possible about the book of Esther, about Purim, and about a possible connection to the Holocaust."

"I see. This is not a question I get every day. Well, do you know anything about either one?" Rabbi Silverman responds, looking right at Jamie.

"I've read the book of Esther recently, and I know the basics of the Holocaust from history classes," Jamie admits with a shrug. "And I've seen *Schindler's List*."

"A friend of mine's grandfather was actually on Schindler's list! And I don't mean the movie—the actual list." Rabbi Silverman's enthusiasm is endearing. Jamie decides she can trust this man.

Rabbi Silverman thinks to himself for a moment, choosing his words carefully. Finally he answers, "In a nutshell, the Purim story and the Holocaust are the same story. Same history, same enemy, and same plot. Very different outcome on the surface, but underneath they are, essentially, the same. You could spend years researching either one."

"I don't have years," Jamie hurries to let him know, "I may not even have weeks...."

"We should get started then. Tell me where you want to begin."

"When I sent out the emails, I copied a few synagogues, and almost immediately I received a response from a rabbi stating that the connection is all science fiction. I didn't even know there was a connection. I had just wanted to learn about each one separately. But it would seem that a connection would be much more illuminating in terms of my work. So..." Jamie drops her briefing-room style and lets some of her curiosity show through as she asks, "Is it true? Are there hidden codes about the Holocaust in the book of Esther? How do these things go together?"

"Like I said before, they are the same story, and, yes, there are fascinating codes in the Megilla. That's what we call the book of Esther in Hebrew. The codes point directly to the Holocaust. But, first, do you know anything about the codes in the Torah and how they work?"

"I've never heard about them until now."

"This will change the way you look at the Torah," Silverman cautions her. He pauses for a moment, contemplating Jamie's face. Then he continues, "You have to see the codes in action to comprehend the connection. Jamie, who wrote the Torah?"

"I was always told it was written by God. Although after a few years in the Bureau and after seeing some of the horrible things people do, I don't really believe in God anymore. I'm not sure if I ever really did. So I guess I believe it was written by man," Jamie tells him candidly.

"It *was* written by God, and I can *prove* it to you," Rabbi Silverman asserts boldly, locking eyes with Jamie.

"I...uh...I appreciate that, but that is not why I am here. I have to solve a crime, not brush up on the Torah," Jamie reminds him.

"Let me tell you about the codes, which is the information you're looking for. Then, after you see them, you may accept them as proof of who wrote the Torah. What I am going to tell you will sound like some recent invention—a mad new theory that there are secret codes in the Torah. But there is nothing new here. We have known about the codes for thousands of years," Silverman explains with a smile.

"Thousands? Come on," Jamie rejoins, her expression disbelieving.

"Yes, thousands," Rabbi Silverman repeats. "The Atbash code, for example, is used openly in the book of Daniel, for all to see. There are other examples as well."

The rabbi picks up a book from the end of the table with the title "Chumash" written on the front cover. "This is a Hebrew/English volume of the Torah. The codes only work if you read it in the original Hebrew. It contains the Torah or 'Five Books of Moses'," he informs her as he opens the book to the first page.

Jamie leans far over the table, trying to see better. Rabbi Silverman spins the book until Jamie can read the writing, now upside-down to him.

"Here—this is the beginning of the Torah. Let's find the first occurrence of the letter 'tav', which is the first letter of the word "Torah." It is right here, at the end of the first word - Breishee**T** - 'in the beginning'. If you count every fiftieth letter from this "tav", or the Hebrew 'T', it spells 'Torah'!"

"That's pretty cool," Jamie admits, actually impressed.

"It gets better," Silverman assures her, then continues, "If you go to the beginning of the book of Exodus and find the first 'tav', and if you count every fiftieth letter from there, it spells Torah again. And it is the same in the book of Numbers, again from the first 'tav', but this time counting backwards towards the center. And also in the book of Deuteronomy, from the first 'tav', going backwards, it spells 'Torah'. But this time it is on every forty-ninth letter instead of every fiftieth. In the book of Leviticus, you find God's holy four-letter name, the Tetragrammaton. So you have 'God' in the middle and 'Torah' spelled out in the first two books going forward towards the center, and you have 'Torah' in the last two books going backward, also pointing towards the center. The odds of this occurring randomly are astronomical."

"Why doesn't everyone know about this?" Jamie interjects, perplexed.

"It's no secret. I heard a reform rabbi say that the Torah was authored by committees over hundreds of years. I asked him about the codes, and he said he doesn't look at them. Just ignores what he doesn't want to see."

"Okay…so how does this connect to the Holocaust?"

"We're not ready for that quite yet. The Holocaust codes are pretty advanced," Silverman explains. "Another thing you have to know is gematria, or Jewish numerology. Before the Arabic system of numbers that we use today, the Jews used the alphabet as their numbers. Each of the twenty-two letters in the Hebrew alphabet is also a number. The first ten letters are one through ten, and the next nine letters are twenty through one hundred, and the last three letters are two hundred, three hundred, and four hundred."

100 = ק	10 = י	1 = א
200 = ר	20 = כ	2 = ב
300 = ש	30 = ל	3 = ג
400 = ת	40 = מ	4 = ד
	50 = נ	5 = ה
	60 = ס	6 = ו
	70 = ע	7 = ז
	80 = פ	8 = ח
	90 = צ	9 = ט

"What if you need a bigger number?" Jamie wonders aloud.

"You can string together more letters, like you would with numbers, but here you always add the total. You don't write thirteen as a one and a three, but as a ten and a three. Seven hundred and fifty six would not be seven, five, and six, but the letters for four hundred, three hundred, fifty, and six.

"Like Roman numerals?"

"Up to a point, yes."

"So couldn't you do this with any text?"

"Yes, you could, but Hebrew is a holy language. When God said "Let there be light" he didn't say it in English or Swahili, but in Hebrew. The Torah is the blueprint of creation, the DNA. An easy example: The word for father in Hebrew is 'av', made up of the first two letters of the alphabet. One plus two equals three. So 'av' has a gematria of three. Mother in Hebrew is 'aim.' Same first letter, one, plus mem, which is forty, equals forty-one. You take "father," gematria three, plus "mother," gematria forty-one; and you get forty-four, which is the gematria for "yeled", which means "child." Father plus Mother equals Child.

אב + אם = ילד

3 + 41 = 44

father + mother = child

"There are so many examples like this."

"Very interesting—father plus mother equals child—and all that. But, I really need to know something specific, about Esther and Purim."

"One of my favorites has to do with the Book of Esther. The word Esther is found in Genesis in the Cain and Abel story. There are no vowels in Hebrew, so the same letters can be pronounced more than one way. This is the only occurrence of the letters that spell Esther in the Torah. With the advent of computers the code researchers looked for the word 'megillas' near the word Esther. We call the book of Esther 'Megillas Esther.' If you skip every 12,111 letters from the letter mem (M) right before this word it spells 'megillas.'

"That's a pretty random number."

"It happens to be the exact number of letters in the book of Esther! So you have the only occurrence of the letters that spell Esther and then encoded right next to it is the word 'the scroll of', with a skip of the number of letters in the book. Now did some committee of authors put this in the Bible hundreds of years before Esther was even written? In the Torah, there are countless examples that will make the hair on the back of your neck stand up."

"I'll have to admit that is very cool. Before I explain any further about my case, I need to evoke the clergy confidentiality privilege and be assured that what I tell you will stay between us," Jamie requests solemnly.

"Not a problem," Rabbi Silverman tells her.

"The core of my problem is that I need to know why the perp is leaving a cryptic note with a name of one of Haman's sons on it at the scene of each crime," Jamie says. She leans on the table with her elbows with her hands hiding either side of her mouth.

"You said 'each crime'? There have been more than one?"

"It's a serial," Jamie admits, hoping she is not letting too much information leak out.

"Cereal? Like Wheaties?"

"I mean a serial killer. He is killing former Nazis and leaving notes behind, each with the name of one of the ten sons of Haman written on them. There have already been six murders. Each body had a note, and each note had a name—from Esther chapter nine, in order," Jamie confesses. She keeps her voice hushed, just loud enough for her words to make it to the Rabbi's ears.

"You don't think the killer is Jewish, God forbid?" Rabbi Silverman whispers fervently back, his eyebrows raised in a mixture of shock and disdain.

"We don't know. The notes also have initials on them, 'J.V.R.', 'W.K.', 'E.K.',"

"Wait, don't tell me the next one, give me a second. I'll be right back," Rabbi Silverman interrupts. He walks over to a small office and starts typing on a computer. A few minutes later, he comes back with a piece of paper he printed off the Internet. "A.R.?" Silverman asks.

"Oh my—," Jamie catches herself, then continues, "how did you know that?!"

"And then 'H.F.', 'W.F.', 'F.S.'?"

"What's going on? What are the initials?" Jamie demands, standing up from her chair.

"I can't believe this," Silverman mumbles, slowly sitting back down. He looks at the paper before him thoughtfully. Looking back up at Jamie with worry he says, "This is deep."

"Can't believe what? What are the initials?

Chapter 31

Eagerly Simon runs along the street to his home. The elementary school he attends is only a few blocks away, and his mother lets him walk. Today he is excited. His feet rhythmically smack the pavement as he sprints. Simon cannot get home fast enough to see his father. After six weeks of being abroad, Dad will finally be home today.

The excitement is almost too much to bear. Simon has so much to show his father. While his father was gone, Simon made him several pictures, and he was proud of his work from school. He had received the highest marks in the whole third-grade class for a shoebox diorama that he had constructed, and he wanted to show his father the chemistry lab set that his mother had bought him last month for his birthday.

As he rounds the corner, Simon's excitement intensifies at seeing his father's car in the driveway. This time he did not come home and immediately drive off to work or somewhere else. So many other times, Simon had run home, only to be disappointed to hear that his father decided to stay a few extra days.

He is only two houses from his own. The grass of the fading lawns is highlighted with light yellow streaks. The wind blows through the neighborhood trees, and Simon runs through a shower of yellow leaves. He skips the long route to his house and instead runs through the grumpy old man's bushes. Simon is usually on the lookout for the mean old man, but today he could not care less.

Imagining himself to be as fast as a lightning bolt, Simon races through his yard, up the porch steps, and into his home. Breathing heavily, he leaves the front door open and drops his backpack right behind him. Looking to his right, Simon sees his father's suitcases plopped down by the side of the entryway.

His mother stands on the stairs, furiously glaring at Simon's father, who stands on the other side of the banister. Simon pauses, feeling the tension in the air. Although his father glances over at Simon, his mother seems oblivious to his arrival. Simon knows he has just walked into something very bad.

"You care more about the dead than you do about the living!" Simon's mother yells, fire blazing in her eyes.

"That's not true, and you know it," Simon's father counters, his voice low and solemn. "But I'm not going to allow these murderers to sleep peacefully while my parents have nightmares."

"You're running this family into the ground! When are you going to see how much this really costs us? It's a lot more than just the money!"

"I already said I'm sorry that I missed our anniversary, but I brought you a present, and we can celebrate tonight," his father tells her calmly.

"Oh, a little knick knack from Europe is supposed to appease me? That is supposed to comfort me for all those nights I spent worrying because you were too busy to call? Or make up for me taking care of Simon all alone, or keeping your silly dry cleaning business running, so you have the money to track these so-called murderers!"

Simon's father looks at Simon. "Let's talk about this later, honey."

"It's never a good time to talk about it!" His mother storms off up the stairs.

"Rachel, please, Simon's...." Simon's father is standing at the foot of the stairs now, looking up as Simon's mother stalks away.

"Don't bring my son into this!" Her voice echoes from the hallway, still thick with fury.

Simon's father gently slumps forward. Slowly turning around, he sees Simon.

"Hey buddy, how are you doing?" For Simon, his father's cheerful voice and huge smile dissipate the tension in the room.

Simon runs to hug his father. "Great, Dad!"

His father gives him a big bear hug. Simon allows himself to relax into his father's arms.

Pulling away, his father asks, "What have you been up to lately?"

"Dad, I got highest marks in the whole grade for my diorama!"

"Really! Let's see this amazing diorama."

"Come on, Dad!" Simon shouts excitedly, rushing up the stairs to his own room.

Throwing the door open, Simon runs over to his dresser where the diorama sits. He proudly picks it up and hands it to his father as he comes in the doorway. His father examines it, oohing and ahhing at Simon's hard work.

"This is amazing kiddo! I'm proud of you." He carefully looks the whole diorama over.

"Check this out, Dad!" Simon grins as he points to the chemistry set he got for his birthday.

"Wow! Mom picked it out well. I told her to get you a nice one, but this is better than I imagined."

"Yeah, Dad! It's amazing. Thank you so much. And here," Simon continues, shoving a piece of paper in his father's hand. "It's my painting of you and me playing ball in the front yard."

"That's great, buddy." His father gives him a genuine smile. "Let's put it up on my wall in the den."

They both head downstairs to his father's den. With a sewing pin, Simon's father adds his picture to the space right above his roll-top desk. His dad stands back to admire the view, and Simon copies his action, putting his own hands on his hips.

"Looks perfect," Simon's father proclaims.

Simon smiles at his Dad.

"So, do you want to help me find some Nazis?"

"YEAH!" Simon agrees, jumping up and down with delight.

His father goes over to the desk and picks up two or three large books that sit on the ground beside it. He grabs the chair by the desk and offers it to Simon, who eagerly jumps at the opportunity to sit in his father's chair. Laying out the books in front of Simon, his father says, "Alright we are looking for the word Kleiss. K-L-E-I-S-S. You think you can help me with that?"

"Sure, Dad!" Simon responds, eagerly scanning the names in the back of the book.

"I'll be right back; I have to get my work from the front door," Simon's father tells him, walking out of the den.

Simon continues down the list of names. He is confused when he discovers that there are rows and rows of Kleisses. Simon turns the book to look at the name. He cannot read the title. Although he knows the letters, the words do not spell anything that Simon is used to reading. As he goes back to the list, his father returns to the room.

"Happy birthday, Simon!"

Startled, Simon turns to see his father standing in the doorway, a large grocery bag in his hands.

"I know how much you love chocolate, so I brought the best chocolate home with me!" Simon's father explains, holding the bag out to his son.

Simon races from his chair to look inside the bag. There are dozens of wrapped chocolate eggs in the bag, along with long chocolate bars, and plenty of gummy candy. Simon eagerly unwraps one of the eggs and is about to bite it, when his father begins to protest.

"Careful, Simon, these are special chocolate eggs. They are Kinder eggs, and each one has a surprise in the middle."

"No way!" Simon shouts with disbelief, then quickly takes a bite of the egg. It cracks open, and he pulls it from his mouth to see pieces of a car and some stickers.

"You can build your own toy and decorate it. Pretty neat, huh?"

"Thanks, Dad!" He finishes off the chocolate and begins snapping together the car.

"You're welcome. Now, how was it going with the list? Did you find Kleiss?"

"Oh yeah! Come see," Simon announces, leading his father to the desk. "See? Look, there are pages of them!"

"That's wonderful, Simon! Can you find a Stefan Kleiss? S-T-E-F-A-N."

"Sure!"

His father picks up some files and begins to open them. He leaves the den and returns with his briefcase. Opening it, Simon's father pulls out the papers and starts sorting them into the separate files.

"Dad?" Simon asks.

"Mmm?"

"I can't read the name of this book. I recognize the letters, but I don't understand the word."

Without even looking up from his filing, Simons father explains, "That's because it is a German census book. And Germans speak another language, even though they use the same alphabet."

"Oh." Simon nods, although he is still confused. "What is a census book?"

"The government likes to keep track of how many citizens it has," his father responds, looking up from his filing.

"Why are we looking for this Stefan Kleiss?"

His father's tone becomes more serious. "He is a very bad man, Simon. During the war he did horrible things to people. To escape punishment, he went into hiding. I found him, but he is using a different name. I am trying to gather proof that he is, in fact, the same Stefan Kleiss, the bad guy."

"Are you like Dick Tracy, Dad?"

Simon's father's mouth twitches with amusement. "In a way, yes. No other detective will go after these bad guys, even though they killed many good guys."

"So does that make me your sidekick? And we are going to fight crime together?" Simon asks excitedly.

"That's right, we are going to get the bad guys in the end, just like Dick Tracy," his father answers, once again smiling at his son.

"I'm going to help you find Stefan Kleiss, and we will catch the bad guys!"

Simon's father beams with pride as he returns to his own work.

*   *   *   *

Simon sits in his usual seat at the Starbucks. His coffee in hand, Simon stares at the laptop before him. He is still thinking about his dad. As he daydreams, he remembers back to when he was sixteen....

Simon unlocks the front door to his home. It's already dark outside, but there are no welcoming lights to greet him. The family car is in the driveway, but Simon doubts his father is actually home. In the last year, Simon has seen his father once a month or so, and has become accustomed to being by himself. Although Simon is only a junior in high school, he has learned to take care of the bills, manage the house, and keep an eye on his father's dry cleaning stores while Dad is out of town. Ever since the divorce, he has been splitting his time between his parents. He goes by his father's house three times a week when he is out of town, to get the mail and collect the circulars that are left on the driveway.

Walking inside the front door, Simon sets his backpack on the ground right in the entryway. There is a small light emanating from the den in the back of the house. Simon's hopes begin to rise. His father is home! He walks down the hallway, past the stairs, and past the kitchen. There, to his right, is the den. Simon's father is hunched over at the desk with a small piano light shining on him.

The den is covered with papers, folders, and newspaper clippings. The walls have several pictures of young men in Nazi uniforms. From each picture is a string that connects it to official documents and pictures of other people and their testimonies. The room looks like it belongs in an FBI office, not the private office of the owner of dry cleaning stores. There are stacks of newspapers on the floor in different languages. The ones in German Simon can mostly read, thanks to three years of high school German.

In one corner of the den, there are two, tall file cabinets, stuffed so full with paper that most of the drawers do not even close properly. Once, the den had been furnished with chairs and side tables, but now it contains only mountains of stacked papers, pictures, newspapers, and official documents. Simon carefully picks his way through the stacks, making sure he does not tip over one of the towers of information.

"Dad? How was your trip?" Simon inquires, pulling on the bottom of his t-shirt.

There is no immediate answer. Simon is unsure whether this is a good sign or a bad sign.

Then he hears a sigh.

"Did you find the government documents on Edward Bayer?" Simon asks, trying to change the subject.

"I have to go to Austria next week to ensure that they provide me with the documents on Eduard Baier. The last letter I wrote them was a month ago, and they still haven't gotten back to me. I have to be in their face to get the information I need," his father snarls bitterly. "Did you send off my letters?"

"Yes. Like you said, I sent them off in the mail every day."

"You would think, after fifteen years of pestering, they would actually look at the evidence I have against these bastards!" his father bellows, slamming his fist on the desk.

The force of his blow knocks a picture down from the top shelf of the desk. The noise of breaking glass fills the room as the frame hits the dark wood. Another sigh escapes his father. Simon watches as his father puts the picture back up with glass shards still stuck in the frame. Without even looking, Simon knows the photograph is of his grandfather and grandmother. His father's parents posing for their wedding picture.

"They deserve better," his father whispers. "The horror they lived through by the hands of these wicked savages, who slaughtered and tortured people they never met, but hated all the same."

Simon stands silently, watching his father's hunched shoulders, as his father stares into the past through the picture of his parents. The body in the chair suddenly seems older to Simon, weak and tired, as his father shakes slightly in the chair.

"She sorted through clothes, thousands of clothes, small and large. Each piece belonged to someone who had a family, someone who was a son or daughter, a wife or husband, a father or mother. The worst was the children's clothing. Mother could hardly hold back the tears as she went through the piles of children's clothes. Little pink jackets, little mittens, small spectacles, and the shoes. The mountains of shoes. And even baby clothing and baby blankets. Could you even imagine, Simon, how that would feel?"

Simon says nothing, and his father continues.

"At first, she could hardly look at each piece of clothing, as she knew it belonged to a precious life that had been maliciously taken. Yet, with time, she became a robot without feeling, doing her job to survive, and ignoring the rest. Mother did what she had to in order to make it out alive," Simon's father whispers to the picture.

"Those memories haunt her even today…You know, she can't forget any of the faces of the guards and capos, the ruthless creatures who burned a number into her like she was cattle? As a boy, I remember her screaming out in the night sometimes. Her cries were blood curdling. Screaming for her mother and her grandparents, all of whom were gassed minutes after they arrived at the concentration camp. Her family eradicated as casually as one kills a simple mosquito.

"The most precious things of your world destroyed in a heartbeat, until you are completely alone in the world, all because you have different religious beliefs, all because of these maniacal butchers. They laugh, even now, Simon, they laugh at me. Each one happily escaping consequences of killing, not just one person, but hundreds or thousands. And now they live among us, free to enjoy lives because they stole their lives from others. The Justice Department claims over ten thousand Nazis 'with blood on their hands' came to the United States after the war. Ten thousand."

Simon nods. He has heard this at least a hundred times, almost verbatim.

"How can they shake hands with their neighbors covered in the blood of thousands of innocent people? They laugh, that's how. They mock us. Coming to America to take over here and reestablish their base. If we let them get away with this, what are we telling them?"

Simon says nothing, but stands still. He is frozen, lost in his father's vision.

"Simon, we are telling them that it's okay to kill Jews. It's okay to murder innocent people. To butcher and mutilate anyone who thinks differently. We are telling them we are okay coexisting with evil. There are consequences to mass murder. And that's what I am here for. To make filthy beasts like Stefan Kleiss and Edward Bayer suffer, instead of basking in undeserved joys. We are here, Simon, to make sure they get the fate they deserve. We have not forgotten what they have done. We will not let them escape punishment for their murders, for their crimes. We will not let them slip through the fingers of Justice."

Simon's father turns around in the swivel chair to face his son. The scarce light casts shadows upon his father's face. Through the darkness, Simon can see the burning in his father's eyes. But there would be no trip to Austria the next week. Or any other week for that matter.

Simon is awakened at 3:30 in the morning by the sound of sirens on his normally quiet street. Police and ambulance are stopping right in front of his house. He quickly throws on a robe and goes downstairs to open the door. The 9-1-1 call had come from his own house. He leads the paramedics to his father's bedroom, where he finds his father lying on the floor next to his bed, the telephone in his hand. His face is so pale that Simon can hardly recognize him. He had gotten up to go to the bathroom and had had a massive heart attack. Luckily, he was able to grab the phone on the nightstand and make a gasping emergency call.

The next day, Simon does not see that same flame in his father's eyes as he stands next to his hospital bed. Now Simon just sees fear and pain. He will spend the next nine days in the Coronary Care Unit before his heart, too badly damaged for any intervention, finally gives out. As the minutes tick by, each one seems to echo in Simon's ears, while his father draws closer to the edge of death.

"Your grandmother. She will put your name on her accounts after I die. Once you are eighteen, you can use the money to finish what I started," his father's hoarse voice explains, breaking the silence.

Simon cannot say anything in return but swallows the lump in his throat. He can only nod his head in understanding.

"Promise me that you will finish the work. That you will see each and every one of these cowardly murderers get the punishment they deserve. Promise me you will finish my life's work. In honor of your grandmother, your grandfather, and their families who didn't survive. Promise me."

"I promise," Simon vows. His notices his own fists are clenched, and a tear slides down his cheek.

His father sighs in relief. His body, pale and drained, seems to melt into the hospital bed, as though a burden is suddenly lifted off his shoulders. Yet there is hardly a pause before Simon's father continues, "Write again to the Department of Justice, to every head and lackey if necessary."

"Yes, Dad," Simon promises. More tears are running down his cheeks.

"I'm proud of you, son." These are the last words his father ever speaks to Simon. The funeral is held the next day.

By the time Simon turned eighteen, his father's estate was settled. Simon was the sole beneficiary. The house and dry cleaning stores were sold. With all of his father's traveling, the stores were not nearly as profitable as they had been in their prime. The lawyer advised selling them while they were still "in the black." The money was put away for Simon, plus $100,000 from Dad's life insurance policy. By college, he had all of the money he would need for quite some time. There were some splurges during Spring Breaks, but otherwise, he was very meticulous in managing his money. Even after he finished graduate school, he had plenty left over. His father had been an only child. He was an only child. He thus became the sole heir to his grandparents' estate, which was worth close to eight million dollars and climbing every year, as his grandfather had amassed his fortune in real estate. Three years ago, Simon sold a parcel of land that had had a fledgling used car dealership to someone who put up a McDonalds. He netted over two hundred thousand dollars. The money would be used to cover his expenses. There is no cheap way to do something, if you want to do it right.

*   *   *   *   *

As Simon returns to the task at hand, he reviews his data on his next victim and the family. This case will be slightly harder than his last one. He takes another sip of coffee and looks at all of the facts before him. August 8 will not be here soon enough. Can he wait that long?

Watching the cars drive by out in front of the store, Simon starts to contemplate the idea to hurry up and get it over with. Maybe it is because he knows these evil men are not long for this world anyway. It would be heinous for them to die before they receive justice. He hopes he has given the FBI enough information to figure out when he will strike next. This is a key to his plan. Could it be that the FBI closing in on him is causing him to sweat a little about finishing the job? No, there is nothing worrisome about the FBI being on his trail. He has planned for this. He is going to play them like a violin.

There is something else that is pushing him to finish. Maybe it is that now-familiar knot in his stomach that makes him to want to hurry. Simon can ignore his uneasiness, though. Besides, he is truly almost done. So close. That thought seems to appease his stomach. "I must get back to work and stick with the plan," Simon thinks determinedly.

He looks back at his facts, checking them over. The next victim's wife is very ill. They live in a small condo, and she has visiting nursing twenty-four hours a day. It might cause some complications, but it should not be a problem for Simon if everything is done correctly. There can be no collateral damage. The wife and visiting nurse are innocent and do not deserve to die.

Drinking the last of the coffee in his cup, Simon starts to feel tired, despite the extra caffeine. Maybe not tired, but irritated. Something is still nagging at him. Simon's fear is that he must have forgotten something important. Thinking back over all of his hard work, Simon is sure he did things perfectly. He has committed the perfect crimes. It is not the crimes that bother him, but the criminals.

Standing, Simon closes his laptop and gets ready to leave. He decides that ignoring the uneasy feeling will have to do for the moment. There are more important things he has to do, and he cannot lose focus. He packs away his laptop and walks out of the Starbucks, wanting to just leave behind the knot in his stomach.

Chapter 32

Rabbi Silverman stares straight ahead, his thoughts blocking out Jamie's voice. A numbing sensation fills his body as he fixates on his discovery. A mixture of unbelief and horror fills his mind. He sits at the table, staring into and beyond his printout, contemplating the unimaginable. That is, until he is jolted out of his thoughts by Jamie's voice, which has become increasingly forceful…and loud.

"What are the initials? How did you guess the next one was A.R.?" Jamie trumpets. She is beginning to draw attention.

"It wasn't a guess," Rabbi Silverman replies, still stunned. He hesitates a moment, then asks softly, afraid of the answer, "Was I correct? *Was* the next one A.R.?"

"Yes." Jamie has also seen that others are curious, and she reins in her emotions. "What is going on? May I see that?" Jamie asks, reaching for the paper. She senses the ominous change of mood in Rabbi Silverman.

He hands the paper slowly over to her, looking as if he is going to be sick. She surveys it quizzically. At the top of the page, it reads, "The List of Nazis Hanged After the Nuremberg Trial in 1946." Jamie glances back at the rabbi, still not making the connection. Returning to the paper, Jamie starts to read the names on the list. There are ten of them in total. Joachim von Ribbentrop, Wilhelm Keitel, Ernst Kaltenbrunner, Alfred

Rosenberg…Jamie suddenly stops. She checks the initials. Sure enough, they match. J.V.R., W.K., E.K., A.R.…

"You did it!" Jamie exclaims, "you solved the initials! But what does it mean? Why would he have a name of a son of Haman with the initials of someone hanged at Nuremberg?"

She puts the paper down on the table and looks to Rabbi Silverman. He is unmoved from when he handed her the paper. His eyes stare blankly into the distance. It is as if his mind is still processing the information. *No, he's uncertain whether I can handle the information.*

"It's complicated, but the code in Esther points directly to the Nuremberg Trials. I'll do my best to make it make sense, Ms. Golding, but it is a lot to take in. I will have to go into a lot of detail. Are you ready for this?"

"That's why I'm here," Jamie assures him with an equally determined and serious stare.

"Okay, here goes. Isaac had two sons, Jacob and Esav, 'Esau' in English. Esau had a grandson named Amalek. The Nation of Amalek turns out to be the archenemy of the Jews. His nation attacked the children of Israel after they left Egypt, and, because of this, even God declared that nation to be Enemy Number One." He takes a deep breath, preparing. "Fast-forward several hundred years, and King Saul is commanded by God to wipe out Amalek once and for all. Saul attacks, but he fails to kill the King of Amalek, Agag. For this, Saul loses the kingship, and it transfers to David. What you need to remember is that the King of Amalek at that time was *Agag*. Now, fast-forward again another few centuries, and we meet Haman, the villain of the book of Esther, which you have already seen."

Rabbi Silverman flips to the back of the volume in front of him, to the book of Esther. He again turns the book so that it is right-side up for Jamie and pushes it over in front of her.

"He is introduced in chapter three as Haman, the son of Hamedasa, the *Agagite*. So now we know that Haman is a direct descendant of Agag, King of Amalek, the mortal enemy of the Jews. Amalek is a different type of enemy. He is not one that wants you to become like him, to become a subject of his kingdom. He wants to totally wipe you out. That's what Agag wanted, and that's what Haman wanted, and that's what the Nazis wanted. Men, women, children—it didn't matter."

"Okay, fine, so Haman was from Amalek, and he felt the same way as the Nazis. Couldn't that just be a coincidence?" Jamie interrupts with an unconvinced shrug.

"Well, wait. Now, if we can also show that Nazi Germany was also descended from Amalek, then we have a more direct connection. Give me a few moments; I need to print something else to show you."

Rabbi Silverman returns to the little office and begins to work on one of the computers. Jamie watches him leave, taking note of his solid black suit. She thinks it is strange that she does not remember seeing anyone wearing those clothes when she went to Hebrew school. Of course, she has forgotten plenty of things about those days. When a few minutes pass by and Rabbi Silverman does not return, Jamie takes out her phone.

Finally, Rabbi Silverman comes back with some newly-printed sheets and a large volume in Hebrew. Jamie puts her phone away.

"Sorry about that. Some of what I need is from the encyclopedia and not found in the study hall. This is tractate Megilla from the Talmud that deals with none other than the book of Esther and with Purim," Rabbi Silverman explains, putting the book on the table.

"In it, Germany is mentioned by name. Of course, the Talmud was completed in the year 500, a long time before Germany came into existence," Rabbi Silverman continues. He opens the book and flips through the pages. "Now then, here we are, page 6b, yep, and I quote:

Rav Yitzhak said, "What is meant by the verse in Psalms?: 'God, do not grant the desires of the evil man, and do not let his plot prosper, lest he raise himself above.'

Jacob our forefather foresaw what his son Esau would do to Israel, and he prayed these words to God: 'Do not grant the desires of the evil man' – he was referring to Esau, and 'do not let his plot prosper' - he was referring to Germamia of Edom, for should they go forth, they will destroy the entire world."

He pauses, watching Jamie to make sure he is not confusing her with all of the information. She nods in the appropriate spots and looks him straight in the eye as he teaches her.

Satisfied, Rabbi Silverman continues, "Now Rashi, who was the foremost commentator on the Talmud and lived in the 11th century, says 'Germamia' refers to the name of a monarchy from the Kingdom of Esau.' In modern Hebrew, Germany is Germania.

"But still, how do we know that what they were talking about refers to our current Germany? The Talmud continues, 'Rebbe Chama bar Chanina said: There are 300 crowned princes in Germamia of Edom...

So, I just printed this quote from the Encyclopedia: 'The political disintegration of Germany had far-reaching economic effects; 300 princedoms and free cities guarded their economic autonomy fiercely.' And here is a quote from The Rise and Fall of the Third Reich: 'By the end of the Middle Ages, which had seen Britain and France emerge as unified nations, Germany remained a crazy patchwork of some 300 individual states.'

"So here we have Haman coming from Esau and Amalek, and the Talmud foresees the nation of Germany also coming from them.

"That being said, let's get back to the book of Esther. This book is unique in that it does not mention the name of God even once. This is very unusual for a book of the Bible. Our rabbis learn a profound lesson from this. It is so clear once you read the entire story that the whole thing was orchestrated by God and that what seemed like a random set of coincidences are in fact not coincidences at all. Likewise, so it is today, when we may not see God in a revealed way, but we know that he runs the show. Okay, so it is interesting that, throughout the Megilla, sometimes you see Achasverosh, the King, referred to as 'King Achasverosh', and sometimes he is only referred to as 'the King'. Our rabbis taught us that, if you want to read the Megilla on a deeper level and see the hidden hand of God, then every time it says 'King Achasverosh' read it as referring to 'Achasverosh', the King; and when it just says 'the King', read it as the 'King of Kings', God."

"One instance where this makes a big difference is in a conversation between Queen Esther and 'the King' after the ten sons of Haman have been killed. The Jews were given permission to defend themselves against the eradicating force. The Megilla says: 'The King said to Queen Esther, 'In Shushan the capital the Jews have killed and destroyed 500 men, including the ten sons of Haman. What have they done in the rest of the King's provinces? What is your petition now, it will be given to you, what is your request and it will be done? Esther said: If it pleases the King, allow the Jews of Shushan to do tomorrow as they did today, and let the ten sons of Haman be hanged on the gallows. The King ordered that this be done—."

"Why hang them? Aren't they are already dead?" Jamie cuts across him with her question.

"Exactly. Now in this whole paragraph it doesn't mention Achashverosh, but only 'the King.' So in the way we mentioned a second ago. It is as if Esther was asking God that tomorrow, meaning sometime in the future, that the Jews of Shushan should do like they did back then and hang ten sons of Haman," Rabbi Silverman replies.

"Yeah, but she said the Jews of *Shushan* should do tomorrow, not Nuremburg, or Germany, or even Esau. Sounds like a stretch to me that she was referring to people a couple of thousand years into the future," Jamie retorts, folding her arms.

"I thought the same thing when I first heard this. So when I got home I did some of my own calculations. If Shushan is supposed to be Nuremberg, then they must be related somehow. Amazingly, 'b'Shushan Habira', the way it is mentioned in this sentence, and 'Nuremberg, Germany', when written in Hebrew, have the same numerical value. Exactly the same."

Jamie's face still shows skepticism.

"Okay, if that is not good enough, here is where it gets really interesting. Your question was, 'How could it be referring to a couple of thousand years into the future when Esther asks the King if the Jews of Shushan can hang the sons of Haman tomorrow?' Why would we think that there would be any connection between the Nuremberg hangings and Esther's words? If you look at any book of Esther, you will find the ten sons of Haman written in a peculiar way. The ten sons are listed in a column on the right side of the page, and the word 'and' is written in a column ten times on the left side of the page. First of all, why do we need to know their names at all? It could just say that the ten sons of Haman were killed. Why list them in such a peculiar way, with the word 'and' in between?

"No idea. I have to trust that this is not the normal way things are listed in the Bible."

"It is not. If you add the numerical value with all of the 'ands' you get a large number, something over ten thousand. Then if you write the ten hanged at Nuremberg in Hebrew, Joachim von Ribbentrop, Hans Frank, Julius Striecher, and add up the numerical value you get the same number! I've verified it myself."

"Exactly the same?"

"Exactly the same. It is only because it is written in the unusual way with all of the 'ands' that it works."

There's more. There are three letters that are written in a smaller font and one letter that is written bigger than the rest."

"What do you mean, smaller?"

"Look inside the book and I'll show you."

ואת	ואבד חמש מאות איש
ואת	← פרשנד ת א
ואת	דלפון
ואת	אספתא
ואת	פורתא
ואת	אדליא
ואת	ארידתא
ואת	← פרמ ש תא
ואת	אריסי
ואת	ארידי
עשרת	← ו י ז תא

"The three small letters and one larger letter point to the year of the Nuremberg hangings in the Jewish calendar. When we say what year it is, we say, for example, this year is 'taf shin ayin gimel'. Numerically those letters add up to 773. Now the year is 5773. We don't mention the thousands, only the hundreds. I guess if you don't know what millennium you are living in, you've got bigger problems," he adds with a small chuckle. He does not get the same from Jamie, who is concentrating on synthesizing all of the information.

"So the three small letters add up to 707. But which 707? Which millennium are we referring too? The big letter is a 'vav', which is, numerically, six."

He puts up an additional finger as he counts off each of these dates. "707, 1707, 2707, 3707, 4707, and 5707 is the 6th time we have the year 707. So the one large letter and three small letters indicate the year 5707. The year 5707 in the Jewish calendar coincided with the year 1946 in the Gregorian calendar. The Nuremberg hangings were in 1946.

"The ten at Nuremberg were all hanged on the same day, just like the ten sons of Haman. And not just on any day either, but on Hoshana Raba, in the year 5707," Rabbi Silverman concludes.

"Hoshana Raba?" Jamie inquires, surprised. "That is on my list of questions. What is it?"

"Hoshana Raba is the 7th day of the Sukkos holiday— Tabernacles in English. It is a special day on which the nations of the world are judged. The Zohar says that 'on Hoshana Raba sentences are issued from the King. Judgments are aroused and executed that day.' It is no coincidence that they were hanged on Hoshana Raba."

"There have been two murders on Hoshana Raba," Jamie tells him quickly.

"Really? I see…"

"Sounds like our guy already knows what you are telling me."

"I'm afraid so. But there is more. Here is a quote from an October 28, 1946, article in Newsweek. I also just printed it. The article gives an eyewitness account of the hangings in Nuremberg, and of how each condemned person approached the gallows and was allowed to make a statement. Here is a quote from the article: 'Only Julius Streicher went without dignity. He had to be pushed across the floor, wild-eyed and screaming: "Heil Hitler!" Mounting the steps he cried out: "And now I go to God." He stared at the witnesses facing the gallows and shouted: "Purimfest, 1946!'"

"*Purimfest*? He could have said anything he wanted, and he says, 'Purimfest, 1946'? Purim, the holiday commemorating the story in the book of Esther? Creepy, wouldn't you say?"

"Yeah, I would. Very creepy."

"So what do you think? Coincidence?"

"The Purim/Holocaust connection or the murders?" Jamie asks.

"The Purim/Holocaust connection," Rabbi Silverman confirms.

"It's not about what I think. I'm trying to figure out what the killer is thinking, and to understand the pattern."

"I see," Rabbi Silverman responds, shrugging his shoulders.

Jamie can see that Rabbi Silverman's excitement ebbs at her statement. She realizes the importance that Rabbi Silverman can play in her case. To mollify him, Jamie goes on, "No, I mean, I do see that there is a connection. I'm just focused on what is driving this guy so I can catch him. There is a murderer who *will* kill again. This is a lot to take in. I'll have time to churn it over for myself later."

"I understand."

"One thing that I am now totally convinced of is that the one responsible for these murders knows this same information, whether he is paying someone to do it for him or he is doing it himself. You have been so helpful," Jamie assures him.

"Listen, this is only the tip of the iceberg. There is more. There are so many other codes throughout the Torah."

"More connecting Purim and the Holocaust?" Jamie asks.

"Well, no, this is about all I know about the Purim/Holocaust link, but there are more fascinating examples."

"I have to focus on the Purim/Holocaust theme for right now. If you think of anything else, will you please call me? Here is my card. Anytime, 24/7."

"Sure, but for me it is 24/6, you know. The Sabbath and all," Rabbi Silverman adds with a smile, taking the card.

"Ha-ha, yeah. So 24/6 it is. Call me if you think of *anything.*" Jamie smiles back.

Rabbi Silverman walks her out to the parking lot and waits until she gets into her car, then disappears back into the Kollel Learning Center.

Jamie takes a deep breath and lets out a long sigh before starting her car. *That was way too much religion for one day.* At least she is walking away with something. Now she has to let it lead her to the killer. *Somehow.*

Chapter 33

Jamie drives back to the FBI campus and returns to her office at the NCAVC building. Before she can even enter her office, Whitehouse is on Jamie's heels.

"Agent Golding? You need to call this number right away," Whitehouse spits out and slaps a sticky note into her hand.

He's in a good mood today. Jamie she tries to hold back a smile.

"Thanks," Jamie calls after him as he runs back into the maze of cubicles. She looks at the number and name written on the sticky note. "Detective Ciborowski of Edison, New Jersey." Curious. Maybe it has something to do with the case.

Hurrying to her desk, Jamie quickly dials the number on the sticky note.

"Detective Ciborowski, what can I do for you?" The voice on the other end is smooth and deep, with a bit of that familiar Jersey accent.

"Hi, this is FBI Special Agent Golding. I'm returning your call," Jamie explains.

"Ah, I'm glad you called back. After I saw the press conference, I was sure that a case I worked on last year is the work of your serial killer," Ciborowski tells her excitedly.

"Great," Jamie manages to say before he continues, undeterred.

"Back in August 2011, an older gentleman was murdered in his home," Ciborowski informs her. "You wouldn't believe the—."

"Right, so what makes you think there is a connection?" Jamie interrupts, anxious to get to the point.

"Despite the decayed state of the body, the coroner has determined that the cause of death was strangulation.

"Decay?"

"Oh, I was trying to explain that. The guy was a bachelor, lived alone. He was quite the hoarder. Hardly came out much. It took a while before the neighbors called the police, noting that something was wrong. It was one of those NCFOs—you know, neighbor complains of a foul odor."

"Yes, I know what you are talking about, but what connects it to my particular case?" Jamie asks, marking that August does not fit the pattern.

"An old man strangled with a wire."

"Was there a note left near the body?"

"Oh, right, there was a note left near the body," Ciborowski beams through the phone.

"What was written on it?"

"In large print, it had the initials 'H.F.' On the bottom right, in a small font, it had 'adal', and 'ya' on the bottom left. On the back of the note was, 'I was here on August 8, 2012', as if he knew he wouldn't be found right away and wanted us to know when it happened."

"That's my perp. So what did the coroner determine for the time of death?"

"Well, the body was discovered on September 5th, and wait…I've got the report right here…Yep, according to the forensic entomologist, the cycle of the blowfly puts the time of death around 28 days earlier. Around the body, and especially the neck wound, were found adult flies, eggs, and half-inch maggots. Basically it means it is quite plausible that Mr. Burton was murdered on August 8th."

Jamie had learned all about the life cycle of the blowfly and how it is used to determine time of death. The fly arrives soon after death and looks for a moist area on the corpse on which to lay eggs—the eyes, the nose, open wounds, and others.

The eggs hatch to maggots within 24 hours, and you have a new cycle to follow, from larvae to pupae to the next generation of flies. What stages of blowfly you find will determine the amount of time since death. About three weeks after death, you see the second generation of adult flies emerge. From there, you can add more time, depending on whether you find their offspring to be eggs, larvae, pupae, etc.…It is a surprisingly accurate method.

"What is the name of the victim?"

"Tomas Burton, no 'h'."

"Could you fax me all of your police reports, pictures, or any other information pertaining to this Tomas Burton that you have? And any evidence or forensics found at the crime scene?"

"I already talked with your secretary, and he gave me your fax number; so we are faxing it all right now, as we speak," Ciborowski informs her. "The victim really was a total hoarder. I mean, stuff was piled to the ceiling in every room. There was literally only a small path through the junk. The place was eventually condemned."

"Perfect.…" Jamie answers, writing down some of the information Ciborowski has already given her. She stops writing as she blurts, "A hoarder like on that TV show?"

"That's right," Ciborowski confirms.

Great, Jamie thinks. All of the other crimes scenes were cleaned of any evidence. Now she might be piled with too much stuff, stuff that probably will not produce any information remotely related to the murder. She rolls her eyes, wishing that she had not cursed the lack of evidence.

"Is there any way I can visit the crime scene?"

"Nope, the place has since been demolished, and a new house has been built. But we do have plenty of crime scene photos, and I could draw you a map of the layout of the house. It's a case I will never forget," Ciborowski adds with a childish snicker.

"Right. Did anyone see anything? Neighbors or friends?"

"No friends, sadly. And, like I said, the neighbors did not hear or see anything. All they noticed were the local county papers stacking up on the driveway. After four weeks of newspapers, the neighbors decided that Mr. Burton did not go on an extended vacation. Besides that, the stench was beginning to reach people walking on the sidewalk in front of the house."

"What about his family?"

"None that we know of. The state disposed of the remains. The guy seems to have been a total recluse, with no family. He was also an immigrant," Ciborowski tells her, then adds, "And, despite being here for years, he never made friends with any of the neighbors. They…well…they tolerated him."

"What do you mean, 'tolerated him'?" Jamie inquires with an arched eyebrow.

"He wasn't exactly known for being the grandpa-next-door. More like the old codger, who would shoot you if you trespassed on his property. We interviewed a few of the children, hoping that they would have seen something while on summer vacation, but all we got were tall tales about the creepy Burton who eats children."

"We had one of those in my neighborhood as well," Jamie muses. She cannot remember how many kites, Frisbees, balls, and other toys were lost to children in the neighborhood when they fell into the old man's yard.

"Well, as he got older, the guy never kept up the outside of his home. It became such an eyesore that people in the neighborhood took turns mowing the guy's yard, just so they wouldn't have to look at it. He was the type of neighbor everyone hated and wanted off of the block, but whom they also felt sorry for."

"Well thank you, Detective Ciborowski. I will call you again if I need anything. And did Whitehouse give you my information?"

"Yes. He did."

"Call me if you discover anything new."

"Will do, but we're not really looking."

"Thanks," Jamie replies, ignoring his sarcasm. She hangs up the phone and looks at her notes. In the chronological sequence of Haman's sons, Adalia and Aridatha had been skipped. *Here is Adalia.*

There is a knock on her door.

"Here are the faxes that just came in from the Edison, New Jersey, P.D.," Whitehouse tells Jamie in his usual monotone, as he sets the papers down in front of her.

She adds Tomas Burton to her notes.

What does August 8th mean on the Jewish calendar? By now she knows better than to think it is just a random date.

Chapter 34

When the Germans arrived in March of 1944, things quickly changed for the worst. I was twenty-two. First, all Jews were required to register, and each of us had to wear the yellow Star of David on our clothing at all times. It could not simply be on a single piece of clothing only. If you wore a coat over your dress, accidentally hiding the yellow star, the punishment was either being beaten close to death or shot. So every piece of clothing I owned had the yellow Star of David prominently displayed. The badge was meant to shame us, but I chose to use it as a symbol to remember God instead.

Second, many daily freedoms and pleasures were forbidden to us by the Germans. No Jew was allowed to use public transportation, go to the movies, visit coffee houses, or be seen out at night. It made it impossible to socialize with my friends. Even Mary, my childhood friend who lived right across the street, began to avoid me and my family. The time was terrible and lonely. Watching Mary live a normal life across the street, having girlfriends, visiting the movies, and receiving suitors—all while I could hardly leave my home without persecution and fear.

Only for a month did these inconveniences last, but what would come next would make those old rules seem kind. It was Passover the day the Hungarian police came by our home and told us to pack. We were being deported to the ghetto. They instructed us to pack a bag and bring food. Our silver was taken right before our eyes. One of my brother's friends older brother was the Hungarian policeman that evicted us. He was screaming at my grandmother, asking her where we hid the money. Before she could even answer, he hit her with the butt of his rifle. My 68-year-old grandmother hit with a rifle in her own home. We packed what we could and were thrown out into the street. Little did we know that whatever valuables we brought with us would be instantly confiscated by the Nazis.

We lived in a beautiful home. What would happen to it? How long would we be gone? Three generations of my family had lived there. That building was more than a home, but a museum of love and memories.

The unknown gnawed at our hearts. So many horrifying rumors had come to our ears that we hardly knew what to believe. Were we going to leave our home country, to never return again? Would we ever come home again? What were the Nazis going to do with us? We trembled in fear of the unknown, our fates not our own, and God our only comfort.

When the Hungarians came to evict us to the ghetto in April of 1944, our neighbors came to watch and laugh at us. Even Mary and her family. Mary had just gotten engaged, and her mother loudly announced, as we were driven from our home, "Look, Mary, you won't have to live with us after you get married after all. You can have their house."

Mary smiled and laughed with the rest of the neighbors at our tribulation. She called to us telling us that we did not need our things where the Nazis were taking us. Seeing her out there, I had hoped that our bond from childhood would still be there. Surely, seeing the injustice of our situation would have softened her heart toward us. Mary, my one-time best friend, would come to save me from the Nazis in some way. I begged my friend to help us, but in return, she used profanities and called me names. That moment in time is etched in my memory forever. The hateful look upon my friend's face as she spat out the words, "Go to hell!"

My mind could hardly wrap itself around such hatred. How had a bond of friendship and love turned into a hate due to a collapsing political situation? How quickly the tides turned against us. I had done nothing to Mary to receive such a response, nor would I have given that response to anyone under any circumstances. The world had changed so much around me, and, at that moment, I came to understand that I knew nothing about evil or the nature of man.

Chapter 35

Jamie savors her opportunity to sleep in on this Saturday morning. She has nothing planned except for a long run. She keeps reminding herself that she should call Barry Shapiro and see how he is doing. If he is going through a hard time, he probably will not admit it over the phone. She decides to plot the start of her route at his house. She'll do a "pop-in." Shap is the kind of guy who loves the pop-in. At least, he used to be. She gets on Google Maps and drags the cursor to change the route, until she has made a loop that is 10.6 miles.

She arrives at Shap's house at 10:30. The lawn is well-manicured and the driveway is blown off. All of the blinds are closed.

Shap opens the door before Jamie even rings the doorbell. He is surprised to see her, and gives a quick glance over his shoulder, as if he is checking to make sure that there is nothing sitting out that he does not want her to see. He clearly hopes she did not notice, and he steps outside and closes the door. He is fresh and clean-shaven. He is dressed in pressed khaki pants and a green polo shirt. Jamie explains how she has not seen him in a while and wanted to stop by. She cocks her head towards the door, motioning that it is time for him to invite her in.

Once inside, Jamie immediately sees that the house is immaculate. Everything is intentionally placed, from the angle of the chairs, to the large art books turned a few degrees to contrast the rectangular shape of the coffee table. It looks like the residence of the most type-A personality imaginable. And it is a striking contrast to the last time she was at his house. Not that it was messy, but it at least looked lived in. This looks like he is selling and having an open house. He does not appear to be hung over and definitely does not look like he is strung-out on drugs. He looks like someone that would be getting to work fifteen minutes early every day and not like someone slacking off.

"Okay, who is she?" Jamie queries sarcastically.

"Excuse me?"

"Who is she? What girl has you cleaning your house like it's part of the Smithsonian?"

"I guess I'm going through a neat phase. About time, right?" Shap responds as he makes a slight adjustment to an already-straight picture on the wall. "Her name is Nikki."

"I knew it."

Barry Shapiro has always been an enigma to Jamie. In college, he was the biggest partier she ever knew. Her first impression of him was of a total stoner freshman, who would probably flunk out his first year. He spent hours every day skateboarding and being the most popular guy in all of fraternity row. To her dismay, he was already a grad student who had finished his Bachelor's with a 4.0. He was either genius-smart, or he had incredibly disciplined study habits when no one was watching. His behavior in grad school convinced Jamie that it was the former.

By the time Jamie started her run home, she had come to the conclusion that, if anything, Shap had become more serious, and not frivolous and lax. She did get him to retell a couple of stories from the wild and crazy days, which brought out the same-ol' Shap. Whatever was going on with him at work was none of her business.

Chapter 36

"Hey, Agent Golding?"

Jamie looks up to see Kim Hammond from Research standing at her door.

"Yes?"

"Here is all the background information we could dig up on the victims and where they were during World War II," she says, handing Jamie a huge stack of files.

"Thanks." Jamie shrugs, pulling the first file off the stack.

She sees that the file has Jules Henning's name on the tab. Jamie begins to read the file.

Jules Henning, born January 11, 1923, in Argentina...

"Strange," Jamie thinks to herself, "not really a Spanish name now, is it?" There is something more to his story. She reads further down the page. It lists the time and dates of his immigration to the United States. It also includes his marriage date, the date of birth of his daughter, and information from his job.

After browsing a few pages, Jamie finds the name Ingrid Schwab circled on Jules Henning's Argentinian visa application to the U.S. Interestingly, she is listed as a relative that lives in the U.S. Henning claims that Ingrid Schwab is his sister living in Albany, New York. Of course, it is possible to have a sister with a different last name.

Next in the file is Ingrid Schwab's immigration papers to the United States, dated 1948. She was born in Pocking, Germany, in 1922. The next set of papers shows birth records of the two children born to Ingrid's parents, Gunter and Erma Schwab. The other child is Fritz Schwab, born on January 11, 1923. The date is circled, and a sticky note next to it says, "see visa application for Jules Henning." It is the same date of birth from the application.

The next document is a copy of an International Red Cross passport for Jules Henning, again with the same birth date. He left Genoa, Italy, in March of 1946, and he arrived in Argentina. Jamie suspects that he had the Red Cross change his name, then acquired false papers in Argentina claiming he was born there. She turns to see military papers for Fritz Schwab, as part of the Einsatzgruppen. Another sticky note informs Jamie that the Einsatzgruppen was the name for the killing squads that followed a few days behind the advancing German troops and rounded up the Jews for slaughter.

The evidence indicates that this Fritz Schwab and Jules Henning are one and the same. No wonder he wanted to hide his past, Jamie realizes. With intense curiosity, she begins to go through the files of all of the victims. Each one places the victims in Europe during the Holocaust. She even finds evidence that Stefan Kleiss, a.k.a. Martin Rossi, was at Auschwitz. A few of the victims are documented as being part of the German army, but without identifying in what capacity.

To Jamie, the most shocking revelation is that many of these Nazis found passage to the United States through Red Cross passports, which were issued in Italy to so-called "stateless" refugees. Those passports were supposed to be for victims of World War II—people in need—not fleeing Nazis. How did this happen?

Jamie sighs, then tries to process the information through the lens of what Rabbi Silverman told her about the connection between Purim and the Holocaust. Jamie does not know what to make of it, but it might help her find the perp, since he clearly believes it enough to craft his murders around it. The sons of Haman were hung on Purim, and the Nuremberg Nazis were hung on Hoshana Raba. Except for two, all of the victims were either murdered on Purim or Hoshana Raba. The ten sons of Haman and the ten at Nuremberg were hanged, and these victims were strangled. It is clear that the perp knows that Hoshana Raba is a judgment day, which might point to him being of the Jewish religion. Jamie doubts that anyone else would know the significance of this holiday, since it is not well-known, even among some Jews. The only thing that does not work is the August 8 murder. He went to such lengths to have the others occur on Purim and Hoshana Raba. What made him change the pattern and choose August 8th? *He even left a note to make sure we knew he did it on August 8th.*

Jamie turns to the Internet and Googles "August 8th." The results produce no connection to anything Jewish. Instead of wasting her time, Jamie decides to ask her expert. She calls Rabbi Silverman, but it goes straight to voicemail. Leaving a message, she requests another meeting and asks about the significance of August 8th.

She calls the team together to reveal her latest findings. Before her meeting, she gathers the information and heads to a small conference room that Whitehouse has reserved for her. On the whiteboard, Jamie charts the victim's names and connects them to their previous names. By the time everyone arrives, Jamie has filled the whole board.

Fredericks is the first to arrive. He takes a seat at the conference table and stares at the whiteboard, intrigued. Jamie sits in the chair across from him, letting him have a full view of the board. Phil and Joey arrive consecutively and also concentrate on the whiteboard.

"You weren't kidding about a Nazi hunter," Fredericks finally concludes.

"Wait, so each of your victims is tied to the Holocaust in Germany?" Joey asks.

"Yes, each one of them has ties to Nazi Germany, and some were even involved with concentration camps. Each one of them escaped into hiding or to the United States and denied their past," Jamie explains, pointing out each of their different methods on the board.

"How does the killer know all of this?" Phil asks with a frown.

"It's not uncommon for people to search for them. Whether they have a personal vendetta or want justice for those horrific crimes, people will do their own research to find such criminals. Just like Simon Wiesenthal," Fredericks replies.

"Our perp actually signed in as 'Simon W.' in Illinois. I think he's a Simon Wiesenthal wannabe, but he is taking matters into his own hands, instead of using the legal system."

"Shouldn't we release this information to the press? It might help us discover the next possible victims and warn them," Phil suggests after a long, quiet pause in the conversation.

"If we do that, will the Nazis come out of hiding? I doubt it. They have been hiding for so long, they aren't just going to give up their secret because we tell them there might be a vigilante targeting them," Jamie assumes.

"Take into account that they are fugitives under the law. They might suspect we are only trying to lure them out to convict them for lying on their immigration papers," Joey muses, scratching his chin.

"I heard once that over ten-thousand Nazis immigrated to the United States under false pretenses. Not just Germans, but Nazis," Frederick tells the group.

"Surely we have files on them," Joey states inquisitively.

"I doubt it. Did any of these victims have files before you requested their information, Jamie?" Fredericks wonders, looking at Jamie.

"Rossi did, but the others didn't."

"It has been so many years since the Holocaust. Most of them are probably dead by now. But how are we supposed to find the ones that are still alive? Didn't we search for them in the sixties and seventies?" Phil questions with a single eyebrow raised. There is a pause while everyone considers the implications of their information, not just that Nazis are being targeted, but that Nazis are living among them.

Phil continues, "Either way, we should warn them that they might be in danger. Maybe they will take steps to protect themselves," he decides, looking at Fredericks. "Maybe one will see someone casing his house and give us a place to look."

"Let's get Research on it and see if they can provide us with a list of people who may have been investigated, and see what they come up with. After that, we will have to narrow down the list and devise a plan. It's possible that one of them will be cooperative and report something suspicious. In the meanwhile, we will go public with this information and see if it provides a lead," Fredericks directs, giving a meaningful look to each of the agents in turn.

Each one present nods in agreement with Fredericks.

"Anything else, Golding?"

"I did find another murder, which happened on August 8th. I'm not sure how it connects with the Jewish pattern. Yet I'm also positive that the perp will strike again on Hoshana Raba of this year, which will be September 25th," Jamie explains, pointing to the pattern on the board.

"Let's get moving. We have to make sure no one blames us for not doing enough," Frederick cautions them. "We'll go public and issue the warning. If the next victim does not seek us out for help, at least we'll have tried to warn him."

Chapter 37

Jamie rubs her forehead thoughtfully. Following the chronological sequence of the initials of those hanged at Nuremberg and of Haman's sons, there is someone missing between the previous two murders. The notes went from "H.F." – "Adalia" to "F.S." – "Parmoshta." According to the chronological sequence, there should have been "W.F." – "Aridata" between them. *We wouldn't want to skip that great humanitarian Wilhelm Frick.* The pattern is Hoshana Raba, Purim, August 8th, Hoshana Raba, Purim, and Purim again.

Following the pattern of the dates, Hoshana Raba 2012 was skipped, and it coincides with the gap in the sequence of Haman's sons and of those hanged at Nuremberg.

Now, it could be that the attack on Hoshana Raba of 2012 was aborted or unsuccessful. Maybe there was an assault of an elderly man on that day, but he survived? But, if that was the case, then the next murder would have borne the note "W.F." – "Aridata", as it is next in the sequence. Unless the killer actually thinks that the deed was done, and therefore, in his mind, the next murder did get the next initials and name in the sequence. If there was a murder on Hoshana Raba of 2012, then either the FBI was not informed about the murder, or somehow it was never reported or misreported. "I have found others," Jamie thinks.

There are close to 7,000 deaths a day in the U.S., with 31% of those, occurring to persons over the age of 85. Finding the correct dead old man will be a challenge. If Jamie narrows the search to males over eighty-five, the number is 782 on that particular Sunday in October. Jamie adds filters: born in Europe (excluding Russia, Great Britain, Spain, Portugal, Norway, Finland, Sweden, and Denmark), immigrated after 1945.

All that information should bring up some sort of match. Indeed, the search this time returns only nine results. That is a number that Jamie can actually research herself. She takes the names and begins to investigate them individually.

The first three on the list turn out to be Holocaust survivors. Jamie gladly rules them out. She is left with six. One of them has to be the missing Hoshana Raba murder. Looking up the first few names yields nothing significant. Then Jamie does a search for Edward Bayer.

Jackpot. The name brings up a bunch of Holocaust-related articles. There are pages and pages of results.

"Businessman Edward Bayer Accused of Being Auschwitz Guard."

"Man Accused As Former Auschwitz Guard, Edward Bayer, May Go to Court."

"Is Edward Bayer Really the Nazi, Eduard Baier?"

"Millionaire Edward Bayer a Nazi?"

"Disturbing Secrets of Edward Bayer's Past."

"Edward Bayer Case Dropped."

Jamie clicks on the first article and begins to read. She discovers that Edward Bayer was a successful businessman who was accused in the eighties of being a Nazi guard at Auschwitz. As Jamie continues to read article after article, she notices that the topic of Edward Bayer as a Nazi was in the news for about a year. In each article, Edward Bayer denies it completely, yet he spent a fortune in legal fees to fight the charges. Eventually, the case was dismissed because there was not enough evidence to prove that Edward Bayer was really Nazi Eduard Baier. Turns out the Justice Department did not want to risk convicting a prominent and upstanding citizen and philanthropist for a crime of which the prosecution had little public support. At least that is what one pundit claimed.

There are many other editorials as well. Many of the authors suspect that the trial was very costly, which was what caused the case to be dropped. Others pointed out that being stationed at Auschwitz was not a crime. A person cannot always choose where his country forces him to serve. A few brought up the possibility that a soldier could either serve at Auschwitz or become a prisoner there. The Nazi government did not give its people options. Editorials also hash out whether or not soldiers get to pick their detail, and the fact that many soldiers are forced to fight and kill against their personal beliefs. The question does bring with it a lot of controversy, Jamie realizes as she moves forward with her search.

Her next move is to find an obituary. "Edward Bayer obituary" yields fruitful results. Died October 7, 2012. Age 93. She discovers that the family had a private service and that he is survived by his sons, Mitchell and Stanley Bayer. Jamie scans down the article to find that Edward Bayer had died after a long battle with cancer. The word "cremated" catches Jamie's eye. Cremated? So much for being able to exhume the body.

On the whole, Edward Bayer seems to have died of natural causes. Jamie sifts through the information in her mind. Maybe he was not strangled? Or maybe no one noticed. Is that possible? There was the near miss in Harwood Heights. The funeral parlor would have seen the wounds on the neck, right? Did anyone check to see if the cause of death was suspicious? He *was* ninety-three years old. Is it possible that no one noticed? Unlikely. But he fits the profile perfectly, and he did die on Hoshana Raba of 2012.

Jamie concludes that there is only one way to find out. Edward Bayer died in Philadelphia, Pennsylvania. Smiling dryly to herself, Jamie realizes that she can drive the three-and-a-half hours to Philadelphia and question the Bayer family.

Edward Bayer made a fortune building apartment complexes in the sixties. He really raked it in when he converted the nicer complexes into condos during the eighties condo craze. Both sons now run his real estate company, still called Edward Bayer Development Corporation. *Or, at least, now his sons cash the checks.* She finds the company information and writes down the address and phone number.

Jamie gathers up her things and leaves her office, locking the door behind her. She needs to get an early start tomorrow to make it to Philly, if she wants to avoid the traffic. As she drives home, her mind wanders. Jamie realizes that she has not heard from her boyfriend in a while.

"He needs a woman who can hold his purse for him!" Jamie tells the empty road in front of her. That is exactly Chris's problem. His needs, problems—and everything else—come before her own. Jamie does not like this idea of being shelved. And that is what Chris is asking her to do with her own problems.

She enters her apartment. It is dark inside, and Jamie is relieved. Although she has not talked to Chris in a few days, Jamie had been worried he might be there anyway.

She is shocked to see arrows on her floor, leading her into the kitchen. Jamie follows the arrows right up to the fridge. There is a note on the freezer door.

Jamie,

I know you have been working hard lately. I thought you deserved a reward. It's sitting in your freezer. Enjoy!

Seth

"No you didn't," Jamie says aloud after reading the note.

She giggles excitedly as she rushes to open the freezer. Her favorite Belgian chocolate ice cream bars greet her with a wave of cold air. Just what she needs with summer on its way. She opens the box and grabs a bar, unsheathes it and throws away the wrapper. Jamie even lets out a sigh as she savors the first bite.

Jamie smiles. "I owe you big time, Seth."

Chapter 38

The beep of her cell phone brings Jamie out of a deep sleep.

Instantly, her discovery from yesterday fills her mind. Jamie grabs a yogurt and banana to eat in the car on her way to Philly. She is on the road by 6:15 in the morning.

While traveling, she keeps track of the time, trying to decide when it will be best to call Seth. After all, she does have to thank him for the ice cream bars. Once the clock shows 8:00 A.M., Jamie makes the call.

"Hey, Jamie, how are you?"

"I got your present last night."

"Oh, good. I wasn't sure if you would sleep in your office again," Seth replies, his voice playful.

"Oh yeah, I do that all the time," Jamie teases right back. "But no, really. I wanted to thank you. I *really* appreciated it. I don't know how you do it, but I swear you can read my mind sometimes."

"I've just known you a long time."

"Well, you nailed it—that was exactly what I needed."

"You women and your chocolate. I'll never understand," Seth responds. Then his tone turns serious. "But you're welcome. Glad I can help you out. I can't solve your case, but I can surprise you with ice cream bars."

"I'll take the ice cream bars."

"So, uh, you want to go out for lunch today?"

"I'd love to, but I'm driving to Philly right now," Jamie laments.

"Philly, huh? What for?"

"Well, I think I found another murder. I just need to go and confirm it. I'm pretty sure something may have fallen through the cracks."

"That's crazy!"

"I'll take a rain check on that lunch though. And I won't let you forget it."

"Sure, sounds great. Okay, I have to get to work."

"Later."

Jamie hits her Bluetooth, ending the call. Seth could use an ear to unload to about his recent breakup. Too bad she cannot be there for him, like he has been for her.

Around ten in the morning, Jamie finally arrives at the office of Edward Bayer Development Corporation. Pulling into a parking spot, Jamie notes that the building is hardly impressive. It is a small, free-standing brick building that probably looks exactly the way it did in the sixties, when it was built. Although the building is ugly, it is situated in a good location—a few blocks away from the city government complex, affording easy access for permits and eviction filings.

Jamie enters the building to find a finely decorated and well-lit office. The decor helps Jamie to forget the outside of the building. A middle-aged woman sits at a desk, typing on a computer.

"May I help you?" she inquires politely, looking at Jamie with a smile.

"I'm here to see Mitchell or Stanley Bayer," Jamie states kindly.

"Do you have an appointment?" the receptionist asks, one eyebrow raised skeptically.

Jamie did not want to have to do this, but sometimes the situation requires it. She flashes her FBI badge and says, "Here's my appointment."

"I see." The receptionist blinks in surprise. "Mr. Mitchell Bayer is out of town; and Mr. Stanley Bayer is with someone, but I will let him know you are here."

The woman scribbles on a sticky note and tells Jamie she will be right back. She then walks down a hallway and disappears from Jamie's view. A gentle knock echoes back to Jamie, contrasting the quiet of the office. Presently, the receptionist returns to her seat and says, "He will be with you in a couple of minutes."

"Thanks," Jamie answers automatically, then walks around the reception area, looking at the pictures on the walls.

Modern art is not really Jamie's favorite, but it provides her something to do while she waits. But, instead of focusing on the art, her mind is working out how to talk with Mr. Bayer. If he or his brother had covered up a murder—no matter the reason—it would be hard to approach the topic. Jamie imagines that it will be difficult to get the information she wants without forcing Mr. Bayer to implicate himself. She will have to be careful.

About five minutes later, two males come around the corner. They are conversing jovially. Stanley Bayer tells his companion that they will wrap things up another time. Bayer escorts his guest out, then turns to Jamie and introduces himself.

"Please come to my office." Stanley guides her to a room around the corner.

Stanley Bayer is tall and lean, well-dressed, with gray hair and blue eyes.

His office is rather large, with a tacky lighthouse theme. From pictures on the wall, to little lighthouse figurines on the bookshelves, Jamie can see Stanley has a *very* strong affinity for lighthouses.

"Please have a seat," Stanley offers, motioning to a chair, then takes a seat in the large chair behind his desk.

As Jamie settles herself into a chair across from the desk, she begins, "Sorry to hear about your father's passing. How long has it been?"

"About six months," Stanley replies, eyeing her carefully. "Did you know him?"

"No, no. I just read about his death yesterday, on the Internet," Jamie admits, pulling out her tablet. She prepares herself to take notes, if necessary. Watching Stanley, Jamie decides that tact will not work with him.

"What can I do for you?" Stanley asks guardedly, putting his five fingertips together.

"I need to know if you have any idea why someone would want to murder him?" Jamie insists bluntly, throwing away her earlier ideas.

"Excuse me?" Stanley stutters, sitting straighter in his chair. His blue eyes dart around the items sitting on his desk.

"I know he was murdered," Jamie persists. "What I don't know is why it wasn't reported."

Stanley shifts again, not taking his eyes off of Jamie's, his stony face revealing no emotion, but a strong mind.

"That's why I am here. To find out why it wasn't reported as a homicide," Jamie finishes strongly. She stares Stanley down. She needs this answer.

Leaning back in his chair and crossing his legs, Stanley tries to take command of the situation with a casual, "I have no idea what you are talking about."

Jamie rolls her eyes at him. "Oh, I think you do. Don't worry—I know you didn't do it. But why didn't you notify the police? That is the part that has me baffled. Someone comes into your father's home and strangles him, and you cover it up, tell people that he died in his sleep. It doesn't make sense."

"Now wait a minute! Where are you getting this from?" Stanley demands, rising partway from his chair and slapping his fist on the desk.

"I mean, I know he had cancer and that he was even on hospice care. Poor guy didn't have long to live anyway, but murder? Someone murders him in cold blood, and you are okay with it? What should I think about that? Is that why you had him cremated? To hide the evidence of murder?" Jamie continues, smoothly turning up the heat on him.

"It was his wish to be cremated," Stanley interjects quickly and sternly. Settling his body again, he picks up a pen and begins to roll it between his forefinger and thumb.

"Oh I doubt that. After seeing all of those defenseless women and children shoved into the crematory at Auschwitz, it doesn't seem like he would want a similar fate."

"Wait a minute now!" Stanley yells angrily, this time standing fully up out of his chair. The pen goes flying across the room. "You have no right to make such accusations!"

"But maybe it could be some twisted rectification for previous sins..." Jamie does not even try to include Stanley in the conversation. "Nah, it wasn't his wish to be cremated. Pretty serious offense, though, covering up a murder." Jamie ends her tirade. Of course, there is no evidence, since the body was cremated, but she goes for the jugular anyway. Stanley does not know what she has.

"What is this all about? What do you want?" Stanley demands, leaning over his desk and glaring at Jamie.

"I'll tell you what I want. In exchange for you not being arrested right here and now for covering up your father's murder, you come clean and tell me what happened and why you didn't report it," Jamie states calmly, yet with a dark undertone.

"I'm not doing any such thing. I want my lawyer," Stanley asserts, once again looking Jamie right in the eyes.

"Call him," Jamie challenges nonchalantly. "I'll wait. I have nowhere else to be but so far up your ass that you will wish you had just cooperated from the get-go."

"Am I being charged with a crime? This is crazy!" Stanley protests, throwing his hands up in disbelief.

"Not yet. It depends on you. I need some facts, and I need them today!" Jamie rejoins firmly. She makes her own face just as stony as Stanley's, hoping she can hold up the façade long enough to get him to fold.

"This is coercion. You've got a wire on you and are trying to trick me into confessing something that never happened," Stanley rants, as he begins to pace behind his desk.

"Settle down. I'll come clean if you come clean. Firstly, on the record, I do not have a wire. I kinda figured you might suspect that. Here is an affidavit testifying to the fact that I do not have any recording devices. We can both sign it," Jamie confesses, pulling out the paper from her bag and setting it on his desk.

That statement makes Stanley stop pacing and stand over his desk, looking her straight in the eye. He briefly glances at the paper on his desk but does not take it.

"Now, that being said, I'm going to be straight with you. We have a vigilante that is killing former Nazis, or at least people whom he thinks are former Nazis. He has operated in a predictable pattern, but there is a gap on the day your father died. I thought maybe the killer skipped one, but the data led me to believe that that was not the case. You confirming what I already know will help us prove the pattern, the profile—and help us nab this guy."

"And if I don't?" Stanley asks slyly, turning away from Jamie.

"There is a hungry D.A. that would love a juicy case like this one. Oh, and the media would have a field day if anyone happened to tell them," Jamie threatens with a smile.

Stanley quickly turns back to her.

"This is extortion! You can't do this!" Stanley protests, his face turning slightly pink.

"No, this is not extortion. It's a great deal for you. You are a felon. I know what happened. I am all about the pursuit of justice. I can use the information you have to catch my killer and get justice for several murders, or I can use the information I have to get justice for conspiracy to conceal one murder. I would rather have the murderer, but I will take you too, if you get in my way."

"Someone all about the pursuit of justice would go after both—not that there is a second crime," Stanley counters, pacing behind his desk again. Every so often, he sends a glare in Jamie's direction.

"Thanks for confirming the first one— that your father was murdered. You know, family members, especially heirs, are always the first suspects," Jamie informs him casually, leaning back in her chair.

"I...I didn't..." Stanley stutters again, leaning forward on his desk, toward Jamie.

"Let's cut the shit, Stanley. I just need to know the answer to two questions, and I, and this whole matter, will disappear. What was written on the note? And how did you get him pronounced dead and cremated without anyone noticing?" Jamie demands, returning Stanley's glare with a firm poker face.

"That's all, that's it. Now, let's hear it, or face the alternative," Jamie finishes, as Stanley remains silent.

"I want my lawyer."

"No, you don't. I am not here to take a confession. I'm here so you can fill in some holes for my profile of the serial killer who killed your father in cold blood. Now tell me, so I can get the hell out of here and go catch this guy. You do want me to catch him, don't you? What about the note that read 'Aridata'?" Jamie pauses at the look of astonishment on his face, and she knows she has him. "I need to know what initials were on the note and why you didn't call the police."

Stanley turns and stares out the window for a moment. He sighs, running a hand through his full head of grey hair. He finally looks up and begins, "My father was very sick. Dying of lung cancer. He was on hospice care. He only had a few more months to live, tops. He had been asking everyone who came to see him since his diagnosis to help him die, so he wouldn't have to linger and suffer. He wanted to die."

Stanley pauses and leans on his forearms on the back of his office chair. He continues slowly, "The pain had been terrible—mets to the bone. I thought someone did it for him, like he wanted. That he had finally convinced someone." He shakes his head and shrugs sheepishly.

"We had sitters staying with him around the clock. That morning, when the night sitter, Julliette, called me, she was hysterical. She kept saying she didn't do it. I told her to tell the day shift assistant that he passed and send her away when she arrived. I came straight away, and she showed me his neck and the note. Yes, it read, 'Aridata'. I didn't call the police because I thought maybe Julliette did do it," Stanley admits.

"I don't know, maybe he had convinced her, and she couldn't watch his suffering anymore. Or maybe he had convinced someone else to do it or had paid someone to do it. He wanted to die. I surely did not want someone going to jail for the rest of their life because they did what my father asked," Stanley finishes, plopping into his chair.

"Well, you would have been the prime suspect. I'm sure you had to cover your own ass as well. He had a large estate, too. Might I presume tens of millions at stake?" Jamie estimates.

"It's more than the money. My brother and I do not see eye-to-eye. He is a big partier and travels a lot, which is fine, because he would squander all of the money and run the business into the ground. He lets me run things," Stanley explains, flipping one hand over, then the other. "See, I'm the type 'A' guy. He would for sure suspect me and then think that he could put me away and have it all. Of course, I knew it would be a huge mess, with life insurance frozen and a disastrous probate. For what? Because he died a couple of months early, probably at his own request. I never thought for a second that he was murdered by some psychopathic serial killer. Who would kill a ninety-three year old man who was already half gone?"

"We'll get to that. Tell me about the note."

"Yes, it read, 'Arid ata', written as two words. The initials were W.F."

"How did you get him past the medical director and the funeral home? Someone had to pronounce him dead."

"Juliette was pleading with me that she didn't do it and that they would suspect her and arrest her or deport her. She wasn't exactly legal—she was from Haiti. So we dressed him in his nicest suit, complete with necktie to cover the wound. Then we called hospice. They sent out the nurse who comes every week, and she pronounced him. Hospice takes care of the Death Certificate and has the Medical Examiner sign it. I asked her if the coroner had to come, and she told me that, in these cases, they sign it without seeing the deceased, since the cause of death is well-documented."

"The rest was easy. I told the funeral home that we had already dressed him in the clothes that he wanted to wear when he was cremated. Pennsylvania has a 24-hour waiting period before someone can be cremated. I can assure you, I did not sleep a wink that entire 24 hours. Not only had my father died, which I was expecting—you are never really ready—but I was also afraid...well, you can imagine," Stanley mutters. Again he runs a hand through his hair.

"So you figured this all out right on the spot?"

"You have to realize that Dad asked everyone who saw him, every day, to help him end his life. It wasn't hard to think that he finally got his wish. I never dreamed anyone would do it, but, like I said, why should someone go to jail for it?"

"Or his fortune get tied up in the courts. So your brother Mitchell does not know about this?"

"He has no idea."

"How fortunate, then, that I caught you here alone at the office today," Jamie opines aloud. "Well, as I promised, I am not going to tell him. Or anyone else for that matter."

"I would really appreciate that." Stanley stares deep into Jamie's eyes, as if trying to see if she is telling the truth. She can almost see the fear he has carried since his father's death, the fear that made him so hostile before.

"You have my word. Besides, you have really helped me out a lot," Jamie confirms with a strong nod.

Stanley's clenched shoulders relax slightly as Jamie stands up to leave.

"I am sorry for your loss. Don't worry, I'm going to get the guy who did this."

"Thanks, please let me know when you do," Stanley replies, also standing up.

"I can see myself out," Jamie tells him and disappears out of the office.

Chapter 39

Our relocation took my family to the Kosice brick factory, which was fenced off to be a ghetto. My older brother, mother, grandparents, and I had to make our home among thousands of other Jews who had also been forced from their homes. The term "home" is a loose term for a space of our own. Later, I would learn that there were around 10,500 Jews packed into the brick factory, which could only house 1,000 people at most.

There were no compartments, rooms, or a modicum of privacy. The brick factory was one large room. There were no curtains, which meant being modest was impossible. No bathrooms, no privacy, and no sleeping with your families.

The Nazi guards did their best to destroy our hope, comfort, and security. We were assigned straw mattresses that separated us from our family. Although we might see our family during the day, at night we were forced to sleep apart and alone. The darkness did not bring comfort, but instead nightmares, to others as well as me.

While we stayed in the ghetto, I spent most of my time assigned to cleaning the rail station in back of the brick factory, which held train tracks that had once transported the bricks. Trains kept passing by, each one filled with people. Through the holes in the cattle cars, I could see eyes staring back at me. Fear, pain, and hunger spoke from the eyes. I'm sure my own eyes held the same emotions. My brother and grandfather were forced to work during the day. They would come back beaten and exhausted. I was so hungry in the ghetto, as we were given rations that would not keep a small dog alive for very long. I was starving, and I had not spent all day doing back-breaking labor, like my brother and grandfather.

On May 15th, we were awakened in the wee hours of the morning to a train stopping at the brick factory ghetto. Within minutes, we heard whistles blowing, dogs barking, and Nazi SS guards shouting out commands. A look in the wrong direction would get you an immediate smack from a billy club. Over 6,000 people were crammed onto two trains that day. We stayed behind to starve. We did not know what to feel. Were we sad that we were left behind? By then, we were almost too weak to feel. We were starving. Surely, the lucky ones who boarded the trains were going somewhere with more food and less suffering. Four days later, the scene repeated itself, with thousands more being crammed onto the trains and getting out of the hellhole we were in. We would be left behind once again.

Our day came two weeks later, on June 3rd.

We were beaten as we were crammed into the railcar. Our car had over 100 people in it. There was no room to lie down, or even sit for that matter. An SS guard put an empty bucket in the middle of the car, and one bucket of water and six hard loaves of bread. We stood there for hours and hours, nearly suffocating, before the train finally started to move. We made several stops along the way, but the door was never opened. Once, the train stopped, and some Germans offered to sell us some water in exchange for something valuable. We had nothing, and therefore they cursed us and poured the water out on the platform. Someone asked where we were going and a soldier gave the "finger across the neck" sign. The trip took three days. Several people died on the train. They were piled into a corner of the car. Finally, the train stopped at the train station of the city Osweicim—Auschwitz. No one on the train had heard of the city before. We stayed at that train station for what seemed like an eternity. Finally, the train started the 4-kilometer trip to hell on earth, Auschwitz-Birkenau.

Chapter 40

Driving back to Virginia, Jamie's head is spinning. She is elated to find the missing murder. It took some work, but she did it. This is the kind of investigative work that makes her feel alive. Excitedly she turns on her Bluetooth and calls Seth.

"Hey," comes Seth's warm voice.

"Guess what?"

"Good news, eh?"

"Yes, I found a missing murder!"

"No way, that's awesome!"

"Yeah, you wouldn't believe the lengths this guy went through to cover up his father's murder. Of course, he had no idea that it was a serial killer—he just thought someone gave his father his last dying wish…literally, he wanted to die."

"That's crazy! We should totally celebrate tonight when you get back."

"That would be great!" It feels so good to know that Seth understands her triumph.

"You want to go out and eat, or just celebrate at home?"

"We could do both," Jamie says, unsure of what she really feels like doing.

"Let's do that, then," Seth agrees.

"How's work for you?"

"I ran a very unusual test today. A guy comes into the ER with abdominal pain and dies in the ICU a couple of days later—

multiple organ failure. The deceased is buried, but his sister is suspicious that his wife poisoned him for the life insurance. He has been embalmed, so, by the time they exhume the body, there aren't any body fluids to sample except the vitreous fluid of the eye. The pathologist reviewed his chart and concluded that his presentation could have been consistent with poisonous mushrooms. I was able to find amatoxin, which is found in poisonous mushrooms, using the Weiland test. Looks like we got her," Seth concludes with satisfaction.

"Glad to hear it. We can celebrate both triumphs tonight," Jamie suggests cheerfully.

"Totally!"

"Great. Let's meet at Crazy Joe's at seven."

"Seven it is. See you tonight."

"Okay, bye."

Jamie hangs up. Turning her attention back to driving, she begins to think again about Seth. He really is a good man. Seth actually cares about helping people and doing the right thing. In a way, Jamie decides, he's like a superhero, but with scientific abilities instead of superhuman strength. He solves crimes and catches bad guys, all from his lab. Not as glamorous as comic book superheroes, but noble nonetheless.

Thinking about the chocolate ice cream bars, Jamie decides she should surprise him with a gift as well. Now all she has to do is figure out what to get for him. As she is driving out of Philadelphia, singing along to her favorite Coldplay CD, she sees an advertisement for a vineyard in Chadds Ford. Wine would be a perfect gift for Seth! She follows the billboards to the exit and makes the detour. In the end, Jamie leaves with a bottle of 2009 Merlot and a 2010 Riesling.

Her mind drifts back to her discovery. She is curious to know the significance of August 8th. She turns her Bluetooth back on and calls Rabbi Silverman.

"Hello?"

"Hi, this is Jamie Golding."

"Ah, Jamie how are you doing?"

"Great, thanks, and you?"

"Thank God. I got your message and was planning on calling you."

"Well, I would like to pick up where we left off last meeting," Jamie explains. "Preferably tomorrow."

"Right, well, the Kollel learns from 9:00 A.M. to 1:00 p.m., so how about one o'clock tomorrow? Will that work?"

"Sure."

"I'll put you down then," Rabbi Silverman confirms.

"I have another quick question, if you have a moment."

"Go ahead."

"I want to know the significance of August 8th, 2012."

"You mentioned that in your message. I don't know offhand. Why?"

"There was another murder, but it occurred on August 8th, and not on Purim or Hoshana Raba. It was done by the same killer, and the note he left had 'adal ya' and the initials H.F. on it. But I don't know the significance of August 8th. It did not coincide with any Jewish holiday that I could find."

"I will see what I can come up with. We will talk tomorrow."

"That's fine. Tomorrow it is."

"Wonderful. I will see you then, *im yirtsa Hashem*," Rabbi Silverman tells her cordially.

"Yes, and thanks again for your help. I really appreciate it." Jamie does not bother to ask what the Hebrew phrase meant.

"It's my pleasure."

"Bye."

By the time Jamie arrives back in Virginia, she is so ecstatic that she can hardly think about going back in to work for the last a couple of hours. Instead, she drives to her apartment to chill before she goes out to dinner with Seth.

Their favorite bar is within walking distance, and the weather is so nice that Jamie decides to take the stroll. Jamie goes inside and sits down at a free table. She does not have to wait long before she sees Seth walking into the pub. With a wave of her hand, Jamie gets his attention.

"Hey! How about a big hug for a great success today!" Seth offers as he approaches Jamie.

"Sure!" Jamie responds, standing up and meeting his embrace. "What a day! All of our hard work and persistence paid off!"

"I can drink to that," Seth agrees, grinning. He looks around and calls a waiter to their table.

They both order beer and an entree. Once the waiter leaves, Jamie pulls out the wine from under the table.

"I have a present for you," she says, presenting the gift bag.

"You didn't have to get me anything...especially since I didn't get you anything," Seth responds, clearly abashed.

"No, no, don't worry—the ice cream bars were perfect. But I thought you might want to celebrate tonight with this instead." Jamie flashes an evil grin.

"Wait, I know that smile, and I don't trust you." Seth grins back.

"Well, you enjoyed it the night we put dish soap in the fountain," Jamie counters, her wicked smile only widening.

Seth instantly begins laughing. After calming himself down, he answers very seriously, "I thought we were never going to talk about that again."

"Well, here, open it already," Jamie encourages, ignoring his playful admonition, as she slides the present across the small, round table.

"Alright, but whatever is in there had better not bite."

Jamie just laughs again at his mock suspicion. "Don't worry—you will love it!"

"Oh, Merlot, my favorite," Seth exclaims, pulling the bottle of wine out of the bag. "And a Riesling! Thanks."

"Found a vineyard on the way home from Philly. Thought you might like a bottle." Jamie smiles from ear to ear.

"You're right! We will have to go home and enjoy this together."

The waiter arrives with their beers and greets them with a smile, "Glad you guys are enjoying yourselves tonight." He takes their order and off into the crowd again.

"For as crowded as it is, at least we are getting fast service," Seth remarks, taking a sip of own beer.

"Well, I guess we aren't the only ones with something to celebrate," Jamie speculates, surveying the crowd.

"Here's your order, the citrus salmon, mashed potatoes with asparagus,—" announces the waiter, putting a steaming plate in front of Jamie.

"Thanks," Jamie replies, startled by his sudden reappearance.

"—And a shepherd's pie with ground beef and mixed veggies, and mashed potatoes with gravy," the waiter finishes as he sets the other plate in front of Seth.

"It looks great, thanks."

"Need anything else?"

"No I'm good," Jamie replies.

"Nope, thanks," Seth echoes.

"Enjoy your meal!" The waiter is off to another table.

"Cheers to our successes today," Jamie says, holding up her beer.

"Cheers," Seth agrees, clinking his beer against hers.

They recap the events of the day. Jamie tells Seth about her impromptu visit to Shap. Seth tells her he seems to have been better lately. Jamie mentions that she has not seen Chris in a while. When it comes time to pay Seth takes out his wallet.

"No way! I'm paying tonight. It's my treat," Jamie protests.

At that moment, the waiter walks by the table. "Are you guys ready for some boxes and checks?"

"Yes," Jamie bursts out before Seth can speak up. "But it's one check, and I will be taking it."

"Great. I will be right back." The waiter again disappears, this time toward the cash register.

"Right. So where should we go for dessert, then?" Seth asks hopefully.

"I've got some ice cream at my place already, or did you forget," Jamie suggests, her grin returning.

"That's a great idea."

"Here's your check, ma'am, and boxes for both of you," the waiter proclaims, as he comes to the table. He puts the boxes down and lowers the check in the middle between Seth and Jamie. Seth reaches out to grab it, but he is just a little too slow. Jamie snatches it up and puts her credit card in without looking.

She hands it back to the waiter and looks at Seth with sly triumph.

"Fine, but I get to pay next time."

"Deal," Jamie concedes with a laugh at his expression.

As they walk through the door, Jamie says, slightly embarrassed, "Since it was a beautiful night, I walked..."

"Good, me too. Guess we are on the same wavelength." Seth winks at her.

"Let's go," Jamie says, threading her arm through his.

Jamie smiles at Seth and really looks at him. He is very handsome in his black slacks, red button-up, and sport coat. One thing Seth had always been good about is dressing well.

"You look nice," Jamie compliments him, as they start walking down the street.

"Thanks," Seth replies, clearly taken aback. "You look great too, as usual."

When they reach her apartment, Jamie unlocks the front door lets them in. "Sorry about the mess. I got back today and didn't really clean up after myself," Jamie apologizes, as she pushes her traveling bag out of the way.

"No problem. I've seen it in worse shape."

"Okay, good point," Jamie concedes. "I'll get some wineglasses. Go ahead and make yourself comfortable."

"Sure." Seth walks away toward the living room.

Since it is a special occasion, Jamie pulls out two of her fancy wineglasses, and a corkscrew, then meets Seth in the living room.

"I'm excited to try your Merlot. The woman at the vineyard said it is really good," Jamie tells him, putting the glasses on the coffee table. She takes a seat next to Seth on the couch.

"Alright then, let's do this," Seth declares, opening the bottle of wine. He pours it slowly into one of the glasses and hands it to Jamie.

"Thanks," Jamie says gently, swirling her cup of wine.

"A toast to our successes, and may we celebrate many more," Seth cries, holding out his glass to Jamie.

"Here, here," Jamie affirms, tapping her wine glass against Seth's and taking of sip of the rich wine. A citrus flavor fills her mouth. Jamie thinks to herself that it has been a while since she had Merlot and that she has been missing out.

She lets out a sigh and puts her feet up on the coffee table. "I did over seven hours of driving today. It was worth it, though."

"Here, give me your feet," Seth directs her.

"What? Why?"

"I bet you could use some more relaxation, since you've been working on such a stressful case," Seth explains. He takes another sip of his wine then puts it back on the coffee table.

"No way, what if my feet smell," Jamie refuses with a giggle of embarrassment.

"Don't be silly. Besides, you have to admit it's been way too long since you got a foot massage."

"Okay, fine." Jamie caves in stretches her legs out across the couch. Seth takes her delicate feet between his strong hands and begins rubbing them. Jamie lets out at a sigh.

"That feels great."

"Good," Seth replies, working gently on the ball of her foot.

"Anywhere else that you're tense?" Seth asks, switching to the other foot.

Jamie reaches for her wine and takes a few, reflective sips. "All that driving really took a toll on my back and neck," she finally decides after putting her glass back down and rubbing her neck.

"Great, I will tackle them next," Seth declares, pausing to enjoy a drink from his wineglass.

"Why are you so good to me?" Jamie questions suddenly. "Looking back, you've always been good to me."

Seth just smiles at her.

Jamie feels warm and content. She goes to reach for her wineglass again, only to discover that it is empty. When did that happen? She sits up to get some more but finds herself, unexpectedly, looking Seth full in the face.

"You have such nice eyes," Jamie tells him, her voice almost a whisper.

"Thanks," Seth whispers back. "I like your eyes too. They're beautiful."

"Here let me get your neck," Seth offers as he moves closer to Jamie.

She turns her back to him, and he begins to rub her neck. Jamie is lost in the touch of his hands on her skin. She feels herself melt under his strong but tender hands. Seth's fingers move down to her shoulders. Jamie groans with satisfaction and catches Seth's right hand between her shoulder and cheek, hugs it tightly. She quickly kisses his hand before he can move it away. Instinctively, she turns to face Seth. The dark brown eyes are sparkling. A delicious chocolate brown.

She feels the excitement of anticipation as she moves closer to Seth's face. His warm, moist breath smells sweet, like the Merlot. He is moving towards her too. So many emotions well up in Jamie. It is almost as if she has been holding back her feelings for Seth, and they are coming to the surface at this moment.

His warm lips brush hers softly, and Jamie immediately wants more. Before he can pull away, Jamie puts her hand behind his head and kisses him again, bringing him to her. Their breath comes in short gasps, as the small brushing kiss grows more intense.

Jamie's mind is whirling with passion. She has not felt this kind of desire in a long time. Jamie wants nothing more than to be close to Seth, closer than ever before. She continues to kiss him, her hands wandering to his chest as she starts to unbutton his shirt. At the same time, one of his hands is caressing her face, while the other slides seductively up her thigh. Jamie yearns for him to continue.

Tonight she will get her wish.

Chapter 41

Jamie arrives at the Kollel Learning Center a little before 1:00 p.m. She slowly approaches to look in through the glass walls encasing the study hall. She is curious to what she might see on her second visit. She finds the four pairs of rabbis sitting at the tables, engrossed in large volumes in front of them. Several of the rabbis are swaying rapidly back and forth in their chairs. There is a loud buzz of incomprehensible banter, some of which seems to be uttered in a sing-song tune. No one looks like they are going to strike another today. She stares idly for a moment, amazed at the intensity of their learning. Based on what Rabbi Silverman told her yesterday, they have been doing this for almost four hours straight. *Haven't they mastered it yet? I mean, they are already rabbis. Shouldn't they know it by now?*

Rabbi Silverman looks casually at his watch, then peers around to where Jamie is standing. He waves for her to come in, and they walk to one of the empty tables. Not one of the other rabbis even looks up from his book. It cannot be every day that an FBI agent walks in, yet no one seems remotely interested.

"Do you guys get to graduate any time soon?" Jamie asks.

Rabbi Silverman laughs. "Nope, no graduation from Torah learning. It's a lifelong pursuit."

"But four hours straight, that's really something."

"Well, in the morning it's four hours; the afternoon study session is only three hours. It's a great job."

"Job? You mean you guys get paid to study?"

"Yes, but we teach, too. Every Tuesday and Thursday, a few of us end at twelve, and we take pizza to various places for lunch-and-learns. Every evening, we teach Torah classes or learn with people from the community that work during the day. It's a fifteen-hour day. Sundays as well."

"Fascinating."

"Speaking of fascinating, what's going on in your world?"

"We had a press conference and came out about the murders. Did you see it? It was on the news."

"No, we don't have a television. Won't allow one in the house."

"Okay…Well, after the press conference, we got a call from Edison, New Jersey, and apparently there was a murder there on August 8, 2011. It matched the others—note and all. Adalia and H.F., or Hans Frank, according to what you revealed. I put together a clear pattern for the occasions when the murders took place, except that he skipped Hoshana Raba of last year. Well, one would think that he did, except that he also skipped that note, for Aridata and Wilhelm Frick. So I did some digging and found out that there *was* a murder this past Hoshana Raba. That puts our total at eight. I'm finding murders, but I'm supposed to be finding the murderer!" She says the last part loud enough for one of the remaining kollel rabbis to look up.

Rabbi Silverman looks around as well, to see if anyone heard what she said. Two of the rabbis are leaving, but the rabbi who looked up catches Rabbi Silverman's eye and tells him, "I have to be somewhere at two, so I can stay until about ten-of."

"Okay, that should be fine." He turns back to Jamie and says, "We may have to go somewhere else if we're not done by then. Don't worry, though, it's no problem to go upstairs. I can give you as much time as you need."

Jamie looks at him, clearly confused. He explains, "Unless someone else comes, then we will be here alone. We don't seclude ourselves with women other than our wives."

"Oh, right..." she hears herself say, still a little disoriented by the exchange. "Like I was saying, there have been a total of eight murders. There were ten sons of Haman and ten hanged at Nuremberg. Am I supposed to believe that there are to be ten here as well? And only ten? Who says he is going to stop at ten?"

"Were all of these victims Nazis?"

"It is hard to tell in what exact capacity they each acted, but, yes, they were all in Europe during the war, and they weren't working for the Allies."

"You know, according to the Midrash, there was an eleventh who died in the Purim story who wasn't hanged, and there was an eleventh at Nuremberg who wasn't hanged. Both committed suicide. Haman's daughter and Hermann Goering. Hermann Goering was scheduled to be hanged with the rest, but he committed suicide a couple of hours before, in his cell. Cyanide or something."

"I read the book of Esther. I don't remember anything about Haman's daughter killing herself."

"It is only subtly alluded to. You would have to read it in the Hebrew to even notice. The Talmud tells us what happened. When Haman was ordered to parade Mordechai through the town on the King's horse, people came out to see what was going on. When they approached Haman's house, Haman's daughter went to the roof to see what the commotion was. She couldn't see clearly what was going on. Someone shouted that it was Haman and Mordechai. Obviously, she assumed that her father was on the horse and that Mordechai was leading him through the streets. She figured she would show Mordechai what she thought of him, so she grabbed a chamber pot and dumped it on his head from the roof. It landed right on Haman. Haman, covered with excrement, looked up and saw his daughter. When she saw the mortified look on her father's face, she jumped off the roof and killed herself. It fits nicely in among the parallels between the two. Eleven deaths, ten hanged and one suicide in both stories."

"What about the fact that one suicide was female and one male?"

"It fits—Hermann Goering was a cross-dresser!" Rabbi Silverman exclaims.

"No way!"

"Google 'famous cross-dressers', and Hermann Goering will be on the list!"

Jamie pulls out her smart phone and searches the name. She finds a website with a list of cross-dressers. Sure enough, Hermann Goering is on that list. "Crazy!" Jamie agrees, putting her smart phone off to one side.

"Okay. But there is still the problem of August 8. There was no Jewish holiday or Holocaust link on that date?" Jamie asks, trying to get back on topic.

"I've been thinking about that since you called and asked about it. Check this out. August 8th is 8/8. Remember when I said that the numerical values of 'b'shushan Habira' and 'Nuremberg, Germany' are the same? They are both 880. So that could be your 8/8. Also, 88 is a neo-Nazi symbol. 'H' is the 8th letter in the alphabet, so '88' equals 'Heil Hitler'. You can Google that as well. I was once driving to Atlanta for a wedding, and, when I was going through North Carolina, I saw a pickup truck with an '88' bumper sticker.

"So maybe August 8th was chosen for that reason."

Jamie Googles "88 as a neo-Nazi symbol" and gets several images of children proudly wearing their 88 t-shirts. Some are even shown making the "Heil Hitler" salute.

"Another interesting thing I found was that executions by the International Military Tribunal are usually carried out by firing squad and not hanging. So one would not have expected the condemned at Nuremberg to be hanged in the first place. In fact, the French judges in the Nuremberg trial wanted death by firing squad and were outvoted. Because of the heinous crimes these men had committed, the other judges thought that hanging would be more fitting for them. Remember that Esther said, 'Let it be done tomorrow as it was done today, and let the ten sons of Haman be hanged on the gallows.' Interesting, huh?"

"I wonder if our guy factored in the suicide," Jamie remarks, not willing to weigh in on whether the ten at Nuremberg were hanged because of the words Queen Esther uttered 2,500 years ago. "If it all started with a suicide on August 8th, it will further strengthen the pattern. With eight murders already committed, and a likely chance the killer is planning ten,

I've got to stop him before he kills the last two. We are going to issue a warning, but we are not expecting a lot of cooperation from hiding Nazis."

"I sure hope there are no more."

"Thank you so much for your help, Rabbi. I think you have explained the August 8th link. It is pretty amazing that 880 is part of the Esther codes, and 88 is now a neo-Nazi symbol."

"Please let me know if I can do anything else for you. When you are done with this case, if you ever want to come spend the Sabbath with our family, you are always welcome. Good food, deep discussions, singing…it's a lot of fun."

"Okay, I'll think about it," Jamie answers, feeling slightly awkward for a moment. "Well, I have to get going."

"Anytime, Jamie," Rabbi Silverman reiterates with a smile, standing up from his seat.

"I'll call you again if I need something else," Jamie assures him, standing up and gathering her things.

"Please do." He escorts Jamie out of the Kollel.

Back at her office, the words of Rabbi Silverman still ringing in her ears, Jamie checks to see if it could have all started with a suicide. Could it be that her perp would try to make it fit by staging a murder to look like a suicide? She turns to her computer and starts looking up suicides that occurred on August 8, 2010. There are plenty of them, but Jamie narrows down the search to males over eighty-five. Now there are four suicides that appear in the results. None seem to match. To be thorough, she includes females over eighty-five and finds another three.

Bingo! An 87-year-old woman, Erna Koch, was found dead in her home, a woman being investigated as a Nazi.

Reading further, Jamie discovers that Koch was being considered for deportation after she lied on her immigration papers. The police concluded that Koch committed suicide because of the defamation that resulted from the investigation into her background as a guard at the Ravensbruck concentration camp for women. There was a typed suicide note found by the body. *Typed and not handwritten?* The file indicates that, in the note, Koch admitted to being a Nazi. It was an overdose of sleeping pills that took her life.

Unbelievable! The perp has taken these codes in the book of Esther so far that he even killed an elderly woman and made it look like a suicide, complete with a note. And not just any note, but a typed note. Although Jamie does not have a picture of it, she is almost sure that it would match the notes found at the other crime scenes.

It suddenly strikes Jamie how much work and thought has gone into these murders. It is not the usual work of covering the perp's tracks and avoiding detection, but the additional effort to make each killing fit the pattern, as well as the book of Esther and the hangings of the ten Nazis at Nuremberg. The perp even went so far as to engineer a suicide to start the murders, then to strangle each victim with a cord, which mimics death by hanging. An unexpected shiver shakes Jamie, and goose bumps break out on her arms. The case has just become creepy to her in a way she had never thought of before.

Ignoring the emotions and thoughts rioting in her head, Jamie pulls out her tablet and reviews the information she has collected from Rabbi Silverman. She has to catch this perp before the next person is murdered. Looking back at the pattern and looking forward on the Jewish calendar, Jamie writes down her eerie conclusion.

Thursday, August 8, 2013—9th victim

Wednesday, September 25, 2013—10th victim

These two men, wherever they are, already have appointments with death. Jamie glares at those dates, promising herself that she will do all she can to save the marked men, despite their dark pasts. At least she has the dates of the future murders; now she just has to find the victims.

Chapter 42

August 8th, 2013

Simon sits in a rental car on one of the side streets to a sprawling condominium complex. He glances at the time again, then looks down the street at the few cars, which are parked in front of their respective condos. His clothing is all brand new, even his socks and underwear. He has a backpack slung over one shoulder. A hairnet neatly contains all of his locks, and he wears a do-rag to conceal the hairnet. He pulls out a burner phone that he bought with cash earlier that day. Using the phone, he dials the number he has memorized just for this moment.

"Hello?" an older, male voice answers, slightly out of breath.

"Hi, I'm Frank Brooks, from your CVS pharmacy. I have a prescription here for Susan Weiss that was called in by Dr. Amanda Hilson. It needs to be picked up as soon as possible as the prescription expires today," Simon says in a professional tone.

"Thank you, I will send the nurse to pick it up," the man on the other end replies. "I'll have her come by now."

"Thanks, I'll be looking for her. Have a nice day." He ends the call and trains his eye on the condo at the far end of the block. A middle-aged woman wearing scrubs emerges. Simon smiles to himself, glad to see the visiting nurse leave the residence carrying an oversized pocket book. Between a wife who cannot walk anymore and visiting nurses present around-the-clock, Simon has had to carefully plan this attack. The condo is a long, two-story stucco building with evenly spaced doors. Each door accesses four condos, two on the first floor and two on the second.

Simon takes his opportunity. He enters the building and places a sticky note over the seeing eye of the condo on the lower level, to his left. He then goes behind the stairwell, removes some newspaper from his backpack and spreads it out on the floor, and places the backpack on the paper. He quickly puts on an impervious coverall suit, shoe covers, latex gloves, fanny pack, and surgical cap. He leaves the backpack under the stairwell and approaches the door of the condo on the right. Simon knocks.

An older gentleman opens the door. He is completely bald and is supporting his weight with a walker. He surveys Simon with distrust. "Who are you?"

"Sorry to bother you. I'm from Nursing Aids Assisted Living Program, and I am doing a routine unscheduled visit. I have come to make sure you are satisfied with the nursing service we provide," Simon explains politely.

"Why are you dressed like that?" the geezer demands boldly, pointing his finger at Simon's chest.

"Due to the nature of my job, I come in contact with many types of illnesses and diseases. For your safety, and for the safety of others, I am required to wear this jumpsuit, to keep contamination at a minimum. And, yes, I put on a new one for each client I visit," Simon tells him eloquently, as though he has made this speech a thousand times.

"The nurse just went to the pharmacy for us."

"Oh, that's fine. I'll only be about ten minutes or so. Can we go in?" Simon asks with a smile.

"Er, right. Come in," the old man concedes, opening the door all the way and moving aside to let Simon in.

"Thank you. Let's sit down," Simon suggests, continuing with his façade.

The old man gestures Simon to his couch, while the old man himself takes the nice easy chair placed opposite.

Before Simon sits down, he says, "I must have left the form in the car. I'll be right back."

The old man rolls his eyes and replies sarcastically, "Take your time."

Simon gets up, watching the old man out of the corner of his eye. He does not move. He seems to be content to sit and wait for Simon. Delighted, Simon removes the garrote from his fanny pack and sneaks up on his prey. Simon slides the wire around the old man's neck and pulls each end. The old man reaches up and tries to grasp the wire, to pull it loose.

Simon then murmurs, just loud enough for the old man to hear, "Alfred Weiss, Zeit für Sie, für Ihre Kriegsverbrechen sterben."

Time for you to die for your war crimes.

Simon then pulls each end tighter and tighter, until he can watch the man's life force fade away.

When it is finished, he removes the garrote and places it back into the fanny pack. He then stares aimlessly at a small, ornate clock on the coffee table. He cannot catch his breath. His chest is tightening, and he is unable to divert his gaze from the clock as his field of vision narrows. He is about to pass out. Suddenly there is a loud thud as the old man slumps forward and hits his head on the coffee table. Simon snaps back to himself and is able to slow down his breathing before he blacks out. He takes a minute to regain composure then exits the condo. He is already at the door when he turns back to place the note on the coffee table. He returns the fanny pack, coveralls, gloves, and shoe covers to the backpack. He removes the sticky note from the neighbor's door and casually walks away.

Chapter 43

Jamie has a list of all living persons investigated by the United States Department of Justice Special Operations Unit. She has contacted them and encouraged them to be on the lookout for anything suspicious.

Jamie paces nervously in her office. She knows she will be getting the call soon. As she had feared, she has been swamped with work ever since the press conference. She has received several leads from police that she has had to investigate. Once the word got out that there is a vigilante killing Nazis across the country, hundreds of people started calling their local police, suspecting the loner neighbor or the grocery store bag boy that has a funny look about him. There have even been women accusing their ex-boyfriends, as an act of spite or revenge. And, of course, Jamie has been notified every time some crazy stopped by his local precinct to confess and demand that he be arrested for the killings.

She has tried to focus more attention on a very vocal, Jewish blogger in Florida, who rants about no one caring anymore about the Holocaust, and about the recent rise of anti-Semitic attacks in Europe being ignored by mainstream media. He also writes that there were more anti-Semitic attacks in Europe in 2012 than there were in 1939. He has published several threatening letters-to-editors of newspapers that he claims have anti-Israel bias. He has clear-cut alibis for several of the dates, so it is impossible for him to be the killer; and he does not appear to have the financial resources to pay a professional hit man. She has also looked into a small group in the Jewish section of Brooklyn, New York. The members call themselves "Nokim", which is Hebrew for "avengers." They have been known to rough up some non-Jewish neighbors for crimes like stealing from Jews in the neighborhood or repeatedly blocking someone's driveway. Several years ago, a pervert flashed a group of teenagers walking home from school. The girls did not call the police, but the Nokim. The next day, the guy ended up in the hospital. Jamie found them to be no more than an overzealous neighborhood watch, and unlikely suspects in her case.

At six o'clock, she leaves. The call did not come.

The next day, when she arrives at work she gets the call. Alfred Weiss, 89. She had personally talked to him six weeks earlier. *Fredericks is going to go nuts. If there is anything good to come from this, maybe, just maybe, the others on the list will wake up and notice something.* The list she received from the Justice Department's Office of Special Investigations has one-hundred-and-thirty-two names. One hundred and thirty two that are still living in the United States and that have been investigated previously. She has tried to shrink the list, but it is impossible. Some of the previous victims were not even on the list. Hopefully this murder will convey the message: cooperate, or die!

Chapter 44

Cousin Edit from Prague had been sent to Auschwitz in 1942. By 1944, all members of her family had been killed. Most people did not survive Auschwitz more than several months. Edit spent three years in that hell. How did she survive for three years? Edit somehow befriended "Dr. Anna", an Austrian Jewish physician. Dr. Anna worked directly with the famed Dr. Josef Mengele, doing his notorious medical experiments. He is also the one that did the "selections" when the transport of new inmates arrived. Edit worked in the "clinic." She knew Mengele well and even called him by his first name. In the clinic, she received better food and lived in a cleaner environment, so she did not succumb to disease, like most.

Edit heard that transports were coming in from Kosice and actually received permission from Dr. Mengele himself to be near the platform when the trains arrived. She searched for relatives when the first two transports arrived, and found none.

The day our train arrived, there had been several other trains that same day, and the place was swarming with people. Edit could not find us. I was separated from my mother and grandparents. They were sent to the gas chambers that very day. My brother and I were selected for slave labor and were sent to different barracks.

I was taken to a room where I had to remove all of my clothing. Then all the hair of my body was shaved off. Then I was forced into a large shower for disinfecting.

After that, I was issued a striped prison uniform. Normally, I would have been taken to another barracks for tattooing. There were so many Jews arriving daily that it took several weeks for me to get registered and eventually tattooed. My number was, and is, A-14191.

Upon roll call, within a few days of finally being registered, Edit walked to one of the guards in the front and handed him a note. He called out my number, and I came forward. Edit said, "Walk with me, and do not say a word." Edit was wearing a solid blue prison dress and not the striped uniform. She also did not have her head shaven, but wore a kerchief on her head. She took me to the clinic, where my brother was waiting. She said not to say a word when I see my brother. Edit gave us each a small piece of bread and then took us to "Canada."

Canada was a section of Auschwitz, not far from the crematory, where they sorted the clothes of the new arrivals. It was called "Canada" because this is where they kept all the clothes and valuables they confiscated from those going to the gas chambers. Canada was dreamed to be a land of unsurpassed wealth.

There was also an area of Auschwitz called "Mexico", which had the worst conditions. A lot of gypsies were sent there.

I was given a job as a clothes-sorter, and my brother hauled clothes from the anteroom of the crematory and brought them to be sorted.

The new arrivals that were selected for immediate death were told to fold their clothes neatly in a stack, and to put any valuables on top, so they would not be lost. It was really so the guards could confiscate the valuables easily.

I, and many other women, sorted the clothes by sizes, and they were then sent into Germany. We checked all pockets and seams for valuables. Occasionally I found something that I could get to Edit, and she would use it to barter for food. That is, if I felt I could hide it from the ever-watchful guards watching me work. If I had gotten caught, it would have been disastrous. The conditions in Canada were horrible, but much better than the rest of the camp. Easier work and a little bit better food. Edit would sneak us food regularly.

Once, I got typhus and was too weak to stand during roll call. Dr. Anna stood next to me and held me up so I wouldn't get selected. We had roll call every day for hours.

We also had periodic selections, and being in Canada did not offer any immunity. Once, after my bout with typhus, I was selected and placed in a line. Edit stepped forward and grabbed another inmate and switched us. When that inmate cried out in protest, a guard came over and smacked her with his club. I was saved, and that inmate, who was actually physically stronger, went to the gas chamber. Hard to imagine, but true.

Chapter 45

For weeks now, Jamie has been monitoring several potential victims. Each one of them has been contacted and warned of the threat. Jamie was not surprised when most of them denied any connection to the Nazis. It does not matter to Jamie, but she can at least make them aware of a serial killer who might target them. Yet many of them dismissed the warning, while others took it very seriously.

She has narrowed the list down to twenty-five of the most likely victims. Her favorite is Bernard Wagner, who was investigated twice for a potential role in the Lidice massacre in Czechoslovakia. He fits the profile completely. They have asked him to report anything unusual and are carefully monitoring his phone lines.

It is less than a week before the expected murder date. Thanks to Fredericks, most of the load has been taken off Jamie's back and shared among several agents, including Phil and Joey. A break came when a Marcel Mueller called and reported some strange phone calls.

Her smartphone starts to buzz. Jamie picks it up off her desk and opens a text from Phil. It reads, "More strange phone calls to Mueller, come now!"

Jamie jumps up from her desk and makes her way through the maze of cubicles to an office with a plaque that reads, "Special Agent Philip Clark." His office is almost an exact replica of her own, except that his room is decorated with framed posters of basketball players and a couple of basketball trophies. Even if Jamie were to forget that Phil had played basketball in college, his office will always remind her.

Jamie stands at the doorway of his office. Phil is on the phone, but he looks up at her and motions her to come in.

"What happened?" Jamie asks, as soon as he replaces the receiver in its cradle.

"So my guy here, Marcel Mueller, has been called several times yesterday and today. Each time it is from a different burner phone," Phil explains, pulling up on his computer the phone records of the potential victim. "First call was at about 10:00 A.M., next at 2:00 P.M., then 8:00 P.M. Today, the calls started at 8:00 A.M., then 11:00 A.M., then we just got one more about ten minutes ago, at 4:00 P.M.," Phil shares, pointing to each time on the screen. "He reported to me, saying that, most of the time, the person immediately hung up after he answered. Twice a man asked if Jack was home," Phil informs her.

"Looks like the perp could be trying to figure out the schedule of his next victim?" Jamie theorizes aloud.

"Exactly my thought. He also said he saw a white car parked at the curb. A white male got out of the car and took pictures of the house and then drove away.

"This is our perp's next victim. There's no doubt in my mind," Phil concludes, smiling proudly. "We are going to catch this guy."

Some of the other victims had gotten some similar calls a week before they were targeted. Jamie is sure that Phil is right—this is their guy.

"I'll inform Fredericks."

"We've got him," Phil repeats with confidence.

"Not yet, but very soon," Jamie agrees cautiously, returning the smile. "I still want somebody on Bernard Wagner."

Chapter 46

Wednesday morning, September 25, 2013.

Outside, a car drives by, doing at least double the speed limit for a quiet neighborhood. Simon ignores the noise and only watches the rise and fall of the man's chest as he snores loudly in his bed. The clock beside the bed reads 2:08 A.M. It is barely two hours into September 25th, but it is enough for Simon. A ten-second pause in the breathing ends with a loud, gasping breath and a snore twice as loud as normal.

You really should have gotten your sleep apnea treated.

László Kovács's poor sleep quality has provided Simon with this perfect opportunity to end his life.

A week earlier, Simon sent a circular in the mail that read, "Does your spouse's snoring affect your sleep? We are studying the side effects of living with a snorer. Participants will receive $1,000 for participating in our 2-week study. You have been randomly selected, and a representative will contact you soon." It was addressed to Mrs. Kovács and, the same evening it was delivered, Simon called, posing as the representative.

Playing the part of a researcher, Simon explained exactly how they could participate in the snoring research study to receive the money. He told her that, as part of the study, they would simply need to sleep in separate rooms for two weeks. Then they would need only to answer a few questions each evening, about their days and overall moods. In return, he promised them a check for a thousand dollars, to be paid as soon as the questionnaire was filled out and returned.

The wife readily agreed. Simon told her that he would be mailing them the questionnaire and to start as soon as they received it. The next day, Simon sent off the fake form. A week later, the wife and husband are still sleeping separately, as prescribed. This allows Simon to finish his task without having to worry about the wife. So far, he has killed no one who was innocent, and he does not want to start, especially not now that he is at the end of his list.

He stands over his last victim. A hellish monster. This frail man used the façade of the Hungarian police force to evict Simon's grandmother and great-grandparents from their home. He was also his great-uncle's friend's brother. He personally knew who he was evicting. He beat Simon's great-grandfather senseless, so that the women had to help him walk away from his own home. The story, told by his grandmother, replays in Simon's head as he looks at the man. The horrible images she painted in his mind, of the beatings, and of how this man forced them into the ghetto, until they would be transported to the concentration camps, give Simon strength to finish his final task. This man sealed their fates. He sent Simon's great-grandparents to their graves.

Oh, how Simon wants to wake up this demon, so he can know what is about to happen to him. So he can know that justice is finally about to be served. But Simon knows, too, that he cannot risk waking the wife in the next room. No, the satisfaction of revenge will have to lie completely in this vicious animal's death.

Simon approaches the bed and carefully slides the garrote under the man's pillow and around his neck. Simon waits for him to exhale completely. With one smooth motion, Simon simultaneously pulls the garrote and sits on the creature's knees to prevent him from kicking. After a few moments, the life leaves the monster, and Simon feels relief. Elation fills him, the joy of knowing that he has kept his promise. As always, Simon leaves a note. This one reads "ASI" and "vizata." On the back of the note, Simon added, "one more to go." As he is leaving the house, Simon places an envelope with a thousand dollars cash in the mailbox.

Chapter 47

Wednesday, September 25, 2013

Jamie waits patiently in the bedroom of Marcel Mueller's home. Phil Clark and Joey Hughes are also with her. Tyler is sitting in an unmarked car down the street. Several local police officers are inside the house, and others are hidden around the perimeter. It is close to 9:52 A.M., and, even though Marcel Mueller is safely hidden, Jamie is nervous, worried that they have tipped off the murderer to their presence. It is quiet. Jamie walks slowly around the home, looking at Mueller's things.

A picture on the wall shows Mueller in a German uniform, standing with his buddies, somewhere near the sea. As Jamie looks around, she realizes that there are many pictures on the wall from World War II. The bookcase in the room next to the bedroom is filled with several books in German. It is strange that Mueller has not tried to hide that he was a German soldier in World War II. None of the other victims had anything in their homes that was associated with Germany. She notices a picture of Mueller standing proudly in front of a Navy vessel. Jamie feels uneasy about her discovery. She leaves the spare bedroom and heads down the hallway to show Phil.

Suddenly her earpiece bursts into life.

"A lone man has just come around the corner onto this block. Car is a late-model, blue Toyota Camry," Tyler's voice announces.

Then, "He is parking his car two houses down," Tyler reports.

And, shortly, "Target is walking toward the house; he is carrying a red rose."

"He is walking up the driveway," Tyler tells them.

"Get ready," Phil's voice adds.

They had left the door conspicuously ajar.

Paul Delaney taps lightly on it as he pushes it wider and steps through to the foyer.

"Hello?"

"FBI, freeze!" Jamie shouts.

"Oh, shit!" Delaney exclaims, as he spins around and pulls a pistol out of his back pocket. Jamie fires immediately, hitting Delaney in the right shoulder and knocking him backwards and onto the tiled floor. Phil steps on the hand holding the gun, immobilizing it. He points his own gun directly at Delaney's face and booms, "One move, and I'll blow your head off!"

Delaney looks up and wails, "You shot me! Dammit! You shot me!"

"Next time, don't pull a gun on the FBI. You're under arrest."

"Under arrest? For what? Reaching for my gun when you scared the shit out of me? Jesus Christ! You shot me!"

Jamie tells him to roll over onto his stomach, then reaches for her handcuffs. As she pulls his bullet-torn shoulder, Delaney lets out an agonizing scream. Jamie is unfazed and quickly secures his hands behind his back.

Phil reads Delaney his Miranda rights. Jamie takes the perp's pistol and searches him for a wire ligature of some kind. The murder weapon. She does not find anything except his wallet, car keys, and cell phone.

"Should we call an ambulance or let him bleed to death?"

"Your call," Joey answers automatically. "I'm fine either way."

Delaney looks up, petrified. Of course, they will not let him bleed out, but they will not give him any sympathy either.

Phil radios Tyler that the perp has been shot and to summon an ambulance. Jamie throws the keys to Joey and tells him to go search the car. At that order, Paul Delaney, still writhing in pain, begins protesting that they have no right to search his car. Jamie informs him that, the second he stepped into the house, he gave them probable cause to search everything he owns.

Joey returns a few minutes later, wearing latex gloves and holding two Ziploc bags each containing a garrote.

"Voilà!" he boasts.

Jamie demonstrates noticeable relief when she sees the murder weapon. "You are under arrest for the murder of Alfred Weiss, as well as eight others," she informs the perp commandingly.

"What?" the man says, "You've got the wrong guy. I didn't kill anyone!"

"Tell it to the judge."

There is an awkward moment of silence. Delaney sort of whimpers in pain and protest, but no one pays him any attention. Finally, they hear the wail of a siren approaching from the distance.

Jamie's cell phone rings. It is Fredericks. Before she can tell him it is all over, he states, "Another victim was found this morning. Elderly male. Strangled. Just across town from where Mueller lives."

Jamie feels a little defeated. She did not save him. The news is like a bucket of ice water poured over her head. "Who was the victim?" she demands. "Was it Bernard Wagner?"

"It was a man named László Kovács."

Jamie raises her gaze skyward, then lets her head slump forward so she is looking at her shoes. "Send me the address."

"Right, I'll text it to you."

"Great, thank you." Her mind spins in circles. *Two murders in one day?* Well, that would explain why the garrote has dried blood on it. She wanted so badly to keep the killer from striking again. Her only consolation is the certainty that László Kovács will be the last victim.

I've finally got the son of a bitch!

Chapter 48

In January of 1945, the bombs, once heard in the distance, came closer. Edit was told they were going to burn the camp down and evacuate everyone. Edit and Anna had made some wraps for our feet, to stay warm. I was also able to get a coat from Canada. Each person was given a small loaf of rock-hard bread as they left the camp. The men and women were evacuated separately. It was freezing cold, and there was snow on the ground. Anyone who could not keep up was shot on the spot. I was separated from Edit and Dr. Anna during the long thirty-five-mile march to Wodzislaw, Poland. So many died along the way, but I made it. I made it! Starving, frozen, but I made it. What would be my reward for making it? I was placed into an open-air cattle car that was full of frozen snow.

You can imagine cold, but you cannot imagine riding in an open-air car, in the snow, already a mere specimen of skin and bones. We finally arrived at Ravensbruck concentration camp for women. After all of that, to actually be sent to another concentration camp. I was frozen and severely frostbitten when I arrived. I was put to work on a potato farm right outside the camp. I worked there until the camp was liberated on April 30th by the Russian army. I made it to Berlin where I met my husband, of blessed memory.

My husband and his brothers were conscripted into the Hungarian labor force. He and his brothers would escape the

Hungarian labor camp, live in the forests of Hungary and Poland, join the Polish resistance, be captured, escape again, and join the Russian resistance. They lived as the Bielski partisans did, in the forests of Europe. He would hide wherever he could. One morning, after hiding in a barn, he would awake to find his brother Shaya hanging from a telephone wire. Killed, probably by villagers or Nazi sympathizers. He would never know.

Amazingly, he would survive the war, and, although having had an extraordinarily difficult journey, he did not have to endure the brutality of a concentration camp—he escaped with his remarkable, humble, quiet strength, having fought and resisted the Nazis at every opportunity.

Chapter 49

Simon sits alone at his favorite restaurant. The waitress brings him a scotch on the rocks. He raises the glass and toasts his success. It is finally over. He played the FBI like a fine-tuned violin. They will not be coming after him. They have made their arrest. He thinks about Paul Delaney. He will be getting the punishment he deserves. In his perfectly executed finale, justice was served twice.

Simon smiles to himself. He remembers sitting at the Starbucks, on his computer, chatting online. He was posing as a fifteen-year-old girl. Paul Delaney was on the other end, devouring everything Simon wrote to him. Simon had him right where he wanted him, eating out of the palm of his hand.

Without an arrest and conviction, the FBI will always be looking for him. Could they find him? Highly unlikely. Yet, a life always wondering if today is the day they come to get him is not the life Simon can live. Someone must be convicted. Sending an innocent man to jail is not Simon's style. Of course, if he could have a criminal who deserves punishment take the fall, then that is a different story. Paul Delaney.

It was three years ago. The case was all over the news. A beautiful high school student was sexually assaulted, and the accused sexual predator walked free. The entire community was outraged by the case because there was an error in the collection of the evidence. The rape kit was mishandled by the nurse in the emergency room rendering it inadmissible in court. The case became her word against his. Paul Delaney was released back into the world, a free man.

Simon's plan was to fix that mistake. Paul Delaney will finally be getting the prison sentence he deserves. Despite the amount of time that has lapsed since the ordeal, Simon has kept track of the rapist. Not only will Delaney's crime be punished, but an arrest and conviction for killing the Nazis will close the case and put a stop to any continued pursuit. He gave the FBI enough information to figure out when he would strike next. He led the FBI to the home of the last victim. The FBI will be waiting for the murderer to show up. He just had to get Delaney there on Hoshana Raba, September 25.

In a chat window, he typed:

"w2m?"

Using the lingo of a teenager chatting online, he convinced Delaney that he was a fifteen-year-old girl totally in love. With this most recent question, Simon had set the snare. *Want to meet, Paul Delaney?* While Simon waited for Delaney's answer, he copied research files about the last three victims onto the rapist's computer.

An answer popped up, "yid", which means, "Yes, I do."

"I'll make it worth your while."

"Parents are working, I can skip school on 9/25. Can't wait to finally meet." He entered the address into the chat window. Delaney fell for the bait and went to the "girl's" house on that day, while "her parents were gone." And the FBI was waiting for him.

"ibt" replied Delaney. "I'll be there."

"gr8 p911 ttyl lysm." Simon typed, which is "great, parent emergency, talk to you later, love you so much."

"lu2" came the rapist's final reply, "love you, too."

Paul Delaney did not realize that the chat came from his very own computer. Simon had hacked it, and Delaney had no way of knowing. First, Simon snatched an Internet bill from Delaney's mail. Second, he called the service provider, impersonating Delaney and using the information on the statement to get through the security questions, Simon asked for the IP address of the Internet router in the rapist's home and received it.

Next, Simon went into the router with the default password, which most people never change. He found an unused port and tunneled through the firewall. Bingo. Simon was in. First thing he did was install a keystroke logger and a packet sniffer. These two programs provided Simon with everything he needed. They told him exactly what websites Delaney visited, as well as his passwords, favorite websites, and all other movement on his computer.

After a couple of weeks of tracking Delaney's computer movements, Simon created an account on one of the chat websites that Delaney frequented. He got Delaney interested, and the rapist took the bait easily. The best part, to Simon, is the fact that, when the FBI checks Delaney's computer, they will find the files on the victims that Simon has stealthily placed. He got a college student to drive to the rendezvous house, park on the street, get out of the car and take pictures, then e-mail it to an account that he made from Delaney's IP address. When he got the photo, he sent the kid a $100 gift card.

Evidence is crucial. For everything to work, Simon had to have a garrote, preferably two, in Delaney's trunk. Timing was everything. If he planted the garrote too early, there was a chance that Delaney might find it. If he waited and missed his opportunity, then Delaney might head to the rendezvous without the damning evidence. Without a murder weapon he could not ensure a conviction. He did not destroy the garrote after the August 8th murder, so he could plant it, and that had caused him his only real nervousness. Although well-hidden, it was still dangerous—he did not even clean it, so it still had Alfred Weiss' blood on it.

Simon broke into Paul Delaney's car several times before, on moonless nights, at 3:45 in the morning. Both times, the apartment complex where Delaney lived was eerily quiet. With practice he could open the driver's door and pop the trunk in twenty-two seconds. This was a great improvement over the almost-two minutes it took him the first time he tried.

After he killed László Kovács, Simon was able to open the driver's side door with ease. Just as he popped the trunk, sirens blasted through the silence of the night. Simon's heart starts to race as he remembers it vividly. He instantly rolled under the SUV parked next to Delaney's car and wriggled on his stomach and out the other side. His throat was tightening, making it difficult to breathe. He crouched low between the SUV and another car and quickly looked in all directions for movement and for an escape route. He centered his weight, so he could spring into attack mode, if necessary. With a sigh of relief, Simon realized the siren was from a police car on the main street and not in the apartment complex. The tightness in his throat took a long time to dissipate as he stayed motionless between the two vehicles. He quickly scanned all of the adjacent windows, looking for lights to come on. There were none. He waited a long five minutes, crouched low, before he quickly placed the last two garrotes and gently shut the trunk. Simon then disappeared into the dark.

Now he can celebrate. His task is done. His promise fulfilled. He has vindicated his grandparents suffering and his father's premature death. Paul Delaney is sure to be convicted and the FBI will go away.

The waitress appears and places his plate before him. He stares at the perfectly prepared steak and is unable to say thank you. His field of vision narrows as he begins to hyperventilate.

"Sir?"

He leans forward and puts his elbows on the table and then braces his forehead in his hands.

"Sir? Are you OK?"

He does not hear the question. In his mind the entrée is his last meal he deserves before they walk him up to the gallows and place the noose around his neck.

"Sir? Can you hear me? Are you OK?"

Simon slowly raises his head and sees the waitress and several of the neighboring patrons staring at him. He removes a one hundred dollar bill from his wallet and places it in the table and then leaves the restaurant.

Chapter 50

Looking out the window, Jamie watches the traffic move along the highway. She turns and smiles at Seth, who maneuvers easily through the traffic, his attention fully on driving. Jamie cannot help but think how adorable he looks, especially right now.

It dawns on Jamie that the last time she had driven on this road was her trip to Philadelphia. That trip had been such a success in several ways—finding a missing victim and then hooking up with Seth. Strange, Jamie thinks to herself, as she realizes it has been three months since Paul Delaney was sentenced to multiple life sentences in prison for the murders of Alfred Weiss and László Kovács.

Jamie was present at the closing arguments at the end of the trial. The Feds' case was tight and convincing. The evidence was incontrovertible. The only part that did not fit was the last victim. Although he was in Europe during the war, Jamie could not find anything that connected him with the Nazis. Kovács was in Kosice, Hungary, as part of the Hungarian Police for the duration of the war. Jamie did not understand why he was targeted by Delaney.

The case drew national attention, and Fredericks gave Jamie a nice pat on the back at a celebratory happy hour on the Friday after the arrest. By Monday morning, it was all forgotten—she passed him in the hallway and did not even get a smile. But that is how it goes in the Bureau. Monday had brought its new cases and new stresses, and she would go on with nothing but the personal satisfaction of a job well done. Or so she had thought. About a month later, Fredericks called her into his office and said that he had recommended her to fill an opening in the Dallas field office. It would include a step-up in GS number, which would mean a raise and an opportunity for advancement.

Jamie likes being at Quantico. She is also getting very serious with Seth. They have now been dating eight months. Jamie turned down the transfer.

"We're almost there," Seth says, smiling at Jamie.

Seth has arranged a day trip to Baltimore. They visited the Edgar Allan Poe House and are now stopping off to see Seth's grandmother, who lives in Baltimore, in a fancy condominium. It is designed for aging seniors who start out living independently. As their needs increase, they can take advantage of added services, all the way up to 24-hour care. Of course, residents pay for what they use. Mrs. Cooper, who will be celebrating her ninety-third birthday in another month, is incredibly independent. She takes advantage of the housekeeping services, has a nursing assistant help her bathe, and has her groceries bought and delivered by the concierge, but otherwise she takes care of herself. Jamie has never met her before. After the visit, they are going to go out for dinner at a waterfront restaurant on Baltimore's Inner Harbor.

Seth pulls up to the front of the building, where they are met by a valet. As they enter a foyer that would make the Ritz Carlton feel ashamed, Seth can see that Jamie is taking in the attention to detail.

"The cheapest unit is over half-a-million, and the basic condo fee is over $1,800 a month. That's without any extra services," Seth explains because he knows Jamie is curious.

"Impressive."

They make their way up the elevator to Seth's grandmother's unit. Seth lets himself in with his key, then knocks on the door and announces his presence. As they enter the spacious condo, Jamie knows that this is not one of the cheapest units.

Seth's grandmother is sitting and watching a large television, which she immediately clicks off.

"Hey, Grandma, this is Jamie Golding,"

"She is beautiful, Seth!" Grandma exclaims. "Come sit. I will get us some tea," Grandma declares, already heading for the kitchen. She is wearing a short-sleeved floral housedress that reminds Jamie of a muumuu. She stops on her way and changes course toward the blinds. "I'll add some light to the room." She pulls the blinds easily, revealing a wall of windows that afford an incredible view of the harbor. Jamie walks over to admire the scene.

"This place must cost a fortune," she says softly to herself, as she motions to Seth to come look. "I'm impressed."

When Mrs. Cooper returns with the tea, Jamie notices a very conspicuous number tattooed on her forearm. She acts like she does not see. They exchange pleasantries for a few minutes, Seth doing most of the talking and Jamie sitting politely next to him.

Seth's cell phone rings. He looks down at it, then at Jamie. "I've gotta take this, it's Barry. There may be a problem at the lab. I'll be back in a couple of minutes."

"Sure," Jamie nods.

Seth answers the phone and walks out of the room. Jamie smiles at Mrs. Cooper, but the silence is awkward.

What am I supposed to talk to her about? I would love to ask her about her tattoo, but I don't dare.

Jamie looks around for something to compliment or use as a springboard for conversation. On the coffee table is a book entitled <u>Memoir of the Holocaust</u>, by Lola Englemann.

Jamie is instantly curious. She gestures to the book with a, "May I?"

"Please, that is why I wrote it."

"You *wrote* it? These are your memoirs?"

"Yes."

Opening the book, Jamie begins to read.

I am a Jew. I was born in the city of Poproc, not far from Kosice, when it was originally part of Slovakia in the year 1921. Later, after World War I, Slovakia became a part of Czechoslovakia. During those days, you either told people you were Czech or Hungarian, since the Slovaks were more anti-Semitic. I was raised by my mother and her parents, as my father had disappeared from our family not too long after I was born. Even today, I don't know what happened to my father. Mother rarely spoke of him, and my grandparents never did.

Jamie pauses after the second paragraph. She knows that city, Kosice. That was where the last victim immigrated from to the U.S.

"So you lived near Kosice?"

"Yes, I was born right outside of Kosice," Grandma confirms with a smile.

Jamie perceives that the old woman is excited to talk about her life. She can hardly hold back the question on her mind. "Did you ever know or hear of László Kovács?"

Instantly, Mrs. Cooper stops cold, as if stuck in a past vision. Her face goes pale, and her eyes darken with a fear that is mixed with defiance. "I will never forget that name," she whispers, barely audible. "I will never forget how he beat my mother, grandmother, and grandfather. How he beat me. Kovács stole everything his filthy hands could take away from my family."

She pauses, her eyes still witnessing the memories of the past.

"Crazy thing was, László was the brother of a good friend of my brother when they were younger. They would play in the fields with us. I remember that, when he turned eighteen, he joined the police force. It's amazing that you can put a uniform on a kid, and he changes into a monster who beats the innocent..." Grandma pauses again, her mind wandering through the images of her pain.

"He was recently murdered."

"Good for him. He sent me to hell; now he can burn in hell. My late son, Milton, spent his life trying to prove that there were Nazis hiding out in America. All I wanted was for him to go after László Kovács. Get him deported or something. That man took my whole family away. I was the only survivor," Grandma continues, unaware of the effect her words are producing on Jamie.

"Your son was a Nazi hunter?"

"A damn good one. It was the system that was the problem. He never took any credit himself. He did the work and handed the information over to the authorities. He had files on hundreds of these monsters."

"Whatever happened to those files?"

"I think Seth has them, or had them. I knew Seth would never keep it up. These things diminish with every generation. It's okay. They'll get what they deserve in hell."

Jamie can only half-listen as her mind puts the pieces of the puzzle together.

Seth.

Jamie can hardly breathe as she looks up and sees Seth standing in the room. When did he come in? Everything is a blur, a tangle of slow-motion images happening outside of Jamie, existing without regard to the devastation being realized inside of her.

Grandma is still talking; unaware of Jamie's struggle, she continues, "I just wanted nothing else but to see justice to those who murdered and maimed. Kovács was the one who evicted us from our home and sent us to the ghetto, and then to Auschwitz. My whole family. Only I survived."

Jamie looks to Seth, asking the question without words, her eyes entreating him to say something—anything—that will stop her from reaching the horrifying conclusion. His face pales considerably, and Jamie's eyes grow wider, desperate for an explanation, begging him not to confirm what she now knows to be true.

Seth stares blankly ahead.

"Seth, dear, are you alright?" Mrs. Cooper asks.

No response. Seth continues to stare straight ahead as he puts his hand on his throat and swallows hard. His field of vision begins to narrow.

Jumping up from her chair and brushing away the memoir, Jamie crosses the room to Seth and demands, her voice cracking under the weight of her emotions, "Give me your keys."

Seth tries to protest, but no words come out of his mouth. He holds out the keys to Jamie.

Jamie reaches for the keys and easily takes them from him. Quickly taking her things, Jamie leaves the condo without saying goodbye. While she waits for the elevator, she glances back, half-expecting Seth to come out and stop her. He does not. Downstairs, she jumps into the car and slams it in gear. Wheels screeching, Jamie pulls out and drives away.

Jamie does not know what to feel as tears start flowing down her cheeks. Her mind is a frantic collection of thoughts. She cannot believe it. He could not have done it. No, her instincts are wrong. Yet, the grandmother, her reaction to Kovács, Seth's father hunting down Nazis, Seth knowing forensics and, most condemning, Seth's pause, his eyes and mind searching for an answer and confessing without saying anything. That confession was all the confirmation she needed. She reaches for her cell, anxious to call someone. Anyone. She briefly considers calling Rabbi Silverman but immediately puts the phone away.

Jamie finds herself pulling into the parking lot of the NCAVC. She enters the building and heads up to her office. She has no evidence and she knows it. Immediately, she boots up her computer, anxious to figure out how she ended up with Paul Delaney. Jamie quickly reviews Delaney's criminal record. She researches further and discovers that he was accused and acquitted of rape, due to a rape kit that had not been properly handled. A conscientious lab tech reported the rape kit as being contaminated. Jamie's eyes freeze on the name of the lab tech. Seth Cooper.

That case alone probably put him onto the fast track to becoming lab supervisor. That is how he got the job and not Barry Shapiro. It showed that Seth is honest, ethical, and by-the-book, and he is not easily swayed by emotion. Why not promote such a worthy candidate? But Jamie is still sure Seth never forgot that his honesty allowed a guilty man to walk free.

Not once has her work made her sick. She grabs the garbage can from next to her desk and throws up.

Chapter 51

Seth walks through the airport, following the masses of people being herded toward the security checkpoint.

This is it. He quit his job and has been in Jamaica for the last two weeks.

Jamie knows, and there was no way to convince her otherwise. He does not need the work. He could never imagine the thought, but what he does need is to be far away from Jamie.

He has the familiar knot of fear in his stomach as he walks up to the security desk and presents his passport. It is his own passport and not a fake. He makes it through with the guard's warm wishes for a nice flight.

As the plane lands at Reagan International Airport, he recalls another flight he once took. As the plane was taxiing to the gate, the captain came on the intercom and asked all of the passengers to remain in their seats and allow law enforcement officers to board the plane. They arrested the man sitting right in front of Seth and escorted him off the plane.

No such request comes over the intercom today.

He makes his way up the gangway to the terminal, expecting to see them waiting for him.

Reaching the doorway that leads outside to the streets, Seth stops and takes a long deep breath. It seems like he has not breathed that deeply in years. He hails a cab and disappears into the highway traffic.

The memoir throughout this book is based on the actual experience of Lola Engelmann-Stark, may she live and be well, who bears the tattoo A-14191 on her left arm as a constant reminder of the horrors she lived through.

All of the codes presented in this book are true and verifiable.

Acknowledgements

The Esther Code has benefitted from many talented people. First and foremost, I must thank Sarah Holst, my co-author, who I met in a most unfortunate setting that turned out to be such a blessing. Paige Stover mentored me from the very beginning and enabled me to build the foundation. Michael Rechtman never believed in me. The drive to prove him wrong got me to this point.

A special thanks to Ilana, Lev, Carmelle, Rafael, and Nissim who are the very fabric of my life and to the Creator of the Universe who has sustained me to see this day.

Wesley Harris of writecrimeright.com read the manuscript for accuracy in FBI procedure. Karen Bonner, Amy Maslia, and Alicia Haley were brutally honest critics.

Thank you to Billy Satterwhite at the English Island for editing. You are terrific!

Thank you to Kristie Birdsong for the cover.

To Ann Stark and Lola Stark for details of holocaust experiences that were the basis of the memoir.

Gene Hollahan read a very rough draft and offered his wisdom. Thank you Jennifer Moore for introducing us.

To the staff of the EP lab who will finally get their copy. No James, I did not put you in the book. You're not mad are you?

Danneman, Michael
The Esther Code

FEB 2016

Made in the USA
Middletown, DE
08 October 2015